BEWITCHING
A
Highlander

ROMA CORDON

BEWITCHING A Highlander

A SCOTTISH HIGHLAND WARRIORS NOVEL

CamCat
Books

CamCat Publishing, LLC
Ft. Collins, Colorado 80524
camcatpublishing.com

Hardcover ISBN 9780744305036
Paperback ISBN 9780744305074
Large-Print Paperback ISBN 9780744305104
eBook ISBN 9780744305111
Audiobook ISBN 9780744305135

Library of Congress Control Number: 2021952250

Cover and book design by Maryann Appel

5   3   1   2   4

CHAPTER

1

"You have witchcraft in your lips. . ."
—William Shakespeare, *Henry V.*

October 28, 1747—Isle of Coll, Scotland

*B*reena MacRae's heart beat out of tune from the cacophony of their wagon's rattling. Sixteen horse hooves trampled the knurled road, pulling them southwest toward the Campbells' keep, a clan she blamed for most of her childhood miseries.

Three weeks ago, she'd awoken from nineteen years of delusions, yet it was no less painful living the truth. Her parents had neither died in some horrific accident nor left because of her. Breena was after all the most deplorable witch the MacRaes and Maxwells ever had the lamentable fortune to beget.

Uncle Craig leaned over and gave her shoulder a gentle squeeze. The clumsy yet affectionate gesture grounded her. It rid her of her punishing thoughts.

"We aught to go over the plan again."

She would always be obliged to him and Aunt Madeline. They'd been her guardians since she was six, although many times since then, despite the fact that she loved them both with all her heart, they'd made her want to either scream or blaspheme.

Sometimes both.

His familiar features reminded her of her mother's, his little sister.

"All right, but understanding the need to lie doesn't make it any less difficult," she said.

"Difficult it may be, but it will keep us alive."

She huffed. He was too cautious. Or was she not cautious enough?

Breena blinked up as the afternoon sun reconsidered slipping past horizontal puffs of clouds.

Mayhap she herself should reconsider her decision to come here.

No. Even if there was a remote possibility her father was alive, she had to attempt to find him. She had to free him. Her heart ached for all he must have endured. She'd believed him dead for the past nineteen years, until three weeks ago, when lovable yet scatterbrained Aunt Madeline had let slip the truth. After suffering from dysentery and a bout of guilt, her aunt had blurted out that Ian might still be alive. Had Aunt Madeline known she wasn't at death's door, she might have been more steadfast in her secrecy. Craig and Madeline had insisted her parents wanted the truth kept from her all this time. The secrecy and deception might have been the stimulant for her childhood misery, but it hadn't been the cause. Nonetheless, it had resulted in long, wasted years.

Her dream from the previous night replayed in her mind. Beloved Grandmother Sorcha, their majestic matriarch, had told her Ian had something to reveal. If Breena believed dreams were a sign of things to come, then it was a sign her father was indeed alive. But she didn't know if she believed in dreams. After all, she lacked the gift of second sight. The revered Sorcha on the other hand wielded her own gift of sight like a true proficient, when she was alive.

A chilled hollowness speared her innards, causing a shiver to run up her spine. It had been her tormentor since she was six. Often she paused and wondered what had slipped her mind, what she had forgotten—perhaps she'd missed something. Then it would hit her. She hadn't missed anything, hadn't forgotten anything, nothing had slipped her mind. It was only that her parents had vanished, without a word, leaving an acute aching void. She pulled her woolen arisaid tighter around her shoulders and prayed not only that their scheme would work on the Campbells but that she could rid herself of this ache in the pit of her belly, once and for all.

She gazed out the wagon as the panoply that was the Isle of Coll rolled by. The crisp October breeze swept her cheeks as she eyed the chestnut-feathered corncrakes scavenging the beachgrass-infested sand dunes. Nature's russets, umbers, and olives, always vibrant at home on the Isle of Skye, were starved for luster here on Coll.

A lone angler in the distance slumped his shoulders in a small skiff, then gazed up at the sky as if beseeching heavenly bodies for a boon before casting a net onto the surface of the ocean. The earthiness of the damp ground below mingling with the briny sea air and the pungency of kelps filled her nostrils as she inhaled a cleansing breath. She was well acquainted with the pain of unanswered pleas. Well, mayhap the tide was changing for them both.

When she caught the incessant tapping of her fingers on the side of the wagon, she pulled her hand back into her lap.

"I'll wager they don't even remember the name Beth MacRae after nineteen years." Breena fought against the agonizing emotions that flooded her every time she said her mother's name.

Craig's brown eyes looked back at her from beneath shaggy brows, the slight impatience that twitched his cheek muscles highlighting his wrinkles. "That's a wager I'll not be taking, for the price of losing is finding our necks at the wrong end of a noose."

George, her uncle's worker, flipped the reins up ahead with a sharp, practiced snap. A throaty intake of breath escaped his mouth. "Holy Saints. It looks haunted."

Breena's head snapped up to follow his gaze. The back of her neck prickled. Castle Carragh loomed grim on the horizon. George was as strong as a feral goat but simpleminded.

"There are no such things as ghosts," she said. But from her sudden inability to swallow, she wasn't sure she believed her own attempt to assuage his fears.

If the builders of this castle had meant to strike terror into its visitors, they'd carried out their goal to perfection. The shadows cast by Carragh against the backdrop of the setting sun stretched out toward them like crooked talons, warning them to keep away.

She ignored the warning and said a silent plea that they were not too late, that her father was still alive.

As they approached the castle's outer gates, Breena made out two menacing sentries dressed in threadbare tartan trews of blue and green, the colors of the Campbell clan. They were each outfitted with a sword, mace, and a flintlock rifle; were they preparing for war?

George pulled their wagon up closer to the gate, reined in the horses, and lowered his head, awaiting instructions. It always caused Breena such disquiet to see such a large man lower his head like that. She had known George for close to a decade, since he'd come to work for Craig, and despite his broad, hulking body he was the gentlest person Breena had ever met.

When one of the sentries at the gate brandished his sword, Breena's dry gulp refused to be suppressed. His flared nostrils and squinting eyes made his pugnacious expression more acute. Did he wish to intimidate them? If so, he'd gotten his wish. The other sentry snarled, exposing crooked incisors, as he scratched his crotch. Breena eased the tension in her face into what she hoped was a pleasant smile, even as her fingers curled against her damp palms. The squinty-eyed sentry scowled. "What's your business here?"

"I'm Craig Maxwell. I'm a healer and spice merchant. May we be of service to your clan?"

Neither Squinty Eyes nor Crooked Incisors was impressed by her uncle's request. Squinty Eyes spat on the ground, his scowl deepening. He sauntered to the back of their wagon and started sifting through their supplies. All of a sudden he lifted his sword high in the air and brought it down in an echoing crash on the lock of a trunk. Breena gasped out loud in surprise.

Craig jumped down from the wagon and stumbled toward Squinty Eyes. "I'll show you whatever you wish, but there's no cause to break our trunks."

Squinty Eyes raised his hand, still gripping the sword, and slammed the hilt down, with a dull thud, into Craig's jaw. Breena's body froze with horror. Her uncle teetered backward and fell to the ground, landing on his rump.

"Unc—Father!"

Dread rose up her gullet as she jumped down from the wagon, almost buckling at the knees, landing with more force than anticipated. She ignored the approaching thunder of hooves and rushed toward Craig. She couldn't lose him too. She just couldn't. She took hold of Craig's arms and helped him from the ground.

"Are you hurt?"

Her uncle's mouth was open, his gaze flat. She took some of his weight as he leaned against her. He was in shock. There was blood at the side of his mouth, at the end of an ugly cut, where he'd been struck. A sharp pang of fear speared her midriff as she reached into her pocket for a clean square of linen and, with a gentle touch, dabbed the blood away.

Her uncle's worker approached them with hesitant steps.

Breena sent him a cursory glance, noting the fear in his bulging eyes when he saw Squinty Eyes.

"George, why don't you remain with the horses?" Breena said.

His head bobbed. "Yes, mistress."

George understood horses, but he had difficulty with people.

She returned her attention to Craig. She took hold of her uncle's chin, avoiding the darkening bruise that was now a stark contrast to his pale skin. She inspected the wound as she gently followed his jaw line with her fingers all the way to his neck. Nothing broken. She closed her eyes and exhaled a breath of relief.

Craig was a graying man of eight and fifty with a slim build, whereas Squinty Eyes was younger and more than twice the size of her uncle. Breena ground her teeth when another drop of blood fell from Craig's mouth. Her pulse raced with heated indignation. How dare this barbaric bully strike Craig? How dare he block them from entering this atrocious castle? It's not as if there were endless visitors clamoring for entrance. Losing her parents and years of this aching void pushed her to retaliate. But she couldn't. They were at the utter mercy of this insolent sentry to gain entrance to the Campbells' keep. He held their fate and her father's life in his hands, a fact he was utterly unaware of.

As she tended to Craig, a loud snigger pierced the air. She swung around to see Squinty Eyes dangling a gossamer shift off the tip of his sword, right above the now-broken trunk. He jutted his flaccid chin in Breena's direction as he addressed Craig.

"You let me have a roll in the hay with the lass and I'll let you in."

Breena's eyes narrowed at the crude proposition. The insult dug in. Her heart rate quickened as self-preservation and a survival instinct unfurled inside her. The heat of it spread throughout her entire body like a wave of sickness, making her shake. "You bastard."

Rationality went out the window as she took two steps forward and dealt a resounding slap across the sniggering face of Squinty Eyes. He was caught off guard, judging by the way his mouth fell open and his head jerked back. His odious stench made Breena want to pinch the tip of her nose shut and breathe through her mouth.

But then, coldness sank into her stomach. Oh no. No. What had she done? She blinked, trying to swallow against the rising bile, and stepped back.

She would never forgive herself if they were barred entrance because of her foolhardy actions. She'd never done anything like that before. What was the matter with her? The earlier mention of a noose burned her ears.

Squinty Eyes recovered. He grunted and swore as he grabbed her. His grip, like cold steel, dug into her soft flesh. He wrenched her right arm forward. Her mouth tightened with defiance as she glared at him. Even as her right shoulder was at risk of dislocating under his granite hold, she held her chin high. She would not give this bully the satisfaction of seeing her cower.

"You brazen wench, how dare you strike me?"

His eyes bulged, and spittle escaped from his mouth. She tugged and pulled to no avail as the pounding of horses' hooves reverberated in the air around them. Out of the corner of her eye, she glimpsed a towering, broad-shouldered Highland warrior dismounting from the blackest stallion she'd ever seen.

He stormed Squinty Eyes from behind.

CHAPTER
2

*E*gan Dunbar, future chief of the Dunbar clan, had always prided himself on his restraint of temper. This was crucial when commanding the most lethal retainers in the Highlands, men he trusted with his life and who now dismounted behind him in a sea of swirling tartan kilts and glinting weapons. It was a shock to Egan, however, that he now experienced difficulty with said vaunted control. Abhorrent behavior by the ornery Campbells shouldn't come as a surprise to him, but somehow it did.

His lips curled, and heat surged through his veins as he grabbed the wrist of the Campbell guard. With deft skill, cultivated while fostering under the warlord Angus MacDonell, he twisted it back toward the man's shoulders. He utilized the guard's natural mobility as leverage.

The man was gutless; why else would he manhandle a lass?

And not just any lass, but the MacIntyres' bonny healer.

Egan had met her several months ago on the Isle of Skye. The meeting was brief but had ignited an esteem within Egan. If it hadn't been for the battle and his subsequent trip to negotiate prisoner releases from the Tower of London, he might have pursued her. But it was just as well he'd been needed elsewhere, for his father would have forbidden him from consorting with a lowborn healer. Although Egan himself never quite understood the need for such division among the classes. Egan fortified his grip on the guard as his seconds-in-command Dougray and Keith advanced.

He gestured with his free hand. "Stand down." He wanted to enjoy a bit of practice after straddling his stallion Heimdall all day.

The guard bellowed as Egan raised the pressure. The man lowered his head and whimpered, still maintaining a grip on the lass's arm with his other hand. But he discovered if he moved even an iota, the grip Egan held him under hurt like the devil. Egan himself had made such a discovery years ago. His foster brothers, Daegan MacDonell in particular, had taken great pleasure in restraining him in similar grapples during endless training sessions.

Was it just a few days ago he'd been surrounded by the Highlands, with their abundance of light, fresh, clean air and snow-peaked bens that towered against the backdrop of bluish white skies? Truth be told, squelching through a smelly peat bog would be preferable to this macabre isle. The stench was unbearable, the scenery dull, and the people less trustworthy than masked highwaymen. But he had orders to follow, despite his reservations.

The Campbell guard ceased his squirms and bellowed, "Let go! Who are you? What the hell do you want from me?"

"I don't want anything from you. But I do wish to greet the lass you are in the process of mauling."

The guard shoved Breena away. She stumbled forward, then righted her step.

"Good man. How thoughtful of you to allow me to have a word with the lass."

Egan eased his grip on the guard then released. He eyed the man, who grunted and cradled his wrist. The guard's contorted expression eased. The pulsating rush of blood through Egan's own veins slowed. But he maintained sharp eye contact with the guard. From his peripheral vision he noted the second guard holding position at the gate. Excellent. He was more intelligent than his appearance suggested.

A crooked scowl stretched across on the spineless guard's face, which somehow managed to make his bulbous nose even rounder. "What's your business with the Campbells?"

The guard had relented, but he didn't like it.

Egan drew back his lips in a smirk. He ignored the guard's question, and he swung around to face the fair Breena. While she'd faced down the guard in spectacular fashion, like a Valkyrie, she could have been injured. She didn't appear asinine or reckless. Several months ago, she'd facilitated their taking on the redcoats at Duntulm. She had also nursed Daegan's then betrothed, now wife, Eva Drummond, back to health. Had it not been for Breena's potent sleeping concoction, administered to the redcoats' food, they would never have had the advantage that garnered their victory. He owed her.

He let his features ease into a smile as the memory of their first meeting sauntered into his head. He'd seen her flouncing in the woods, outside Castle Duntulm, at point-blank range of a rifle-wielding redcoat. Chivalry had been called for: he'd rescued her from the blackguard by knocking the man out with a cudgel-sized branch.

Now, what in Hades was a skillful healer like Breena doing on Coll?

CHAPTER
3

*T*he pinch in her lungs prompted Breena to breathe. She'd been rendered utterly speechless by the Highlander's skilled offensive move. He'd stopped Squinty Eyes's brutish body with quick precision. Then when she'd been shocked by recognition and the fact that she was gaping at the striking Egan Dunbar, it had slipped her mind to breathe. No, not gaping. Admiring. *Admiring?* Squinty Eyes must have shaken her with such vigor, she'd become disoriented.

Several months ago, Egan and three armies had showed up at the MacIntyres' castle to negotiate their release from the redcoats' siege. The redcoats had trailed Charles Edward Stuart, leader of the Jacobite Rebellion, to the MacIntyres' castle. Even though the Jacobite uprisings had been curtailed by British forces in the year since Culloden, there were still isolated attacks in the Highlands. Heat flooded Breena's countenance at the memory of their first meeting.

Egan Dunbar had slipped out from behind the trees and disarmed her captor with a single blow. As rationality is always the first to go in a panic, she'd bolted. Egan had given chase, no doubt worried she would inadvertently alert the redcoats. He'd smoothly slid his arm around her waist to restrain her escape. His body had been hard, and his grip felt like she was being held against a warm monolith. Daegan had stepped out from the stealth of the woods in time to reassure her that Egan was a friend. He'd returned to his army, and soon after the battle, he'd disappeared. She'd speculated more than once if she would ever lay eyes on him again.

Now as she gazed at him, rays of the evening sun gilded him in a surreal light as he released Squinty Eyes and swiveled around to face her. From the quality of his ebony coat with its silver buttons and embroidered cuffs, the Dunbars were prospering. The visible frilled neck and cuffs of his white léine were of the finest linen. Instead of breeches as she might have expected because of the recent Act of Proscription, which proclaimed kilts illegal, Egan Dunbar wore a kilt of emerald green and cherry red, the colors of the Dunbars. The pristine garment ended at his knees, where his riding boots took over. No flimsy ghillie brogues for this imposing Highlander.

"Are you hurt?" His eyebrows were drawn together with concern. There was something about him that not only stunted her breath but jumbled her wits.

"Just my pride, sir. Other than that, I am unharmed." She offered deference to Egan, surprised and pleased at the relative calm of her voice.

His thick rufous hair had golden hues as if sun-bleached, it had been pulled back in a queue. His bladelike nose, linear forehead, and sculpted cheekbones had been darkened by prolonged exposure to the sun. He no doubt had an affinity for the outdoors. A whitish scar ran from his right earlobe down to his Adam's apple. She recalled that from before and had pondered on its origin.

Eva had commented that the Dunbars had Norse ancestors, and she decided Egan looked like a Viking warrior of old. Just the Viking helmet, a fighting polearm, and a wolf's-pelt cape were missing.

Goodness, she was disoriented.

"Then I'm relieved you are unharmed."

Something coiled in Breena's stomach. What if Egan picked up on their scheme? It would be only a matter of time before the MacIntyres found out. Would they still place their trust in her as their healer?

Two weeks ago she'd given in to her curiosity and had performed a sideromancy divination spell. She'd first practiced this spell a few years ago in lieu of reading tea leaves, which she'd never been good at. The movement of the flame, smoke, and the pattern of yarrow stalks pressed against the searing iron frying-pan had hinted at danger in connection with Coll. Breena hadn't told Craig, of course. She hadn't wanted to dissuade him from making this journey. But in addition to the obvious danger posed by the Campbells, could that danger refer to possible discovery by Egan Dunbar?

"We are much obliged to you, Master Dunbar. We meet again just as we're in need of assistance."

He threw her an affable grin. "Delighted to be of service."

Breena went to her uncle's side and schooled her features for the lie.

"Master Dunbar, I'd like to introduce my father, Craig Maxwell. He is a healer from the village of Kilmuir."

Egan considered her for a split second more than was necessary before amiably reaching out to shake hands with Craig. "Let's not stand on ceremony. Please, call me Egan. It's a privilege to make your acquaintance."

She shook her head. He couldn't possibly have remembered.

Egan eyed both Craig and Breena. "Whatever brought you to this wretched isle?"

Squinty Eyes's loud affronted snort behind Egan was ignored.

"We have herbs and spices for sale. And we also came to visit an old friend," Breena said. She let the second half of her answer fall in pitch to avoid Squinty Eyes's overhearing.

"How do you know my daughter?" Craig directed the question to Egan, even as his eyes widened with interest at Breena.

"Your intrepid daughter aided us in bringing the redcoats to the negotiation table several months ago at Castle Duntulm. As a result, we were able to get the MacIntyre prisoners released."

"Ah yes, I remember Breena telling me of the battle. She also promised me not to be that reckless ever again. Those merciless redcoats kept her under guard the whole time, despite the fact that she was only there to help the wounded."

"Yes, I can think of a few choice descriptions besides merciless. It appears you are trying to gain entrance here. Would you fancy an escort into Castle Carragh? You can properly attend to that cut inside." Egan gestured to Craig's bruised mouth.

"We'd be much obliged. Please, lead the way." Craig reached up to touch his bruised lip and winced. The color of his mouth was darkening to a most disagreeable shade of purple.

Egan gave a curt nod, then swiveled around to address Squinty Eyes. "Inform your laird that Egan Dunbar, son of the Dunbar chief of Kintail, and his guests are here. We seek an audience."

A flash of unease crossed Squinty Eyes's face. But, despite the way his Adam's apple bobbed, as he seemed to be having difficulty swallowing, he offered no apologies.

He swung around and headed into the keep.

Breena's gaze strayed toward Egan as he swaggered over to his men to exchange a few words. She recognized his squire Alban, whom she'd met previously at the MacIntyres' Duntulm.

Her eyes took in Egan's easygoing manner and his strong and confident posture. It was clear from their attentive nods that his retainers respected his authority.

Breena jerked her head away to consider the gates as her uncle's quiet voice snapped her out of her thoughts. The warmth of embarrassment settled on her cheeks. Had she been staring at the man?

"Do you trust this Egan Dunbar?" he asked.

She considered for a moment. "From my first encounter with him, I gather he's loyal to his friends. Let's not put him in a position to have to reveal to Laird MacIntyre that his healer has infamous parents."

The MacIntyres relied on her; they needed her healing abilities. And somehow that bond of trust had become sacred to her. She fully intended to do whatever it took to keep that bond intact. She'd moved to Castle Duntulm seven years ago and now counted many of them as her closest friends, despite keeping a large part of herself from them.

"With Egan or his men escorting us amongst the Campbells, it'll hinder our search of the dungeon," Craig whispered.

"We can keep up the pretense of looking for an old friend."

"In the Campbells' dungeon? Egan Dunbar will certainly question that."

"We won't require their escort at all times. Mayhap it's best to look for my father in the dark of night, when both the Dunbars and the Campbells are asleep."

CHAPTER

4

*A*n hour later, the sound of their footsteps bounced off the walls of a narrow, musty corridor. The pitch of Breena's breath had risen, and her stomach churned with anticipation. No, not anticipation. Dread. Portmanteau in her right hand, she trailed after Egan alongside Craig. She held her head high despite the urge to make herself small. The absence of almost any lighting around them made her half expect to spot bats hanging upside down from the ceiling.

The Campbells they passed on the way eyed them with a mixture of chilled stares and curled lips. It was no great puzzle why the rest of the Highlands considered this clan hostile.

She valued the fact that Egan and three of his men escorted her and Craig as they followed Squinty Eyes, whom she'd learned was called

Finlay. She prayed she didn't cast up her accounts now, for she didn't want to face the Campbell. She told herself it was because he would question the purpose of their presence. But she knew that wasn't the whole of it.

Craig gasped out loud. Breena swiveled around in time to see him stumbling over debris lying in their path. Unable to right his step in time, Craig fell, landing on his knees. Breena dropped her portmanteau and was at his side in a trice.

Poor Uncle Craig.

Breena took hold of Craig's arm and was helping him up from the filthy floor when Egan trotted over to their side. He grasped Craig's shoulders to hoist him up, bumping against Breena in the process. Stark awareness tinged with something a little more tangible than interest shot through her body at its contact with Egan's. His body felt like steel that had been heated by a summer's sun. She blinked and found herself staring up into the gold-flecked eyes of Egan Dunbar. The depths of those warm globes pulled her in. His scent, a mixture of soap, leather, and the rugged outdoors, was undoubtedly male. Heat burned her cheeks and she quickly stepped away.

"Thank you for your assistance, once again," Craig said as he brushed dust off his knees.

"Take care where you step," Egan said, eying Craig.

Egan moved his gaze to Breena, giving her a cursory glance, and resumed his stride behind Finlay.

"How long do you both plan on availing yourself of the Campbells' fine hospitality?"

Breena wasn't surprised at the tinge of sarcasm in Egan's tone at the word *hospitality*.

She picked up her portmanteau and continued onward with Craig.

"As long as it takes to sell our spices," Craig said.

"Can I inquire with the Campbell after your friend?"

"No!"

"No!"

Heaviness sunk into Breena's belly as she shot a questioning glance in Craig's direction. He'd cried out at the same time she had.

Egan's arched eyebrows left no doubt they'd piqued his interest. But he seemed to let it go, for the time being. "I don't anticipate staying on Coll for more than two or three days. If your purpose is achieved by then, may I escort you back to the Isle of Skye?"

Breena presumed Egan made the offer because he'd recalled she was dear friends with Eva, his foster brother's wife. And while his offer was gracious, even generous on its own, it complicated matters, considering their plans.

"We're yet unsure how long it will take us to unload our stock. Perchance we let you know in a day or so?" Craig said.

"Of course."

They navigated four flights of slippery stairs and turned into a chamber that served as the laird's private solar. Two sentries stood guard, one on either side of the entrance, armed with Lochaber axes, broadswords, and flintlock pistols. One of the sentries scoffed in disgust as Finlay announced them. He needn't have bothered. It was already quite clear they were unwelcome.

After they all gathered in the solar, the sparse chamber still held space for an additional fifty men. The furnishings consisted of a single discolored trestle table with its single candle, quill pen, small inkwell, and strewn-about papers. Alongside it stood six equally run-down accompanying chairs, the tallest one occupied at present. She avoided looking at its occupant. The furniture looked hard and unwelcoming, like its users. Remnants of a single meal were spread on the table, as if the Campbell had eaten alone.

The chill in the colorless room seeped into her bones as she eyed the water streaks on the ceiling and the dark soot stains above the two lit torches on the wall. Despite the spaciousness of the chamber, Breena felt boxed in.

Confined.

That boulder of dread growing on her chest.

"Get back to your post." The command was sharp.

"Aye, sir." Finlay scrambled to offer deference to the Campbell as he backed away.

Wasn't it the Unready who said when God closes a door, he opens a window? It seemed the door to the outer world slammed shut when Finlay pulled the door closed behind him. Her eyes followed the uneven lines of the brick wall to the single window; this eased some tension from her neck, not that she anticipated the need for escape through the high, narrow opening.

She lifted her chin, straightened her back, and turned to face the man seated at the table, whom she'd attempted to avoid until necessity demanded it. Breena tried to push past the resistance at the back of her throat, but her mouth had gone dry.

Egan stepped forward. "Laird Alasdair Campbell, we thank you for receiving us. I'm Egan Dunbar."

Alasdair Campbell looked to be Craig's age. His slim frame was half a head taller than Breena. His skin was wrinkled with an unhealthy tinge of sallowness. His thinning ash-gray hair clung to the top of his forehead and temples. The pinch of his lips showed nothing but disdain.

His fashionable léine, waistcoat, and Campbell-colored trews spoke volumes. The rest of his clan, at least the ones she'd observed, wore nothing but threadbare garments.

Did he also feast on mutton and venison while the rest of his clan chewed on dry bread?

Breena took in a long, slow breath and exhaled in a controlled manner. She'd never expected this to occur. After all this time, she'd managed to come face-to-face with the man who'd taken her parents. Rancor oozed through every single pore of her body; it rose like acid to burn her gullet.

"I ken who you are. What do you want?"

"Did you receive my missive?" Egan's tone remained even.

The Campbell's affirmative grunt metamorphosed into a series of guttural coughs as he rose and clutched the table. The hacking racked his frame as his shoulders curled forward. Was the man ill? Her healer's instinct battled her rancor.

"Well then, you're aware I'm here to discuss the deaths of two of my men."

When the Campbell's coughs ceased, he straightened and took note of Breena for the first time.

"Who is the woman? Is she your mistress . . . your leman? I don't conduct clan affairs in front of women."

His scornful tone coupled with the verbal insult grated against the pain and anger that swarmed inside of her. Without knowing it, he'd managed to rid her of the last vestiges of her healer's instinct. The boulder on her chest made her tongue move like sand in her mouth as she swallowed.

She took a long deep cleansing breath and kept her chin high, her countenance amenable, and her mouth shut.

"Craig Maxwell here and his daughter Breena are my guests. I expect them to be treated with some measure of decorum." Egan's tone was stony despite his relaxed demeanor.

Something fluttered in Breena's chest at Egan's defense. But mayhap his response was more about a male power struggle with the Campbell and less about defending her virtue.

The Campbell replied with another grunt; more earsplitting coughs followed. What ailment manifested in such coughing? Breena raced through a list in her head, starting with consumption and ending with winter fever. But then the heat of shame that should have assailed her for her aloofness to the Campbell's illness never came.

"You're championing merchants and healers, Dunbar?"

His sneer dripped with derision. His tone made the word *healers* sound unclean. Finlay had no doubt informed him of what they were and their purpose.

Egan scoffed, narrowed his eyes, and crossed his arms over his chest. "You're trying my patience, Laird Campbell. I insist we stick to the issue at hand."

Something Grandmother Sorcha had told her once rang loud in her head. Victims are exploited. Never cower.

Breena pulled back her shoulders, drew herself up to her full height, and eyed the Campbell head on while feigning a smile. "Laird Campbell, my father and I are honored you have allowed us into your keep. We do apologize for our unexpected appearance at your door and beg of your kind benevolence a place to sleep and some food, so we may take our leave, allowing you and Master Dunbar to discuss clan affairs."

Breena fought to keep her gaze unwavering even when his eyes bulged and his face reddened. She'd no doubt been impertinent for opening her mouth. If Egan Dunbar, accompanied by the fifty Dunbar retainers outside, hadn't been their escort, she'd be about to suffer a good lashing or worse.

The Campbell gave her the cut direct. He barked at one of the sentries to take her and Craig to the head of household in the kitchen. Well, at least they wouldn't starve.

She shouldn't care that the Campbell hadn't deigned to address her. Had she intended to exchange a few meaningless words with the man who had robbed her of her parents? No. Not a man. A murderer, one who insulted without provocation, dismissed for the sheer pleasure of it and threw hostility about like it was good cheer.

Her intention for this introduction to the Campbell to mean more than it should was inconsequential, just as she was insignificant standing in his solar. Nothing would ever alter the cold hollowness that had shredded her innards since she was six, because of what he'd done.

As the Campbell sentry accompanied Breena and Craig to the kitchen, loud footfalls tailed them. Breena peeked backward. Alban and a frighteningly large Dunbar retainer, whom Egan had ordered to escort them, followed.

Breena nodded at the Dunbar retainer and eyed Alban as the corners of her mouth turned up. "Alban, I thought that was you. It's a pleasure to see you again."

A smile stretched across Alban's face as he blinked, and shyness pulled his gaze down. "It's nice to meet you again too, mistress."

She cringed at her second lie. "It's such a comfort to have you and the Dunbar retainers with us. Are you to escort us at all times?"

"Master Dunbar said we are not to leave your side under any circumstances." Alban puffed out his chest and lifted his chin. Despite his eagerness, she hoped evading them wouldn't prove difficult or land him in a pickle with Egan.

Upon arriving at the kitchen, the guard ordered them to wait at the entrance. He disappeared into an adjoining scullery where muffled voices could be heard. The pitch rose, but the actual words were masked by the adjoining walls. From the crescendo of a woman's voice, she was not pleased.

The guard exited the room and walked past them with a pinched expression. Behind him came a tall older woman, her grimace adding to her already severe aspect. Breena figured that even a tornado couldn't remove the ramrod straightness of her posture. She now understood why the keep was unkempt; the woman's harassed appearance hinted at little help and a mountain of work.

She turned her hooked nose up at Craig. "My name's Hilda. I'm the head of household. I'll show you where you can bed down for the night. As your arrival is late, the kitchens are closed, but I'll ask the cook if there's aught left."

"We are pleased to meet you, Hilda. We are healers traveling with the Dunbars. I am Craig Maxwell, and this is my daughter."

"Healers?"

She eyed them as if she'd detected a foul stench. Breena recalled the Campbell's reaction. Did all the Campbells dislike healers?

"Yes, we are," Craig answered with nonchalance.

"Follow me. I'm to treat you as guests of the Dunbars," Hilda said, her tone clipped as if she wanted to add *regardless of my thoughts on the matter*.

Breena hurried after Craig, who rushed to catch up with Hilda. "We have several spices, herbs, tinctures, salves, and poultices for sale. We cultivated and harvested them ourselves—only the highest quality, mind you."

Hilda kept marching at the pace of a small charging battalion, without a word or a backward glance.

Craig carried on with his pitch. "Could we interest you in some fresh citronella and mint tinctures? They are good for headaches. We also have dill and hyssop tinctures for cough and colic—they've gotten rid of my coughs countless times. Then there are the marigold poultices for burns and dry skin. And we—"

"We have no need for such things." Hilda's terse response silenced Craig.

As they followed Hilda to their bedchambers, Breena couldn't help comparing the woman to the chatelaine at Castle Duntulm. The latter a warm summer's breeze, and the former a frosty winter's hail. It looked like Breena would need a few extra layers of backbone, a warm cloak of cunning, and a cap of confidence to get through the days to come.

CHAPTER
5

Egan flexed his fingers against the onslaught of irritation as he eyed Alasdair Campbell. The man's indignant scowl was even darker now than when he'd first arrived. His peevish attitude was proving an obstacle.

Alasdair was known for his deceit and cunning. Egan didn't trust him, or anyone on Coll, for that matter. This distrust had demanded he send Alban and Keith to watch over Breena and Craig.

Egan's duty to his sire to keep the peace wrestled with his aim for justice for his dead men Callum and Brodie. This craving for action almost overpowered him. But though the Campbells had killed his men in the most dishonorable way possible—in the dead of night when they were unarmed—he had to honor his sire's wish for peace. It took all his fortitude to push the images of the grief-stricken faces of the widows and fatherless bairns to the back of his mind, where they joined a burdensome conscience.

Egan leaned against the hearth, one hand on the mantel and the other on his hip.

Alasdair took a swig of ale and slammed his mug down on the wooden table, causing it to rattle. "The men who were part of the skirmish on your lands are out hunting. I don't ken when they'll return."

The cords twanged in Egan's neck. "Customarily, how long do these hunting trips last?"

"It depends if the hunt is successful or not, doesn't it? It could be two days. It could be a fortnight. I'm no gypsy fortune-teller."

Egan didn't succumb to the posturing. A judicious clan chief wouldn't demonstrate such a blatant disinterest in his men's whereabouts. And Alasdair was judicious if nothing else.

"How long ago did they leave?"

"Two days."

In all likelihood, Alasdair ordered them to a hunt to avoid their presence when Egan arrived.

Adrenaline pulsed through Egan's veins, grating on his patience and propelling heat through his body. "Did they leave before or after you received my missive?"

"After. How the hell was I to know you'd want to speak with them? My word should be good enough. I know my men. They are honorable, therefore fault for the skirmish has to lie with your men."

What utter bollocks! Egan was quite certain Alasdair had not only arranged for his men to attack on Dunbar territory two weeks ago but was fully aware and could account for their every move.

He itched to put his fist through the other man's jaw. "Then I am your guest until your men return. If their hunting trip takes longer than three days, I'll be forced to go find them."

Alasdair's eyes bulged at Egan's threat. He backhanded his wooden mug, which flew across the solar in a wide arc. It crashed against the stone wall. Rivulets of amber liquid streamed down the wall, making tiny puddles on the stone floor. Both the Campbell's guards shot up at attention. Alasdair slapped one hand against the tabletop and clawed his chest with the other as his loud breathing ripened into coughs.

Egan failed to see the levity, despite the tug of a sardonic grin. The solar door swung open, and Dougray, who'd been standing guard, scanned the chamber, sword in hand, eyes alert. Dougray was one of the strongest and most astute of the Dunbar's retainers, when he wasn't itching for a fight or chasing lightskirts. The two Campbell guards fumbled for their swords. Their ineptitude caused Egan to grin again, this time with genuine levity. If he'd given the command, they'd both be dead before they'd even drawn their weapons.

"Stand down, Dougray, Alasdair just has a little indigestion," Egan said.

Alasdair's hacks grew louder, as if in protest.

Dougray nodded and stepped back outside, but not before scoffing at the two Campbell guards.

"You expect me to feed your men for three days?" Alasdair said, after the coughs subsided.

"My men are skilled hunters. They can feed themselves."

The glare in Alasdair's gaze flattened despite the persistent sneer. The coughs had taken the fight out of him. He was averse to feeding them for three days from his own larder but didn't object to them hunting on his lands.

Egan halted his discussion and exited the solar.

Dougray strolled alongside Egan as they accompanied a Campbell guard to locate the head-of-household. The eerie passageways and foulness of the keep made Egan wish for a night out in the fresh air under the stars.

Dougray appraised their surroundings, then whispered, "Not a lot of Campbells about."

Egan kept his voice low. "Alasdair claimed a number of his men are out on a hunt."

"For Jacobites or food?"

The lack of crops, livestock, and other means of food production on Campbell territory suggested the Campbells made their coin fraternizing with the British. They presumably earned bounties for Jacobite hunting or the British could simply forgive their tax obligations. One thing was for certain, the Campbells weren't industrious enough to make coin by other means. Some clans coordinated shipbuilding ventures, while others got involved in small-scale production of local goods like distilleries.

Egan raised a hand to rub the back of his neck when thoughts of butchered neighboring clans flooded his head. They were simple farmers, trying to raise their families. Their only crime had been to lend a supporting hand to Charles Edward Stuart, leader of the Jacobites. In the end, the unhappy truth was "the Butcher" Lord Cumberland, leader of the British army, had trained his men well; they were too many and too well funded to lose to his countrymen.

Some were of the opinion that the Battle at Culloden had crushed the rebellion, but others, like Egan, still had faith that wasn't the case.

"If they are hunting for Jacobites, then they have no need to hunt for food, do they?" Egan said.

"Then they're not simply traitors to Scotland, they're lazy traitors?"

Egan smirked. "That sounds about the whole of it."

"There's a rumor the Campbell himself not many days back knifed one of his own men in the back after the man dared question him."

"Never trust a Campbell," Egan muttered.

"From your scowl after the meeting with Alasdair, I presume we'll be staying longer than was planned?"

"I'll make it as short a stay as possible."

"The Campbell will never admit his men were responsible."

His father's edict for peace rang in his head. He exhaled in slight frustration. "This journey was necessary, nonetheless."

Dougray had been hankering for a fight since Callum and Brodie's deaths. His lips lifted to bare his teeth. "Their incompetence will make the win less satisfying, but just give the order and we can annihilate them."

"Let us not get down in the muck with them. At least, not yet."

When they arrived in the kitchen, the Campbell guard bid them wait for he had to locate the head of household.

Egan assessed the kitchen. The utensils, pots, and pans were old, crooked, and sparse compared to their kitchen at Eileanach Castle. Breena and the old man wouldn't have much success selling their merchandise to a clan that couldn't afford decent kitchen supplies. What about this friend of theirs? Curiosity crept into his gut.

He hadn't missed the way something seethed beneath the surface when Breena addressed Alasdair. It was clear Breena was built with mettle and tenacity, taking on sentries and lairds alike. But what was she and the old man about?

Daegan had presented her as a MacRae several months ago, so it baffled him that she introduced Craig Maxwell as her father. Did it not occur to her he'd remember the details? Or was he the one who was mistaken? Should he send a missive to Daegan for clarification as to whether she was a MacRae or a Maxwell? Too intrusive. He could simply ask her. But that'd put her on guard if she was dissembling, and Egan didn't want her to caution herself, at least not around him.

He mulled over her amber eyes, the color of his favorite *uisge-beatha* and the way she'd bitten down on her lip, giving it the hue of a ripe peach. Getting the lass to give up her secrets stirred something primal inside him.

CHAPTER
6

Hilda showed Breena into a tiny windowless bedchamber, which was more like an oversized closet. The candle Hilda lit threw the stifling space into flickering light. A small pallet with its coarse blanket eyed Breena from a corner. The sight of it made Breena's skin itch. She was about to deposit her portmanteau atop the stool at the foot of the pallet but reconsidered when she noticed the left leg was slightly shorter than the right. Stale dust hovered in the air. Breena rubbed her nose in anticipation of a sneeze that didn't come.

Breena set her portmanteau on the floor and turned to face Hilda, trusting her smile was adequately amiable.

"Since the cook has retired for the night, I could go down and scrounge up something to eat myself. There's no need to disturb the cook."

Maybe she could determine something about the guards' schedule or even the location of the dungeon if she could strike up an accord with Hilda.

Hilda narrowed her gaze. "We don't allow strangers to scrounge in our kitchen."

Breena cleared her throat, grasping for another approach. "We'll be here for a few days. I'd welcome the chance to make myself useful, if your keeper of the wardrobe has extra mending or general sewing."

Hilda pinned her with a stare as if she were a skunk.

"We are quite capable of performing our own duties."

From what she'd observed, that was not the case, but Breena wasn't going to point that out.

"Well then, mayhap I can do the—"

"I'll have the cook send up your supper," Hilda cut in, then made an about-face that would have made a field marshal proud.

Keith, the large Dunbar retainer Egan had assigned to escort her, stood outside. The man was built like a mountain and could hold a conversation like one as well. If it were at all possible to sleep in this keep it would be with this man guarding her door. It was unfortunate however, that safety wasn't her only worry at the moment.

Breena gave the man a cursory nod and slid her chamber door closed. With the lightest fingers possible, she slid the bolt shut, ignoring the tremor in her hands. If the Campbells found out what she was about to do, they wouldn't hesitate to execute her. Breena took in her surroundings, hoping that she would see some sign of her mother. She did not. Had her mother been in this chamber? Had they taken her life in this very keep?

She swallowed the rush of emotions that preceded the memories of past witch hunts. And then there were the ghastlier stories Sorcha had told her to impress upon her the repercussions of witchery among non-witches. The worst of her memories involved her childhood friend Rowan MacNeil. The MacNeil family had been driven out of Kilmuir village. They'd been branded witches after a jealous friend of Rowan's grandmother had reported her as a witch to the authorities.

She hadn't seen Rowan since. She missed her.

With Hilda on her way to instruct the cook to send supper, she had to be quick. Breena swore a long time ago she would never use witchery for healing, for personal gain, or in places where she would be discovered. The consequences were too high a price. She didn't want to meet the same fate as her mother or Rowan. Nonetheless, it appeared necessity was about to make her break part of that oath.

Was her father being held in the Campbells' dungeon? Since she was six, she'd been led to believe her parents had been in a fatal accident. But then three weeks ago she'd found out that her mother in fact had been executed for witchcraft and a murder that never happened and that her father had been thrown in the Campbells' dungeon by Alasdair.

Perspiration formed on her brows now, and tears welled up in her eyes. Why had Craig and Madeline waited nineteen years to tell her this? Because her parents didn't want her to know, they'd said. Why? She blinked the tears away.

Well, she needed to know.

She picked up her portmanteau and flicked the two latches open. She inhaled the familiar assortment of herbal scents, ranging from earthy to sharp and exotic. Breena grabbed the nettle leaves, the sprig of rue, cumin seeds, and the red hair ribbon. She planted them on the table with its water-filled chipped ewer and burning tallow candle.

Ignoring the tightness in her chest and dryness in her mouth, she poured three cups of water from the ewer into the basin, then added the nettle, rue, and cumin. Breena lifted the candle from its holder and placed it to stand in the center of the basin, now two thirds filled with water and the floating herbs. She knotted the red ribbon around the middle of the candle.

Clearing her mind, she focused on the candle and its melting wax.

"Is my father in the Campbells' dungeon?" Her voice was a strained whisper.

As the wax melted, it dripped into the herb-sprinkled water. The droplets formed two separate lines, then one of the lines branched out and touched the other. Breena's eyes narrowed at the familiar H. The rune symbol *Hagalaz* foretold of destruction and change. She exhaled in a rush of impatience. But destruction and change of what?

Since she'd been taught the art of divination by Sorcha, the signs had plagued her with endless ambiguities. Not to mention the fact that her question was almost always ignored, and instead a vague indication of future events was provided. Sorcha would be disappointed her skills hadn't advanced. Would consulting with the stones yield a clearer answer? She reminded herself she wasn't eager for more ambiguities. Nor did she relish discovery by the Campbells. She removed the ribbon and returned the candle to its holder.

Breena plopped down on the pallet, not surprised at its hardness. She rested her elbows on her knees and let her forehead fall into her open palms. If the Campbells' keep was in such a poor state, she didn't like to think of the condition of their dungeon. She shuddered as coldness coated her spine. She had to find her father and take him away from this horrid place.

CHAPTER
7

Breena sat her uncle down in the chamber across the hall from hers to tend to his cut lip. He'd returned with Alban and their trunks after leaving their wagon with George, who had decided to camp outside with the Dunbar retainers.

Healing was more than Breena's livelihood. It gave purpose to her life, not to mention the gratification of healing the sick and injured. She'd be at a loss if it were taken from her. If Egan found out about her witchery and her family's history, it could threaten all she held dear. She couldn't let that happen.

She wouldn't.

Then there was her dream of having a family of her own, a husband and bairns who belonged to her, the same as she belonged to them. A dream she'd had since her parents had vanished. It had filled the void and given her hope for her future. If her witchery was revealed to the MacIntyres, she'd be shunned.

No one would take her to wife then.

Something sharp gnawed at her insides, as if her future tilted precariously on the proverbial edge of a cliff. She pushed the thought aside as she tilted Craig's chin up to apply the alcohol.

Craig eyed her. "You've fussed enough, lass. It doesn't even hurt. Besides, I can do that myself."

"If I left it up to you, you'd let it fester. You are a grand healer for others, just not for yourself."

She ignored a dismissive wave of his hand and sprinkled some alcohol onto a piece of linen. With care she patted the damp linen on the cut.

"Ouch!"

"I thought it didn't hurt."

He huffed. She was well acquainted with the male tendency to act tough. It was a tendency she ignored.

Breena finished cleaning the wound and reached for the St. John's-wort salve. Not wanting Keith or Alban to overhear her next words, she strode to the door and closed it before returning to Craig's side.

As she applied the salve, his eyes flicked up at her.

"What is it?"

"Since the Dunbars are all taken up at present and Egan is otherwise occupied, we should have a look around the grounds," she whispered.

"And what about our guards outside?"

She ruminated for a second. "We could make a pretense of looking for the bathhouse."

"Now is as good a time as any, I suppose."

Something in his tone made her pause. "I am obliged you consented to us coming here, despite the dangers."

"I hope it's a decision I don't regret, for both our sakes."

A short while later, Breena strode into the courtyard beside Craig. She fetched linen and a heather-pressed soap in the event they were interrogated. Alban and Keith were close behind. The waxing moon shed meager light on their surroundings despite it having swelled since she'd last seen it a few days ago, much like her hope of finding her father. And while there was a chill in the air, it wasn't the kind that seeped into your bones, like in the Campbell's solar.

Breena and Craig assessed their surroundings. Then Breena's posture perked up at the burning torch by the side of the building across from where they stood. The most she'd garnered about dungeons was that they tended to be close to the guard house, and if she was not mistaken, the burning torch signaled guards on duty.

Breena flicked a purposeful glance at Craig and inclined her chin in the direction of the guardhouse. Craig gave a discreet nod.

Breena cleared her throat. "I'd wager that's the bathhouse."

"That's not the bathhouse, it's the guard—" said Alban.

"Yes, it looks like the bathhouse. If not, I am sure they can point us in the right direction," Craig said, his words unnecessarily loud.

She was beholden to Craig for interrupting Alban, who no doubt wanted to set them straight.

Breena ignored Alban's puzzled expression and darted for the entrance to the guardhouse, forcing everyone else to keep up.

The guardhouse was an improvement, for unlike inside the keep, out here she could identify the stench, a particularly ripe version of horse manure, sweat, and the outhouse. Archaic and unpolished broadswords, maces, and axes hung on the walls. The walls themselves looked like they hadn't been whitewashed in years. Two Campbell guards were seated at a table across from each other in the midst of a card game. Their heads jerked up at Breena as she entered.

From their bulging eyes and gaping mouths, Breena ventured to guess that women did not frequent the guardhouse. After a moment's awkward silence, both guards jumped to attention. Their stools fell over with simultaneous thuds.

One of the guards was tall and lanky, like a beanpole, with a flat gaze. The other guard, who was short and beefy, had a shrewd look about him. Breena scanned the guardhouse and spotted an arched doorway toward the back, blocked by a barred iron door, which seemed a promising start.

She threw on a toothy smile at the shrewd guard in an attempt to flirt, hoping her inexperience didn't show. She sauntered toward him just as Craig, Alban, and Keith arrived.

"Good evening, kind sirs," Breena said.

"Mis . . . mistress, how can we be of service?" the shrewd guard said. His blinking eyes signaled uncertainty, which she pounced on by gently brushing invisible dust from his right arm.

"We arrived today from Kilmuir. Can you believe it took three days to get here?"

The guards exchanged a look of uncertainty at the same time that Breena shot Craig a calculated glance while inclining her chin in the direction of the barred iron door.

Breena snapped her head back with a feigned smile to the guards, concentrating on the shrewd one. She reached out as if to touch his arm again but then paused mid reach, lowered her chin, and brushed some imaginary dust from her décolletage as she thrusted out her chest. It was wicked of her, but it was all for a good cause. She was taken aback when it worked.

She regaled the guards with step-by-step details of their journey. Giggling and twirling her braid did wonders for the animation of her story. Out of the corners of her eyes she kept track of Craig as he pressed on to the back and examined the doorway. When he started back toward her, she wrapped up her story. Breena blinked, bit on her lip, and looked around as if taking note of her surroundings for the first time.

"Why, this isn't the bathhouse. Can you good gentlemen direct us to the bathhouse? We are quite lost."

"It's in the keep, behind the kitchen, mistress. Separate ones for the laddies and the lassies," the taller guard said, showing yellow teeth.

"I am indebted to you. I bid you good night."

Later, after her bath, Breena scuttered up the stairs toward her bedchamber, grinning as she recalled the guards' astonishment at her appearance in the guardhouse. Breena wasn't a feckless woman, but she'd enjoyed acting as one today. It was a strategy she'd used on occasion to get her male patients to drink their tinctures or promise to stay off an injured leg or broken arm. She was now keen to speak with her uncle about what he'd found.

She tilted her head up as she reached the top of the stairs.

A falcon's wings expanded in her chest. Egan stood on the landing. Next to him was a monolith of a Highlander she'd observed him speaking with earlier. His eyes narrowed, which made her clutch her linen and soap tighter.

"Is aught amiss?" Egan said.

"Pardon me?"

Had Alban or Keith said something to Egan?

"The Campbell's head of household sent up food with a chambermaid, but the maid couldn't locate either you or Craig. And as it happens, I am unable to locate both Alban and Keith."

Breena exhaled in a rush of air. So, he didn't know about her visit to the guardhouse. "I left them at the bathhouse. It slipped my mind to inform Keith or Alban I was finished. Forgive me if I caused any worry."

"I need to speak with both you and your father."

She blinked. What could he possibly want to speak to them about?

"Craig . . . my father is in the men's bathhouse."

"As he is unavailable, do me the honor of taking a turn with me out-side?" His words would have been gracious if he had chosen to return her attempt at a smile.

CHAPTER
8

*E*gan's suspicions refused to be crushed by the quiet calm of the night. In fact, after Gregor from the Dunbar camp informed him of what Craig's coachman had said, he felt vindicated from his earlier hunches. As the story goes, Craig's coachman, George, guilelessly let it slip that Craig and Breena were here to rescue someone.

The subtle floral notes of earthy heather imbued with something exotic flirted with Egan's nostrils, sidetracking his purpose. It conjured up the deep pink and purple glens behind Eileanach in the springtime, fragrant and stunning, some with sinuous winding lochs—lakes—and others with freshwater creeks. It was all wild and untamed, and so unlike this place. He'd swived his first lass in one of those glens, almost fifteen years ago—Lucy with the bright green eyes.

Turned out, Lucy did quite a bit of swiving, and not just with him.

He eyed Breena now before he asked his question, curious about her reaction.

"Were you and Craig in the guardhouse tonight?"

She kept her head straight, but the fingers of her right hand popped up to tap her parted lips. Although nothing changed in her overall countenance, he detected a stiffening of her shoulders.

Gregor had also reported seeing them leaving the guardhouse.

"We mistook it for the bathhouse," Breena said.

No one in their right mind would make that mistake.

Her guard was up. A subject occurred to him that might bring it down.

He shot her a glimpse and offered a smile. "How long have you been a healer?"

The rigidity in her shoulders eased. "I started practicing seven years ago, although I apprenticed for Craig in the beginning."

Egan noted with no little interest that she referred to her father by his first name, if he was indeed her father.

He took a step back. "You started practicing when you were what, ten?"

She shot him a dubious glance. "Is that question designed to flatter me?"

He feigned a look of shock. "Why ever would you say that?"

The curve of her jaw relaxed a little bit more, but it wasn't quite a smile. "Meaningless endeavor, your attempt at flattery. I am no young miss."

"You're not exactly an old spinster either."

She continued as if he hadn't spoken. "I started observing Grandmother Sorcha, who was also a healer, when I was six. But my formal training didn't start until I was older."

Six? Didn't she take time to enjoy childhood? Come to think on it, training on his own responsibilities as future laird had started at an early age as well. In addition to arithmetic, Gaelic, philosophy, and the arts, his tutor had taught him the subtleties of addressing peerage for those rare social occasions when he had to converse with his grandfather.

The duties of their squires, marshals, seneschals, retainers, pastoralists, and the lot had been drilled into him at a young age. As a boy, Egan hadn't understood why he'd had to learn more, practice harder, be smarter, tougher, and faster than the other lads. It had taken him some time to work it all out.

He, too, hadn't had a typical childhood.

"Have you always wanted to be a healer?"

She nodded, as she bent down to pluck a piece of tall meadow grass.

"And you're quite accomplished, from what I've seen."

"I suppose," she mumbled absently, twirling the grass around her pointing finger.

"And modest as well."

This time a genuine smile broke out. He'd achieved his purpose. He scrutinized her as he asked his next question.

"I was surprised to find you here on Coll. I'd have thought as the MacIntyres' healer, you'd be quite busy at Duntulm."

Her eyelids fluttered as her mouth opened to speak, but no words came out. His eyes lingered on her lips, taking in their heart shape for a bit too long before he blinked away.

"My unc . . . father and I told you why we were here: to unload merchandise and see an old friend."

Egan had negotiated enough clan disputes for the Dunbars to know when someone was lying. Something clicked in his gut, and he took a chance.

"Are you here to find your uncle?"

"No. We're here to find a friend." The pitch of her voice had risen, conspicuously so.

"I misunderstood. Forgive me. What's your friend's name?"

The delicate muscles at her throat worked as if she was having trouble swallowing. Why was she hesitant to discuss this friend?

A look of resignation etched its way across her soft feminine features. "His name is Ian."

Egan sensed that was the truth.

He chuckled. "Is this Ian infamous?"

He'd meant it as a jest, but her widening eyes suggested she not only found no humor in his question but that he'd hit some thread of truth. It was clear she was poor at dissembling, particularly when nonplussed.

"No."

Egan made a mental note, he needed to work more on his wit and charm.

A thin layer of sweat had formed on her forehead despite the coolness of the night. The name MacRae, which Daegan had used several months ago, bounced back into his head.

"Is he a MacRae?"

"Yes. No! Why all these questions?" The bluster in her tone shot up.

The wideness of her eyes reminded him of a scared little bird. Egan tried not to be too pleased with himself.

It was distinctly possible she and Craig were looking for someone named Ian MacRae if he believed her slip of the tongue more than her actual answer. He was inclined to, in this instance.

A distant look washed over her face, wiping away the scared little bird. Something akin to fear settled there, that quickened into straight-out panic. Was the lass in trouble? Her expression elicited something foreign in Egan. It grabbed hold of his gut and twisted. It was difficult to identify what it was. Protectiveness?

The unexpected rawness of it hit him, shattering his senses.

When Egan was seventeen, his grandfather, Sir Donald Lindsay, Baronet, had called his own daughter, Egan's mother, common. The insult had riled Egan, and his protectiveness had caused him to lash out at his own grandfather. They'd never exchanged more than two words again.

Was that protectiveness resurfacing now? It was difficult to reconcile himself to it, considering he knew so little about Breena.

"Let me help you," he said, before he could stop himself or consider the ramifications of what he was offering. He'd stopped walking and was facing her.

Breena stared at him wide-eyed and shook her head. She let out a laugh, but he doubted she meant for it to sound strangled.

"It's unnecessary, I assure you. I thank you for that and for your concern, but it has been a long day, and I need rest. I bid you good night." Her abrupt words held gratitude, but her tone lacked any.

She whirled around and raced back to the keep.

Her thick hair, the color of a raven's wings and still damp from her recent bath, glistened in the night, and cascaded down her back like luminescent waves of silk, ending just above the gentle curve of her pert bottom.

The shade of her burgundy overdress, the color of a French Bordeaux, was a stark contrast to the eggshell white of her underskirt, peeking out at the hem. The material swayed like a siren's call as she darted into the Campbells' keep.

Egan stared at the spot where she'd disappeared. Well, he'd just done a fine job of it. At least she hadn't told him to go to hell.

CHAPTER
9

A short while later, Egan strode into his bedchamber but then stopped abruptly. A full-figured chambermaid was turning down his bed. She threw him a bold come-hither glance; however, her plump lips and generous cleavage left his nethers cold.

"May I be of any service, sir? Any service at all." Her tone husky and honeyed.

Egan skimmed past her voluptuous bosom and rounded bottom straight into the plain chamber, with its unlit brazier, tattered writing desk, and mismatched chair.

"Can you light that?" he said, nodding in the direction of the brazier.

Her lips thinned into disappointment.

Egan sauntered toward the desk, giving her a wide berth.

He leaned over to the smudged windowpane and threw it open. He had to clear the cobwebs in his head.

He shifted around to scan the room as the maid busied herself with the brazier. The hideous counterpane atop the uneven mattress eyed him. Egan feared the frail wooden frame would collapse with even the lightest weight. A few days ago, he would have taken immense pleasure in breaking the damn thing as he took the chambermaid up on her offer, but for some reason, that held no appeal tonight.

<hr />

The next morning, a cockerel somewhere crowed out for dawn, two hours before the sun ignited the horizon with its customary fiery hues.

Upon concluding his ablutions with the cold meager water in the ewer by his bedside, Egan stepped out of his bedchamber.

He surveyed the hall. Where was Alban? The lad almost always awaited instructions on the day's tasks right outside his chamber. Alban's pleasant demeanor, unassuming ways, and eagerness made him perfect for a clandestine mission Egan needed accomplished.

"Have you seen Alban?" Egan said, as he strode pass Rory.

Rory was one of his youngest retainers, who'd taken guard duty the previous night. He was the size of an elk, large enough to lug the various weapons he had strapped to his body with space to spare.

"He came by earlier, sir. He headed in the direction of the guard-house."

Egan trotted down the stairs, strutted into the courtyard and headed for the guardhouse. He welcomed the cool dewiness of the predawn air against his face. Except for the calls of the black and white gannets and the sharp whistles of the white-bellied guillemots nestled in the trees, nothing stirred.

It appeared the Campbells were late risers.

He stepped into the guardhouse with the aim of asking after Alban but stopped precipitously and froze.

Alban, Craig, and two of the Campbell guards were in the middle of a card game at a wooden trestle table. From the empty trenchers and goblets around them, they'd broken their fast already. But that was not what made him stop all of a sudden. The last person he'd expected to see in the guardhouse was Breena.

Egan's eyes swept the full length of her. She stood dressed in the same gown as the previous night, except this time her glossy hair was dry, plaited, and the ends held together with a wide red ribbon. In the blackness of the previous night, he'd failed to catch the way the burgundy dress emphasized the rose hue of her cheeks or the paleness of her décolletage, now revealed under a flickering torch.

Breena pointed at a card in one of the guard's hands.

"But how can an ace be both a one and an eleven?" Breena asked, her lips pinched together. Something in her posture looked practiced, as if she were a thespian onstage.

"It's vingt-un card rules, mistress," one of the guards said, then gave the widest and longest open-mouth yawn Egan had ever seen.

Egan cleared his throat with drawn-out exaggeration. Five heads swiveled around to face him. The two guards nodded in his direction, their movements slow, their eyes heavy. Had they been up all night, or was drunkenness involved? If he lived in a dung pile of a castle like this, he'd drink before dawn too. Alban stood up, staggering in the process. Egan lifted an eyebrow.

"Good morning, sir. How may I be of service?" Alban said. His words slurred.

Egan narrowed his eyes. Alban too? "Come find me when the game is over."

Alban plopped himself back on his stool. Had just one night at the Campbells' keep driven Alban to drink and gamble? In contrast to the others, Craig and Breena looked quite alert and attentive.

Egan didn't miss the way Breena avoided his gaze. The panic that had been imprinted on her features from the previous night was now replaced with determination. Craig, on the other hand, had blanched when his eyes had connected with Egan's. He now seemed intent on studying the cards in his right hand, which he had lifted like a shield in front of his face.

One of the guards, whose head bobbed far too much, landed head down with a loud clunk on the table. Egan gaped, but no one else seemed to notice. When loud throaty snores, which threatened to bring down the roof, started to vibrate from the felled guard's mouth, then it hit Egan.

Had he thought her a Valkyrie the previous day? No. She was more like Loki, a trickster.

Egan's heart rate quickened as adrenaline pulsed through his veins. "Breena, may I have a word outside?"

"I am busy at the moment, perhaps later?" Her chin inched outward with obstinacy.

Egan shot her a steely gaze. "I insist we speak now."

He'd opted for a chastising tone. The same one he had used in the past with his sister Phoebe and little brother Alex whenever he'd wanted to impress upon them the error of their mischievous ways. Of course, it never worked with them.

His eyebrows shot up when Breena stepped around the table and sauntered toward him. Craig threw them both a questioning glance as Egan ushered her outside. The dullness of the predawn sky cloaked them in shadows. He stayed close to the wall of the guardhouse. He didn't want anyone who came out of the keep witnessing them. If his suspicions were correct, they'd need the stealth.

When they were out of eyeshot and earshot of the guards, he swung around to face her. He glared as she scuttered to catch up, stopping two paces away. Her movements brought her face into full illumination by the torch's light. He took in the pursed lips and the deep crease between her brows. Her attempt to appear disinterested in his interest was having the opposite effect.

"It's no coincidence you're both at the guardhouse again, is it?" His whisper was sharp. He hoped no one overheard.

"Pardon me, Master Dunbar?" He didn't believe the blank look she threw him.

"I've given you leave to use my name. It's Egan. And diffidence will not serve you well in this conversation."

"Forgive me, Egan, I don't follow."

The determination in her chin turned to full-blown sassiness with a hip jut to the left. For a moment Egan was speechless at her reaction. His eyes lingered a bit too long on the apricot glow of her lips under the torch's light. He swallowed back the flood of moisture to his mouth.

"I'm returning to the game," she said with an impatient huff and turned around.

Egan reached out and swung her back around. The buzz of a shock sizzled through his body at contact with her arm. Egan jerked back and released her. Her eyes widened, surprised as well.

Egan exhaled in a rush, hoping to rid himself of the heat building up inside him. "If the Campbells find out what you and Craig are up to and you're lucky, you'll find Ian for sure, because you'll both be joining him in the dungeon. And if unlucky, neither of you will leave Carragh alive."

Her eyebrows shot up and her jaw ground down in what looked like obstinacy. She lowered her eyes, examined her shoes, and flattened the fronts of her skirts. When she faced him once more, the determination was back.

"Master Dunbar, whatever are you referring to?"

How purposefully obtuse could a lass be? But then recalling their conversation last night, something like understanding speared Egan's gut as he blinked.

Considering the ardor with which she had defended Craig against the Campbell guard yesterday, Craig might not be her father, but he was important to her. Perhaps a close relative? This Ian MacRae was important too.

"The name is Egan. I am referring to the fact that you laced those men's food with a sleeping tincture. Have you taken leave of your sanity?" Egan struggled to keep his voice low, despite the thumping in his chest.

She worried her lip, but she remained silent.

Indecision fanned out from his midriff, even as something else tightened his nethers. His need to take hold of her shoulders and shake until she saw reason warred with his desire to draw her in, hook those apricot lips away from her teeth with his own tongue, just so he could have a taste.

She was utterly and completely unaware of the type of man the Campbell was, the things he was capable of, what he would do to her if she were caught breaking into the dungeon.

Egan made a move to turn. "I'll just go and inquire with those guards if Ian MacRae resides in their dungeon."

She darted in front of him. Her whiskey-colored eyes shot him a glare.

"Why are you meddling?" Every syllable was exaggerated.

"If Eva or Daegan found out what you two are doing, they would no doubt tell you how irresponsible you are, and if they found out I stood by and let you do it, they would have my hide."

Perhaps it was his harsh tone or the fact that he returned her glare with one of his own. Whatever it was, her expression sobered. Egan's eyes followed the movement of her slender jaw as she swallowed. His unwitting gaze found her lips again. Bloody hell, the devilish things he could do to lips like those.

Perhaps it was just that she was so bloody irksome, or the fact that she was standing too close, but her floral scent threw a heavy, sluggish haze over his senses. His lungs fought for air, as if he'd stepped into a steamy hut with a thermal bath.

He lowered his gaze to avoid leering. Her gown was plain, yet it somehow managed to look regal on her tall, slender figure. The lass tended to hold her head high, her chin up, and her back straight.

An image of her without that gown, every fair luminous inch of her exposed, with unbound hair, hit him like a cudgel to the chest. Egan had to shift his stance for a more comfortable one. He took a deep cleansing breath and shoved his hands through his hair. What the hell was the matter with him?

"I apologize."

He blinked. Why was she apologizing? He was the one staring at her like a lecherous bastard about to pounce and ravish her senseless.

"What for?" He needed a good dunking in a frigid loch to clear the fog in his head.

"I had to lace Alban's food with the tincture as well. It was unavoidable."

His brows knitted, recalling Alban's slurred words. "Why was it unavoidable?"

"Your Alban is too keen. He would have figured out what was happening. We have at most a mere hour before the rest of the keep awakens and someone wanders into the guardhouse. You must leave. I beg you."

The plea in her voice was interwoven with a raw apprehension that clawed at Egan's chest. Was this her way of giving in, and taking him into her confidence? Or had he forced her hand?

"Why did the Campbells imprison Ian?"

"Because he dared go against the Campbell. I found out three weeks ago. I'd thought him dead all these years." Skin bunched around her eyes, adding something gut-wrenching to her plea.

An intense urge to protect this lass blazed through his body with such vehemence, it made Egan unsteady where he stood. She was going to poke the angry wasps' nest.

And if the determination he saw in her face was any indication, she was prepared to get herself stung in the process.

His sire's words boomed in his head. *We lost too many in the old Clan Wars, countless fatherless bairns and grieving widows left. We can't allow this to lead to another war.* His duty to his sire warred with this strange, bur-geoning need to protect this lass, for she would no doubt do this with or without his assistance. And the only way to protect her was to assist her. However, in doing so, he also risked poking the angry wasps' nest himself. And a war between the Campbells and the Dunbars goes against his sire.

Egan turned away from her and mumbled a few choice expletives. He had to resist the urge to stomp his feet like a rebellious boy of ten.

The truth was, Egan himself wasn't against war with the Campbells, but every molecule, bone, and cell in his body fought against disobeying his sire. Still, assisting the lass didn't necessarily mean that war would follow. Not if it was done in a well-planned, clandestine manner. If it was, the Campbells would be none the wiser. He took a deep breath, prayed he wasn't making a monumental error in judgment, and turned back to face her.

"There is no way I'm allowing you or Craig to go prancing around the Campbells' dungeon. It's far too dangerous."

She drew herself up to her full height, her chin lifted, and she crossed her arms over her chest.

"Are you going to inform the Campbells?" she asked, mutiny etched in her delicate features.

"I'm coming with you." Bollocks! Had he just offered to break into the Campbells' dungeon and rescue a prisoner? He had taken leave of his bloody senses.

Her brows creased in puzzlement. "You . . . expect to come with me as I inform the Campbells we're breaking into their dungeon?"

"No. I'm coming with you into the dungeon. We're not informing the Campbells of anything." His whisper was laced with impatience.

Egan expected the panic in her gaze to ebb, given that he'd not only agreed to say nothing to the Campbells but also extended his services in freeing Ian, but instead she shook her head, the whites in her eyes gleaming.

"No. No. If you'll please just leave, we are quite capable of—"

"This is not a negotiation." His voice was resolute.

Egan was as sixes and sevens that she seemed more panicked at his plan to help than at Craig and herself alone breaking into the dungeon. It occurred to him that she didn't trust him, which made even less sense, since she was the one dissembling.

It grated at his nerves. Why had he allowed himself to get caught up in this charade? And what a cold punch in his face that his help was unwelcomed and somehow distasteful. But hang the debt he owed her, the fact that she was Eva's friend, his duty, and the fact that she was lying through her teeth; he just couldn't stand back and let harm come to a woman. Barely discernable footsteps hitting the soft grass sounded behind him. Egan's hand went for the hilt of a dirk as he swung around. He exhaled in a rush of breath. It was Craig. Egan let go of the dirk and swore inwardly. He'd been so taken up with the maddening lass in front of him he'd failed to keep an eye on their surroundings. What if it had been a Campbell?

Craig padded toward them with a questioning look.

"Is aught amiss?"

"I was just pointing out to Breena that if you two have taken leave of your senses enough to break Ian out of the Campbell's dungeon, you will both benefit from my assistance."

Craig's eyes bulged. He then scratched his chin. "How did you—"

"It's not important. What is important is you understand I'll not allow you to proceed with this absurd plan unless you accept my help. Because otherwise, you'll both get yourselves killed. I don't want that on my conscience . . . I have enough there already." Egan swallowed the unpleasant taste of guilt as Alex's face hovered on the periphery of his mind.

A host of emotions played across Craig's face, from shock to acceptance, then settling on resignation.

"We accept and appreciate your help. Ian MacRae is innocent. The Campbells cannot be trusted, whatever they claim he did."

Egan glanced at Breena, scrutinizingly, at the very moment she chose to rub the back of her neck and look down at her shoes. She'd been caught in a lie, for she'd said the prisoner's name wasn't Ian MacRae, even though he'd gathered as much.

"I happen to agree with you about the Campbells. That's another reason why I'm prepared to lend a hand," Egan said.

"Then it seems we're indebted to you yet again," Craig said.

"There's no debt . . . even if by some miracle we manage to free Ian and leave the dungeon undetected and unharmed."

Egan was no knight in shining armor, and he'd balk at anyone who thought him such. But if not a show of esteem for the fact that he'd just agreed to perpetrate a prisoner breakout and risk igniting an already volatile situation with the Campbells, then he at least expected some degree of relief on the faces of Breena and Craig.

So why did she still look panicked, and he still look resigned?

CHAPTER
10

reena stomped into the guardhouse as a riot of emotions surged through her. She was met by two additional sets of snores bombarding the air inside. She took in the fact that Alban and the second guard had nosedived into sleep. Craig and Egan slipped in after her. Breena's chest had squeezed at having to drug Alban, but it'd been unavoidable. It was a harmless draft, however, except for its potent sleeping properties.

"How long will the effects of the sleeping draft last?" Egan said.

She gave Egan a cutting glance. Irritation flooded her. He meddled where he wasn't welcome. Annoyance heated her insides at the way his perfectly sculpted nose and cheekbones took charge. Who had such ridiculously wide shoulders anyway?

"Two or three hours, if they're undisturbed," she said.

"Then let's hope they remain undisturbed until we return. I doubt the Campbells are fastidious enough to change guards before then," Egan said.

"What's the plan?" Craig eyed Egan.

"It's safer if Breena accompanies me into the dungeon, while you remain here on lookout."

For a brief moment, Craig looked as if he would object. But he ended up nodding in acquiescence.

What if Egan learned of the reason for Ian's imprisonment and her mother's death? Then it was just a matter of time until his friend Laird Rossell Macintyre found out. Breena's insides squeezed. She swallowed the bile threatening to crawl up her gullet. Her life, her future, her livelihood, her reputation as a healer, and her chances of finding a decent husband and having a family of her own would be lost.

"What do I do if a Campbell wanders in?" Craig looked at Egan.

"Since there seems to be one entrance, you will have to come and find us."

"Why don't we all go down?" Breena shook her head free of its mulling.

"We need to be sure none of the Campbells have wandered in here, and that we can return with Ian MacRae, if we find him."

Breena regarded Craig. In his raised eyebrows and thinned lips Breena read worry and doubt. She'd seen those there many times before, like when she'd asked him seven years ago if she could leave Kilmuir to go work for the MacIntyres at Duntulm, or when she'd cried for two days straight after Grandmother Sorcha's death. She tried to squelch the worry from her insides—worry that they would be found out by the Campbells, that Egan would come to know of her family's history, and of the likelihood that her father was indeed dead.

But it refused to be quelled.

A few minutes later, cold sweat trickled down Breena's body as she followed Egan down a narrow, musky corridor. She kept her eyes trained on their path, not wanting to trip on the uneven dirt beneath their feet. When Breena stumbled into something akin to a stone wall, she gasped aloud, and her head jerked up. The stone wall was Egan's hard-muscled chest. He'd stopped his trek and was considering her.

"I will not let anything happen to you." His voice was a whisper.

"Pardon me?" She wrinkled her nose at her own gruff voice.

Why did his nearness addle her thoughts, her senses, and her ability to form words? She shook her head to garner some clarity.

"I can see the fear in your eyes. I will not let any harm come to you." He then turned and continued his trek.

She sprinted to keep up with his long strides. Was she that transparent? She didn't know if it was the fact that her fear showed, that he had spotted it, or that he chose to mention it, but her back shot up to its full height.

She spoke before first considering her own words. "I'm not afraid."

"Why are you lying?" This time his voice was laced with irritation.

Did he ask that question because he'd seen her fear, or because Craig had revealed they were looking for someone named Ian MacRae when she'd denied that very fact just last night? She needed to settle on a story with Craig once and for all. But then again, that was neither here nor there. She refused to apologize for lying to protect her family, especially when all she held dear in this world might be taken away.

"When lies are necessary to safeguard my family and to protect our livelihood, I will gladly spin them."

Egan eyeballed her. His darkening gaze reminded her of the skies when a dangerous storm was brewing. Her skin tightened.

"Is it the Campbell who scares you?" He left her to consider that question as he circled around and resumed his trail.

The Campbell wasn't the only one she was afraid of. She was afraid that Egan would learn of her family's past. That it would bring her shame.

Heaven help her. Was she ashamed of her family's past? Something cold clenched her chest.

"You accuse me of lying, then ask me another question? Aren't you afraid I'll just lie to you again?"

"Point taken."

Breena was having difficulty breathing, and she suspected it wasn't all together due to the dank air in the passageway or the anticipation and dread of what they'd find, but without meaning to, she held her breath, awaiting further questions from Egan.

While she trailed after Egan, she eyed the length of his back. He was an interesting dichotomy of elegance and ruggedness. He held a position of power, as future chief to the Dunbars, and he wielded it with honor. If that wasn't awe-inspiring enough, there was always his imposing physicality.

"Don't tell me gilded lives of future lairds preclude lies and liars?" she said, when no other question came.

Egan snorted. "Is that what you think, I lead a gilded life?"

"Don't you?"

He shot her a wry glance as he continued his trek down the passageway.

"I can understand why you would think that, but it doesn't mean my life is any less complicated or holds fewer responsibilities or burdens than others."

Breena recalled their previous conversation. "You alluded to a burdensome conscience earlier. Is that what you refer to now?"

Egan muffled a chuckle. "You have your secrets and I have mine."

An iron-framed wooden door came into view at the end of the corridor. It was held closed by a heavy padlock. Egan used the ring of keys he'd purloined from one of the snoring guards, and on the third try, the padlock clunked open. The door's metal frame grated against the ground, and its hinges creaked as Egan pushed it open.

He raised his hand. "Wait here."

He padded ahead, disappearing beyond the door. She quietly stood there, even as coldness coated her spine and her eyes widened. She strained to detect sounds, expecting a Campbell to pounce on Egan, for the sharp clash of a sword's blade against another, for angry shouts to erupt. But instead, Egan returned alone.

"Follow me."

Breena heaved a sigh of relief, not realizing she'd held her breath the entire time he'd disappeared behind the menacing door.

She obeyed. As the light from the torch Egan carried struggled to fight the darkness, Breena made out a locked wooden hatch in the ground. The tiny round space they'd just entered could have held six or seven people, with no room to spare. The stone walls and floor were bare except for the hatch.

Egan reached around her and pushed the door closed behind them, then handed her the torch. The heat of its flames hovered over her curled fingers, but it did nothing to warm the coldness in her body. Was her father beyond that hatch? Was a Campbell guard? She considered Egan, at the way his head almost touched the grimy ceiling and the way his shoulders seemed to fill the space. A sliver of calmness settled in her chest. When had her irritation been soothed into gratitude? He did seem to want to help, regardless of his reasons.

"I don't know many lasses who'll go for a stroll in a dungeon. None in fact," Egan whispered, as he surveyed the small space around them.

Breena raised her chin. "I assure you, it's out of necessity."

"You have conviction and mettle, which I admire. It almost makes up for my momentary lapse in judgment in bringing you here."

"I'd be here with or without you."

"I'd guessed as much." His tone held a smile.

Breena lowered her gaze. "But I'm grateful you're here."

The ring of keys jingled as Egan stooped down and tried the first key in the lock that held the hatch shut.

"Even if you and Craig disapprove of me? Or is it my assistance you disapprove of?"

Her eyes flew up to meet his. "We don't disapprove of you."

"I'm thrilled. Then why do you object to my assistance?" Egan attempted to open the lock with another key.

She swallowed against the tightness in her throat. "It's complicated. Suffice to say it's a private family matter."

He shot her a poignant glance. "I've never been accused of being indiscreet."

His devilish grin made her forget herself for a second. Her stomach did funny little summersaults as some of the tension eased from her shoulders. He was more dangerous than she'd originally pegged him. She had to be careful not to reveal anything further.

"I will hold you to your claim of discretion."

"I promise to reveal to no one yours and Craig's penchant for storming the dungeon." Egan whispered as he tried yet another key.

The enormous, rusted lock clanked open. Egan removed the lock and lifted the hatch. An odious smell, something akin to hopelessness and the inevitability of death, hit Breena head on.

The force of it pushed her back against the stone wall; the cold dankness of the rocks seeped through her clothes and sank into the flesh on her back.

A weakening tremor vibrated through her limbs. How could her father survive this for nineteen years? She steadied herself, swallowed, and lumbered forward to look into the opening. It was dark, but she just made out the end of a manila hemp rope dangling below. The rope was tied to a metal ring fastened into the ground where they stood. She shot a curious glance at Egan.

"I've seen enough dungeons to know what lies below is no place for a woman."

"But you can't mean to stop me now, after we've come this far." Something akin to panic speared her gut.

In truth, she felt faint. Was it the noxious smell or the apprehension of what they'd find? Whatever it was, it weighed like rocks, heavier by the second, on her chest, and hit her with a sensation of drifting between reality and the blackest of nightmares.

As a healer she'd cleaned gangrenous legs, soiled bedpans, sores filled with discharge, and burnt flesh, so why did the smell of this dungeon affect her? Why was it difficult to breathe in here? Because it wasn't just the smell. Dejectedness stifled the air, it coiled around, like a serpent waiting to strike, and the fact that her father had been subjected to this for nineteen years made her want to scream, cry out, and strike back at every single Campbell.

"I will go and look for Ian. You shall wait here. And on this I will not yield." His voice was low.

"This is not your decision to make."

"I suppose as a healer you've seen many unpleasant things. But have you ever seen prisoners after they've been tortured, bloodied, and left for dead?"

Her eyes widened, and she swallowed. "I've treated prisoners before, but not in that exact condition."

His chin jutted toward the hemp rope. "Are you capable of climbing down that rope to the lower level?"

She sniffed. Stifling a groan, she hated that he had a point, maybe two.

He seemed to take her silence as agreement of his dictate. "How will I know it's Ian MacRae, if I encounter him below?"

She took a deep cleansing breath, exhaled, and pulled on a distant memory of her father.

"The last time I was with Ian, I was six years old. He towered over me, like a great big oak tree. He had dark hair, kind eyes, and a caring face. That was nineteen years ago." Breena swallowed back the lump as emotion flooded her.

"How old is he?" Egan scrutinized her.

She shifted in discomfiture. "About Craig's . . . my father's age." Her low voice cracked. She was revealing too much, and it unsettled her. But they'd reached the proverbial crossroads where she had to trust him, to a point. There was no other choice. Besides, he'd said he was discreet. Could she trust that? Should she trust him? She broke eye contact and looked away.

"What about scars? Eye color?"

"His eyes always reminded me of warm chestnuts. I don't recall scars."

Egan grabbed one of the silver-handled dirks from his belt, flipped it up into the air, caught it by the tip of its shimmering blade and handed it to her. She took it with raised eyebrows.

"Wait here for me. I won't be long. If a Campbell surprises you, the pointy end of the blade goes into his gut." He winked.

He twisted, took hold of the rope, and lowered himself into the dark abyss below. As the muffled scrapes and scratches of his palms against the rope sounded, her breathing kicked up a notch at what he would encounter on his descent. When faint footfalls sounded on the earthen floor below and the rope slackened, she held her breath, her hand squeezed around the handle of the torch. Were there guards down there? But receding footsteps were all that echoed up from below.

She took a step back and leaned against the stone wall. Her muscles tightened at its coldness. All was silent except for the crackling of the torch in her hand. She closed her eyes, and a memory, like a distant dream, came to her. In it, her parents were together, and the clear azure skies housed a brilliant marigold sun. Their warm smiles eased her insides as they looked down at her. They'd then reached to envelop her in a bear hug while she giggled and squirmed. The softness of her laced day-dress almost touched her skin now, the tenderness and love of their embrace and the warmness of the sun a hairsbreadth away.

That memory now filled her with a wretched emptiness. It curdled her insides. She'd never hug her radiant mother again, never surround herself in that warm safety. They had taken her. Breena stifled an overpowering urge to howl just so the rawness of it would dull the pain. But amid it all, there was now hope that her father was down there, steps away, in this miserable place. Hope that this ever-present hollowness, which had plagued her since she was six, would ease.

The sound of climbing rustled from below. Breena's eyes flew open. The rope had gone taut. She pushed herself away from the stone wall and brandished the dirk in one hand and the flaming torch in the other, even as fear rooted her to the ground.

When auburn hair held in a queue started to ascend from the abyss, she relaxed and let out a breath of relief. The rest of Egan's body rose from below, hand over hand, on the rope. She stared at him as he climbed through the opening and stood in front of her, his expression impassive.

Why was he alone?

CHAPTER
11

*A*larm shot through her as she craned her neck to look behind him. She bit down on her lips and shot him a questioning look.

"He's not in the dungeon," he said.

She tilted her head. *What does he mean, "he's not in the dungeon"?*

Iciness stabbed her gut. "You have to go and look again. You must have missed him."

"He's not there. I checked twice."

"How many prisoners are down there? How can you be sure? Did you search thoroughly? You must go back." Her voice was a strangled rush of words.

"There're just two prisoners down there, one much younger than Ian and the other is fair haired."

Breena pushed past Egan and grabbed the rope. It couldn't be too difficult. She'd just seen him do it. She'd just have to go and look herself.

"What are you doing?" he asked.

"I am going to look for him."

She tightened her grip on the rope, hesitant as to what would come next. She was about to step into the hole when his hands reached over and covered hers. His hands were much bigger and warmer than hers. They were steady on her tremulous ones.

"Look at me," he whispered.

Breena's eyes welled up. She tried to blink the tears away. A pathetic shriek escaped her lips. She looked away.

"Breena, look at me."

When she did raise her head to face him, she'd lost focus on his expression, for tears blurred her vision. She wanted to pummel him for the concern weaved into his calm voice. Logic must have left her again.

"Ian MacRae is not down there."

She wiped away the tears. Her shoulders dropped, and coldness washed over her body. Something in her soul sank like a boulder dropping to the bottom of the ocean. She was grateful she hadn't broken her fast yet, for nausea kicked in. Bile rose, and after several attempts she was able to push it down.

"I'm sorry," he said.

Hollowness tightened its relentless grip on her stomach and twisted. She wanted to curl into a ball on the filthy ground and wail until rationality left, until numbness set in and nothing remained, even the cold.

She somehow released the rope and managed to put one foot in front of the other as she stumbled after Egan back the way they'd come.

Breena was a hairsbreadth away from more tears when they returned to the guardhouse. She was in no mood to answer Craig's questions.

"You didn't find Ian?"

Egan wordlessly shook his head.

The grimness etched in her face must have dissuaded Craig from asking any more questions. He tilted his chin down and frowned.

Breena and Craig trudged after Egan in silence toward the keep, after they'd relocked all the doors and gates and returned the pilfered keys to the snoring guard. The sky had turned to a light gray. They stepped through the keep's main door just as two Campbell guards exited and headed in the direction of the guardhouse. If they'd taken a minute longer, they would have been discovered.

"Will you join me at the Campbells' high table to break your fast?" Egan asked, eyeing Breena and Craig after they were back in the great hall.

Craig shook his head.

"It's more fitting that we sit at the low tables," Breena said.

Breena and Craig took seats at a trestle table across from two Campbell chamberlains carrying on a hushed conversation. The woman sitting next to them was a laundress, if the blue washing dye stains on her graying pinafore were any indication.

Breakfast, with its hushed conversations and downcast eyes, was a dismal affair. Even the morning sun was missing, through the single smudged window. The serving women edged around with stiff shoulders and bleak expressions. The pleasant scents one would expect to waft through the air as breakfast was being served never came. It didn't occur to Breena why everyone looked like they were attending a funeral rather than breakfast until sounds of the Campbell's sharp nasal voice resonated. Breena veered around toward the high table as the Campbell flung a trencher of food at one of the serving women. The woman's head and shoulders collapsed inward as she shrieked away and burst into tears. From the Campbell's diatribe thrown at the woman, it appeared she'd dared serve him cold food.

Just at that moment, Hilda scurried past their table, instructing a young maid who proceeded to place several bannock cakes on their table.

"May I be of help?" Breena asked, standing up to face Hilda, ready to lend a hand.

Hilda's withering stare made it clear she was impeding the serving process.

"With serving the food," Breena explained.

"Only Campbells serve food in the Campbells' great hall," Hilda said, her mouth twisting like she'd tasted something bitter.

There was no thawing that frigid iceberg. Breena swallowed and dropped back down on her seat next to Craig. The truth was she didn't fault Hilda for her horrible attitude. If she lived in a dreary keep with bullies and barbarians in charge, with few to no supplies and even less help, she would be in a perpetual foul mood as well. And she wouldn't put it past a prideful personality like Hilda's to view her attempts to help as a statement about Hilda's ineptitude at her job.

"Stop trying to soften her up. It's useless," Craig whispered in her ear.

As Breena bit into a piece of tasteless bannock cake, she eyed the wall above the high table where there was the head of a boar and, beneath it, low relief letters inscribed on a gray stone plaque. *Ne Obliviscaris.* Forget Not. Breena stifled a scoff. If she were fortunate enough to leave this pitiable place with her father and Craig, that is one thing she would never do. For the moment they were away from Coll she wanted to forget. Forget it ever existed. Except they'd taken her mother from her, thus she'd never be that blessed.

Breena's gaze scanned the high table just as a pair of hazel eyes, the color of smoky quartz, trapped hers. Something had shifted today between the two of them in the dungeon. It was there in the hitching of her breath and the warming of her cheeks as she stared back at Egan. She dragged her gaze away with some effort. Was she coming down with a fever?

———————

Breena let her shoulders drop as she sat outside the curtain wall on a flat slate outcropping. The rippling turquoise sea crashed into the sand and ashen rocks of the shore in frothy white waves, dissipating like her hopes. Its pungent salty scent reminded her of Tulum Bay, just beyond the MacIntyres' castle on the Isle of Skye, where she took her evening constitutional. The chill breeze tousled the hems of her skirts and cooled her ankles. The rawness of the predawn events still rattled and twisted her insides.

Craig, who sat next to her, exhaled in a disheartening rush of breath.

"I, too, am disappointed we didn't find Ian. But from what Egan told me this morning, I don't like to think of your father spending nineteen years in that hellhole, even if one could survive it for so long."

"Did he tell you he refused to let me go down?"

The setting sun made its way further down the western sky, taking with it the warmth and marking the coming end of day, as it also marked the coming end of her rescue mission.

"That was wise on his part. He was trying to shield you from its horrors."

Breena harrumphed. *Does he no longer think Egan a hindrance?*

"Do you think he is dead?" she asked, speaking her fear out loud.

He was staring down at his hands. "I—I do. I'm sorry. I know how much you wanted to have your father back." There was something in Craig's flat monotone that made Breena look at him.

"You've been my father and Aunt Madeline has been my mother these past nineteen years. And I love you both. But I also don't like to think of my father being down there either and I'd hoped for an opportunity to get to know him, to find out what happened. . . . Why was he on Coll?"

"I understand. And your aunt and I love you too. We were never blessed enough to have bairns, but the truth is we think of you as our own."

Breena's vision blurred as tears welled up again and emotion squeezed her throat. She turned in her seat and gave her uncle a bear hug, which he returned with an awkward pat on her back.

"What was he like?" she asked, releasing Craig.

"Ian? Your mother was the love of Ian's life. He'd have done anything for her. And you were the apple of his eye."

The warmness of his words seeped into her, but she lowered her head.

"What if he's not dead? What if they're keeping him elsewhere?"

"Where else can he be?"

"I don't know, but we should scout and snoop around some more."

◆━━◆━━◆━━◆━━◆

A short while later, as Breena trailed after Craig back in the direction of the curtain wall surrounding Castle Carragh, her gaze was drawn toward the Dunbars' camp. She hadn't seen Egan since breakfast.

Breena spotted a group of the Dunbar warriors sparring in pairs. The two mountains among them, Keith and Dougray, stood out. The sounds of grunts and punches carried in the air to where they strolled. Echoes of swords clashing against swords rang out, as did the loud thuds of blades slamming into battleaxes.

Breena's breathing momentarily ceased. Heat ran down her spine when her gaze was drawn to one formidable Dunbar in particular.

Whether it was Egan's height or his easy grace and assuredness of movement, she wasn't sure, for she was too busy gawking at his golden sinewy nakedness from the waist up. A restless sort of power surrounded and vibrated in the air around him. A sheen of sweat on his skin in the evening light gave him the glistening aura of a great Norse warrior god.

He'd tossed aside his léine and coat while he practiced with his men. His hair was pulled back in a queue. Even from a distance her gaze was held captive by the modicum of ruddy hairs on his chest, which trailed a path down his midriff and disappeared in a single line below the waist of his kilt. Her eyes widened, and she swallowed against the rush of moisture flooding her mouth. His upper body was magnificent, all granite looking, well-defined musculature on his arms, chest, and washboard abdomen.

The hem of Breena's dress snagged on something, pulling her back as she dawdled. She looked down at the offending thorny gorse bush. Gathering a handful of her skirts she tugged. A rip sounded. Her uncle stopped and turned around.

"Is aught amiss?"

"My hem's ripped." Breena eyed her skirt.

Craig trailed back toward her, narrowing his eyes at the skirt. Just then, a movement ahead made Breena's head jerk up toward the Dunbar camp. One of Egan's men came at Egan with a two-handed sword at least five feet long, while Egan held one of the foot-long silver-handled dirks in his right grip. She gasped aloud as Egan stood in ready position, feet planted wide apart, knees angled and arms out, every bit a fierce Highland warrior. The sheer force of Egan's iron will, steely determination, and lethal resolve chiseled in his features at that moment made Breena sorry for the retainer who now charged him.

"Quite an impressive bunch," Craig said.

"Uh-huh." Breena swallowed, unable to speak.

The Dunbar retainer lifted his sword above his head. A roar echoed from his mouth as he swung down hard toward the nape of Egan's neck. At the speed of lightning, Egan spun on his left heel, taking two steps back from his opponent's trajectory and at the same time tangling his dirk's cross guard with the blade of his opponent's sword. A sharp clash of blade against cross guard pierced the air. A few of the other Dunbar retainers stopped their sparring to witness Egan and his opponent. With fluid movements, Egan thrust his dirk outward, its cross guard trapping the blade of his opponent's sword with such force, the sword was ripped from the other man's hands and sent flying. The sword landed a few feet away with a dull thud. Egan lurched forward and pressed the blade of his dirk against his opponent's throat.

"I've never seen his equal," Breena said, wide eyed. She cleared her throat to mask the breathy sound of her voice. What must Craig think of her?

Guttural cheers and barks of laughter erupted from the Dunbars. A few of the Dunbar retainers trotted over to Egan, dealing out good-natured slaps on the back. Breena was too far away to catch their exact words. Egan barked out a congenial laugh and in a teasing manner cuffed his opponent's back, who was stunned from the training but after a few breaths threw his head back and joined the revelry.

"Come along, let's head back," Craig said, as he continued in the direction of the keep.

As if Egan sensed he had another spectator, he turned, and his dark gaze locked with Breena's. Time stopped. Her world was reduced to just the two of them as her heart rate picked up the pace enough for her to hear it booming in her ears. Was it indecent to stare at a half-naked Highlander? His gaze pierced her straight down the middle, heating her core and scalding every inch of her body. The fire in his eyes pilfered her ability to look away.

"You're lagging behind." Craig called out to her.

Breena blinked. She was ailing from a strange fever. Her entire body burned as if she'd just jumped through a bonfire. She turned away, grabbed her skirts, and sprinted to join Craig.

"Do you fancy the lad?"

"Don't be absurd." Egan's question from their predawn scout through the Campbells' dungeon rang aloud in her head. *Why are you lying?*

"Well, it's just as well: he's highborn and we're lowborn. I don't have to tell you, that's oil and water."

No, he didn't have to tell her that.

They plodded through the Campbells' gates. The few Campbells they passed ignored, even avoided them. As they headed toward the keep, guttural coughs rang out ahead. Breena peered into the distance.

"I spotted her retching earlier," Craig said.

She followed her uncle's gaze.

A young woman leaned on a tall birch tree toward the back of the keep. One of her hands rested on the trunk for support, while the rest of her was bent over retching behind the trunk. She raised her head for the briefest of moments as if to catch her breath, but then heaved and bent over again. From her long golden hair and her gray working dress, Breena recognized her as one of the women seated in the great hall during break-fast. If it weren't for her dull complexion, with its grayish tinge, she'd be quite pretty.

Breena ran through a list of possible causes in her head, starting with dysentery and ending with food poisoning, considering the conditions and food supply of the Campbells. But then something entirely different occurred to her.

"Can she be with child?" Breena asked.

"From her pale skin, I thought it more along the lines of something she ate."

"Spoiled food?" Craig scratched his chin. "Even though the Campbells' cook has no talent for cooking—the bannock cakes were hard as rocks and the black pudding tasted like mud—the food wasn't spoiled."

The soft ground beneath their feet silenced their steps as Breena and Craig edged toward the woman. The retching had stopped, and she now leaned back against the gray trunk with her eyes closed. She seemed to be collecting herself. As Breena inched forward, Craig stood back. Breena threw him a questioning glance.

"I don't want to scare her," he whispered.

Breena nodded at him. She surveyed their surroundings. The only Campbells about were the men speaking with the guards. They either hadn't noticed the sick girl, or they'd noticed and didn't care. She snorted with contempt and continued toward the young woman.

From her girlish features she could be five or six years younger than Breena's five and twenty.

Breena cleared her throat to alert the girl she wasn't alone. "Are you unwell? May I help?"

The lass's lids fluttered open, and she stared at Breena. Confusion dimmed the aquamarine of her eyes. She blinked several times, after which the cloud seemed to disperse.

"It's happening again. I don't ken what it is," she said, her face twisting in misery. Breena's chest tightened with concern.

"Could it be something you ate?"

"I don't rightly know."

As she spoke, Breena scrutinized the almost imperceptible bluish tint to the lass's lips and the redness of the collarbone area.

Breena offered a warm, affable smile. "I'm a healer. I can help you. My name is Breena."

But the woman's eyes widened in revulsion. Or perhaps she was going to be sick again. "A healer? Please . . . go away."

Breena gazed at the girl in surprise but still took another tentative step forward. Did all the Campbells hate healers? First it was the Campbell himself, then Hilda, and now this poor lass.

"Leave me be!"

Stunned by the girl's outburst, Breena's tongue refused to work, but only for a few seconds. "But . . . I think you were poisoned. Please, I can help you."

The lass wobbled one step back away from Breena, her eyes bulging as she shook her head in disbelief. "Poison? That can't be."

She swerved and staggered toward the curtain wall.

Breena stared after her. "Please come back. Wait! Let me help you."

But the lass kept stumbling toward a gap in the curtain wall, and then she was gone.

Breena's mouth slackened with incredulity. Who would want to poison such a helpless-looking lass?

CHAPTER
12

*E*gan considered a succulent piece of mountain hare before popping it in his mouth. The spiced smell of the meat and the scent of burning oak from the camp's fire mingled with the earthy evening air as purplish-pink clouds drifted across the sky.

His senses were assailed by his men's loud chatter. Half his men bellyached about giving up the last harvest, Samhain, to be here. The other half prayed they'd get back at the Campbells for what they'd done to Callum and Brodie. Many in his clan wanted justice and revenge for the two families now left without fathers. But Egan had to honor his father's request. His words rang aloud in his head. *We lost too many in the old clan wars—countless fatherless bairns and grieving widows left. We can't allow this to lead to another war.* His father's orders were sacrosanct, and he intended to carry them out despite the gnawing in his gut that said the Campbells should pay. Mayhap he would always be a bairn of ten, doing whatever he had to get his father's approval.

Dougray's resonant voice encroached on his mulling and he shifted to eye him. He was describing to the men his latest partner in bed-sport, who had a penchant for screaming like a banshee.

"I always forget to put my hands over my ears when she comes. Then her yowls puncture my eardrums, and I remember."

Half his men barked out in laughter.

Egan had decided to have his eventide meal with his men at the Dunbar camp. Anything to dodge eating food prepared by the Campbells' cook.

Why was it that the entire thirty-odd Campbells in the great hall earlier that day hung their heads as if they'd rather be anywhere but there? Alasdair Campbell. The few words they'd exchanged during the morning meal had cemented the Campbell as a hypocritical, callous despot in Egan's mind. The Campbell had introduced his half-brother, William, and then had proceeded to insult the man.

"My father disgraced our family by taking up with the local whore from Arinagour. William's the result," Alasdair had said.

It shouldn't have surprised Egan that the Campbell had dished out insults to his own half-brother with such imperiousness and nonchalance.

Even though William had remained quiet and stoic, Egan hadn't missed the way his nostrils flared, or the way his hands curled around his goblet at the Campbell's words.

A serving woman had tripped and nearly fallen off the dais as she poured ale in their goblets. The speed and agility with which William reacted, grabbing the woman by the arm and saving her from a fall, had stunned Egan. Not only was the man quick on his feet but he was gallant as well, not traits Egan had ever expected to see in a Campbell.

"I'm a generous person, willing to give a man a chance in spite of his black origin," the Campbell had carried on.

Impatience had needled Egan even as disgust made him shake his head. From the way Alasdair treated his clan, he was anything but generous. The man had gone on to pontificate as he took a mouthful of food and wiped his mouth on his sleeve. "I am so generous that I've brought William here to better his future by serving as my head of retainers. My father had him trained as a warrior from a young age. He can now put that training to good use."

Egan had later inquired of William if he'd been on Dunbar territory two weeks ago and if he recalled what had happened between the Campbells and the Dunbars.

"I wasn't with those Campbells. I am sorry you lost two of your men," William had said.

A gallant and sympathetic Campbell. More than likely, it had started to snow in Hades.

Rory's loud voice jarred Egan from his musings.

"The scullery maid I tupped a few weeks ago left nail marks all over my back. While she screamed in pleasure, I screamed in pain!" Rory bellowed with laughter.

Egan curled his lips as Rory elaborated on the particulars of the story. He refrained from scoffing. Where did his men find these women?

Egan leaned back on the hard cold outcropping where he sat as his mind flashed to Breena. Something had squeezed relentlessly in his chest at the devastation on her face when he told her Ian hadn't been in the dungeon. He'd made the right decision in asking her to wait on the upper level. Egan wasn't squeamish, but if it wasn't the rank smell that sat in the air, then it was the two crumpled dead bodies that had made his stomach churn. He'd told her only of the two prisoners who were alive. The dead men, who could have been Jacobites, were too young to be Ian

MacRae anyway. The question remained however: If Ian MacRae wasn't in the dungeon, was there a chance the Campbells had him locked up elsewhere?

Why the hell did the paralyzing indignation of the whole predawn episode unsettle him so? Because he had to help her, even though it went against all he'd come here prepared to do, to prevent a war. The cost had been too great the last time he'd ignored someone.

Alex's death had been gnawing at his insides for the past fifteen years. His little brother's death had wrecked him. And try as he might, he recalled the good times with less and less clarity. They'd climbed trees together and swam in the sea together. He'd taught Alex to fish in the loch and to skin a mountain hare after their first hunt. But what ended up sticking out in his memory with unblemished recollection was the day he'd ridden home after receiving the missive at Inbhir Garadh, where he'd been fostering. The day he'd seen Alex's lifeless little body. The air thinned around him. Even now, the sharp pain of it speared his gut despite the intervening years. He ought to have given Alex more of his time and not let his duty get in the way.

But he'd been too busy with his own bloody self-importance.

Egan flexed his fingers against the sting of guilt, cracking a few of his knuckles in the process. He'd do whatever he could to help Breena and Craig. His conscience couldn't take the extra load.

He heard footfalls and turned. Dougray approached.

"How will we know if the Campbells return during the night from hunting?"

"Besides the fact that our current position here gives us a bird's-eye view of who enters and leaves the Campbells' keep . . . the Campbell said he'd inform me," Egan answered.

"It won't surprise me if that slips his mind," Dougray said, his voice laced with derision.

Egan wrapped up his meal, then left camp with Dougray in the direction of the Campbells' keep. At the keep they took the stairs, two and three steps at a time. On the fourth level, they headed to Egan's bedchamber. Dougray was to stand guard tonight outside Egan's door. But even without Dougray, Egan wasn't concerned at the possibility that he'd encounter any one of the Campbells with ill intentions at night. With years of training under the MacDonell's tutelage, a feared and revered warlord, he was an adept warrior himself. His men, however, would never allow him to be unguarded in the keep of a hostile clan.

When they stepped into his bedchamber, Alban was waiting with an eager smile plastered on his face, bouncing from foot to foot like a bairn dying to share news.

"Is aught amiss?" Egan said.

It seemed the reconnaissance mission he'd given Alban, after the lad had awoken none the wiser to what had caused him to fall asleep in the first place, had been successful.

Alban peered at the door as if to confirm that only Egan and Dougray were about. He scampered up to them with wide eyes. Dougray closed the door. Both Dougray and Egan regarded Alban with questioning looks. Alban did love the dramatics; if he failed as a warrior, he'd make a splendid thespian.

He leaned toward Egan's ear, placed his palms halfway across his mouth, and spoke just above a whisper. "I overheard two Campbells in the guardhouse. They are holding more prisoners in the gabled garret of the cylindrical flanking tower."

"Strange place for prisoners." Egan scratched his chin, even as a spark of hope crept into his belly.

"These prisoners have each incurred the personal wrath of the Campbell. And he takes pleasure in torturing them himself," Alban said.

Dougray bared his teeth. "The man's demented."

Egan's mind raced with the ramifications of Alban's news. If Ian MacRae was in the flanking tower, what in Hades could he have done to incur the personal wrath of the Campbell himself?

His sire's orders precluded him from striking back at the Campbell for the deaths of Callum and Brodie, but who'd know if he struck back at the Campbells in a surreptitious manner for their imprisonment of Ian MacRae? Of one thing he was certain: anything that would give the Campbell grief would fill him with satisfaction, as it would his men.

"Is this regarding the healer's search of the guardhouse?" Dougray said.

Egan cocked an eyebrow at Dougray. How had Dougray found out that Breena and Craig had interest in the guardhouse?

Dougray cleared his throat and answered the unspoken question. "Keith might have mentioned that the healer and her father were interested in the dungeon."

There was a reason Dougray was Egan's second in command. In addition to possessing the strength of ten men, he was damn astute.

"If you are planning to cause trouble for the Campbells, it would be my absolute pleasure to assist you," Dougray said, a smirk lighting up his face.

Egan snorted. "You and every other Dunbar retainer, I'd venture to guess."

Egan was surprised that a strange protective streak for Breena chose that moment to hit him in the midriff. Breena had asked for discretion, so he had every intention of saying as little as necessary to his men. Then he recalled her unapologetic attitude regarding her lies. Had there ever lived a man capable of deciphering the bewildering ways of women?

He eyeballed Alban. "Did you learn anything else?"

"No, sir, not about the prisoners. However, regarding your other request, one of the Campbell guards said he was looking forward to joining the hunt with the redcoats. And he mentioned the MacDonell lands, in the western Highlands," Alban said.

"This is confirmation these bastards are working for the Sassenachs!" Dougray growled.

"Bollocks!" Egan swore, curling his lips. "Keep your bloody voice down. Do you forget where we are?" His voice was a barely contained whisper as he shot Dougray a sharp look.

Egan had used that gibe himself before, referring to the British as Sassenachs, but that wasn't what chafed his nerves. Dougray, it appeared, had forgotten that his outburst could possibly be overheard by the Campbells, alerting them to Egan's interest in their prisoners.

"Apologies, sir." Dougray's shoulders sagged in a contrite manner.

Egan fisted his fingers against the dark emotions the redcoats always elicited from him. He had to warn the MacDonells.

"I want you to go to Gregor at camp. Have him send two of our men posthaste to Daegan and Angus MacDonell at castle Inbhir Garadh with the news. Leith and Camdyn are our quickest and most skilled riders," Egan said.

Dougray headed for the chamber's door but paused. "When I leave, you'll be without a guard, sir."

"You're my right hand, Dougray, not my nursemaid."

"Yes, sir."

The truth was Dougray was too impetuous, bordering on reckless, to have around for any type of covert mission.

"Also, have Gregor send someone to relieve Keith from guard duty, and have Keith join me." A plan formed in Egan's head as his mouth curved up in anticipation.

Dougray gave a curt nod and departed the chamber.

Alban gave Egan a questioning glance. "Can I arrange a bath and dinner for you this evening, sir?"

"I ate at camp. And there's no time for a bath. We have more important things to do tonight."

Alban quirked an eyebrow. "We do, sir?"

Egan strode over to the single window in his bedchamber. He grabbed the windowsill, straightened his arms, and leaned out, studying the view. Grayness had blanketed the world outside. There was something about dusk, when it was neither day nor night as yet, that caused uncertainty to linger in the air, as one awaited the coming blackness of night.

His gaze traversed the courtyard and came to rest on the entrance to the flanking tower. That wasn't covert enough. Far too risky.

Egan's eyes then roved the distance between his window and the flanking tower, pausing with particular interest at the connecting point between the keep and the gabled garret. He grinned. Difficult but not impossible. He was about to pivot away from the window when he spotted two Campbell guards patrolling the perimeter. He'd have to deal with those blighters.

A wide smirk broke across Egan's face. For the first time since arriving on this godforsaken isle, things were looking up.

CHAPTER
13

*N*ight had arrived as Breena and Craig strolled toward the stairs of the Campbells' keep. The flickering light from the torches held in sconces on the stone wall of the corridor cast eerie, quivering shadows across their path. Footfalls thumped against the stone floors, approaching them. Breena swung around as William Campbell came toward them. Dark circles sagged under his eyes as if he'd been ill at ease for some time. He stopped across the corridor from them, his breathing labored. Breena hadn't missed the way he'd saved the serving woman from falling off the dais.

William didn't strike her as the typical barbaric Campbell. He was similar in age to Egan. Tufts of his dark hair stood out as if he'd run his hands through it a thousand times. And from the looks of his stubbly chin, he hadn't shaved in days. He was as broad shouldered as Egan, but somehow not as imposing.

He nodded at both Breena and Craig but directed his address to Breena.

"My wife's ill. She says you're a healer. You must come, quick."

Breena's mind flashed to the pale young woman who had been retching earlier. She prayed it wasn't too late to save her. It all depended on how long she'd been exposed.

"Wait here. Let me fetch my medicinal bag."

Breena darted up the stairs. She snatched her portmanteau and dashed back down to where William and Craig waited. Another Dunbar escort had replaced Keith at her bedchamber door, who now hurried after Breena.

"Take me to her," Breena said to William.

She shot a single-minded glance at Craig. "I'll send for you, if I need you."

Craig nodded his assent.

She then sprinted to keep up with William as he left the keep, her Dunbar escort close behind.

William, it seemed, didn't share the same grudge or hatred for healers as other Campbells. He didn't have that aura of oppression and animus hovering over him either.

Breena had to gather as much information about the lass's condition as possible.

But first she had to make sure. "Your wife has golden hair? Blue eyes?"

His expression softened for a split second. "Aye. That's my Rosalin."

If Breena had to guess, she'd say he cared a great deal for his wife.

"How long has she been ill?"

"Since yesterday." The skin around his eyes bunched.

"I tried to help her earlier, but she ran away."

He glimpsed her way for a brief second. "She said you'd approached her. But the Campbells dislike healers. She was scared."

"Don't you share the Campbells' opinion?"

"I grew up in Arinagour. I don't share the Campbells' singularity of opinion or their peculiarities. Besides, that is of little importance now, I just want Rosalin to be well again." William's voice had taken on a hard edge, laced with something like panic.

Peculiar? Was that how he referred to murderers?

"What are her symptoms?"

"She can't keep any food down since yesterday. I've been beside myself. I can't lose her."

Breena raced to keep pace with him as she stumbled on every few steps. The moon shed paltry light on their path, which was rather unhelpful in spotting the small rocks, twigs, and clumps of earth on the trail.

"Is it possible she's with child?"

"Nay, her courses came four days ago. Can you help her?" The plea in his voice was clear but it was his pained expression that tugged at her gut and tightened her chest.

"I will do my utmost." Breena tried for her most soothing and confident voice while internally praying her best was enough.

After they cleared Carragh's curtain wall, they did a fifteen-minute sprint north of the castle. They then arrived at a simple yet pleasant wattle-and-daub cottage nestled between two towering spruces. The Dunbar escort stationed himself at the door while Breena went into the cottage with William.

From the back door, they went past a charming living space, which appeared to serve as both kitchen and dining areas. The crackling fire, from the far corner hearth, along with the lit cast-iron lantern, which sat atop a simple golden oak dining table, cast a warm glow. What struck Breena was the sharp, sweet scent of spruce, and despite the burning wood from the hearth, the delightful freshness in the air around them. What a contrast to the cold foulness of the Campbells' keep.

As Breena happened to look back while she trailed after William toward the bedroom, she spied a bowl with red apples, yellow plums, and what looked like dark scarlet berries atop the dining table. Breena frowned. *It can't be.* She'd recognize those deceptively juicy-looking berries anywhere.

It was a simple business spotting poisonous plants and fruits. Treating a patient for ingestion, however, was not as simple.

Breena rushed to catch up with William. Did he realize what those berries were? He didn't seem the sort who would want to poison his wife.

Rosalin, the same pale young woman from earlier, lay atop a hand-carved fourposter bed asleep. Her dressing gown reminded Breena of bluebells. She was even more pale and ashen now, by the light of the lantern that stood on a nightstand, than she had been earlier. Her lips were dry and cracked. Small beads of sweat sat around her lips and forehead. William lifted Rosalin's hand in his and planted gentle kisses on her knuckles as he knelt beside the bed. He lightly brushed errant strands of hair from her forehead.

"Rosalin, my love, the healer is here." His voice was laced with something akin to anguish. It caused a heaviness to settle in Breena's belly.

Breena was a good judge of character, and she'd never expected a burly isle warrior to be brought to his knees as fast as William Campbell had been by the sight of his sick wife. He couldn't have known about the devil's berries.

Breena's gut tightened, her adrenaline surged, and her healer's instinct took charge. She stepped around to Rosalin's side and felt her forehead to gauge her temperature. Afterward she lifted her eyelids one after the other. Her pupils were dilated. Breena then attempted to nudge Rosalin awake. She woke after a fashion, but she was lethargic and unaware, and her eyes were unfocused.

Breena shot William a firm glance. "Help me to sit her up."

Rosalin mumbled unintelligibly as William and Breena hoisted her up to a seated position.

"It's imperative we keep her from falling back asleep until we have purged her stomach," Breena said.

William jerked his head up to face Breena.

"Purged?"

"I know it's intolerable, but we need to get all the poison out of her stomach."

William shot her an agitated look. "Poison?" Something dark then settled on his features.

There wasn't time to discuss it just yet.

"You have to help me now." She opted for a commanding tone. Past experience dictated the need for such a tone. It helped to impress upon the loved ones of her patients the necessity of quick action.

William blinked, then nodded. "Tell me what to do."

"Help me hold her."

While William held Rosalin up, Breena washed her hands with water from the ewer by the bedside. She then opened Rosalin's mouth and stuck her pointing and middle fingers as far back as possible, careful to not hurt her. As Rosalin started to heave, William positioned his wife's head over a chamber pot. They repeated the process until nothing came but dry heaves.

"Will she get better?" William asked.

Breena tried for as confident a smile as she could muster.

"I believe we got the immediate poison out of her body, but I can't be sure how she'll respond. Some patients fare better than others."

Breena then reached into her small medicinal portmanteau for the dried leaves to make the tea. It was the best she could offer on the spot to neutralize the poison already in Rosalin's bloodstream and at the same time replenish fluids in Rosalin's body. She didn't believe in bloodletting, especially when a patient was in a weakened state. Breena left William to tend to Rosalin while she went to the kitchen to make the tea.

As the water started to boil in the copper kettle over the hearth, William trailed into the kitchen.

"Are you sure it's poison?"

"Yes. I can show you."

"The . . . poison is here?"

Breena shifted from the hearth and strode to the dining table. She picked the bowl up with its fruits and gestured at the berries.

"Those berries are devil's berries. Eating up to six of them will make you severely ill. More than twelve will kill you."

William stared at the berries, locked in some private thought. He approached Breena, and she muffled a shriek when William yanked the bowl of fruit from her and hurled it, along with its contents, straight out the open window. He did it with such force the bowl smashed into the huge trunk of the spruce tree outside. Pieces of the bowl along with the fruit fell to the ground. A collage of fruity mess remained on the pale tree trunk.

"Those were left at our front door yesterday morning. I ate a couple of apples and Rosalin had some of the berries and plums."

Breena couldn't fault William for his reaction, especially because she sensed that whoever left the fruit did it with the intent of causing William and his wife harm.

She returned to Rosalin's bedside with the tea, and with William's help, despite Rosalin's unfocused condition, they got her to drink all the warm liquid before laying her back down to sleep.

As Breena departed the bedchamber, she turned back for a brief moment in the doorway. William sat in the bed with his wife, running his fingers along her temple and hairline with gentle strokes, his face tight with worry. Breena didn't miss the tremor in his hands. He had the countenance of a man who was in love with his wife, and who tortured himself over her weakened state.

Breena was familiar with that look.

It was the same look on her uncle's face when he'd cared for her aunt during her bout of dysentery. And she'd witnessed it on the faces of husbands who cared for their sick wives at Duntulm, whom she'd treated over the years.

Would she find a husband to care for her in such a way?

The adrenaline that had powered her actions since she'd stepped into the cottage subsided. Realization hit her that she was so tired her bones ached. She strolled to the kitchen, sat down, and rested her head on folded arms atop the table.

Two hours later she got up and went to check on Rosalin. William had dozed off, but his head jerked up when she neared.

"How is she?"

Breena touched Rosalin's forehead, then lifted her eyelids one after the other to inspect her pupils. She then studied the skin around Rosalin's neck and collar bone.

Breena let her mouth curve into a smile. "She's not worse. And that's always a good sign."

William raised his head toward the ceiling, squeezed his eyes shut, and let out an audible sigh as if thankful to the heavens. He glanced at Breena.

"Please stay here with us. We have two spare bedchambers. I am selfish in making that offer, mind you, because I need you to show me how to care for Rosalin."

Relief settled in Breena's chest, since the truth was, she didn't want to sleep in the Campbells' keep. "I had planned to stay with Rosalin until she's well. So, I thank you for your offer. I accept."

The dark circles under his eyes were more pronounced now, and his hair was a mass of tangled tufts, but his expression was more relaxed than it had been before.

Breena cocked an eyebrow at him. "Who do you think left the fruit?"

William exhaled out loud. "We came from Arinagour after the Campbell offered me a position as head of his retainers. In the beginning, we stayed at the keep, but Rosalin didn't like it and insisted we have a place of our own. We moved to this cottage a few weeks ago. We thought someone left the fruit to welcome us to the cottage."

"Having spent just one night in the Campbells' keep, I can understand why she'd insist on such a thing. But do you think the poisonous fruit was deliberate?"

He looked away, saying nothing. She didn't know him well enough, but she instinctively sensed, if the shadow of an underlying dark mood in William's countenance was any indication, the person who'd left the poisonous fruit wouldn't escape their comeuppance.

CHAPTER
14

*E*gan leaned out his bedchamber window, his palms on the rough wood of the windowsill. Waiting. The stillness of the air might have been calming on any other night; tonight, however, it made him restless. His gaze traversed the courtyard. It was close to midnight, and too quiet.

Faint chortling joined the hoots of the owl. Egan peered into the darkness. How many were there? Then he spotted them. Three figures cast stretching shadows as they left the guardhouse staggering toward the gate. Two Campbell guards stumbled alongside Dougray. Egan sniggered when one of the Campbell patrols took a hearty swig from what looked like the jug of *uisge-beatha* he'd instructed Alban to bring from their camp. This was the signal he'd been waiting for. Egan turned to Keith, who was sitting on a rickety chair.

"That's my cue."

Keith jumped up.

"I wish you'd let me go instead, or let one of the men from camp go. They're on alert, waiting for you to give the word."

Egan exhaled a rush of breath. "I thought we'd settled this. Besides, I'm the best climber we have."

"Yes, sir, that is so, but we can't afford to have the future chief of the Dunbars get caught for breaking into the Campbells' guarded tower."

Keith's exacting tone caused Egan to narrow his eyes. "I have no intention of getting caught. Besides, Dougray is doing an excellent job of distracting the guards."

"What if the patrols come back before you return?"

Keith fussed like a mother hen.

"You yourself said you could climb down to the gabled garret and back thrice within the span of time it would take them to complete one inspection of the perimeter. That's plenty of time. However, in the unlikely event that happens, let's settle on a signal should there be the faintest hint of trouble. Dove's cooing?"

Keith nodded as Egan proceeded to tie the end of a three-story length of hemp rope to a grappling hook.

"Don't you plan on returning with the prisoner?"

"Not this time." Egan shook his head.

"You plan on doing this again?" Keith's eyes widened.

"At least once more." A smirk broke across Egan's face.

"This is because of that healer, isn't it? You are of a higher social ranking than she is—you must see how your association with her appears to others? The men are jabbering about the way you two eyed each other this afternoon."

Egan bristled at Keith's words. He quelled his rise of annoyance. "Why, Keith, you never struck me as being a snob. Besides, I am sure you and the rest of my retainers have better things to do than gossip like a bunch of fishwives."

Keith harrumphed and turned away.

It was none of their bloody business who he eyed.

"Then at least let me go with you." Keith's voice was interwoven with worry.

"You know as well as I do it's easier for the Campbells to detect two of us than just one."

Keith's shoulders sagged. "Well, if you are sure."

"Never surer. Besides, I have a need to stretch my legs."

He gave Keith a wry smile as he fastened the grappling hook on the windowsill and then let go of the rope outside the window. Keith leaned forward and gripped the hook. He held it in place on the sill. Egan scrutinized the rope below. It ended at the third floor of the flanking tower.

Perfect.

With a wink of his eye and a grin on his face, Egan saluted Keith and climbed onto the windowsill, then rappelled off. Excitement surged through his veins as he lowered himself hand under hand on the rope. His booted feet clenched the rope below as he descended toward the roof of the flanking tower. The night air was cool as it brushed against him.

When Egan stepped onto the roof of the flanking tower, he was not expecting his foot to go straight through.

Bollocks!

Coldness shot down his spine as he pulled himself back up, gasping at the Campbells' shabby roof. He exhaled in a rush of breath and mumbled a prayer of thanks that he hadn't plummeted to his death.

Egan glimpsed upward. Keith's mouth had dropped open, his eyes bulged, and his neck was bent precariously out of the window. He was such a worrywart since he'd become a father. Egan gave him a thumbs-up, and Keith visibly relaxed.

Egan strained his ears for movement below, aware his breathing had become audible. He was relieved when he heard nothing. He tested the roof with his booted feet. Finding its wooden frame, he edged along one of its beams to the periphery of the roof, while he kept a firm grip on the rope. He then lowered himself down.

Egan dangled from the rope outside the third floor of the flanking tower, reached for the open window, then released the rope. Without making a sound he crept through the window.

Loud, rhythmic snores resonated around him. Egan made out the dark silhouette of a hulking Campbell sentry slumped over on a bench about ten paces away. Both the bench and snoring guard were in front of a wooden door at the end of the landing. The door was padlocked, and a ring with a single key hung on the side of the door. If Egan were a gambling man, he'd bet that door was the entrance to the confinement area, where the prisoners were kept.

Tiptoeing, he gave the sleeping man a wide berth. Egan took the key, opened the padlock, and pushed the door back. The door screeched, and Egan paused, but the snores of the guard remained even and steady.

The first thing to hit Egan when he snuck into the confinement area was the smell. Burnt flesh and the metallic scent of blood mingled with a stench not unlike that of the dungeon. But then Egan froze mid step.

Bloody, bloody hell.

He had never witnessed anything like it before. Righteous indignation vibrated through his entire body as he fisted against its onslaught. He took a deep breath, swallowed, and forced himself to slip past the two hanging bodies. He'd seen a Judas cradle before, but not one as worn. He recognized the rack and the two iron chairs, but the rest of the contraptions were foreign to him. He pushed himself to keep moving, for stopping to fixate on what degenerates the Campbells were would benefit no one.

Egan's muscles tensed when something scurried across the floor. He grabbed one of his dirks, but when he identified the rat, before it disappeared into a hole, he replaced the dirk in its sheath.

He crept toward the swaying iron cages at the back. When he stepped in something slippery, he looked down. Egan had never been squeamish before, but it appeared the Campbells were proving him wrong. He stepped out of the red viscous substance and kept moving toward the two dangling cages, which were fastened by ropes from the rafters.

The first caged prisoner was asleep. The second was turned away from Egan as if he hadn't seen him, which was unlikely. Egan was being ignored. From the prisoner's lanky, gaunt profile, he appeared to be the right age. His hair, long and gray, hung limp over his ears, along with his bushy beard. The man's clothing was nothing but tattered rags, their original colors indistinguishable amid the dirt.

"Ian MacRae?" Egan whispered.

The man continued to look sideways, away from Egan.

"Breena sent me."

The man blinked but didn't budge. The likelihood that any mind would be weakened after enduring these conditions for nineteen years occurred to Egan. Would hearing the word "trust" encourage the man to speak?

"I'm here to help you. You can trust me."

A jolt of relief shot through Egan's belly when the man shifted to face him.

The man's long, hollow face had more wrinkles than Egan had ever seen on any one person. Skin bunched around his eyes in a pained stare, and his shoulders curled over his chest as he looked down at Egan from his perch in the hanging cage. The man's frail body seemed to be in a constant state of tremulousness.

"Who are you?" His voice was a hoarse croak, as if he'd not used it in ages. Egan noted his warm chestnut-brown bloodshot eyes, even though they currently glared, untrusting, above a long, prominent nose.

"A friend."

"What do you want with me?" The man's eyes narrowed atop thinned lips.

"To take you to Breena."

A hopeful smile tugged at the man's lips.

"You are Ian MacRae then?"

The man nodded. Egan exhaled a rush of breath. However, the relief didn't overthrow the underlying horror of this place. Or the rage burning inside him at what these prisoners must have suffered at the hands of Alasdair Campbell.

"How is wee Breena?" The dry skin of his cheeks looked to be cracking into a genuine smile as crow's-feet etched their way next to his eyes.

"Hale. Although she's not so wee anymore." An image of Breena's tall, slender figure flashed across his mind's eye.

"Where is she?" His corrugated eyebrows arched.

"Not far from here."

The wrinkles on Ian's face hardened.

"It's not safe for her amongst the Campbells. Craig was to keep her away from this place."

"What?"

Something cold and heavy settled in Egan's chest. Of course, the moment Breena decided to orchestrate a Campbell dungeon break-in, it became unsafe for her here. But why did the man's comment make it sound like there was more to it?

He made a mental note to put on additional guards to watch over her.

Just then Egan caught a rustling from the entrance. His head snapped around.

Bloody hell! The sentry was awake.

"I will return for you within three days' time."

Ian nodded.

He hoped the sentry remained ignorant that the door was unlocked, even though it was pushed in. Keeping close to the wall for the stealth of its shadows, Egan inched toward the entrance. He peeked through the keyhole as what sounded like water trickled against stone. From the pungent scent, he guessed what the sentry was doing, even though his back was toward Egan.

Too bloody lazy to visit the garderobe.

Egan nudged the door slowly. The guard emitted a sigh of relief. Egan's head swiveled around, looking for something, anything. Then he spotted it. A sneer broke out on Egan's face as he bent down and picked up a shoe-sized brick. Holding the brick with a firm grip, Egan neared the guard from behind. He raised his hand and brought the brick down hard, making a dull thud as it connected with the sentry's skull. The sentry's body tottered, then lost its balance and fell forward. The man landed with a crash. Egan didn't envy him for the aching head he'd have when he awoke.

CHAPTER
15

*S*nowy white clouds lay like a painter's coordinated brush strokes against the backdrop of the bright azure sky. And just where the tips of the brownish conical hills of the Fairy Glen on the Isle of Skye touched the eastern heavens, fiery reds and pinks rippled outward like dissipating waves around the brilliant rising yellow sun. She stood on the soft green grass, in the center of a circle of stones about nine feet in diameter, gazing at Sorcha. Her grandmother's beautiful, lined, knowing face smiled back at her. A gentle breeze brushed her cheeks. It carried with it the earthy smell of the ground. The sight of Sorcha filled her with a warmth she hadn't felt in years. And peace and calm sank deep into her bones, as if it was all going to work out.

But she didn't know that, did she?

"I miss you, Grandmother. I've been fumbling so since you . . . you died," Breena whispered.

"You shouldn't worry so about the dead, my child. Not while you are amongst the living,"

"But am I doing the right thing, bringing Uncle Craig here?"

"You must speak with Ian MacRae."

Somewhere, the sharp piercing crow of a cockerel sounded. Breena's head snapped up. She blinked. Was it the cockerel that had awoken her or Sorcha's insistent voice?

She shook her head and pushed the dream to the back of her mind while scanning her surroundings.

William's kitchen was cast in dark shadows. The candle had burned down on the dining table, where she sat. The last thing she recalled was laying her head on her folded arms. Just for a moment, she'd thought. Exhaustion must have caught up to her.

She and William had taken turns keeping vigil over Rosalin. Breena had been thankful that sometime during the late night into the wee hours of the morning, Rosalin's color had started to return.

Breena rose and inhaled deeply, attempting to rid herself of drowsiness. The fire in the hearth had died down. In its wake, red-hot coals emitted the faint scent of smoke into the air mixed with the freshness of the coming dawn. Breena rummaged around the kitchen as quietly as she could for a new candle. After she located one, she lit it and tiptoed toward the master bedchamber to check on Rosalin. Both William and Rosalin were fast asleep. A relaxed smile eased across Breena's lips when she took note of Rosalin's improved color. Warmness suffused her chest. The lass was on the mend.

Breena returned to the kitchen. She eyed the iron frying pan hanging over the hearth and the broom made of straw lying against the wall in the corner. Did she dare conduct a sideromancy spell? This gnawing need in her gut to find her father was starting to outweigh her fear of discovery. It even started to outweigh her deep frustrations yielded by the ambiguities in her spells.

But what if William caught her conducting witchery? Would he string her up by a noose as her mother had been? Even though the Isle of Coll was a dangerous place to perform witchery, if she had to conduct a spell, she'd rather take her chances in William's kitchen. She could always feign cooking if he strode in.

Despite that thought, her heart started to hammer against her chest.

If the Campbells were holding her father in another location, she had to know. After having come all this way, she simply could not return without being completely and utterly sure.

One thing she was certain of, this gnawing feeling in the pit of her belly couldn't be ignored.

Nor could her dreams of Sorcha.

Breena revived the fire in the hearth by adding more kindling and logs from a nearby pile. Heat started to permeate the space around her. Admittedly, when her palms began to sweat, she questioned if the heat was from the renewed fire or from anxiousness over discovery.

She scanned the kitchen again, making sure she was alone. Breena then lifted the iron pan from its hook and set it directly on the brilliant red-and-orange flames, which crackled and snapped as they danced.

She hissed and pulled her hands back when they came too close to the fire.

As the pan heated, she plucked nine strands of straw from the broom.

When the pan was hot enough that its edges emitted smoke, she tossed in the straws. They landed together with a light clatter and the heat from the pan consumed the straws.

Breena swallowed against the pounding of her heart, and she whispered, "Where are the Campbells keeping my father?"

Nothing happened, and Breena sighed in disappointment, until she saw fat lines of dark gray smoke slither up from the heated straws, like coiling snakes in the air.

Breena blinked and looked for familiar shapes amid the smoke and flames. But she deciphered nothing. She exhaled in a rush of annoyance. The straws themselves snapped and jumped, bombarded by the heated iron. It was then she realized the straws had moved to form the letter P connected to a backward facing P. Breena's eyes widened as she stared at the rune symbol *Mannaz*. The symbol foretold of friends as well as enemies.

But what did this have to do with Ian MacRae?

Was he among enemies? It certainly couldn't mean he was among friends. She let out a frustrated snort. Saying Ian MacRae was among enemies was overstating the obvious, wasn't it?

She paused. Realization settled over Breena, even as her heart rattled against her chest.

This meant he was alive, didn't it?

She closed her eyes and inhaled a shaky breath. She said a silent prayer that it was indeed so, as she proceeded to return everything to its rightful place and remove any trace of a spell.

◆──◆──◆──◆──◆──

The loud morning whistles of the small reddish birds were sounding by the time Breena had finished tidying up and making coffee. Resting her elbows on the tabletop, she let her forehead fall into her open palms to block out the blinding rays of the sun, just for a second. Tiredness flowed through her body and stiffness cramped her neck. With the warm sun's rays and the fresh dewiness of morn seeping through the window, it was unnecessary to rekindle the fire in the hearth. Every part of her ached from tension.

Breena's head jerked around when there was a loud knock at the cottage door. She rushed over before whoever knocked woke up both William and Rosalin. Breena swung the door open. Her breath hitched as warmth settled over her body.

"Egan, did you want William? He's asleep." She chided herself at the breathlessness in her voice.

"I'm here for you."

Something fluttered in her belly. "You are?"

The flecks of shimmering browns and sparkling greens in his hazel eyes caught her attention. Had they always glinted like that? Then her eyes dropped to the parting of his moistened lips and the sculpted lines of his hard jaw as he considered her. She blinked away, but not before taking in his immaculate dark jacket, crisp white léine, and pristine kilt. *Does he have to look so resplendent, first thing in the morning?*

She swallowed the unexpected rush of moisture in her mouth.

"One of my guards informed me you were here . . . caring for William's wife?"

Ought she to tell Egan someone was trying to poison William and his wife with devil's berries? She decided against it. She'd treated enough patients to know confidentiality was paramount. It was William's and Rosalin's choice to disclose that fact, should they choose.

"Rosalin ate something that didn't agree with her. But she's doing better now. William stayed up to help me keep an eye on her. He fell asleep a bit after midnight."

"I'm relieved she's doing better. But I do need to speak with you. Will you take a turn with me outside?"

She inclined her head in assent. What could he want to discuss with her?

Had the Campbells somehow found them out?

"Of course. Let me fetch my arisaid."

Breena hastened to the guest bedchamber and plucked her arisaid from the trunk, which George had dropped off just an hour before. She wrapped it around her shoulders, then hustled back to the door to join Egan.

She briefly scrutinized the extra Dunbar guards. "Is aught amiss?"

He followed her line of vision. "Just a precaution."

He led them in the direction of the sandy shoreline.

Besides the few Campbells they passed with axes in hand, who seemed to be heading into the forest to chop wood, there was no one else about.

Any other place besides here on Coll, it would be diverting, pleasing, even venerating that a future clan chief paid her attention. In fact, given the way her skin heated at the nearness of said future clan chief, she'd be thrilled. But not here on Coll, not where the skeletons in her family's cupboard threatened their safety, their livelihood, and even their lives. She had to keep those skeletons where they belonged.

She pulled herself out of her woolgathering. "I'm exceedingly grateful for what you did yesterday, in the dungeon. I don't believe I ever expressed my gratitude."

"No, you didn't. You mostly glared at me." A wry smile crossed his lips.

The sight of the sea breeze tousling his thick auburn hair and the sun's rays dancing off its highlighted strands did funny things to her stomach. But it was his smile that started to erode those walls she'd just built up, in much the same way the cobalt-blue waves crashed against the sandy shore just beyond where they strolled, eroding it bit by bit.

"In that case, I'm much obliged for your assistance," she replied, a contrite smile easing her mouth.

"That's why I wanted to speak with you. I'd hoped for a more convenient venue for our discussion, but as it's important we're not overheard, this will have to do."

She lifted an eyebrow at Egan. He stopped his stroll and shifted to face her. He appeared to have something important to say as he ventured to formulate his words. Anticipation speared her gut as she eyed him.

"I bring good tidings. Last evening, it came to my attention the Campbells are holding additional prisoners in the flanking tower."

Her pulse quickened as she processed this bit of news. Had the sign from her spell been correct? Was he alive and here?

Egan continued. "I stole a peek of the flanking tower last night, a climb rather, and I met Ian MacRae himself." A wide grin settled on his features.

Breena took a step back, almost stumbling.

It may have been the implosion of her heart or the quick breaths inside her chest, but she couldn't be sure she'd caught the words.

"Pardon . . . pardon me. What did you say?" Her body froze. Heat warred with the chills swirling through her.

"Ian MacRae is in the flanking tower."

Tension left Breena's entire body in one powerful plummet, the rush of it so fast, light-headedness sank in. Her hands flew to her mouth to muffle a loud screech. Her breath came in fast, shallow gasps, yet no air reached her lungs. Her limbs lost all their strength. Then they stopped supporting her altogether as she fell.

But she didn't hit the sand, for warm, steely arms enveloped her and held her up.

"I can't believe he's alive. We came so far looking for him, but there was always a voice in my head that said it was impossible he'd survived all this time. It's a miracle." Breena sniffled as the light-headedness ebbed.

She became aware of the dampness on her cheeks as she looked at Egan. He was carefully considering her.

"Are you sure it's him? What if you're mistaken?" The questions rushed out mirroring her fears.

"It's him, as you described." The whitish skin of his scar all at once seemed pulled taut as a bowstring.

Something new swirled around Breena, an unmitigated awareness at being held against a large and powerful chest. The delectable heat from his body started to wreak havoc with her already jumbled thoughts.

"How is he? Where do they have him? . . . Is he hale?"

"He's a bit worse for wear. But I've no doubt once he's rescued and has had a few proper meals, his health will be restored."

What her father must have gone through at the hands of these vicious Campbells.

Breena glanced up, but it was a mistake. She found herself tumbling down into the depths of Egan's hazel gaze. Something dark and feral pulled her deeper still. Something that caused her dress to shrink two sizes too small for her body.

"Will your peek . . . ah . . . climb in the flanking tower not jeopardize your standing with the Campbell?" Her mind slowed to the unhurried pace of dark, thick honey. Why was he still holding her? And why did she not want him to stop?

"Nothing is jeopardized if they don't find out." His voice sounded gruff.

Her eyes lowered to Egan's lips. A man shouldn't have such full, supple lips. His movements ceased and his body went rigid. It might have been his divine, heady scent, a mixture of leather, soap, and the rugged outdoors, that filled her nostrils, making her knees unsteady all over again. And the fact that their lips were mere inches away from each other sent delicious tingling throughout her entire body.

She had to get her thoughts out before his closeness caused her to lose them entirely.

"I must tell you that in finding Ian, you've started to fill a nineteen-year-old void in my family's heart. But I don't know why you, a highborn future laird, singled me out to bestow your attentions and kindness upon."

His gaze pierced hers. "Certainly, you must have some sense of why?"

Her fingers curled into the soft, refined texture of his jacket as she searched through her jumbled thoughts. But she just shook her head hesitantly, coming up empty-handed.

When Egan's eyes fell on her lips, her eyes widened, and something sultry washed over her senses, heating intimate parts of her body. Perhaps she did have a sense after all.

Her gaze lingered on his eyes. Their smoldering intensity looked like that of a caged beast. An animal about to pounce. Breena should have broken free and run in the opposite direction at seeing the dangerous hunger in those eyes, but an unexplainable and un-ignorable pull caused her feet to rise up onto her toes instead, as his head came down.

The kiss was raw and demanding. Her reaction instantaneous, fierce, and visceral. Her chest tightened and sharp prickles of excitement shot down her spine all the way to her toes. Heat burned her skin. It was unlike anything she'd ever felt before. It caused a cloud of emotions and chemical reactions to explode, not only in her body but in her very being. Stark desire and unexplainable wonderment collided with a sensuous shock.

His lips searched, probed, then devoured hers, they were warm, strong, sinful, and wicked against hers. The taste of mint leaves on his lips made her delve further into the kiss. Breena fought to breathe, caught up in this whirlwind of luscious emotions that tugged and flooded her. It was like what she'd imagined happening if she drank an entire bottle of port wine, multiplied a hundred times. The guttural moans that ensued stunned her, even more so when the realization hit that they came from her.

She matched his hunger with her own, mimicking the movements of his lips, for she was an inexperienced kisser. Yet raw need made her bold; the need to taste more, touch more, experience more overpowered her. Her arms extended up and around his neck, pulling him closer, just as one of his hands clasped her nape and brought her yet nearer to him, to deepen the kiss as his head tilted. His hands blazed a slow, fiery trail up and down the length of her back.

The carnality of the kiss squeezed her chest. It frightened her. The kiss moved too fast, and she had trouble catching her breath. How did her knees still hold her up? They were like the legs of a wobbly foal that had just stepped out from its mother. Her heart, blood, and breath raced ten steps ahead of her mind. A powerful riptide pulled her under, and she struggled for air.

And then it all stopped. Egan broke the kiss. His breath as audible as hers. When Breena blinked up at him, the rawness there gripped and twisted her insides on a primal level. He released her, stepped back, and swore under his breath. Her body screamed with a thousand needy sensations, one of them deprivation at the loss of his heat. Her insides quaked. What was the matter with her? Her breath was labored and ragged, as if she'd just run fifteen miles without stopping.

He raked his hands through his hair. "Forgive me, I took advantage of your vulnerability." His voice was hoarse.

His words were like a pail of frigid water tossed at her.

CHAPTER
16

*W*hat in Hades just happened?

His heart pounded and reverberated like the vespers bell against his chest, and his breath came fast and shallow. Reining in the pressure at the base of his spine and his stiffening arousal proved difficult. One moment he'd kept her from falling, and the next he'd kissed her. He'd been under siege by a powerful inferno charged with a singular surge of energy, like lightning during a storm. His heart spiraled with a perplexity of emotions. Lust. Fears. Fantasies. But yet, he had to be the worst kind of lecher, taking advantage when she was inundated with emotion over the discovery of Ian MacRae.

But having her in his arms had scorched him to the bone, boiled his blood, and robbed him of his senses. Nonetheless, he'd overstepped. The days of his baser instincts getting him into trouble were supposed to be behind him. He was almost thirty! But he couldn't remember ever having such an unbridled desperation to taste a woman's lips before. And if he was honest with himself, having tasted her, he wanted more. Bollocks!

Egan scrubbed his face with his palms in attempt to calm his raging desire.

He eyed her. She looked as undone as he felt. Her mouth opened and then closed without speech. The look of her lips devastated him, plump and moist, with a deeper blushed hue because he'd just thoroughly kissed them. Her cheeks were flushed, their crimson stain adding to her delectable appearance. His mind made the leap to picturing her naked and in the throes of passion. That did nothing to remedy his stiff and painful arousal.

He needed to get ahold of himself. Egan rubbed the back of his neck and glanced heavenward as he muttered yet another expletive under his breath.

After a few deep breaths, Egan faced Breena once more. "It was my fault—"

"We share equal blame." Her voice was rushed. She cast her gaze downward, seeming to take interest in her shoes.

"I'm not in the habit of . . . of taking such liberties. It won't happen again."

Did he have the strength to follow through?

Her lips pressed into a tight grimace, and her shoulders dropped. Did a sliver of disappointment just cross her face? No. That wasn't possible. He was letting his baser instincts cloud his mind again.

"Why don't we pretend it never happened?" she said.

Pretend he'd never tasted those honeyed lips, or held her supple curves in his arms, distracting him to wild madness? That was bloody impossible.

He nodded. "Agreed."

She cast her gaze out to sea, avoiding his. She inhaled sharply. He'd come to equate her avoidance of eye contact with her telling a lie. But now he wasn't so sure.

"Please know I'm forever indebted to you for all you have done for us, as Craig will tell you himself when he finds out about Ian."

"It's my absolute pleasure. I gather Ian is a close friend of yours. You seem to care a great deal for him."

"I do." Her eyes followed the flight of a seagull, avoiding his yet again.

At that moment it struck Egan. Discomfiture caused her to avoid eye contact—any type of discomfiture—as when she lied or whenever the topic of her family came up.

"Forgive me, but I get the impression Ian MacRae is more than a mere . . . friend."

She pressed her lips together in what appeared to be uneasiness. His question was not an unreasonable one, considering he'd broken into the Campbells' flanking tower and was now prepared to do it again.

It was a few long moments before she shifted to look him square in the eyes.

"Ian MacRae is not a friend. He is my father." Her voice was just above a whisper.

His jaw slackened. The revelation shouldn't shock the kilt off him, for he'd come to gather the lengths to which she'd go to help family, but it did.

"Your father? Then who is Craig?"

"He's my uncle, but he's been my guardian since I was six. He is . . . like a father to me."

Egan raked a hand through his hair. Breena and her family were ensconced in more riddles and mysteries than the Druids.

"But . . . why the charade?"

She visibly winced, he wondered if in regret. Was she going to be honest with him this time around?

"We didn't want the Campbells to find out why we were here, since it was our intention to leave with my father. I didn't expect to encounter any acquaintances here on Coll. It was never my intention to lie to you, Egan, just to the Campbells."

Her tone was sincere, almost pleading. It invoked that protective streak again.

This time it rattled in his belly as he eyed her.

"You don't have to fear the Campbells, not while I'm here."

Egan's own words echoed in his chest and vibrated in the air around them.

He'd just made a promise to her, which he intended to keep for the sake of his conscience, for the sake of Alex's memory, for the matter of the debt he owed her for Duntulm, and for the indisputable fact he was drawn to her like a parched man was drawn to a freshwater burn.

Her expression softened, a warm smile easing her features. It loosened the knots and tangles inside him. "I'm much obliged, not just for your protection but for your discretion as well."

He sensed an opening and chose the opportunity to ask the question he'd wanted to ask since he'd first chanced upon her on Coll.

"Is your name Breena MacRae, then?"

"I was hoping you hadn't recalled Daegan's introduction when we met at the gates."

"I recalled the name MacRae but thought I had imagined it when you introduced Craig Maxwell as your father."

Her chuckle was cheeky, yet it managed to be bold and confident all at the same time. It cast her face in an inviting warmth and her cheeks in a most becoming blush.

"My mother is a Maxwell and my father a MacRae."

He might not have remembered her original clan, but he certainly hadn't forgotten her.

They strolled along the soft sand for a few quiet minutes, nothing but the steady sounds of the waves, the whistles and piercing calls of the gray and white seabirds, and the rustle of the breeze circling them. Egan didn't mind the salty air or even the smell of kelps, which tended to make him breathe through his mouth, as he considered whether to ask her why the Campbells had imprisoned her father.

She slowed her pace and shot him a determined glance.

"I have to rescue my father . . . take him away from here."

The wind tussled a thick lock of her ebony hair free of its braid. Egan touched it. He let the soft silkiness of it brush against his fingers with the aid of the wind. A faint floral scent teased his nostrils. It sent something raw snaking through his gut. He gently tucked the soft lock behind her right ear.

"I know you intended to. But I will do this for you, so my debt is settled." Egan's voice was resolute and even though he'd never considered himself a person who took chances, he was taking a big one that the Campbells would be none the wiser.

"But we have a plan—"

"I was out of my mind to take you to the dungeon. I hope to conclude my negotiations with the Campbell within the next couple of days. The night before we depart Coll will be the best night to rescue your father." Egan's jaws were set as he planted his feet in a wide stance in front of her.

"My uncle and I had a foolproof plan to break him out." A gleam darkened her whiskey-colored eyes.

"Foolproof?"

She nodded.

"Tell me."

As Breena laid out the plan she and Craig had concocted to rescue Ian, a wide grin tugged on his lips. Then a loud laugh bubbled up from his gut, past his chest, and straight out of his mouth.

"That's crafty. The Campbells will never expect it. I'll tweak it of course, but I think it will work."

◆——◆——◆——◆——◆

Egan sat with his men for the midday meal at the Dunbar camp and sliced a piece of fire-roasted trout from its skewer with his *sgian dubh*. The voices of several ongoing conversations from his men swirled around him, as did the sounds of shuffling feet on the soft earthen ground and the rustle of nearby trees.

Rory and Gregor, who sat behind him, heatedly discussed the advantages of skewering uncovered fish over an open flame versus encasing the fish in oak or chestnut leaves. Keith, who sat next to Egan, stifled a grin as he eyed the two, no doubt finding their domesticity amusing.

Something in the consistency of the sounds around camp shifted. Egan paused, as did his men. There was an almost imperceptible rumble from the ground where they sat. Egan knew the sound well. He turned in its direction.

"Riders approaching," Keith said.

The rumble grew louder and louder. Keith stood up from his seat atop a gray boulder. He held a half-eaten skewered trout in his left hand, and his right hand went up to hover over the hilt of his sword, strapped to his back. Many of the other men shifted to a similar stance.

"Steady, men," Egan said in a conversational tone laced with steely authority. He remained seated on the boulder as he chewed his food. The rumble didn't sound like it came from more than fifteen to twenty riders. Nothing he and his men couldn't handle. A few seconds later, the riders came into view in the distance. He counted twenty of them, half dressed in stark red coats and the other half in Campbell tartan. All of them outfitted in various weapons. Their horses' hooves kicked up dirt, creating a dusty cloud around them as they neared.

"Gregor alone can take them without breaking a sweat," one of Egan's men said above the rumbling. The rest of the men sniggered.

"Good, then the rest of us can finish our meal," another one said.

The men roared with laughter. Egan felt the hard tremor beneath his feet as the riders bypassed their camp on the way to the castle gates. His men continued with their conversation and their meal; some spat on the ground while eying the redcoats.

Egan didn't laugh.

He glowered at the redcoats who rode with the Campbells as they entered the courtyard. There was a time when he and his sister Phoebe had pleaded with their father to grant them permission to join the Jacobite Rebellion, but he had forbidden it. Another desire Egan had pushed aside, for the sake of his duty to the clan.

Duty to the clan comes first, son.

Egan flexed his fingers. He took a bite from the skewered fish he held in his hand, despite the souring of his stomach.

As future clan chief, he had to put the safety of the Dunbars before his personal desires. Joining the Jacobite Rebellion would have placed the entire clan at risk of an attack from the British. That didn't stop him from celebrating with his men after the Jacobites' victory at the Battle of Falkirk Muir. They'd gotten howling drunk after every triumph of the Jacobites against Lieutenant General Henry "Hangman" Bolingbroke, right hand to the Duke of Cumberland, leader of the British army.

When the Jacobites had fallen at Little Ferry, and then again at Culloden Moor, his sire chose that opportunity to crow how prophetic his decision to disallow them to join the rebellion had been.

He grunted and flung the bare skewer away. It flipped in the air and landed a few feet away from camp on the soft grass. Thoughts of the rebellion always put him in a foul mood.

Keith sat back down beside Egan, his voice jarring Egan from his ruminating. "This is proof the Campbells are doing the bidding of the redcoats. Bloody traitors to Scotland." Keith scowled as he eyed the riders.

"Now that the Campbell hunters have returned, let's hope we can conclude our negotiations and leave this wretched place," Egan said.

Since he'd arrived on Coll, the colossal burden of Egan's duties as future clan chief to the Dunbars weighed on him, almost stifling him. He took a deep, cleansing breath. One duty in particular had been gnawing at his gut ever since he'd kissed Breena.

"Music to my ears, sir. I know the men are as anxious to depart as you are."

"Should I conclude my discussions with the Campbell today, we'll have much to do tonight, before we leave tomorrow."

"Tonight?" Keith's eyes widened.

"Tonight." Egan nodded.

CHAPTER
17

The prismatic afternoon sunlight trickled through the window of the master bedchamber. Hope of seeing her father again billowed anew. This was a chance that the ever-present inner hollowness would cease its torment of her innards. But hope was tinged with the pain of regret for lost time. And sorrow pierced her belly for the life that had been stolen from her father, while ire simmered somewhere deep inside with thoughts of the Campbells.

Breena sat at the side of the bed as she fed soup to Rosalin. The piquant scent of the food Breena had cooked from dried meat, neeps, and tatties, infused with various healing herbs, permeated the air.

Rosalin was propped up in bed, and she eyed Breena as she pressed fingers to smiling lips, chewed, and swallowed. She tugged closed the lapels of the periwinkle dressing gown over her muslin chemise, which had slackened. Her pale golden hair was a delicate contrast to her sapphire eyes. Breena ventured a guess that Rosalin was a sheltered, shy young woman with a sweet temperament, which shined through as she stepped more and more outside of her shell.

"It's marvelous you're better," Breena said, in her soft, amiable bedside tone.

"I'm sorry I ran away, but the Campbells despise healers."

"It was good of you to change your mind and let me help you."

"The Campbells were unpleasant when William and I first arrived on Coll. I begged him for us to leave their keep and have our own place. It was a blessing when they let us have this cottage. It belonged to the previous head of retainers. He died from a knife wound to the back. Some say the Campbell himself did it."

Hearing that about Alasdair Campbell didn't come as a surprise to her.

"The Campbells are disagreeable to outsiders, in particular, healers," Breena said. The Campbell's scathing tone and the image of Hilda looking down her hooked nose at them the night they'd arrived flashed across her mind.

"They haven't liked healers ever since a healer killed the laird's wife . . . almost nineteen years ago." Rosalin's affable countenance became solemn.

Something tightened in Breena's chest, hearing her mother referred to as a killer.

After Madeline had blurted out that her father might still be alive, Breena had begged Madeline and Craig to tell her what happened. They had said the Campbells executed her mother for Lady Campbell's death, calling it murder by witchcraft, when in fact Lady Campbell had died of natural causes. They had thrown Ian in the dungeon after he stood up to the Campbell. But her aunt and uncle refused to say anything else, despite Breena's protests and belief that there was more to the story. They'd said it was for her own good. How could keeping her in the dark be for her own good? Why had her parents been on Coll?

What reason could the Campbells have for vilifying her mother as a killer?

Breena cleared her throat in an attempt to rid herself of the excruciating thoughts. "Alasdair Campbell had a wife?" She tried for as steady a tone as she could muster, wanting to know the Campbells' version of the story.

"It's difficult to believe, isn't it? He's so rotten. But Elsie, the laundress, told me he was married twenty years ago. His wife was from a wealthy clan. Their marriage was arranged. He married her for the torcher—dowry, of course. Lady Campbell became with child soon after but died during the birthing. The bairn was stillborn. They said the healer who did the birthing was a witch and killed them."

Breena stared at Rosalin. She had to stay focused and not let the ire rising up her gullet get the better of her. Her fingers tightened around the spoon.

"But why would the healer kill Lady Campbell and the bairn?"

Rosalin's brows rose, and she twirled the end of her braid with her left hand as if anxious. She then leaned forward and whispered, as if she feared someone would overhear, "The Campbell and the healer were lovers. The healer sought to eliminate her competition."

Breena froze even as dizziness danced before her eyes, and something squeezed the air from her chest. Lovers? Nausea kicked in and when a loud, echoing clank sounded, Breena realized she'd dropped the bowl of soup.

She blinked and looked down. The bowl's contents had spilled on the floor and she noticed the tremor in her now empty hand.

"I'm . . . I'm sorry, I'll clean that up. Let me get a rag from the kitchen." She winced at the tremor in her voice.

She rose from the bedside as the bottom of her world fell out from under her. Had she fallen asleep only to awake to a nightmare? This can't be.

Her legs were like jelly as she staggered toward the kitchen. Despite last seeing her mother nineteen years ago, Breena recalled a gentle woman with a tremendous capacity for kindness. She'd been an ethereal beauty with warm, brown eyes and a softhearted smile that illuminated all that was around her. With her, Breena had been safe and loved. Warmth still suffused her insides every time her mother came to mind, even though it was now tinged with the pain and emptiness of the loss.

But what now shook the very foundation under Breena's feet was the fact that her mother could have been lovers with a vile piece of excrement like Alasdair Campbell. What about her father? They would have been married at that time. Breena would wager her life on the fact that her mother would never betray her father. Never. Which left only one other possibility to explain Rosalin's story. It wasn't true. It simply was not true.

Breena entered the kitchen and flattened her palms on the tabletop, letting her neck and head hang down. She swallowed the rising uncertainty and closed her eyes, taking deep cleansing breaths, in an attempt to settle the tumultuous emotions within.

Mayhap it was time to consult the stones for some answers. But every cell in her body rebelled against the vagueness and ambiguities her spells yielded.

Breena's lashes flickered open and she eyed her hands splayed on the rough surface of the tabletop. Their tremors had eased.

She grabbed a rag and headed back to Rosalin's bedchamber to clean the spilled soup.

"You are tired. You should rest, you have done so much already." Rosalin's forehead puckered with concern.

Breena waved Rosalin's concern away, feigning a smile. "Nonsense. I just had an instance of butterfingers."

Rosalin seemed to accept her explanation. Breena persisted, as she stooped down to clean up the mess.

"What happened after Lady Campbell and her bairn died?"

"They executed the healer for witchcraft and murder. And her husband was imprisoned."

When she'd thought both her parents had been lost in an accident, she'd been miserable, yet there had been simplicity in that misery. Now she longed for that simplicity. It was better than this nightmare. Rosalin's earlier words echoed in her head.

The Campbell and the healer were lovers.

She now wished the events of three weeks ago hadn't taken place. That her aunt hadn't blurted out the truth. But then she wanted to hide her face, as her cheeks burned with the shame of her own selfish thoughts. No. No. She slapped the cleaning rag against the floor. Now wasn't the time to have doubts.

A soft tap on Breena's shoulder made her glance up from her stooped position. Amiable sapphire eyes studied her.

"You seem distracted. Is all well with you?" Rosalin said in a soft tone.

"Yes, of course. I apologize. Just woolgathering." Breena attempted a chuckle, which sounded hollow to her own ears.

"William will not return for another few hours. Why don't you have a lie-down till then?"

She stood up from her stooped position. When Breena had told William she would be leaving with the Dunbars in a couple of days, he'd decided he didn't want his wife staying alone at the cottage anymore while he trained the Campbell retainers. He'd left for Arinagour to bring Rosalin's cousins.

Breena heaved a sigh. "You're correct, of course. I think I'll do just that."

⋆—⋆—⋆—⋆—⋆

Later that evening, Craig showed up at William's cottage. Despite the questions that whirled around in her head, a lightness settled in Breena's chest at the sight of her uncle.

His relaxed countenance made him seem happier than she'd seen him in a long time.

"Did Egan tell you? I wanted to tell you myself, but I couldn't leave Rosalin alone."

The corners of Craig's mouth turned up as he drew her in for a hug. "It's marvelous news, isn't it? Egan said you told him of our plan. He approves."

Craig grinned, released her, and pivoted around. "This is much more inviting than the Campbells' keep. And I am sure the fare tastes better as well."

He sniffed audibly at the air in the kitchen, then his head veered toward the cast-iron pot over the fire. He sent her a hopeful glance.

Taking the hint, Breena took a clean bowl and filled it with soup. She placed it in front of him with a spoon as he sat down at the table. He threw her a wide grin as he rubbed his palms together. He licked his lips as he picked up the spoon. "I always said you were a gifted cook. I haven't had a proper meal since we arrived. The Campbells' food tastes like dirty dishwater."

A smile tugged at Breena's mouth as she eyed him eating like a starving man.

"It's most certainly the best news I've ever had in my entire life, that he is alive, albeit a prisoner," she said.

Breena again recalled Rosalin's words. *The Campbell and the healer were lovers.*

How to broach the topic of her parents, specifically her mother, with Craig? During the past three weeks, he had switched topics, become tongue-tied, or simply refused to discuss them, saying he was doing her parents' bidding.

"Ian always had a quiet sort of unbreakable core. It was one of the things my sister admired about him. I can only imagine that's how he survived this long."

Breena leaned against the wall and folded her arms across her chest.

Craig paused his eating to regard her.

"What is it? I can tell you are happy about Ian, but you have something else on your mind."

Breena eyed her uncle. Where to begin?

Even though Rosalin was asleep, Breena kept her voice to a whisper.

"Rosalin told me that Alasdair Campbell and the healer . . . witch . . . who killed his wife were lovers."

Her uncle choked on the soup. He coughed out loud, then covered his mouth with his hand. The spoon dropped to the wooden tabletop with a dull clank.

"Uncle . . . ?" Breena scrambled toward Craig.

He raised his arm for her to stop. "I'm fine. Your words just startled me."

Breena eyed him. He cleared his throat and opened his mouth as if to say something but sighed out loud instead. He closed his mouth without a word. Something dark crossed his features. It caused Breena to swallow against the tightening in the back of her throat. *Why doesn't he say something? It can't be true. It just can't.*

He rubbed his wrists, then touched the fallen spoon, but gazed at it instead of picking it up.

Breena had hoped for a categorical denial to such outrageous Campbell gossip. But when it didn't come, coldness settled along her spine.

"Uncle . . . is it true?"

"No. Beth loathed that bastard. And she loved Ian. Your mother would never . . . Beth was a gentle soul, loyal to the core. Ian wasn't a witch himself, even though many in the MacRae clan were witches. But when he met your mother, a Maxwell witch, they formed a connection, almost as if fate had conspired with the craft to bring them together. Ian understood her, accepted her, loved her. They were true to each other."

The soft emotion in Craig's voice eased some of her fears, but not all of them.

"But then why—"

"No. It's not true." Craig squeezed his eyes shut as his expression hardened.

Even though part of her settled as relief washed over her, countless questions swirled around in her head.

"Why would the Campbells lie about—"

"There is nothing else to discuss. This is for your own good." His tone was clipped, sharp, final.

Keeping her in the dark wasn't for her own good—it was driving her mad. Frustration to the point of vexation stabbed her innards. She resisted the urge to pound her fists against the wall and scream. But she'd already done that three weeks ago and several times since. It had been futile. Then there was the fact that whenever Craig talked of his sister, his face twisted into something dark. Agony. It pained her when he was like that, so she hadn't pressed.

He picked up the spoon and carried on with his meal, although with less fervor. She huffed and turned away.

Her uncle's sharp tone always reduced her to a child all over again. A child who'd been reprimanded because she'd stayed out too late playing with her best friend Rowan or because she'd muddied her dress running after Balor, her childhood deerhound.

Craig cleared his throat, breaking the tenuous silence.

"How is William's wife faring? Knowing how you are when tending to patients, I imagine you haven't slept since you arrived."

"She is recovering. We were able to get most of the poison out of her stomach."

Setting aside her own inner battles, Breena recounted the origination of the poison. She didn't think their discussion constituted a breach of patient and healer confidentiality, as Craig was a fellow healer.

"You think it was the Campbells? But why would the Campbells bring him here to be head of retainers and then try to poison him and his wife?"

"It's certainly baffling. William is closemouthed about it. But I suspect he knows or has a strong notion of who did it."

"Come to think on it, I'd not put it past the Campbell to have some nefarious plan in mind. The man is Mephistopheles himself. Who knows what motivates such a mind?"

After Craig finished his meal, he bid Breena good night and left the cottage.

◆——◆——◆——◆——◆——◆

Breena saw to Rosalin's dinner, then with a lit candle in hand made her way to her own bedchamber. She was pleased with Rosalin's progress.

When she stepped into her room, her eyes fell on the bed nestled in a small alcove, its soft fur throw beckoning her taut muscles and tired body. She placed the candle on a small oak table and proceeded to undress.

Breena removed her fingerless mittens and her woolen outer dress. But then her fingers lingered on the delicate frilled sleeves as her mind sauntered toward Egan Dunbar and their kiss. The hard, inviting length of him against her, the lush feel of his capable lips and the luxurious long strokes of his tongue with the promise of wickedness.

Despite the heat suffusing her skin, she scoffed.

There were no doubt scores of beautiful women he'd kissed that way before, who held either peerage title or were highborn and more suitable for kissing the future clan chief of the Dunbars than a lowborn healer. She pulled on her plain underskirt, yanked at her hip-roll, and jerked her tight corset stays off. He'd no doubt already forgotten about that stupid kiss. She should do the same. Breena harrumphed at her shift, then tugged at the laces of her nankeen half boots. She tossed the boots one after the other on the floor, then wrenched off her stockings.

But as she took a square of linen and the piece of heather-pressed soap from her trunk and started to perform her nighttime ablutions, an unbidden memory of the kiss returned. His lips had been strong and sure as they'd melted her insides. Even now her knees weakened, as she wiped her damp body with the linen. She shook her head. She had to stop thinking about that damnable kiss!

She donned a white gossamer night rail and was about to blow out the candle and slip under the fur when a knock sounded on the cottage's door. Breena frowned as she grabbed her green woolen dressing gown.

CHAPTER
18

*E*gan nodded at the guards and knocked on the door with one hand while the other rubbed his tense, stiff neck. He'd just come from an ineffectual back-and-forth with the Campbell and four of his retainers who'd returned from their so-called hunting trip. The Campbell hunters mimicked the exact same claptrap as their laird. They claimed the Dunbars attacked first, and the Campbells were just defending themselves when Callum and Brodie were killed. Egan didn't for a second believe their claims.

If he didn't leave this godforsaken place soon, his frayed nerves would unravel. But what had he expected? For the Campbells to admit they'd attacked his men like cowardly revivers in the dark of night? Egan feared if he stayed on Coll any longer, he was at risk of dishonoring his sire's orders and declaring war on the Campbells. Egan's duty as future clan chief weighed on his conscience. If only he were made of the kind of fiber to toss it all aside. If only he could feed this need for vengeance against the Campbells strumming deep inside of him. But he exhaled in a rush of frustration. He couldn't. His sire fought for justice in the old clan wars; he had integrity and was right-minded. And Egan could never cross those things.

Egan raised his hand to knock on the door again just as it was pulled open. Something raw and heady washed over him at the sight in front of him.

"I apologize for the lateness," he said, finding his voice.

Breena stood at the door, lit candle in hand. His eyes catalogued every little inch of her, and it detonated equal parts torment and titillation through every inch of him. He'd never before beheld anything or anyone lovelier; her raven locks unbound, a stark contrast to her unblemished alabaster skin and her kissable cherry-blossom-pink lips. Keith's words about their difference in social ranking came back into his head, pulling him into a turbulent vortex of frustration. He swore under his breath.

"It's quite all right. Is aught amiss?"

She stepped aside, and as he swaggered past her, the tantalizing earthy tones of heather caressed his nostrils. Egan inhaled deeply as images of his home in the Highlands flashed across his mind and something else entirely made his skin tighten.

She closed the door and shifted around.

"I just came out of a negotiation with the Campbell and his men."

She strolled to the dining table and deposited the candle on top. Egan's gaze was drawn to the translucent material of her night rail, only partially concealed by her hastily tied dressing gown.

"You don't look like the outcome was favorable."

"It was not."

"I am sorry. Having seen what type of a man the Campbell is, that comes as no surprise."

Her back was now to the wall, her hands resting on a chair, as her eyes perused the length of him, then blinked away. The light blush of her cheeks stoked his male pride. There was something warm and palpable in the air between them.

Was it because of their recent kiss?

He eyed the way her hands rested on the back of the chair as he pulled out the one next to it and sat down. Why did he get the distinct impression that that chair was a barrier of some sort? Was it to keep him from her, or the other way around?

"The Campbell has the ability to try the patience of a saint. And a saint I am not."

In fact, his thoughts were quite devilish at the moment. His eyes fell on her lips, recalling their innocent brushes and sweeps. Yes, he craved more, his duty as future laird be damned.

He took in a deep breath, attempting to clear the heat of his lascivious thoughts. "How is your patient Rosalin faring?"

"She is asleep . . . doing much better."

As her face brightened, it occurred to Egan that she cared about her patients. Or perhaps she had formed a bond with William's wife.

"I'm sure William is pleased," Egan said, as his eyes dipped from the tip of her head to the ends of her unbound hair. It was almost as wild as he'd imagined it, when loosened from its braid. What would if feel like to tangle his hands in those silken tendrils?

"He is. He left early today for Arinagour to bring Rosalin's cousins. He should be back soon."

"Arinagour?" Egan's eyebrows arched.

"Yes. William didn't like the thought of Rosalin remaining here alone when I've left for Skye and he's out training the Campbells."

An enigmatic pull caused Egan to stand up. He took a leisurely step toward her, his movements smooth but deliberate. The last thing he wanted to do was to frighten her. If she moved away, he would retreat. But how he wished she wouldn't. Her eyes flickered up, and her mouth entrapped the tip of her tongue in a corner of her lips. However, she didn't budge.

He eyed her closely. "I have been meaning to ask you. Why did the Campbells imprison Ian?"

She raised a brow.

He wasn't sure if it was at the question or the fact that he now stood a single step away from her. The increased rise and fall of her chest didn't go unnoticed by Egan. She took a deep breath, and the tip of her delectable pink tongue licked her bottom lip. Bloody hell.

He was in trouble.

"I'm . . . I'm not sure it's my story to tell."

The pull to touch her was intense, overwhelming, and could not be disregarded. Every muscle in his body clenched to the extent of pure agony. His desire for her thundered through him like an animal in and of itself. But now wasn't the time to contemplate designs on a bewitching healer from Skye. He ought to find a nice suitable Laird's daughter or a lass with a peerage title. Another one of his damnable duties. Mayhap for that exact reason he took the final step toward her, or mayhap he didn't know how to stop himself. His heart slammed into his chest and heat pulsed through his veins. And then, like Icarus flying into the sun, Egan found himself incapable of resisting the temptation to his own destruction, for he would no doubt incur his sire's wrath for entangling himself with a lowborn healer.

The reflection of the candle's flame flickered in her eyes and shimmered like liquid gold. That wasn't the only reflection he caught in those amber globes as they darkened. He shifted the chair out from between them. The warmth from her body and her floral scent stirred something primal deep inside him. Egan reached out and flattened his palms against the cool wall on either side of her. And as heat threatened to consume him, he slowly lowered his lips to hers.

Her mouth tilted upward to meet his and he groaned with approval as lust fired through his blood. Her lips were soft and inviting. They tasted of a sweet, forbidden nighttime rendezvous.

Her hands edged up around his neck and pulled him closer to her. His lips caressed, lapped, and nibbled hers. Her taste was exquisite. The sound of her quickening breath hit him like wildfire to kindling, fueling his movements, his entire body one pulsating raw nerve. His hands drifted down the length of her back as he drew her closer. Their bodies fit like a dagger in its sheath as he pressed into her.

His lips trailed kisses along the delicate line of her jaw.

"You've changed tactic." His ragged voice made him sound inebriated to his own ears.

Her hands traveled up to twine themselves in his hair. She was pliable and limber in his arms. His craving for her convulsed inside of him as duty battled desire.

"I fail to follow you, Master Dunbar." Her husky tone melded into his heated senses.

His hands traveled up to gently cup her firm mounds.

His mouth found hers once more. Her lips were sultry and pliable beneath his, allowing him to explore her taste. The innocent yet hesitant movement of her pelvis against his, in conjunction with her taste, worked in tandem to give him the sweetest and most erotic gesture he'd ever experienced with the fairer sex. His breath raced, his blood boiled, and his vision tunneled when her hands reached into the opening of his léine, splaying their heat on his bare chest.

"The name is Egan."

Egan had a maddening urge to have her flat on her back as she writhed and moaned with pleasure. He lifted his head and glanced around. The kitchen table would have to do.

One of his arms encircled her shoulders as the other went around the backs of her thighs. He scooped her up into his arms. She gasped.

He swung around and placed her on the edge of the table, her arms hanging around his neck. Her skirts bunched around her thighs as he slipped his body in between her knees. He held her in his arms, and his mouth descended on hers for a slow, prolonged kiss.

Craving to taste the rest of her, his lips trailed down to the delicate, soft skin of her décolletage.

"I fail to follow you, Egan."

The throaty sound of her voice saying his name just about undid him.

He tugged at the top of her night rail and freed her breasts. As he proceeded to pay homage to their splendor, her head slid back, and her fingers tugged at his hair.

He raised his head to look at her. The loveliness of her half-lidded gaze, her lips swollen and moist from his kisses, her wild hair, and her exposed chest put his imaginings to shame.

"Instead of dissembling, you're now being evasive."

His hands caressed their way down her legs, which dangled off the table. He then trailed a teasing path back up to her bare thighs. Satisfaction speared him at the slight tremor of desire in her body. His hands moved farther up her thighs, savoring the luxuriousness of her smooth, velvety skin. Delight pierced his chest, for she wore no small clothes. Her breath hitched and for the briefest moment, her legs locked together. Egan paused. She was still a maiden, as he'd suspected.

He lowered his head and captured her lips once more. This time his kisses were soft and decadent; they cajoled and seduced.

"You lied as well," she whispered as he raised his head to look at her.

"How so?" Egan's head was stuck in a sultry fog as he slowly caressed his way back up her thighs.

Her legs remained open, and he was rewarded with a delicious, soft moan as he caressed her.

His lips closed over hers again, this time with more purpose. As Egan's tongue made a slow silken sweep of her mouth, his forefinger slipped inside her body.

He raised his head again, wanting to take in her responses.

"You said we ought not to kiss again." Her breathing was heavy and sultry. As he slipped two fingers inside her, she gasped, and her eyelids dropped.

Desire roared and howled in his veins but he drew in a long, deep breath to calm the screams of need inside his body. He wouldn't take her. Not here. Not like this. His esteem for her wouldn't allow it. He wouldn't dishonor her.

He bent down and whispered in her ear. "You're bewitching enough to drive any man to lie."

He looked down at her heavy-lidded eyes.

"Open your eyes. Look at me, *leannan*."

Her eyes fluttered open, their color darker than he'd ever seen before.

"I want you to let go for me. Do you understand?"

She blinked up at him, taking in his meaning. She nodded. Egan kept his ministrations deliciously slow yet calculated and relentless on her softness. Then he felt her body coming apart, and she squeezed her eyes shut. She made the most delightful little sound, somewhere between a whimper and a soft moan.

She raised her head, brushing aside errant strands of her hair to gaze up at him. Her sheepish grin touched something deep inside.

Her gaze traveled down. "What about you?"

"This time was about you."

She cocked a brow at him. "This time?"

Then she frowned as she reached out and with a gentle touch traced her fingers along his old scar. The touch of her fingers was cool on his hot skin. "What happened?"

Egan was about to answer her when approaching footfalls sounded from outside the cottage's door. Bollocks!

He grabbed her by the waist, lifted her off the table then planted her on her feet to stand behind him.

"We are about to have company," he whispered.

He stood in front of her to shield her from view of the door. She started to put to rights her bunched skirts, smooth down her night rail and tie her dressing gown just as the handle on the cottage door rattled before the door swung open.

CHAPTER
19

*I*t'd been some time since Egan was caught in flagrante delicto. But then the night, eleven years ago, when an angry Angus MacDonell had crashed through the door of a Loch Alsh Inn's room, where Egan had been swiving a barmaid senseless, looking for Daegan flashed across his mind. They'd both skipped training curfew and had to pay the price with double cleaning duty at the stables. Weren't days such as those behind him? Evidently not.

Egan clenched his jaws and stood arms akimbo in the kitchen as William strode in. The steamy air in the kitchen resisted the chill that rolled in from outdoors. William's eyebrows shot up when he caught sight of Egan and Breena.

"Dunbar? To what do I owe the pleasure?"

William's eyes flicked up and down Egan's length, and Egan muttered an expletive, even as a half-cocked grin tugged the right side of his mouth. He was sure his shaft still made a tent with his kilt. Why hadn't he worn a sporran today?

William frowned as his eyes found Egan's again.

Egan cleared his throat. "Campbell. I'm here to speak with Breena."

Egan lifted his chin as he met William's stare, daring the other man to call him out.

Just then Breena stepped out from behind Egan.

"William . . . how was your journey?"

Egan caught sight of Breena's flushed cheeks, red swollen lips, and mussed hair.

Bloody hell!

She'd had time to right her clothes, but the rest, Egan was sure, would leave no doubt in William's mind as to what he'd interrupted.

William's eyes narrowed and his lips thinned as he took in Breena's appearance.

"My journey was fine. Is all well with you?"

Egan didn't miss the trace of concern in his voice. Did William think he'd taken advantage of Breena? Egan didn't give a shite what William Campbell's opinion of him was, or any other Campbell's, but he didn't want a cloud cast over Breena's character for what he'd done. Or what William imagined he'd done. He flexed his fingers against the surge of heat in his belly.

"Yes, all is well. And Rosalin continues to improve. She's asleep."

Just then two fair-haired, lanky teenagers rushed through the door, almost at the same time. They stopped short before colliding with William, who stepped away from the doorway. They were each fresh-faced with cornflower-blue eyes. In effect, they'd be identical with their amiable smiles, except that one was a lad and the other a lass.

William introduced them as Ethan and Chloe, Rosalin's twin cousins from Arinagour. Owing to the awkward self-awareness of youth displayed on both their faces, Egan doubted they noticed anything else.

Breena went to the twins, her lips turning up into a wide smile. "It's a pleasure to meet you. Rosalin told me quite a bit about you both."

Both teens beamed at her. "Hello, mistress," Ethan said. Chloe echoed him seconds later.

Egan nodded at the teenagers, but then the original purpose for his visit to Breena hit him.

"Breena, I came by to pick up the . . . sleeping draft and clothes you were mending for my man Ian?"

He hoped she interpreted his veiled request as intended. Since William and Rosalin's cousins stood in the kitchen, he was unable to elaborate.

Breena swung around to face him. Her eyes flickered with confusion, then understanding seemed to settle on them as her heart-shaped lips formed the most delectable O.

"Will he need those tonight?"

Egan winked at her. "He'll need those tonight."

"I'll go put them in a bundle and be right back." She sprinted toward the back of the cottage.

"Will you two fetch the trunks from the wagon? When you're back, I'll show you which bedchamber is yours," William said to Chloe and Ethan.

When the two teenagers scrambled out of the cottage, William spun around to glare at Egan. From the flare in William's nostrils, Egan had a good handle on what William was about to say.

"Did you molest her, you bastard?"

Egan restrained a laugh, for this situation was not without its irony. Here was a Campbell accusing him of misbehavior when they represented the epitome of treacherousness. But he had to admit William Campbell was not a typical Campbell. He seemed to possess scruples.

"I care about her. And no, I didn't molest her. Not that it's any of your damn concern."

William cleared his throat and straightened his shoulders.

"She's a good lass. She saved my wife's life. I don't want you taking advantage of her, and in my own home." William's voice was hard and had notched up a few decibels.

Had he taken advantage of her? Something sharp sliced through Egan's chest, and the air thinned around him. She'd stuck her hands in the fire as much as he had, although she was an innocent. Had she been as willing as he'd interpreted . . . or had his baser instincts clouded his judgment? Egan exhaled out aloud. At the very least he'd seduced an inexperienced lass.

"I didn't take advantage—"

"You're a future chief. And she's a baseborn healer. I doubt your intent is to marry her."

Egan's breath accelerated. He clenched his fists so hard, a knuckle cracked. He wanted to hit something. Hard. And right now, William Campbell's face would do. No one had ever accused him of taking advantage of a woman.

Egan took a threatening step toward William. "I didn't take advantage, nor did I molest her. Other than that, it's none of your goddamn concern what I did. Are you accusing me of something?"

William stepped back and let out a heavy sigh.

"No. But it was obvious what you two were doing. And if I hadn't walked in when I did, perhaps you would've shamed the lass. I am asking you to leave her alone. Does her father know what you're about?"

William no doubt thought Craig was her father.

Egan avoided William's gaze as guilt tightened his ribs and a cold quiver settled in his belly. What was his intention with Breena? And would she have allowed him to kiss her, to do the things he'd done to her if he hadn't found Ian MacRae? If Egan pursued Breena, her virtue and integrity, which were paramount for a good marriage, would be lost. Even the appearance of impropriety would do that. The need for propriety had been drilled into his sister's head by his parents enough times that even Egan was now painfully aware of its importance. In a way, William was right.

He needed to keep his wits about him. But would his body's desire cooperate?

"Look, Campbell, I'll not do anything to shame Breena. It's noble of you to want to protect her honor."

Had he just called a Campbell noble? A snowstorm must have descended in Hades.

Egan would've laughed if he didn't feel so culpable.

William Campbell approached him and slapped him cordially on the back.

"You're a decent sort, Dunbar. Let's share a pint sometime, eh?"

Just then Breena walked into the kitchen with a bundle in her hands.

"Excuse me, will you, Dunbar? I have to go check on my wife." William inclined his head then strode toward the back of the cottage.

Breena handed Egan the bundle.

"The clothes we discussed are in there. And the tincture in the vial is to be mixed with something to mask its taste, perhaps whiskey. Fifteen drops to one goblet will do the trick."

Egan took the bundle from her. "I have a couple jugs of *uisge-beatha* set aside for this very purpose."

She touched his arm, and her eyes flickered with something soft. "What you are doing for me and my family means . . . everything. You are giving me back my father, who has been lost to me for nineteen years. I don't know how, but I will repay you somehow. Until then, I'll be in your debt."

The sincerity of her expression and the twinkling warmth in her eyes did something to quicken his pulse. He wanted to take her in his arms, but then William's words came back to him and he stopped his hands.

"It's a debt repaid."

Egan swallowed, fighting against a strange new emotion tightening his throat. It threatened to scramble his thoughts.

She reached up and with the lightest of touches traced the scar on his neck. Her touch was a taunt. He resisted the urge to lift her fingers and put each one of them to his lips.

"You never answered my question, how'd you get this?"

Her question jarred his senses. The memory flashed before his mind's eyes. He glanced toward the low flames dancing in the fireplace, not seeing anything. He fought against the rumble of darkness that flooded him whenever the redcoats were a topic of conversation. Was it because, in their estimation, they'd come to Scotland to tame the backward Scots, to convert the Roman Catholics to Protestants, to uproot and destroy hundreds of years of rich Gaelic culture? Or was it because they'd plundered, pillaged, raped, and murdered hundreds, no, thousands of his fellow countrymen all in the name of the Rebellion? And there wasn't a damn thing he could do about it. Because of his bloody duty to his clan.

He exhaled in a rush of breath, shifting to face her again. "I defended my sister's honor from a redcoat who made improper advances toward her . . . unsolicited and unwanted advances. He came at me with a dirk. We fought, almost killed each other. He escaped with his life, and I was left with this scar."

Her eyes widened with concern and what looked like admiration. "I'm sorry your sister was the recipient of unwanted advances, but she is lucky to have a championing brother such as yourself. This cut could've severed your larynx and inhibited your ability to breathe."

"You should tell that to Phoebe. In her opinion, I was meddling."

Breena chuckled. "Do you have other siblings besides your sister?"

Tension settled on Egan's neck and shoulders as the familiar coldness of guilt coated his spine. He stepped away from Breena.

"No." An urge to deflect further questions took him over. "Do you have siblings?"

She gave a heavy sigh and lowered her head. "No."

Following the thin line of her lips made him wonder if she'd been a lonesome child. "You're welcome to my sister then."

Her feminine giggle at his gest was unassuming. It lit up the kitchen and warmed him from the inside out.

She playfully poked his chest. "If I ever meet your sister, I'll tell her you said that."

And he liked the sparkling tease in her eyes. This was a new side of her he hadn't witnessed before. "Just so."

She glanced toward the back of the cottage, where William had disappeared, then whispered. "What you have planned for tonight is dangerous. I don't want you to get hurt."

"It's a simple rescue. Don't worry, *leannan*. We'll get Ian tonight and leave here at first light. Be prepared." Egan resisted the deafening impulse to take her in his arms and kiss her good night. Instead, he took her right hand in his, brushed her knuckles with his lips, and left.

◆──◆──◆──◆──◆──

Close to two in the morning, Egan snuffed out the candle with his fingers. His dank bedchamber fell into a shadowy blackness. He strutted to the door and eyed Rory, his guard for the night.

"When Keith returns, knock three times. Besides him, I don't want to speak with anyone, least of all a Campbell." The last part he whispered.

Rory nodded. "Aye, sir."

It was unlikely that a Campbell would come calling; nonetheless, it was wise to ensure he not be bothered.

Egan bolted the door and threw open the window shutters. The chill of the night air flooded in. Except for the croaks of tree frogs and buzzes of insects, nothing else broke the silence of night. His gaze scanned the entire courtyard, confirming no one was about. In response to the dryness in his mouth, he pressed his lips together. There wasn't any reason to believe everything wouldn't go according to plan.

Egan removed his weapons and clothing. He pulled his hair into a queue and donned the black léine and kilt with the weapons he'd need. A wave of uncertainty washed over him, which had nothing to do with the pending rescue. His esteem for Breena warred with his sire's expectations. Uncertainty was Egan's enemy, for he'd never encountered it before in this light. It was like lumbering around in quicksand. He'd never had cause to doubt his duty before, and while he had disagreed with his sire on occasion, it had never weighed on his chest like this. Then there was the fact that he wanted the Campbell's head on a pike after seeing what the man was capable of, regardless of his sire's edict.

Three knocks sounded. He shuffled over to the door, unbolted it, and pulled it open. Keith stood in his doorway. From his broad smile, Egan ventured to guess he had good news. Egan stepped aside. Keith slid in, and Egan closed the door behind him.

"You are ready, sir?" Keith said, as his gaze fell on Egan's clothing.

"Almost." Egan trotted over to the lit brazier.

He grabbed the poker, which leaned against the wall, and scooped out some charcoal.

As he waited for it to cool, he shot an inquiring glance at Keith. "Report?"

Keith straightened. "Alban and Gregor took the coins, jug of *uisge-beatha* with the tincture, and playing cards and struck up a game with the guards on the first floor of the tower four hours ago. As luck would have it, one of the Campbells has a penchant for gambling. He couldn't resist. As of half an hour ago the players were asleep like wee trusting bairns. Dougray has been working on the two patrol guards with the second jug of *uisge-beatha*. Same dolts from last time. As of a few minutes ago, they were almost finished with the second jug."

"Well done. Anything else?" Egan tapped the black charcoal with his fingers. They had cooled. He proceeded to smear the soot across his face and exposed parts of his arms and legs. It had been difficult to get this off his skin the last time, but it was a small price to pay for the camouflage it provided.

Keith's quietness caused Egan to shoot him a quick assessing glance. Keith broke eye contact and blinked. Egan was well acquainted with that expression.

Egan glanced heavenward and exhaled in a rush of annoyance. "Speak freely."

"The men think you've gone soft in the head over the healer. They say that your sire will certainly not condone your fraternizing with a lowborn lass. And it's causing you to take unnecessary risks with your personal safety by breaking into the Campbells' dungeon to rescue this prisoner for the lass. They each volunteered, including myself, to go in your stead and rescue the prisoner."

Egan scowled. His men were worse than chaperones. And he suspected why they volunteered to go instead. Half were chomping at the bit to get back at the Campbells for the deaths of Callum and Brodie, no doubt hoping the Campbells would discover what was going on and full-out war would erupt. And while part of him wanted that as well, part of him had the voice of his sire ringing in his head.

We lost many during the clan war. There were too many fatherless bairns and grieving widows.

And while the genuine concern of the other half of his men did ease something inside of him, he couldn't allow them to question his actions.

"Well, it seems my men have too much free time on their hands, nattering like a bunch of old biddies. I'll have to find something more constructive for them to do. I want you and Gregor to oversee the doubling up of sparring routines. And tell Dougray, I want him to conduct an extra weapons inspection, unannounced. The usual extra duties for the men who don't measure up."

Keith frowned. "But . . . but the men are busy, getting ready for our departure."

"Next time they'll consider carefully before grumbling about what I'm doing."

Keith's shoulders slumped as he let out a pathetic groan. He at least had the good sense to look contrite. "Yes, sir."

Egan draped a dark sack containing the items Breena had given him across his back.

Keith bent down and pulled the grappling hook and its connecting rope from under the bed and carried it to the window.

Just then the familiar call of a dove came from outside. Egan popped his head out of the window. Dougray stumbled from the direction of the guardhouse giving a stealthy nod and thumbs-up.

"That's the signal. And from the looks of it, the patrols weren't the only ones imbibing," Keith said, glancing out the window as well.

"It appears weapons inspections will be delayed until Dougray sleeps it off."

Keith cleared his throat longer than was customary. "I'm sure he took a few swigs of the whiskey to be sociable."

"Sociable my arse." Egan chuckled, knowing full well that Dougray would never pass up the opportunity to have a good time.

Keith fastened the grappling hook on the windowsill and dropped the rope outside. He then took a firm grasp of the hook to keep it in place.

"I'll be here if you need me, and the rest of the men are but a shout away. Please be careful, sir."

"Keith, you are worse than a bloody nursemaid."

"Yes, sir."

His alertness sharpened into a pointed focus as Egan lowered himself off the windowsill with the rope coiled around his body.

All went well until he entered the window of the flanking tower's third floor. He wasn't sure what to expect after the first time. Would the guard be asleep, or would the man be more diligent at his duties?

The second his booted foot touched the hard stone floor, Egan sensed something wasn't right.

CHAPTER
20

A voice cracked through the dark, like a rumble of thunder.

"Get the bastard! I was right. It wasn't a damn brick from the roof!"

Egan's pulse shot up tenfold, spurring him forward. He didn't have time for his eyesight to adjust to the pitch-blackness of indoors before he faced the direction of the voice.

He made out two menacing shadows lumbering toward him. He grabbed one of his dirks from his belt and sent it slicing through the air at the shadow closest to him.

"The bastard got me!" First Shadow said.

Good. He'll be busy for a few seconds. Egan took up a defensive position against Second Shadow's advance. The man's heavy footfalls thumped against the floor like a bass drum during a highland charge.

Egan ducked as Second Shadow sent a right hook toward his face. Before the man righted his swing, Egan aimed for the man's ribs and slammed his fists into the man's left side in two successive punches. A dull grunt sounded, then a deep howl. Anticipation and adrenaline surged through Egan's belly when he marked Second Shadow as big but slow. While Second Shadow clutched his side, Egan rammed a left hook hard into the man's jaw. The crunching of bones sounded. Nothing was more satisfying during a fight. Second Shadow dropped to his knees, his howls reduced to a pathetic whimper.

Just as Egan's head jerked around to locate First Shadow, something connected hard with his skull. Sharp pain reverberated from his head and shot straight down his entire body. Stunned, Egan lost his balance and landed on his right knee.

"You all right, Glenn? I got the bastard."

Well, if the jackanapes thought that was all it took, he was mistaken.

Egan pulled his second dirk from his waist and jabbed it deep into First Shadow's thigh. First Shadow yowled. It took all of Egan's strength to stand up and slam his right fist hard into First Shadow's jaw. Egan followed up with a left hook to the man's ribs. The second sound of grating bones tugged a grin from Egan. First Shadow fell, and his whimpers joined Second Shadow's, but his were colored with expletives.

Egan staggered forward. His head throbbed like a hundred arrows had struck his skull, splitting it into a million tiny pieces. He made out a stone block, the size of a large jug, two feet away. Was that what First Shadow had struck him with?

He needed to quiet them in case they alerted other guards, if they hadn't already. He picked up the stone block and walloped the two shadows in the head, one after the other. They both stilled. Egan retrieved his dirks and ripped strips from the bottom of the guard's shirts which he used to bind and gag the two men. He didn't know how long that would hold them after they came to, for they were huge, hulking fellows. He had to act fast.

The key was in the same place as the last time. He opened the door and hurried toward the cages at the back. This time he was more prepared for the pernicious smell and the abhorrent sights that met him. Egan's hand shot up to his head. It throbbed like the devil. A damn goose egg had formed where First Shadow had struck him, but he had no time for that now.

Egan approached the hanging cages and looked up at Ian.

"I thought I'd dreamt you." Ian stared down at him.

"Are you ready to leave?"

Egan took the sack from his back and tossed it up to Ian. Ian barely grabbed hold of it through the iron bars. Egan was pleased at Ian's spryness despite the man's skeletal appearance. He hoped that spryness continued for the next half hour, at the very least.

"If you take me from here, Alasdair will come after you . . . come after Breena. I don't want the lass to get hurt."

Egan's brows lifted. The man sounded more concerned about Breena's safety than his own freedom. Egan supposed that was a father's prerogative, but it still cemented Ian as one of the most selfless men he'd ever encountered.

"I'll protect her. You have my word," Egan said.

Ian studied him for a second as if determining his trustworthiness. After a few seconds, the other man nodded and looked in the bag. He pulled out the clothing, then tossed Egan a baffled glance.

"You want me to don these?"

"Yes. There's a straight shaving razor in the bag and a small vial of lather; you'll have to shave that beard of yours. In the meantime, I need to go hide the two sleeping guards outside."

Ian cocked an eyebrow. "Sleeping?"

Egan cast a wry grin in Ian's direction. "Bump-on-the-head-induced sleeping."

Ian chortled. Most of his front teeth were gone and those that remained were stained. Egan tried not to imagine what this unfortunate man had suffered.

"There's an unlit hearth in the back. You can hide them there."

"It'll have to do."

Egan turned to go get the guards but paused as he caught sight of the prisoner in the second cage. The man was about Ian's age, perhaps a few years younger, and wore a tattered Jacobite uniform. It wasn't difficult to guess why the Campbells had imprisoned him.

Ian seemed to mark Egan's concern as he followed Egan's line of sight.

"Don't worry about the Jacobite over there. They took his tongue out."

Regret overwhelmed Egan, for he would've liked to take the Jacobite with them. But he hadn't brought extra resources, nor did he want to run the risk of jeopardizing Ian's rescue with the delays caused by freeing a second prisoner.

Egan made quick work of dragging the guards into the hearth. He was about to leave when he saw three small bundles of hay and kindling. An idea struck him as he grabbed them and returned to Ian. The man's change of clothing was complete. Egan put his hand over his mouth to muffle the laughter that bubbled up from his stomach. A shift, gray outer dress, stockings, and women's shoes. Egan didn't even want to consider where Breena had procured the Campbell arisaid. Egan had to admit that due to Ian's thin frame, the disguise was not terrible, except from the neck up, which was a dead giveaway, even though he'd shaved the beard.

"Why, Ian, you're quite fetching."

"Get me the hell out of this cage. The sooner I can take this ridiculous disguise off, the better."

This was only his second time meeting Ian, but he already liked the man. "Hold on to something. I'm going to lower your cage."

After he unhooked the cage, lowered it, and unlocked the door, Ian stepped out. Egan then took Ian's old clothes and stuffed them with the hay and kindling, turning the bundle in such a way that the back was facing the room's entrance and the limbs were curled in.

Ian looked askance at him. "Is that supposed to be me?"

"Since the Campbells aren't too fastidious, at a quick glance they may mistake it for a sleeping you."

"I can see why Breena asked you to come get me. You are quick on your feet," Ian said.

Egan decided not to elaborate that he'd volunteered, and rather forcefully. He hoisted the cage up to its former position, then he locked the door to the torture chamber after they exited and returned the key to its hook on the wall.

As they walked toward the stairs, Egan shot Ian an assessing glance, catching the man's unsteadiness.

"Are you all right to walk out of here?"

"My feet were in a Malay boot. I haven't been able to walk straight ever since."

Egan had seen a Malay boot before. It was a gruesome contraption. Some of that old righteous indignation speared his gut. But he hadn't the time to dwell on it.

"Put your arm around me. I'll take your weight, pretend you're in your cups and we've been on a tryst. Hold the arisaid so it covers your face should we encounter anyone."

When they reached the ground level, loud snores cascaded off the walls. Egan barely made out two motionless Campbell sentries slumped against the wall in the dark, remnants of a card game on the ground next to them.

Ian's body went rigid next to Egan's when Gregor stepped out of the shadows, followed by Alban.

"Any trouble with these two?" Egan asked.

Gregor was built like a monolith, with facial features just as hard and unyielding. Egan had seen him kill a man with his bare hands. He could count on one hand the times Gregor had smiled.

"No trouble at all. We even won some coin," Alban said, flashing a wry grin.

Egan felt Ian's body relaxing next to his.

"Excellent. I don't want to attract attention with the four of us leaving together. Ian and I will head for the keep. If there's no trouble from the Campbells, the two of you can head back to camp."

Egan led Ian out into the stillness of the predawn morning. He looked heavenward and let out a low sigh of relief. Now they just had to make it up the stairs of the keep to his bedchamber.

CHAPTER
21

*B*reena twisted and turned, but sleep never came. She sat up and swung her legs over the side of the mattress. The night was silent, except for the bed ropes beneath, which squeaked and groaned as she stood up.

She didn't want to consult the stones. The stones revealed things to her. They made her hope for things, want things, things that weren't there, until the need drove her out of her mind. Sometimes the stones left her cold and empty, sometimes raw with frustrated agony. The stones showed her the things they wanted to, not the things she asked of them. Sometimes they unveiled to her the past, the future or alternate realities that would never come to pass. It got particularly gnarly when there were several versions of each. But she had to do it, even though the moon was void of course, according to the almanac. She couldn't just sit here wide awake all night. This torment of waiting to find out if her father would be freed and if Egan would survive the night unharmed was worse than all the frustrated agony put together.

It tipped the scales.

The coldness of the wooden floorboards seeped into her bare feet. She tiptoed to her door and pushed the bolt closed. Its metallic unevenness grated against her frayed nerves. She hoped no one came knocking.

She was taking a risk by seeking answers from the stones. If someone witnessed her, she could well end up like Rowan MacNeil. She and her family had been chased out of the village by their angry neighbors waving pitchforks, wooden staves, and torches because they were accused of witchcraft. And if not driven away, she could always be executed, as her mother had been.

She dragged open her trunk, grateful it didn't squeak. She grabbed all the supplies she needed and deposited them on the oak table with the lit candle, the one source of warm light in an otherwise crisp, lonely night. She drew out the stool, wincing when it dragged loudly against the wooden floor.

Her fingers trembled as she unknotted the strings and tugged open the velvety yellow pouch. Something fluttered in her belly. Was it in anticipation or apprehension? Perhaps both. The air around her thinned. She took in two deep breaths to settle herself. The strong scent of the cinnamon wafted up, overpowering the light freshness of the juniper and woodsy yarrow. She sprinkled fresh dashes of everything and breathed out her warm witch's breath onto the stones, like Grandmother Sorcha had taught her. After drawing the stings closed, Breena shook the contents of the pouch. The stones clanked as they grazed and hit each other.

She whispered her first question.

"Will I see my father again?"

Breena closed her eyes, pulled the pouch strings open. She reached in and lifted the first stone that touched her fingers. Its smooth coldness registered in her palm, even as her fingers tremored. After inhaling a cleansing breath, she opened her eyes. Black onyx. The stone nearly slipped through her fingers. A weak whimper escaped her lips. Her left hand flew up to clamp down on her mouth, quieting any more sounds that might escape. A cold shiver ran up her spine. She closed her eyes and breathed until composure returned. It couldn't be true. It wasn't true. She wanted to cry out, scream out aloud, yell at the top of her lungs, pound her fists on the tabletop.

Why couldn't she have her father back?

She put the black onyx stone back in the pouch. She wiped at the hot tears that wet her chilled cheeks with the backs of her hands. Were the stones answering her question or an altogether different question? Self-doubt at her skills gave her a small measure of comfort. She wasn't an expert at divination like Grandmother Sorcha, who had been a master at the art and tried without much success until the last to sharpen Breena's skills. It wasn't just for divination; she lacked great mastery. Her spell casting and ability to raise energy were marginal, her connection to the elements and nature tenuous, her communication with spirits nonexistent, plus she had no desire whatsoever to dabble in hexes or black magic; one of the fundamental principles of witchcraft was to harm none, after all. Breena gave a heavy sigh and shook her head.

She repeated the steps and asked her second question.

"Will any harm come to Egan Dunbar this night?"

There was a foreshock in her whisper, as her breath and blood flow picked up. Her mind unwittingly flashed to their last kiss. The intoxicating taste of him still lingered on her lips, on her neck, and on her fingers. The memory was so fresh, it was as if he still touched her core. A hot shudder ran down her spine. The woodsy pine scent of him, she knew, was still in her hair where he'd threaded his fingers as he took her lips with his. She'd smelled it earlier as she'd braided her hair before attempting sleep. How she'd relished his intimate invasion. She'd never craved anything or anyone like that before. Desire had shaken her to her core, rattled her soul, and shifted the ground beneath her feet. Then he'd called her *leannan*. Sweetheart.

Had it been a slip of his tongue?

Breena yanked her mind out of its reverie and looked down. The red tourmaline eyed her. Her eyes widened as she stared at its fiery sheen. Its sparkling surface glistened against the candlelight. The jagged-edged stone was hot, almost burning a hole in the palm of her right hand. She dropped it back into the pouch and drew the strings closed. This time she knew without a doubt the stones hadn't answered the question she'd asked—they had simply chosen to reflect her thoughts. But she didn't need the stones to tell her about the burn in her blood.

When the first light of dawn was an hour from splashing its way across the eastern horizon, Breena was packed, dressed, and ready to depart William's cottage. The morning air was cool, so she donned her black hooded cloak over her travel gown.

Portmanteau in hand, she unbolted her bedchamber door and took one last glance around to ensure everything was packed away in the trunk. Then she walked to the kitchen. The pleasant, creamy smell of warm oat porridge filled the air. William sat on one of the chairs, eating.

"There's breakfast in the pot," he said.

"I'm not hungry. But thank you."

Her stomach was twisted into tiny painful knots, and she could barely catch her breath from worry. The last thing she wanted to do was eat.

Was Egan unharmed? Had her father been freed? As always, the stones had confused her.

After she said her good-byes to Rosalin, Chloe, and Ethan, Breena set out for the gates of Castle Carragh with William as her escort. Four Dunbar guards trailed behind them with her trunk.

The dampness of the morning swirled around Breena as she took in the grayish-blue light of the predawn sky. Their boots crushed dried grass, snapped twigs, and pushed aside short tufts of bushes as they neared the gates. Her palms were sweaty, and her hands trembled. She prayed the stones were wrong. She thought of all the things she wanted to talk to her father about, centered around her mother. Would she get that chance today, would she even recognize him? But then perhaps he would be concealed from the Campbells for now.

Tall torches stuck into the ground cast a warm glow around the Dunbar retainers. The mingled scents of smoke and horse drifted through the air. Countless conversations bounced around, and wagons rattled as they were loaded with supplies. Neighs of horses filled the air as did the slap of saddles being settled into position and the champing of bits being slid into place. Breena pivoted around as she scurried. She made out Dougray and Craig. She waved at her uncle. His trunks were already loaded onto a wagon.

Breena blinked when she made out Egan among the Dunbars. She exhaled in a rush of relief. Some of the knots in her stomach eased. Egan was unharmed and braw. He stood with Alban and Keith, engrossed in conversation. She marveled at the potent sort of energy that surrounded him, as if the air were charged just being near him.

Egan turned and seemed to notice her and William's arrival. He left Alban and Keith and swaggered toward them. His ebony unbuttoned overcoat covered most of his dark waistcoat and white léine. She'd never seen him in a cravat before. It was a stylish traditional knot, but then the realization hit her that she preferred his bare neck. Her eyes were drawn to his exposed knees, where the edges of his Dunbar tartan kilt flickered in the light breeze meeting the tops of his riding boots. Her eyes lingered there before she realized she was ogling him.

Just as Egan approached them, William turned to her. "May I carry that portmanteau for you to the wagon?"

She nodded and handed it to him.

He took the small trunk with one hand, placing the other hand on her shoulder. "Rosalin has grown fond of you; she'll miss you."

A smile stretched across Breena's lips. "And I her."

Egan stood a foot away from them. A single muscle twitched at his right temple as he glanced sharply at William's hand, still lingering on her shoulder. She caught what sounded like a low growl from Egan's direction, or perhaps it was just the rustling trees nearby.

Egan's lips relaxed when William released her.

"We thank the Campbells for hosting our short stay," Egan said to William.

"I hope you accomplished all you intended."

"Enough for now."

"You are all more than welcome to return, should the need arise."

Breena bit down on her lip as she skimmed her surroundings for an aged version of dark hair and warm chestnut eyes. How would nineteen years have changed him? Were the stones correct? Did the negative response of the black onyx answer her question about ever seeing her father again?

Or was it answering something entirely different?

When she tasted the iron saltiness of blood, she released the bite on her bottom lip and turned to Egan.

"Egan, I trust your man Ian found the clothes to his liking?"

He arched an eyebrow, then his mouth curled up.

"Yes, he did. And the tincture did a fine job. Ian feels much better this morning."

The remaining knots in her belly loosened as a wide smile tugged at her mouth. "That's marvelous!"

A weightlessness settled over Breena's entire body, and heat warmed the insides of her chest. She fought the urge to throw her arms around Egan's neck and kiss him. She was going to have her father back. The stones had been wrong.

The Dunbar escorts carrying Breena's trunk arrived and were depositing it in the wagon, when someone's voice pierced the air, sounding more like a pig's squeal.

"Halt! You there, stop."

Breena recognized the voice even before she turned to observe the corpulent, tetchy-faced Finlay. He barreled toward the men with the trunk. Was it just three days ago he'd laid his meaty hands on her? Her head practically spun with the knowledge that her entire world had changed since then.

"I have to search the trunks, as is customary when outsiders depart," Finlay said, a hideous scowl etched into his features.

Breena had many things to be grateful for today, not the least of which was that she wouldn't have to see him ever again.

Something shifted in the air as Finlay approached the trunks on her uncle's wagon. Was it her imagination or had the Dunbar retainers stilled in unison as Finlay laid a hand on the first trunk? She turned in time to observe an almost imperceptible shift in Egan's countenance. His chin rose and his eyes narrowed from relaxed to alert. She didn't imagine that.

A sharp voice stilled Finlay's hands. "How dare you speak to guests in such a manner?" William marched toward Finlay.

"'Tis customary. Orders from the Campbell himself." Finlay's face twisted in disdain.

Breena whirled around. Only the Campbell sentries were present. She wasn't surprised to discover that Alasdair Campbell was nowhere in sight. The man wouldn't deign to bid farewell to his guests. Or perhaps his illness had gotten worse. She was ashamed of herself for not caring about that in the least.

"Then I'll conduct the search myself. You return to your duty. Post-haste." William's voice left no room for argument.

Finlay's sneer and rigid shoulders showed what he thought of William's dictate. Nonetheless, he stomped back to the gate and his post.

William walked to the wagon, slipped Breena's portmanteau inside, then turned to Craig. "I need to take a quick look inside these bigger trunks."

Craig nodded his assent to George, who appeared nervous. He fumbled first then managed to open and remove the lock from Craig's largest trunk. William grabbed the lid and lifted it, and from the corner of her eye, Breena saw Egan shifting his stance. He went from arms folded over his wide chest to arms akimbo. Breena blinked, and her shoulders tightened when she noted his hands were now that much closer to the two dirks on his belt. Her limbs shook, and the air thinned around her. Something was happening, but she didn't yet know what. All the Dunbars' attention seemed focused on William Campbell's movements now.

When the lid was thrown open by William, Breena's mouth dropped and a gasp escaped her lips.

"Steady, *leannan*."

The low rumble of Egan's voice, the kind used to calm a colt about to bolt, caused Breena to close her mouth. She stared at what, or rather who peeked out from inside the trunk William had opened.

It was a man with long gray hair pulled back in a neat queue. His clean-shaven face emphasized his sunken cheeks and numerous wrinkles.

But even from thirty paces, Breena recognized his kind chestnut eyes. Her hands clamped over her mouth as tears welled up.

She trained her eyes on William, holding her breath.

The Campbells' sentries were too far away to witness any of this. Would William alert them? If he did, war between the Campbells and the Dunbars was inevitable, for the Campbells would attack, and the Dunbars would defend themselves. William stared at Ian MacRae for what seemed like an eternity but in fact must have been less than ten seconds. He closed the trunk, his expression unreadable.

"Looks good to me. Can you open this second? There's a padlock on it." William's voice carried as he pointed to the lock and eyed George, who in turn looked at Craig for approval.

Breena bit down on her lip as her stomach constricted. It wasn't possible that William had missed her father. Had he then unilaterally decided against a war between the Campbells and the Dunbars?

With shaky hands, Craig rubbed his brow as he nodded. George mutely opened the second trunk.

Breena's voice was raspy when she looked at Egan. "But he must have noticed—"

"Yes, he did."

"And he didn't call the guards?" Breena felt faint from all the emotions rushing through her head.

A slow smirk broke out on Egan's face. "It looks like William Campbell is not of a mind to start a war today."

Her head whirled back to William, who seemed to have finished with his inspection of the second trunk. "All seems in order. Thank you."

As the remaining trunks were loaded into the wagon, William approached Egan and Breena.

William whispered, to Breena. "I'm pleased to return the favor so soon, for you saving my Rosalin's life. I wish you a safe journey."

The emotions surging through Breena's veins propelled her to throw her arms around William and kiss him on both cheeks before releasing him.

"I am grateful for what you just did."

Egan had a strange expression on his face as he glanced from her to William. But then, his features stretched into a wide smile as he stepped forward and clasped forearms with William. "You are a good man, William Campbell. You'll always have allies in the Dunbars."

William's countenance brightened as he returned the smile. "I owe you a pint or two, one of these days."

"I'll hold you to that."

After the wagon was loaded and ready, Craig and George went to the front of the wagon. Egan took hold of Breena's waist and lifted her onto the back. She grabbed the tips of his shoulders to steady herself, surprised at his gesture. His shoulder muscles flexed beneath her grip. She resisted the urge to tell him it was improper for him to grab hold of her in public, because the truth was, she longed for his touch and the way it heated her insides.

Craig didn't seem to have witnessed Egan's move, but the same could not be said for several of the Dunbars, who glanced their way, some with grins and smirks as they mounted their horses, others with disapproving looks.

She gazed up at him. "You now have my undying gratitude, Highlander, for what you did for my father. I would kiss you if we didn't have an audience."

She expected some wolfish remark from him, or at the very least a simple "It was my pleasure."

Instead, his lips curled.

"I want to do much more to you, but my favors are not given as gratitude."

His face had the expression of a hungry lion just before it unsheathed its claws.

Heat and shivers alike swarmed her body.

Breena swallowed as her brows furrowed in confusion. "You don't approve of my gratitude?"

"I welcome gratitude, just not in the way you're offering it up."

Breena's face scrunched up. *What does he mean, offering it up?*

As realization slammed into her, she gasped in shock.

"You think I let you kiss me . . . let you do those things to me, because I am grateful for what you are doing for my father?"

His face was a stony façade. "Didn't you?"

Something red and blistering unfurled inside her. Her palm shot up and dealt a sharp resounding slap across his cheek. His face was like marble, causing her wrist to bounce back in pain. Except marble was cold, not scalding like his skin. Her palm stung from the contact. She regretted her action almost the very instant she'd done it. What was the matter with her? She'd never slapped anyone in her life, yet here on Coll she'd done it twice.

Had this horrid isle driven her mad?

Her eyes speared him as she bit down on her bottom lip. Egan's hardened expression didn't budge for a second, he simply glowered at her. A red mark appeared on his cheek where her hand had connected.

She wanted to scream at him, to pound her fists against his chest, except they would bounce off as well. Of all the emotions that swelled inside her, regret and anger stood out. She actively restrained her hands to her sides, so she wouldn't do anything else that was foolish, like throw her arms around him and beg until the glower was erased.

A shuffle sounded from the front of the wagon. "Is aught amiss?"

Breena looked back. Her uncle eyed them, his brows arched. Had he witnessed their exchange?

"All is well," Breena said. Her voice sounded strangled to her own ears.

She turned back just as Egan walked toward his black beast of a stallion. Heimdall seemed the kind of horse that could get you to Hades and back without breaking a sweat. Breena didn't miss the uncomfortable stares and clearing of throats from some of the Dunbars.

Hadn't they both garnered some esteem for each other? How could he think that of her? Breena took in her stinging palm as George snapped the reins and the wagon creaked and started to move. She shook her head as her shoulders slumped. No, they didn't know each other at all. He was a future chief and she a baseborn healer, their worlds hugely different. He mingled with lairds, peers, and the highborn, while she mingled with merchants, tradesmen, and the lowborn.

Her spine started to coat itself in something like ice. This departure was special. She should be ecstatic; she had her father back after all these years and she was leaving Coll. Then why did she have to blink away threatening tears?

CHAPTER
22

Breena clutched at then smoothed down the pleats of her cloak with anxiousness. The woolen material was soft yet uneven under her fingertips. She crossed her legs as she shot an inquiring glance at Craig, who rode in the front of the moving wagon. He seemed quite relaxed, facing forward. The bright magentas, fiery reds, and coppery yellows of dawn had started to even out against the lightening azure sky. Castle Carragh had been reduced to a speck on the horizon.

Her gaze spanned the fifty-some impressive Dunbar riders who flanked their wagon, their powerful horses clopping the dry dirt. The dust being kicked up made her sneeze. The Dunbar riders looked disgruntled and testy on their horses. They seemed restrained by the gait of the wagons, which they were forced to keep pace with.

They'd no doubt rather be chasing the wind.

She didn't think the Campbells could see them this far away, plus she could wait no longer to speak with her father. She took a seat alongside the trunk that held Ian. She shot her uncle a determined look.

"Isn't it safe to open the trunk now?"

Craig shifted around to face her, then nodded. Holding on to the sides of the wagon, he made his way to sit next to her.

He lifted the lid. The grayed head of Ian MacRae jutted out from the trunk. His warm chestnut eyes lit up as he eyed Breena.

"Thank you, my dear, for championing an old man. I am sure if it were left up to Craig here, I'd be in this wretched position all the way to Skye."

His croaky voice was not the exuberant one she recalled. Tears stung Breena's eyes, not just for the charismatic, larger-than-life man who had been reduced to the tremulous, frail body in front of her, but for the six-year-old girl who had sat at home many days and nights waiting for her father's return. Her thoughts scattered, and the warm expansion of her chest was bittersweet. She knelt next to the trunk and threw her arms around his torso. His frame felt thin in her arms.

"*Athair*—Father!" Breena's body quaked with a mountain of emotion as she held him. His arms came around her; they felt insubstantial somehow.

"Do I look that dreadful?" Ian said, the intonation of his voice diverting. It tugged Breena's lips into a smile.

She brushed her tears away. "Quite frightful."

"Breena!" Her uncle's voice was laced with a reprimand that somehow didn't ring true. But she didn't mind because a warm smile stretched across her father's face. Her dear father who was finally here. At long last, she could look upon him and gorge her eyes. She swallowed back some of the emotions that strangled her throat.

"I agree with you. But I'm as delighted as a lark to see you, my dear. And I suppose with time and proper food, I won't look like a *glaistig*— ghost." Ian exchanged a glance with Craig. Something ambiguous passed between them, but Breena didn't pay it any mind.

Craig and Breena each took an arm of Ian's. Their bodies swayed and jerked with the movements of the wagon as they helped him out of the trunk. Breena tried not to stare at how Craig's clothes sagged on Ian's wiry frame.

"I thank all the saints you survived. But how'd you manage it for nineteen years?"

A rueful stare crossed Ian's face. "I can only imagine that Alasdair took immense pleasure in the act of torture. So much so that they made sure to keep me alive over the years so he could continue."

Breena lowered her head as a dull ache registered inside her belly. "I would have come for you sooner, but I only found out three weeks ago. I thought you dead all this time."

"That's the way your dear *màthair*—mother wanted it."

"But why?"

"She didn't want your life tainted. She wanted to give you an unblemished start."

"But neither you nor she was guilty. She was accused of a crime that was never committed." Breena's voice sounded like a strangled plea to her own ears. She still didn't understand. Didn't comprehend why her parents had even gone to Coll in the first place.

Before Ian could answer, Craig cut in. "Your mother had her reasons. We should not question her. Why don't we let Ian rest for a while before we pepper him with questions?"

"Forgive me. Of course, Uncle."

Frustration settled on Breena's chest. She pinched her lips together. Was she too impatient to learn what'd happened? It'd been nineteen years, after all. She huffed. And why did Craig insist on leading the conversation elsewhere whenever she sought answers?

"Are we off to Skye then?" Ian said, after a few silent minutes.

"You are coming to Kilmuir to stay with Madeline and me," Craig answered.

Ian's eyebrows arched. "And Breena? Does she not live with you as well? Or does she have a family of her own now?"

Breena had never been called an old maid outright, but for the past couple years she'd gotten used to the pitying gazes of people, above all the women, when she said she was not yet married at five and twenty. However, nothing but kindness was displayed on Ian's face.

"No, Father. I am not yet married. I live at Castle Duntulm. I am healer to the MacIntyres now."

"Healer for the MacIntyres? That's a great honor. You have done well for yourself. Your mother . . . she would be proud."

Briefly etched in his haggard features was a grief-stricken expression. A sharp pang hit her in the chest. She hated seeing her father like this, graying and forlorn. She took hold of his hand and gave it a gentle squeeze.

"Thank you, *Athair*."

After that she kept the conversation light and avoided any mention of her mother. Even though she was delighted to have her father back, her insides itched and burned. On the one side, she wanted to know more about her parents, why they'd gone to Coll, and her mother's supposed affair with Alasdair. But on the other side, she understood Craig's concern: she should not inundate her father with questions, at least not yet.

White, frothy waves crashed up against Arinagour's rocky shore as gulls flew down to perch on docked fishing boats. A cool breeze brushed

Breena's cheeks. Egan and the Dunbars went to work to hire the local fishermen for transport of their group. They were to travel from Arinagour across the Sea of the Hebrides to Loch Brittle on the southern tip of Skye. Breena took Ian for a stroll along the sand. She took some of his weight, as he leaned on her because of his injured legs.

Breena's furtive glances were drawn to Egan, across the sand. He was deep in negotiation with a short, stocky fisherman. She couldn't help but admire the way Egan's muscles bulged under his coat as he raised his arm and pointed north toward Skye. Her eyes followed the leisurely way his other arm rested on the hilt of the dirk at his waist.

Egan glanced back to their traveling party, and his eyes found hers. Her breath hitched, but she was unable to break away from those piercing eyes. Despite the heat of anger and the sting of hurt that swirled inside her, something hot settled in her core. There was no mistaking the heat in his gaze as his eyes raked the length of her. How dare he look at her like that after accusing her of "offering it up." Without saying the words, he'd branded her a lightskirt.

Her eyes narrowed. She huffed.

Offering it up indeed.

After what seemed like an eternity, she dragged her eyes away. Her skin was feverish, and she tried with great difficulty not to recall strong, rough hands on her willing flesh, the sensuous teases and compelling taste of his decadent lips, and his wicked fingers. She'd made the decision to erect a wall between them when she'd first met him on Coll, for fear he'd learn her family's secrets, her secret. She had every intention of reinforcing said wall.

As Ian held her forearm for support, he shot her an inquiring glance.

"Does the lad share your affection?"

Had he witnessed her staring at Egan?

"Pardon me?" She forced an impassive expression.

Ian placed a gentle hand on her shoulder. "I've seen the way you look at him and the way he looks at you. Forgive me for saying it, my dear, nonetheless, please be more guarded in your associations with Egan. Even the appearance of impropriety will blemish your good name. Once lost, it can never be regained. While Egan Dunbar is a good man, his world is different from ours."

Breena lowered her head to absently inspect her hand. She fought the emotions his words elicited in her. Rebelliousness and anger at the world for always putting her in her place. Fear of Egan discovering her witchery roots and their implications. And longing. Longing for things that can never be. If only her heart understood what her head already knew.

She blinked up at Ian. "We are mere friends. Nothing more."

He sent her a pointed stare. "He said you were friends when he came to rescue me. But you two give the appearance of more than mere friendship when you are together." His brows were drawn in concern, but there was no judgment in Ian's face.

"He felt obligated to help on Coll because I assisted him and his men several months ago with a battle against the British redcoats. That is all there is to it. And I tended to the injuries of his foster brother's wife, who happens to be my friend. This is all in the line of duty to the MacIntyres."

Ian's eyes widened. "You took part in a battle?"

Despite herself, Breena chuckled at the astonishment displayed on her father's features. "I didn't do battle, *Athair*. I don't even know how to hold a sword. I simply added a sleeping draft to the redcoats' food and drink, rendering them ineffective on the battlefield."

Understanding settled on his features. "Oh, I see. That was clever of you. You remind me of your dear mother. She was bonny, clever, and a bit fearless as well."

Breena harrumphed. "I'm not fearless."

Her gaze fell. If she were fearless, she wouldn't hide her witchery out of pure dread of discovery. And that dread wouldn't rule every action of her entire existence until, she feared one day, it would drive her completely and utterly mad.

She surveyed their surroundings; not seeing Craig, the question she'd been meaning to ask slipped past her lips. "What did the Campbells do to her?"

She felt Ian stiffen. A pained expression flashed across his face.

"Lady Campbell came from a powerful clan who claimed to be direct descendants of the old Somerled. Alasdair married her for her dowry. When Lady Campbell became pregnant, your mother started to attend her as her personal healer. Alasdair lost interest in his wife and became enamored with Beth. Your mother rejected him, of course, but that enraged him. And when his wife died in childbirth, giving birth to a dead bairn, Lady Campbell's clan blamed Alasdair. He needed a scapegoat. Beth was the most suitable candidate, she was close to Lady Campbell, and Alasdair hated her because of her rejection."

Breena frowned. "But didn't the wife and bairn die of natural causes? Why wouldn't the Campbell say that instead of accusing my mother of a nonexistent crime?"

Ian exhaled out loud, sounding helpless. "I've often wondered that myself. The answer I came up with was Alasdair Campbell wanted to punish Beth for her rejection. His hate was greater than the need to tell the truth."

Iciness took hold of Breena, it corded her neck muscles and tightened her shoulders. Craig had never told her, but she so desperately wanted to know.

"How . . . how was she executed?"

She eyed Ian even as tears stung the backs of her eyes. They'd stopped walking now and stood facing each other. Ian balanced himself on his better leg. The wrinkled skin on his face bunched together, and he shook his head. "My dear, it's not a pleasant—"

"I have to know," she said, her voice a whispered plea.

She was prepared to beg, having had extensive practice with Craig. Much good that had accomplished.

Ian cleared his throat, as if he were trying to find his voice. "She was burned alive at the stake, branded a witch."

Breena gasped. Her hand flew up to cover her mouth. Nausea gurgled in her stomach, the pain of it shot to the back of her throat, momentarily impeding her breathing. She'd had countless torturous nightmares from which she'd jolted awake in a screaming, sweaty mess from seeing both her parents shot and hanged. But never that. She imagined her bright, beautiful mother, an innocent child of nature, shackled to a stake as red flames scorched her alabaster skin. Breena squeezed her eyes shut. She willed the torturous image with all her might to leave her.

The serpent-like sneer of Alasdair Campbell popped into her head. She turned to her father.

"How could he let her burn at the stake for a crime she didn't commit?" Her voice was low and cold, foreign to her own ears.

Ian tilted his head and gazed out to sea. A distant expression washed over his face. "The man is evil to the core. There's no doubt about that. But the weapon he used to murder Beth was created a long time ago by that so-called man of God, Heinrich Kramer."

Breena had read a copy of the three-hundred-year-old treatise called *The Hammer of Witches*, which was nothing but an account of a senile old man's prejudices. Most pagans blamed it for their persecution by the Church, the reason they had to practice their religion in secrecy. It not only called witchcraft heresy but encouraged burning alive at the stake as the preferred punishment.

Breena gazed out to sea alongside Ian.

A shuffling sounded behind them.

"Is aught amiss?"

Breena and her father swung around as Craig approached. Breena schooled her features into impassivity. She was sure if Craig found out she was asking Ian questions he would disapprove. *No good can come from revisiting this past*, he'd said more than once before. Well, she disagreed.

"Athair was telling me about his tannery business before he was taken by the Campbells." She took in Ian's quirked eyebrows, but he said nothing to the contrary.

"Egan wants us to board one of the *birlinns*. We are about to make our way to Skye," Craig said.

Breena and Ian trailed after Craig, who led them toward a long wooden vessel that was propelled on the water by sail and oar. The Dunbars had already started loading their wagons and horses onto the vessel.

◀─◀──◀─◀──◀──

Breena thanked her lucky stars she'd worn her cloak, for an eerie sea mist and rain followed them on the Sea of the Hebrides as the small fleet of *birlinns* made their way north. The sight beyond the hull of their *birlinn* included the thick mist and big curling waves that rocked them up and down. But true to the Islanders' saying, if you don't like the weather, just wait a few minutes, the whirling sea breeze blew the fine rain and mist away after a short period.

It was past nightfall when they approached Loch Brittle, on the southern tip of the Isle of Skye. The silvery rays from the full moon glowed in the cobalt sky, guiding their way. Breena took in the hazy light reflecting off the familiar towering hills and rugged landscape. She was almost home.

As that thought crossed her mind, she breathed out a long, heavy sigh that released some of the tension she'd carried on Coll.

They disembarked the *birlinns* in the dark and the men led the horses and wagons onto the sandy beach away from the water. After neighing horses and creaking wagons were mounted once more, their party's journey was underway. Breena sat with Ian, while Craig rode at the front of their wagon with George.

Ian's mouth curled up in a smile. He appeared more relaxed now than Breena had seen him all day. "It's good to be back on Skye. I thought I'd die on Coll."

She was speechless on how to respond to that, except to silently thank all the saints she could name that he didn't.

Their wagon trailed the Dunbar riders away from the beach, with its massive crashing waves, heading toward the firmer ground of Glen Brittle Forest. The sounds of the water receded into the background, and the chirping of crickets and croaking of frogs took over. They circumvented lean, crooked sycamores and fragrant pine trees.

"Is it like you remembered?" she asked.

Ian considered their surroundings, then inhaled deeply. "I fought every day to remember the simple things, the crisp woodsy scent of the forest, the sweet-smelling purple thistle, and the cool wind against my face. It was the only way to be free, in a cage."

Breena considered her father for a few breaths. "Craig said you had a steely core. I now start to understand what he meant," she said.

Breena was drained from the journey. All her energy had abandoned her. Although it was a mild night, a shiver ran up her spine, and gooseflesh covered her limbs. It took her a few minutes to understand why. Between the fine drizzle and the splashes from the waves earlier, her cloak was soaked and had doubled in weight.

They stopped at a grassy glade in the forest.

While some of the Dunbars went hunting, Breena helped feed, brush down, and tether the horses. Craig and George unfolded the canvas flaps at the sides of the wagon's canopy to allow for privacy within the wagon.

When the Dunbar hunters returned, Breena helped to prepare the grouse and mountain hare for roasting. After the meat was skinned and cleaned, she used a few sprinklings of dried rosemary, thyme, and sage from her portmanteau for flavoring.

Breena regarded the Dunbars while they skewered and roasted the meat over the crackling fire. But her gaze kept straying to their future laird, who stood speaking with Dougray and Keith.

"I don't mind missing Samhain back at our keep," a young Dunbar said.

"Scared of the ghost?" An older man clucked.

"He appeared to me once, pale as white linen and eerie as a crypt at midnight. Made the hairs at the back of my neck stand up. He was dressed like a Spanish pikeman and floated in the air down the hall of the east wing at Eileanach Castle," Alban said.

Breena eyed Alban. "Oh, come off it. You don't in actual fact have a ghost, do you?"

Some of the Dunbar retainers chuckled, but no one answered her question.

Samhain was celebrated each year on the last day of October to mark the end of the harvest season. Many Highlanders believed it was a time for purification, cleansing, and remembrance. On the night of Samhain, many in the Highlands believed that the veils between the worlds of the spirits and the living were thinned.

"Why a Spanish pikeman?" Breena asked. She hoped someone would answer her this time.

"He died in the Jacobite rebellion of 1715 when Spain was an ally, fighting for the rebels. They say he haunts the halls, looking for his lost love, a bonny lass," Alban said.

A few of the men made piercing wolf calls while others laughed out loud. A cold shiver ran up her spine. It took her a second to realize it had nothing to do with a ghost, but the fact that her cloak was still wet.

Breena decided to wash up before dinner. She walked to the wagon, where she took a clean piece of linen and soap, then followed the hazy moonlight to a nearby babbling burn.

When she found a copse of trees that allowed for a modicum of privacy, she took off the wet cloak and spread it on a thicket of gorse bushes. At the water, she folded up her sleeves, untucked a few buttons on her dress then stooped down. She splashed the cool water on her arms and neck and started to unlace her boots, with the intention of unclipping and rolling down her stockings.

A movement behind her caused her to gasp out loud and spin around.

CHAPTER
23

"*I*t's not safe to be alone out here."

Her muscles stiffened, and for a few angry breaths she was unable to process any thoughts. She gazed up at the foreboding, hard lines on Egan's features.

"I don't recall asking for your opinion."

She scowled, then swung back around. She was about to unroll her stockings, but then she huffed out a breath and turned back around. "I require privacy. Please leave."

Even though he stood four paces away, she could feel the heat radiating from his body, as if she were standing next to a bonfire. How had he come up behind her without making a single sound?

"I see. Now that you have your father back, all pretense of cordiality is gone. No need to tolerate my company or moan with need for my kisses anymore."

His voice was low and dripped with derision.

Breena shot up and spun around. "How dare you accuse me of offering it up as gratitude."

He glared at her. But then his eyes flickered to where she'd undone the first few buttons on her dress. The heat of anger fused with an entirely different sort of heat on his granite features. His grin was mocking. "Wasn't that what you've been doing ever since I told you Ian was alive?"

His words were cold, causing fire to shoot through her veins. Her entire body shook with the force of it. She'd never been this insulted or riled up in her entire life.

"How dare you insinuate I am a lightskirt!" Breena didn't care if she was shouting.

Before he could respond, a shuffle sounded from a few paces away.

"Breena, where'd you disappear to?" Her father bored through the nearby copse of trees.

"I'm just washing up before dinner." Her attempt to make her voice airy failed miserably.

"You shouldn't leave camp by yourself, my dear." Ian approached her with a pronounced limp, using a walking staff Craig had fashioned for him from an oak branch earlier. Ian's eyes flickered toward Egan and he offered him a nod.

"That's what I was trying to explain to her," Egan said.

The arrival of her father cleared the angry haze from her head. Something needled her and she shot a firm glance from Ian to Egan. "You are concerned the Campbells will follow us?"

"It's simply advisable for us to be prepared," Egan said.

"We'll wait for you behind the trees, my dear."

Egan and Ian moved behind the copse of trees and Breena continued her washing. And even though the water refreshed her, remnants of hurt, anger, and uncertainty swirled around her with regard to Egan. After he escorted them home, would she ever see him again? A knot formed in her belly, and she had trouble swallowing. A heaviness weighed on her while she finished up. She then rejoined Egan and Ian, and they strolled back to camp.

◆—◆—◆—◆—◆

Breena was perched atop a rocky outcropping next to Ian and Craig near the campfire as curly lines of smoke floated up into the air. She bit into a tender piece of roasted grouse and inhaled its spiciness, listening to the conversations of the Dunbars. Their voices and laughter mingled with the hiss, and pops of the fire. She couldn't seem to muster any interest in their jests.

Her gaze kept finding its way to Egan, who stood looking out at the periphery of their camp.

Why did his opinion of her being a lightskirt not only grate at her nerves but tighten her chest every time she inhaled?

Ian shifted next to her. "Do the folks on Skye still carve faces onto hollowed-out turnips and beets and light candles inside for Samhain?"

She tilted a smile in Ian's direction. "Yes. They leave them to burn all night outside their windows, along with the bannock cakes for the spirits."

"When I was a child, I used to sneak out of my bed and steal those bannock cakes and have a feast." He smirked.

Breena feigned horror with an audible gasp. "You were a mischievous child, Athair."

Ian shrugged, grinning. "Not mischievous, just hungry."

Even as Breena smiled at her father, a tingling spread across the nape of her neck as Ian pivoted backward to greet someone who approached from behind. Breena knew who it was before he stepped into view.

"You look better than you did last night. The taste and smell of freedom agrees with you." Egan handed Ian a large jug of ale.

Ian nodded his thanks with a huge grin and took the jug. "As it would with any free-thinking man."

Ian took a hearty swig of the ale, then wiped traces of the amber liquid from his mouth with the back of his right hand and handed the jug to Craig.

"You are right, of course. But I'm sure being back in the company of your family is also responsible for improving your health." Egan threw her and Craig a cursory glance.

"Staying on Coll is bad enough for anyone's health. But being imprisoned there without just cause . . . I would imagine there is no worse kind of hell," Craig said, before he put the jug to his lips, leaned his head back, and drank.

"I am blessed to be free, with my family and amongst friends," Ian said.

"That's all anyone can ask for," Egan said.

After everyone was sated and their thirsts quenched, one of the Dunbars pulled out a fiddle and started a rhythmic rendition of "Hey Tuttie Tatie."

The melody, as old as Robert the Bruce himself, filled the camp. Several Dunbars stood at attention exhibiting their national pride. Breena didn't miss the dark expression that passed over Egan's face as he stood next to Dougray eying the fiddler. She hoped the Jacobites would rally again after Culloden, although most thought it unlikely.

After "Hey Tuttie Tatie," the fiddler started the livelier tune "Frog Went a-Courting," to which animated chatter and laughter broke out.

A tap on Breena's shoulder made her turn around. A beaming, pinked-faced Alban smiled at her. His right hand was upturned and held out toward her.

"May I have this dance, mistress?"

A smile tugged on Breena's lips. She took his hand, and he pulled her up from her seat. She curtseyed, and then he led her to a small clearing near the campfire where they took each other's arms and started a Highland schottische. As Breena moved, she was aware of some of the Dunbar retainers' eyes on her and Alban, along with their encouraging cheers and whistles. Breena stepped to the tune, right, left, then twirled around on her toes as she held on to Alban. The movements made her giddy and light-headed. Her rapid breaths came out in spurts of giggles and laughter. The last time she'd done this was at the Beltane fair at Duntulm, with Eva, over a year ago.

"Alban, where'd you learn to dance?" Her voice was breathy.

"My mother taught me, and I never wanted to thank her until now." His mouth turned up in a shy grin.

Breena was still laughing when the tune and dance concluded. She turned to walk back to her seat, still looking at Alban, and walked straight into a rock wall, a muscled wall that smelled of woodsy pine and maleness. She stepped back, a little dazed, and glanced up into hard, hazel eyes.

Egan's lips curled at her even as the vein twitched at his right temple. "May I have the next dance?" He inclined his head toward her and held his hands out.

Breena opened her mouth with the intention of declining. "I am actually not—"

"Of course, she would like to dance with you, sir. She's an excellent dancer." Alban cut in.

Breena's eyes narrowed at Alban, but she said nothing. Why call unnecessary attention to herself? She extended her hand to Egan as her chin tilted upward. The fiddler started to play "Greysteil." She wondered at the fiddler's choice of song, from the old epic romance, as her head turned in his direction. His bearded face was stretched into a conspiratorial grin.

She glared at him.

All else melted away as Egan's left palm held up her right arm. His touch sent feather-like tingles down her body. His other arm came around her waist, causing her breath to hitch. She felt small in the arms of such an impressive physique yet protected somehow. The granite hardness of him, coupled with his male scent, went to her head like an intoxicating elixir. The longer his hand held her waist, the more heated she became.

It made her want to press against him and purr like a cat. Goodness, was she coming down with that strange fever again?

They moved together in a Highland schottische. He twirled her around, and everything in the background spun in a blur. Nothing existed but Egan, the music, her audible breathing, and a pulsating energy between them.

The glare in his eyes heated to the shade of cool gray cabochon gemstones slicing through her. It stripped her bare. "Why've you lost the smile you had when you danced with Alban?" His voice was edged with something raw.

"Because Alban never cut me to the quick." Her answer came out in a rush of breath.

"And I have?"

Her nostrils flared; she wasn't sure if it was from the dance or the man. She bared her teeth and held her chin high. She wanted to scream at him but decided against it considering where they were.

"I thought you honorable once. I've since changed my mind." The second the words left her mouth, she regretted them.

She jerked her head back and straightened when his fingers pressed into a ticklish spot, not enough to hurt her, but certainly enough that she might normally giggle. However, she was not in a giggling mood.

Had he done that on purpose? She narrowed her eyes at him as he continued to lead her in the dance.

"And I thought you a liar once. I've yet to change my mind."

She gaped at him, then stepped hard on his toes as they moved together in the dance. She was going to give as good as she got. She straightened on the next turn, her lips thinned and curled, as she glared at him. She wanted to stick out her tongue at him.

Then she made the mistake of looking at his lips. A heated sigh escaped her mouth. She recalled their soft, luxurious feel. Something melted inside her. Something changed. The heat of anger was replaced with a different sort of heat. Her body wanted to melt like a boneless mass at his feet, and she almost lagged in the next twirl, but he held her steadily in his arms and moved her along to the tune.

"Stop looking at me like that. Everyone can see you." His voice was low and raspy.

She blinked away the sultry, hot images and looked him in the eyes.

"Like what?"

"You know like what."

She became aware of several things all at once, the music had stopped, and they'd stopped dancing, but he still held her. And she stared at him as he gazed down at her.

She shook her head to clear the hazy fog and stepped back, out of his embrace.

"Thank you for the dance." His voice had become hard again.

Her breath was labored, and her head felt light as she curtseyed, then walked back to her seat next to Ian. She ignored the curious gazes directed at her.

Breena jerked awake with a start. Her body trembled and shook; her night-rail clung to her damp skin, except for the fabric bunched up in her fists. She uncurled her grip and blinked into the blackness of night.

What had awoken her? A dream. Grandmother Sorcha's voice came back to her.

The Highlander needs protection.

Breena sat up on her makeshift pallet in the wagon, rolled her shoulders, and shook her head. It was just a dream. She took deep gulps of air to calm her ragged breath. It was a dream, wasn't it? She'd never had the gift of second sight. She was almost sure she didn't.

But what if Egan was in danger? She harrumphed. Why should she care? It wasn't as if she couldn't breathe each time the thought that she'd never lay eyes on him again after he escorted them home entered her mind. It wasn't as if she was in love with him. A pathetic groan rumbled in her throat, and she squeezed her eyes shut. Love?

God help her.

Breena peeked through the narrow opening of the flap at the back of the wagon. The Dunbar retainers, covered in their plaids, lay on the ground around the campfire, which was now reduced to mere embers. Loud snores mingled with a long, solitary hoot overhead, no doubt an owl declaring its territory.

Breena donned her dressing gown and arisaid. Thankfully, she'd never removed her half boots or stockings. She spotted her portmanteau in the corner of the wagon. It had everything she needed. She grabbed it, pushed back the flap on the back of wagon and slid down. The night air was cool as she peered around in the dark. No one stirred. She tiptoed away from camp and followed the hazy light of the full moon into the forest. The damp air mixed with the earthy smell of the forest made her alert. Insects squeaked and hissed, and the breeze rustled the trees as she walked deeper into the forest.

She stopped when she encountered a small glade surrounded by swaying sycamores and towering pine trees. It was no Fairy Glen, but it would do. Warmth spread through her as she took in the yellow and dark purple primrose flowers growing by the root of a sycamore tree. They'd been Grandmother Sorcha's favorite.

The first time Sorcha had taken her to the Fairy Glen, she'd been six. The day had been mild, with clear blue skies and golden sunlight glimmering off grassy hills. She could still smell the fragrance of the vibrant and colorful wildflowers. Sorcha had turned to her, unabashed confidence etched in her lined smile as if she were unveiling the secret of life to Breena. Her beautiful gray hair was unbound, swaying with the wind. "I'm going to teach you about your heritage, child," she said. And in that moment she introduced Breena to the seven stones of divination.

"Should you pluck the clear white quartz from the pouch during your spell, that foretells of peace and tranquility in the coming days. The yellow citrine means you've an important lesson to learn, and the orange carnelian is for luck," Sorcha said.

Six-year-old Breena pouted. "Does the carnelian mean good luck or bad luck?"

Sorcha chuckled. "That's an important distinction, isn't it? It means good luck."

That day, Breena was most fascinated by the orange stone. The sun's rays somehow intensified its sparkle as she herself plucked it from the pouch. It shined brighter than any of the other stones.

The truth was, since that day, she'd never again managed to pull the carnelian from the pouch. She'd often wondered if the orange had in fact indicated her good luck that day at having Sorcha pass these teachings on to her.

Sorcha continued. "The brown jasper means a gift is in your near future and the green aventurine means love."

Breena scratched her head. "Love? But does it mean you love someone or that someone loves you?"

Sorcha sent her a knowing smile. "Well, my dear, as your skills sharpen, you'll be able to make that distinction. You see, it's different for every witch."

Breena had often mulled over Sorcha's words, for she'd never actually been able to make the distinction.

She smiled at the memory.

She plucked a few Primroses and used the flowers and four rocks to mark a circle nine feet across in the center of the clearing. Breena stepped into the circle with some remaining flowers and her portmanteau. After she ignited a small flame with the flint and steel she'd brought, Breena used a few twigs and small branches to get the flames up to a healthy crackling.

The heat from the fire started to warm her, so she removed her arisaid and dressing gown. She withdrew dill, fennel, and vervain from her portmanteau for the protection spell and sprinkled them into the fire. The fire fizzled as tiny sparks rose into the dark air like fireflies. The familiar grassy scent of the dill, the licorice aroma of the fennel, and the woody whiff of the vervain filled the air.

She stood up, stretched her arms out toward the silvery glow of the moon, and said a silent prayer that this would work. The heat from the fire started to make her body loose and limber. She faced the east, and then started to twirl clockwise around the fire as she recalled the earlier tune from the fiddler. Grandmother Sorcha always said dancing increased the potency of any spell.

She mulled over what she wanted to say. Then she pictured a healthy and unharmed Egan and spoke.

Blue fire and heat, I call thee,
Earth God, giver of life, attend me,
Rage, wind, rage with my humble request,
Hear the beating heart in my chest,
Listen! Dark depths of the stormy sea,
Irksome and vexing, as he may be,
Keep Egan safe, so mote it be.

CHAPTER
24

*T*he silvery glow of the full moon cast a hazy path amid the still blackness of night as Egan trudged back to camp in somnolence, having just relieved himself. He sent a cursory glance in the direction of Craig's wagon as he passed by.

Egan stilled.

Why is the flap thrown back?

Egan's heart picked up its pace as he moved closer and peeked inside. It was empty.

Where was Breena?

Something like fear slammed into his chest. The Campbells. No, it couldn't be. Someone would have sounded the alarm. He swung around, trying to locate Ian and Craig. Perhaps they could shed some light on

Breena's whereabouts. Egan walked gingerly around the sleeping bodies, he had to lift tartans that were covering faces, but only identified his men,

Relief washed over Egan when he spotted Ian and Craig fast asleep on the periphery of the camp. But where was that infuriating lass? And had she taken an escort?

Some of Egan's men started to stir.

It was then that Egan spotted Rory, who looked like he was just waking up, having slumped back on the ground against a large wheel of their supply wagon.

Egan clenched his fists and marched over to Rory, who shot up at attention. "I ought to wring your bloody neck! You are supposed to be on watch duty."

Rory's eyes bulged. "Ah . . . sorry, sir. I must have only dozed off for a second."

Egan's nostrils flared as he narrowed his eyes at Rory. "Where is the healer?"

Rory craned his neck to look past Egan in the direction of Craig's wagon. "Isn't she in the wagon?"

Blood rushed through Egan's veins at a deafening pace, yet he fought to rein in his anger so he didn't throttle Rory senseless. "She isn't," he said through clenched teeth. He turned and sprinted back to the wagon. It was then that he noticed a single set of tracks beginning at the back of the wagon, heading deeper into the forest.

Rory had come to stand next to him, his face now registering worry. "Should I sound the alarm, sir?"

Egan pushed past the raging heat of his anger and the cold chill of fear slithering down his back. *Think.* he said to himself. He raked a hand through his hair.

Perhaps Breena just needed a bit of privacy to relieve herself and he was overreacting.

He turned to Rory. "No. Wake Keith and Dougray, tell them what has happened. Have them post extra guards. I'm going after her."

Before Rory could respond, Egan was already picking up on Breena's tracks venturing farther into the forest.

Breena's tracks were easy to follow in the moonlight. After scrambling through the forest for a full fifteen minutes, during which his heart had dropped to the depths of his stomach, Egan came upon a small glade surrounded by towering trees.

When he spotted Breena, he stopped. The lass looked perfectly hale. The coldness of fear seeped out of him. However, the heat of anger still sizzled in his blood. Something else sizzled inside of him when he took in her state of partial undress. He made a move toward her, but stopped instinctively.

He shook his head and scratched his chin. One question circled in his mind: Was he still dreaming?

His dreams of her the past three nights had so far involved tangled, sweaty limbs and bodies writhing in pleasure. However, the scene in front of him conjured up witches, fairies, and forest nymphs. He took in the way she danced around the fire, her inky tresses unbound and wild, the gentle curve of her swaying hips, and those long, graceful legs as they moved with the translucent material of her shift.

Despite himself, his nethers stirred. Egan groaned and closed his eyes. He couldn't take himself in hand again as he'd done the nights before. It wasn't to be borne.

Egan was unsure what he now witnessed. A pagan ritual of some sort? Witchery? Was this one of her secrets? Witches were either vile aggressors or vulnerable prey for religious zealots. But Breena fit into neither of those categories: she was a compassionate healer who'd helped many and was far from prey for anyone. He couldn't pick up her words as she danced, for he was some distance away, behind a sycamore tree.

But then she stopped, put out the fire with sand, and started to dress. He straightened. The second she picked up her portmanteau and turned in the direction of their camp, he stepped out from the shadows, and within a few strides, he caught up to her. He grabbed her arm and whirled her around.

"Are you out of your damn mind, leaving camp unescorted in the middle of the night?" His voice sliced through the stillness surrounding them.

Her eyes widened, and her mouth opened as if to scream, but then a rush of breath escaped her lips as she held her chest.

He shouldn't have run up to her like that, but damn it, after what she'd put him through, kissing William, dancing with Alban, and then the shock he'd suffered when he'd discovered her gone from camp. She deserved it.

She narrowed her eyes and wrenched her arm free. "Why do you insist on following me?"

"Because you insist on leaving camp unescorted."

"I am not one of your retainers. I don't have to follow your orders." Her nostrils flared, and her chest rose and fell at a pace that distracted the hell out of him.

"You will follow my orders, because I am responsible for your safety." He'd never thought to shout at a woman before, but then he'd never been irritated beyond endurance by one before either.

"I don't have to do anything you tell me." Her mouth was mutinous. She had the audacity to fling his help back at him. He'd just about had it.

Egan didn't like using his size to intimidate anyone, least of all women, but he couldn't help himself. She brought out the beast in him. He pulled himself up to his full height, like a bull fighter preparing to battle. She didn't back down. Instead her chin rose and she glared at him. He shouldn't find that surprising, considering how he'd first encountered her on Coll.

But then something happened.

Her eyes dropped to his lips, and her stubborn mouth slackened. A tooth bit into the plumpness of her lower lip.

"Stop looking at me like that," he said.

"Like what?" Her gaze softened but remained on his lips.

Egan couldn't take it anymore, none of it—her damn secrets, her infuriating attitude, her sultry glances, and most of all, the way she burned his blood. His very sanity unraveled with the full force of a tidal wave.

He grabbed her shoulders and pulled her against his chest. She rose on her tiptoes and brushed her lips against his. The touch was as soft as a rose petal. Her soul-melting tenderness shot though every fiber of his being like an explosion of cannon fire. Without hesitation Egan's lips took hers.

Jesus Christ, she is sweet.

His hands encircled her waist. Her body slackened as if in surrender and shaped itself against his hard frame. Her raw, husky gasps wreaked havoc on the stability of his senses as her arms slid around his neck. Her soft suppleness was like black gunpowder to Egan's raging internal inferno. Her feminine fragrance was a delicious torture that almost brought him to his knees. Heaven knew why, but he craved losing himself in her curves. He wanted to let her surround and consume him. He was sure of one thing, he'd never wanted to protect, defend, ravish, and scream at a woman all at once before Breena.

Her breathy moan made him not want to think anymore, just feel.

Egan lifted his lips from hers. "Your gaze is direct, bold . . . seductive."

She blinked at him. "I . . . I had no idea."

He drank in the desire on her face. It was for him. Male pride ballooned in his chest, as did something infinitely more feral. It was something born of the earthy wind, musty soil and the dark forest that encircled them.

"What thoughts go through your head when you look at me like that?"

She cocked her head and grinned provocatively. "I like the look of your lips."

Raw desire hit Egan head on. "I like the look of yours."

With an urgency that pounded the last vestiges of sanity out of his head, his lips captured hers once more. He traced, savored, then devoured her lips with his.

The kiss removed all thoughts except one. That he didn't want to say good-bye to her once he escorted her to Duntulm. Even as the red-hot blaze of desire pulled him under, the thought lingered. But when she tugged him toward her to deepen the kiss, his mind stilled altogether, as the need for her raged within.

His hands slid down her back. The feel of her fed the pandemonium inside him. Her throaty mewls fueled him on. He ached to satisfy this need that threatened to explode. When she started to move her hips against him, he growled like a hungry beast. The innocent yet suggestive movement tugged and squeezed his insides.

The heated touch of her fingers splayed on his neck fed his madness. She yanked at the buttons on his léine. He paused to divest himself of the infuriating garment. Her soft hands kneaded his chest, lingering and tweaking the sprinkling of his chest hair. His muscles flexed in response.

Egan captured her lips with his once again. This time the kiss deepened to something infinitely more carnal.

His hands slipped under her silky dressing gown. The gossamer material of her night rail caused an exasperated grunt to escape his lips. He tugged it down toward her waist, along with her dressing gown and arisaid. He met her cool alabaster skin with his eager lips. He framed her delightful bottom with his hands and lifted her up. She wrapped her legs around him. At the crux of it all, Egan struggled to keep the untamed animal within him under control. He placed her back on her feet, against the nearest tree, but kept his hands at her back, so the roughness of the trunk wouldn't hurt her.

"Egan . . ."

It took a minute for her voice to fight through the haze of his desire.

He gazed down at her. "Yes?"

He was convinced a lifetime of tasting her wouldn't satiate this raw hunger deep inside him. He took in the sultry desire displayed on her delicate features. Everything else spun around him, like he'd drunk five bottles of whiskey. His body hummed and his brain slowed, even as his heartbeats raged on.

"I want you to be my first . . ."

It took a moment for him to comprehend, his mind moving at the pace of a truly inebriated man, but then her words hit him. His knees weakened, something he'd never experienced in his life. He didn't know what to say, so he just blinked and nodded. He knew what that meant: he had to make it bloody spectacular for her. He had to temper his urgency in favor of her pleasure. And he was going to do just that, even if it killed him.

"I am honored, *mo ghaol* . . ."

Mo ghaol. . . my love. He'd never used those words with any other woman before. He tried not to consider what that meant.

He swept her off her feet and placed her on a soft bed of primrose. He grinned. What he had in store for her was better served with her flat on her back.

He knelt beside her and relieved her fully of her garments. Egan's hunger was almost his undoing when he discovered she wore no small clothes.

Her body was spectacular: pert breasts just the right size for his palms and a tiny waist that he could span with his hands. Her hips curved gently, housing a creamy cleft dusted in alluring jet curls. An uncharacteristic tremor took hold of his hands as he unlaced and removed her half boots.

It took a particular kind of raw control Egan wasn't even aware he possessed. But he proceeded to lavish meticulous and careful attention to every little bit of Breena's bewitching body.

By the time he was finished tasting, nibbling, and feasting on the entirety of her loveliness, he'd learned something new about himself. He'd learned that Breena not only had the ability to bring out a wildness in him he'd never experienced before, but that he had the ability to rein that wildness in, in favor of her pleasure.

His ministrations left her body shuddering beneath him. A weak, breathy whimper escaped her lips while she squirmed and writhed. She'd completely surrendered to him. The fingers of her left hand tangled themselves in his hair while her right hand ran over his shoulders and raked down his back. Egan never wanted to please a woman as much as he wanted to please her at this very moment. This was new. This was different. It was important. She was important.

Amid the chaos that raged inside Egan, the most prominent feeling was the one that tugged at his heart when he looked down at her.

Egan quickly divested himself of his remaining clothes and returned to her.

"Look at me," he said.

She tugged on him to bear down on her body. He knew she was ready. But he had to hold it together just a little while longer.

CHAPTER
25

*B*reena had never been taken on such a blissfully wicked journey before.

Air rushed in and out of her lips in an attempt to relieve the pinch in her chest. Her heart thrashed and boomed against her ribs. Blood coursed through her veins at a dizzying speed. Her body was a decadent mess after it'd shattered. After his shrewd yet erotic ministrations to every part of her body, particularly the secret parts, he had propelled her over the edge. The white-hot pleasure had been unlike anything she'd ever experienced.

Her body was slickened with sweat. Her sluggish senses were capable of one thing only: reveling in the delicious hum of pleasure that still sizzled inside her.

She marveled at his impressive physique. It was a masterpiece, akin to a naked Roman sculpture chiseled from raw stone. A sound rumbled in his chest, very much like approval, when she dug her fingers into his granite-like shoulders. Piqued, she ran her hand down the bulging muscles of his arms and gently raked his hard chest. The sound he made intensified. Encouraged, she proceeded to graze his flat nipples, scoured his tight midriff, then landed on his firm lower abdomen. His eyelids dropped halfway, even as they remained on her.

"Are you going to look at me?" His voice was gruff.

She noted the vein mirroring his racing heartbeat at his right temple as her eyes flicked back up to his.

Had he said something? Perhaps it was his rugged male scent that left her head in the clouds, but when she felt his weight on top of her, it answered a primal need deep inside her she never knew she had every inch of her body tingled with aching sensitivity where he'd kissed and nibbled.

But Breena yearned for something more.

His rushed breath tickled her cheeks.

"Are you sure this is what you want? Your virtue will no longer be intact."

Breena had never been more sure of anything.

"I want you for my first."

"A lass's first time can be painful, *mo ghaol.*"

Mo ghaol . . . My love. This was the second time he'd used that phrase tonight.

"I do know something about the mechanics of the female form. If not because I am a healer, then because I am a woman."

"That you are." He took her lips again in a demanding kiss.

Anticipation speared her and she broke the kiss.

"It's all right. I trust you," she said.

A tumultuous vortex of emotions surged through her as Egan joined their bodies with a slow gentle thrust. Among the emotions, curiosity, desire, and anticipation stood out. "Are you in discomfort?" His eyebrows drew together as he scrutinized her.

Breena grappled with the strange sensation within her passage.

His consideration and gentleness soothed her and tugged at her heart. She sensed that he held himself back for her, and she loved him for it. Love? There was that word again. Breena took a few deep breaths. After the strangeness subsided, she wrapped her legs around him.

She blinked up at him. "Not discomfort—it feels rather peculiar."

His lips eased into a sultry grin. "Let's see if we can change that."

Egan began to move. The invasion was curious yet, in an odd way, natural. Her panting sped up as the pleasurable, aching sensation returned to her body. She reached up and curled her hands in his hair. They started to move together as if in a sensuous dance, one that felt instinctual and as old as time.

Breena had a feeling that he still held back, but she yearned for him to unchain himself. She tightened her legs around him and started to move faster, which forced him to respond in kind. Her lips curled up in a smile when after a few thrusts Egan seemed to let go. Sublime heated tingles spread throughout her body as her blood raged and roared. The hazel depths of his eyes revealed a carnal intensity that mirrored the pulsating emotion surging through her own veins.

The heat of his body enveloped her as she started to climb, higher and higher to the peak of some invisible precipice. Then her body contracted and shuddered. She cried out as she shattered into a million little pieces. Breena fell off that invisible cliff into a mindless, weightless, formless sea of pure ecstasy. Egan growled out his own release seconds after hers. She fell back on her dressing gown like a lump, all the energy spent from her limp, sweaty body. She lacked strength for movement and for rational thought. Egan rolled off to lie by her side, then nudged her into an embrace. The gesture was filled with tenderness. Something contracted in her chest. The sounds of their labored breaths started to even out and quiet down, to be replaced with the whirs of night insects and the gentle rustling of the leaves above them.

Breena had never imagined lovemaking could be this cataclysmic.

She'd lost her head. Had she lost her mind too? Making love with Egan was better than she'd envisioned, and she'd envisioned something quite incredible.

She'd been branded, indelibly marked by Egan Dunbar. And why did that not bother her in the least? On the contrary, the raw carnality of it was satisfying. Freeing. Odd. The question was, what was his opinion on the matter?

Then the undeniable solidity of reality punched Breena in the gut. Egan had filled her with new intimate pleasures, and for a stretch, naught else existed. But now it was back, like a vulture that circled above her, her father's stolen life, the unspeakable end her mother had endured at the hands of the Campbells, and a gnawing feeling that her uncle held something essential back from her.

There was also the undeniable fact that no matter how much she'd come to care for Egan, he would never be hers.

Had he seen her cast that spell?

She turned to Egan. Something fluttered in her belly, for he'd been studying her.

His lazy smile warmed her, despite her thoughts. "That tiny mark on your left inner thigh, in the shape of a wee horseshoe, does that mean you are good luck?"

She was obliged he didn't call it a witch's mark or something similar. She leaned over and gave him a kiss on the lips, enjoying his taste. "That's for you to decide."

What was going to happen now? Would he still leave for Eileanach, and she return to Duntulm to take back up her position as the MacIntyres' healer? What if a child resulted from this union? Breena's courses weren't due for another two weeks, so she couldn't be sure until then. Would her dream of a family of her own, a husband and bairns who belonged to her as much as she belonged to them, come to fruition if she had Egan's bairn? Something hollow settled in her belly. She was under no illusion they'd marry; an ocean of unsuitability stormed between them. There was a vast difference between the strata of society they each belonged to. Neither of them could change that, even if she wished it. Did he?

Then a hot wave of something ripped through her body. "Your opinion of me as a lightskirt is now realized." She hated that she sounded bitter to her own ears.

His brows gathered. "I never used the term lightskirt."

She eyed him. "You said I offered it up as gratitude." Even now the rawness of the comment needled her.

He considered her for a moment. "Yes. But those two are not one and the same. Pray tell, why did you allow me to make love to you?"

Breena swallowed and her muscles tightened as her mind blanked. How was she to answer that? She shrugged, even as a smile tugged at her lips. "I didn't want you to stop."

His body vibrated with a chuckle as he held her. Had she said something amusing?

"If I hadn't freed your father, would you have let me make love to you?"

She was flummoxed by the question. She shifted her position to face him, even as his arms continued to encircle her. "That's impossible to answer. That's asking me to opine on an alternate reality. Because you rescued my father, we shared experiences, became friends. At least I hope we have. I couldn't begin to know what would have happened if you had not. It's possible we may still have shared similar experiences, or it's possible I might be dead, if the Campbell had learned what we were about."

He seemed to contemplate this for a few moments, then spoke. "I recall you saying you liked the look of my lips. Does that still hold true?" He bent down and gave her a soft kiss, which curled her toes.

She lifted her head and sent him a questioning smile. "How is this relevant to our discussion? Or are you attempting to evade the issue at hand?"

"Apologies for digressing. It's entirely possible I owe you an apology." His tone held a hint of playfulness.

Her cheeks warmed, and her muscles relaxed. She waited for said apology. And waited. After several long minutes had passed, she quirked a brow at him. "Well?"

"I'm attempting to formulate the right words. In the meantime, I still don't know why your father was imprisoned by the Campbells."

His last sentence jarred her. Something cold replaced the warmness of her current position. She made a move to rise, but he placed his hands around her waist and drew her back down on top of him.

What did he want from her?

"After what I did for Ian, I think I deserve to know." His tone, while gentle, had lost some of its mirth.

She swallowed, then chewed on the inside of her left cheek. What could she tell him? She still didn't know how much of her spell casting he'd seen. She took a few seconds to mull over her words before she spoke.

"Alasdair wanted my mother for himself, and Ian stood up to him."

Egan's body stiffened next to hers. "Where's your mother?"

Something akin to a dagger sliced through her stomach at his question. This wasn't a conversation she could have like this. The truth of the matter was, this wasn't a conversation she could ever have with Egan

Dunbar, not when he could expose her and her family. Tears stung her eyes, but she blinked them away.

This time, when she tried to get up, he didn't stop her. She put some distance between them, then proceeded to pull on her woolen stockings, not because she was cold—the heat generated by his impressive body was enough to warm her from her disheveled head to her wiggling bare toes. And even if the heat from his body wasn't at present close enough, she only had to take in his handsome nakedness, and her own salacious thoughts would make her burn. No. She needed to keep her hands busy. And say as little as possible.

A way to redirect the conversation hit her. Why had he reacted in that odd manner when she'd asked him about siblings in William's kitchen? If he wanted her to speak of her family, he'd have to respond in kind.

"Tit for tat. I got the sense that you were holding something back when I asked if you had any other siblings besides your sister."

Her eyes were drawn to his hands as he flexed his fingers and averted her gaze. His expression shifted into a stony façade. He lay there, propped up on one elbow, not making any movement or indication he intended to answer her question.

Just when she'd convinced herself he wasn't going to answer, he did.

"I failed my brother Alex fifteen years ago. He died."

Something constricted in her chest at the emotion in his voice, even as puzzlement caused her brows to furrow. Egan was honorable; she found it difficult to believe that he would fail anyone, least of all a brother.

"You told me how you defended your sister's honor. I witnessed you fight for your foster brother at Duntulm, without regard for your own life. You rescued my father from an unjust imprisonment, despite the threat of war with the Campbells, because it was the honorable thing to do. I've seen the way your men respect you. It's not in your nature to fail anyone."

He seemed to gather his thoughts for a few breaths, then he spoke. "Alex had written to me at Castle Inbhir Garadh, saying he wanted me to come to Eileanach to take him riding for his tenth birthday. He wanted to show me how much he'd learned. I'd been away fostering with the MacDonell. I should have gone home to be with him. He sneaked out of Eileanach on his own and headed toward Inbhir Garadh to find me, to make me keep my promise, no doubt. He was thrown. He broke his neck."

Breena gasped. Heaviness seeped into her heart for his loss. She left her second stocking halfway up and took a seat next to him. She placed her hands on his shoulders, half expecting him to move away. When he didn't, she stooped down and held his face in between her palms.

"You cannot blame yourself for that. How could you have known he'd go riding by himself?" Her voice was soft, she hoped comforting.

"He would've celebrated his twenty-fifth saint's day a few months ago if it weren't for me. There isn't a damn day that goes by that I don't see his little face in my head. . . ." His voice cracked with emotion.

The heaviness in her heart tightened, making it ache for him. She wanted to soothe him somehow, to make him understand it wasn't his fault. She put her arms around him in a soft embrace. Warmth settled in her chest. She liked holding him.

The day Egan had happened upon her and Craig in the guardhouse, he'd said he didn't want their deaths on his conscience because he had enough there already. Now she understood what he meant.

"It was a tragic accident. No one's to be blamed," she whispered gently.

She was trying to soothe him, but when he slid his arms around her in return, it comforted her. She felt as if she were shielded somehow, like nothing could hurt her, safe enough for her to break her own outer defenses. The wall she'd built between them had cracked when they'd made love, and now pieces of it started to crumble and fall to the ground.

"My mother died. And like you, there isn't a day that goes by that I don't see her in my mind. It leaves this painful, cavernous void which never goes away."

She felt his muscles tighten as he lifted his head to consider her. His eyebrows drew together.

"When did she die?"

"A long time ago."

"I am sorry."

His voice slid over her like steely strength and soft empathy.

They stared at each other. Something passed between them, a deep searing desire for something that would alter their lives, something so wonderous her blood simmered, and her bones melted. The taste of this sweet notion warred with the bitter reality of their situations. She swallowed against the tightness in her throat. It was only an illusion.

Breena cleared her throat, trying to push the emotion down. What was the matter with her? She pulled away from him, tugged on her second stocking, slid on her boots, then started to don the night rail before she was settled enough to look at him again. "Did you meet Daegan Mac-Donell while you fostered at Inbhir Garadh ?"

He grabbed his léine and pulled it over his head. "Yes. Without hesitation, I'd give my life for him, for any of my foster brothers. Although, come to think on it, we got into many fights during our years of fostering with the MacDonell, and I remember wanting to kill him on more than one occasion."

Breena's mouth curled up, almost picturing it. She'd never understood why so many Highland clans sent their sons to foster with neighboring clans. It deprived the parents of their bairns and the bairns from the comfort and familiarity of their homes for many years. But then, it was no doubt necessary to prepare them for their duties as men and lairds.

And the bonds and partnerships forged during those years no doubt benefited their clans.

When they were both dressed, Breena braided her hair and grabbed her portmanteau. Then they both took off in the direction of camp.

"Didn't you miss your family while at Castle Inbhir Garadh?"

"Yes. But duty to my clan came first. After a while Daegan and my other foster brothers became my family."

"My friend Rowan MacNeil was like a sister to me, after I lost my parents. But I haven't seen her in over fourteen years."

He sent her a questioning glance. "Oh. What happened?"

Breena pushed through the tightness in her throat. "Rowan's grandmother was an elder in our village. After she had a disagreement with another elder, the woman accused her of being a witch. She was imprisoned, then sent to a tollbooth in Auldearn to stand trial. The villagers turned against the entire family. They were forced to flee."

"What happened after her grandmother was sent to Auldearn?"

"My Uncle forbid me from inquiring; he said it would land us in hot water with the villagers. I did manage to get my hands on a number of old newspapers from Auldearn which detailed the punishment of those found guilty, but it never listed the names."

"I remember my sire speaking some time back with our old pastoralist about a well-known old witchery story out of Auldearn . . . a witch claiming to commune with fairies. Although I can't rightly recall her name. . . ."

Breena shook her head and sent him a knowing glance. "Yes, the story you recall was probably that of Isobel Gowdie, a famous . . . or infamous woman from Loch Loy. But her trial was about eighty-five years ago, well before Rowan's grandmother. They found Isobel Gowdie innocent of devil worship after she'd been coerced into confessing. They'd no doubt made the poor woman delirious enough after subjecting her to a witch pricker, thumbscrews, and metal boots for her to confess to all sorts of outlandish things."

Grandmother Sorcha had told her the story, in all its terrifying details, in an attempt to impress upon Breena the risks of being caught. Sorcha had also spoken of the two hundred people accused of witchery in Salem, Massachusetts, fifty-four years earlier, in the colonies.

Egan laid a gentle hand on her shoulder, scattering her morbid thoughts. His touch reassured her somehow. "I'm sorry you've lost touch with your friend. The Dunbars condemn such behavior at Eileanach Castle, even more so since the Witchcraft Act of 1735 abolished witch hunts." Even though his voice was firm, it was laced with empathy.

Breena was well aware of what the Witchcraft Act of 1735 had accomplished. One hundred and fifty-five years prior to the Act of 1735, thousands of people were burned at the stake in Scotland and fifty thousand people executed across Europe in total. But since 1735 it had been illegal to claim that anyone was guilty of practicing witchcraft. The act, for all intents and purposes, repealed previous witchcraft acts in Scotland that laid out harsh punishment for witches.

Something eased the tightness in her stomach as she considered Egan for a few breaths. Egan's impressive stature and commanding presence usually surrounded her with a sense of safety and security, but this was the first time that sensation hit her while they discussed witchcraft. The wall she'd erected between them crumbled yet further.

They walked for several long minutes in companionable silence, but then Egan paused and his body went rigid as he held an arm out to stop her. He turned around as if scanning their surroundings for something.

"Be still, don't move." His voice was low and steely.

"What is it?" Breena's eyes widened as she came to a halt. Her gaze took in nothing besides tall trees and underbrush. But something in the air shifted , and the sounds of the night insects quieted. It was then that she heard it—a set of low, bone-chilling, scratchy growls. She snapped her head toward the sound. Four sets of beaming yellowish eyes emerged from the tall, dark undergrowth to the left of them. Coldness shimmied down her spine as her pulse shot up. The tallest of the four wolves advanced in silent steps, his upper lip raised to expose the longest set of sharp teeth Breena had ever seen. They gleamed white in the dark of night, enough for her to see the spittle hanging off the side of its mouth.

Egan slid between her and the wolves. "Back up slowly, no sudden movements."

Breena did as she was told, while raising her portmanteau high above her head, getting ready to strike. Despite the animals' pinched, lean bodies, they were bigger than she'd imagined wolves to be. How long had it been since they'd eaten? There'd been rumors about wolves on Skye, but she'd never thought she would come face to face with any. She might even have thought their immense grayish-brown bodies majestic if they didn't look so hungry, if their growls and vicious snarls didn't chill her spine.

Egan shot her a glance as they both continued to back up slowly. His face held something she'd never witnessed before: sharply focused eyes in a stark, ashen face. The lines of his upper body had become rigid and his hands formed an X at his midsection as he slowly slid his dirks out of their sheaths.

Breena's eyes were on the largest of the wolves—the alpha—just as she stumbled over something hard on the ground. She immediately righted her step, but the alpha wolf's snarls became louder and more aggressive as he advanced, the other three branching out to flank him.

Then Breena's heels hit something else.

She gasped loudly as she lost her balance and went flying backward, her portmanteau slipping from her grip.

The leather bag made a muffled crash as it landed some feet away, just as her own body slammed into the hard earth. The wolfpack's asynchronous growls erupted into loud, vicious barks. Breena's eyes widened in bone-chilling terror as three of the beasts sprang at Egan. One leaped for Egan's neck. Another sprang at his right shoulder. And the alpha wolf lunged for Egan's left flank. A raw scream tore from her throat. It was like no other sound she'd ever made.

Breena scrambled to stand back up as she reached for her portmanteau. Egan cuffed away the wolf that aimed for his neck and jabbed his dirk into the neck of the one that had sunk its fangs into his right shoulder. Both animals whimpered and crawled away from him. The snarling alpha wolf, however, had ahold of Egan's left flank and held on despite Egan's punches.

Leather bag raised in hand, Breena went for the alpha, just as the fourth wolf leaped out of nowhere and sunk its fangs into her right arm.

Her blood-curdling scream sounded the same time as another piercing howl of pain penetrated the furor of the wolfpack's attack. She wasn't sure if it was from Egan or the alpha wolf. Half blinded by the pain in her arm, she punched, hit, and kicked at the beast that had attacked her.

Then out of nowhere two loud shots reverberated at the same time. She swung around. Through her tears, the dark silhouettes of Keith and Dougray, reloading flintlock rifles, came into focus about twenty-five paces away. The animal released her arm and fell to the ground with a low whimper. Breena pivoted toward Egan. The alpha wolf still had its fangs in Egan's bloodied left flank, hell-bent on ripping it apart. Glacial fear and an agonizing terror speared her through her core as she struggled to breathe.

Dear God, he must triumph over the alpha. He had to. She couldn't lose him.

Egan raised his second dirk and plunged it into the animal's neck. Once. Twice. Just then, two other shots cut through the air and the alpha wolf whimpered as its body jerked off Egan and dropped to the ground.

Clutching her bloodied right arm under her breast, she scurried to Egan, who turned to her and stumbled.

"You are safe . . . you're safe." He exhaled aloud. His eyes started to lose focus as he fell to one knee.

"Me? And you!?" she cried. Hot tears burned her cheeks.

"It's just a wee bite, *mo ghaol* . . ." His voice trailed off.

Her eyes flickered to Egan's left flank. The dark red blood had soaked through his tattered léine and most of his kilt below. For the first time in Breena's life, the metallic scent of blood made her want to retch, for it had never been coupled with such a deep, twisting fear in her belly before. She hooked her left arm under Egan's right as she tried to hold up his toppling body. Her head jerked in the direction of Keith and Dougray, who were drawing near.

"Dear God, help me!" For the second time that night, she didn't recognize her own voice, as her knees buckled under Egan's weight.

CHAPTER
26

*E*gan's side throbbed like he'd been skinned, gutted, and filleted. And why in Hades did his stomach rumble like a starved bear? He'd eaten a hearty meal just a few hours ago. Although his mouth was now dry, as if he'd eaten cotton instead of roasted grouse. Forcing his heavy eyelids open, he blinked a few times as his vision came into focus. It was still dark, but a glow from a nearby light source cast warm shadows where he lay. He inhaled the scent of smoke from a campfire and caught the distant chatter of conversations, which he recognized as belonging to his men. Egan cocked an eyebrow at the brown tarp roof above.

He tried to haul himself up, but gentle hands nudged him back down. It was a good thing, since his body lacked the strength to make itself move. His right shoulder was dead weight.

"Don't try to move, or you'll rupture the stitches. How do you feel?"

The corners of his mouth turned up at her voice. He shifted to take in Breena. The tiredness in her smiling eyes and the tremor in her voice did nothing to detract from the brightness of her bonny face.

"Like I was speared in the gut." His voice was a raspy croak.

Then an image of the wolfpack attack came crashing back into his head. Chills shot through his body. His mouth soured. Bollocks! Fear had never hit him like that before, fear that she would be hurt. It had almost crippled him, rendered him useless. But then strength had come from somewhere deep inside, just before he'd plunged that first dirk. He wouldn't fail her—he just couldn't—like he'd failed Alex.

"Were you hurt?" He wanted to hold her, but his body was sluggish. He instead scanned her up and down, his eyes widening at the bandaging on her right arm.

"I'm quite hale. Except for a few shallow teeth marks."

Some of the tension seeped out of his body at her declaration that she was hale.

His head sank back down.

He considered the tarp roof again. "Where are we?"

She touched his forehead with her palm. "You're in our wagon, because of the rain."

He frowned. He didn't recall the rain. Then several things needled him at once. "How long have I been here?"

"Three days."

Egan's jaws slackened, and he moved to get up again. "Three days?!"

But she nudged him back down again, her brows bunching with concern. "Lay back down or you'll wreck your stitches."

Egan's flank was stiff, and it pained him like the very devil. He groaned at his own helplessness. She moved to push something firm under his head and neck to elevate him. For the briefest moment, her chest was two inches from his lips. He recalled her breasts' suppleness in his palms and their dulcet flavor. He groaned again.

Breena stopped moving him. "Did I hurt you?"

"My virility and prowess as a Highlander are being called into question, but other than that I am quite well."

A smile warmed her features. "In addition to your bruised virility and prowess, you also have bites on your shoulder and several deep puncture wounds on your left flank that just missed your vital organs, including your entrails."

"Doesn't sound too bad. I've had worse." He shrugged but then flinched when a sharp pain stabbed his arm.

She mumbled something about acting tough, then brought a goblet to his mouth. He drank in deep gulps, for he expected the taste of cool water, but when the bitterness of some congealed devil's brew registered on his taste buds, somewhere between what he'd imagine the dry bark of a tree and horse manure to taste like, Egan coughed and sputtered. He decided if he swallowed the remaining liquid, it would lessen the time the vile stuff stayed in his mouth. He gulped it down, then wiped his mouth with the back of his hand.

"What in Hades was that?"

"It's a healing tincture. It will help with the pain. The worse it tastes the better it works."

"Then I should be healed as we speak." He wanted to lick grass or mud or anything, just to get the taste out of his mouth.

She rolled her eyes, then offered him another goblet.

He kept his lips firmly closed and quirked an eyebrow at her.

"Water," she said.

Egan took huge gulps, but she pulled it away before he was finished. "Take small sips, you haven't eaten or drunk anything substantial in three days."

He shot her an inquiring glance. "Was I asleep all that time?"

Her cheeks reddened. "You thrashed about and mumbled unintelligible things, but most of the time you slept."

From her blush, Egan doubted his mumblings had been unintelligible. He just hoped it hadn't been too vulgar.

"Your fever broke just a few hours ago."

He studied her and took in the dark circles under her eyes. Had she slept since it happened? Had she been worried for him? Something warmed inside Egan's chest.

He took in the bandage on his shoulder and considered his clothes. He was dressed in a clean white léine and fresh kilt. His last memory was of bloodied, tattered clothes. He lifted the léine and peeked at the bandages wrapped around his mid region.

"My thanks for the clean clothes."

"Craig cleaned and stitched you up. I made a promise to myself a long time ago not to serve as healer to the people I care for. I lose all objectivity, you see. Plus, after the attack, I wasn't in any state to hold a needle. But I did tend to your bandages, applied the poultice and salve. Keith brought your change of clothes."

She lowered her eyes, avoiding his gaze. Was that an attempt to hide something from him again? Her emotions this time, perhaps: she'd just said she cared for him. The warmth in Egan's chest ballooned.

"Come to Eileanach with me . . . to continue tending to the bandages, of course." The words were out before he could stop himself.

Her features softened as she glanced at him. The warmth in her gaze melted every bone in his body. "You are not going anywhere for at least a fortnight. If you get back on that beast of a horse of yours now, you'll ruin the stitches."

He blinked. That wasn't the answer he'd expected. He searched her face for what she hadn't said. Did she need to consider it first? He shouldn't have said he needed her to tend to his bandages—they had healers and access to physicians at Eileanach Castle. That wasn't why he wanted her with him at his home.

"If I'm not going anywhere for a while, can I have something to eat at least?"

"Of course. It's a good sign you're hungry. I'll fetch you something."

She made a move to leave. But he stopped her, reaching for her left wrist. The contact jarred his senses. His calloused thumb brushed over the soft skin of her palm. He reined in his need to pull her down and touch his lips to hers. "You look like you can use some rest. I'd ask you to come lie next to me, but that wouldn't be decent, despite how much I wish it. Ask Gregor to bring me some food."

"All right. But you're not to get up, and nothing more substantial than bone broth."

"It's now my turn to thank you for taking such good care of me." He gave her hand a tender squeeze before he released her.

The corners of her mouth turned up. "Since you saved my life, and freed my father, it's the least I could do."

◆──◆──◆──◆──◆──◆

After Egan had had a measly cup of broth, which he'd complained wasn't enough to fill a wee bairn's stomach, Dougray and Keith hung their elbows over the rail of the wagon and eyed him.

"How do you fare?" Keith asked.

"I've been better."

Keith glanced in the direction Breena had disappeared. "She didn't leave your side for three days."

Egan let that fact sink in. He inhaled deeply. The settling herbal scent of the broth still lingered in the air. He wanted to close his eyes and grin like an untried lad over his first sweetheart because of what Keith just said. But he couldn't do that in front of his men. So, he cleared his throat sharply instead.

"Well, she is the healer." Egan said.

"Aye. And a bonny one at that," Dougray said, the right side of his mouth quirking up.

Egan shot a glower in Dougray's direction out of irritation. If he didn't have stitches, he'd probably punch him. He didn't like to think Dougray looked at Breena the way he did. "You ought to pay more attention to your damn duties and less attention to the healer."

Dougray's eyes widened even as his mouth quirked further up. He then awkwardly avoided Egan's stare.

Was Dougray goading him? Bloody mutton head. Egan scoffed.

His men had made remarks about women before, but Egan didn't want his men to talk about Breena, even in jest. It struck him as disloyal. He wasn't entirely sure why that was.

Was he jealous? He suspected that was part of it, but he also suspected it had to do with his curious need to protect the lass. It dawned on him that he'd also reacted out of jealousy when Alban danced with her and when she'd kissed William on the cheek. Damn. He'd never been jealous of a woman in his entire life.

"Although the lass's actions are tempting gossip and threading on the edge of propriety, it's obvious to everyone that she cares for you." Keith's words jarred Egan out of his mulling.

Egan relished the latter part of Keith's comment but purposefully ignored the former. On the one hand, he was aware of Keith's penchant for acting like a chaperone. But on the other hand, Egan was too glutton for Breena's attentions to entertain any notions to the contrary.

He took in the contents of the wagon.

"If I'm sleeping in their wagon, where is Breena sleeping?"

"We set up your tent for her, although I think she just headed there for the first time."

Egan traveled with a tent but used it only when the weather was bad. Most of the time he slept alongside his men under the stars. He liked the idea of a night shift-clad Breena lying in his tent.

Egan shook himself out of his reverie.

"Report?" he said sharply, eying both Keith and Dougray.

Keith straightened. "I have fifteen of the men dedicated to clearing our tracks each day. There's always four scouts patrolling the area around the camp at any given time and reporting back here every hour—"

"I want you to triple the scouts and I want two guards each on Breena, Craig, and Ian. They are not to be left alone or to leave camp unescorted."

Dougray eyed him. "Are you worried about the Campbells?"

"I think you'd have to be a vile, twisted son of a bitch to imprison a man for nineteen years because you wanted free rein with his wife," Egan said.

Dougray frowned. "That's why the Campbells imprisoned Ian? Alasdair wanted his wife?"

Keith bared his teeth. "Twisted bastard."

Egan tried to ignore the hardness in his belly, which had nothing to do with his injury. The same thing had happened to him when Breena had told him Alasdair had wanted her mother. The look on her face had quelled his need to ask what had happened, even though it hadn't quelled his desire to know. Her pained stare when she'd talked of her mother struck a familiar chord deep inside him when he thought of Alex. But he knew his need to protect her wouldn't change the past, even if he wished it.

Egan clenched his jaws. "I want us to be prepared if the Campbells come looking for Ian."

"We'll be ready, sir," Dougray said.

CHAPTER
27

*B*reena pushed through her drowsiness, opened her eyes, and blinked. How was Egan faring? Worry caused her belly to tighten in knots. And where exactly was she? She sat bolt upright on the pallet, then it came back to her as she looked around.

Dawn's gray light cast hazy shadows inside the ridge-tent. It was a comfortable size, with an expensive coating of wax for proofing against the elements. The highest point of the roof seemed a head or two taller than Egan's height. Besides her own trunk and portmanteau in the corner with the pallet, there was a decorative cast-iron brazier and an ornately carved wooden table and stool in the opposite corner. Quite luxurious for a tent, but then again, Egan was a future laird, and the Dunbars purchased only the best.

Her stiff neck, achy muscles, and sore shoulders from the past three days were less pronounced. Breena's stomach grumbled, reminding her she hadn't eaten much since that night. She squeezed her eyes shut when images of the wolfpack assailed her. Breena had never been so frightened, nor had she ever prayed as much in her entire life as she'd done in the past three days. When she hadn't been wiping down the sweat from Egan's fevered body or tending to his injuries, she'd paced like a madwoman and tried to refrain from pulling all her hair out with worry. He'd mumbled, asking for Alex and for her. She'd been shocked when he'd called out her name one night as he'd thrashed about.

Would he have been injured if she hadn't left camp, forcing Egan to follow? Guilt and misery washed over her at the possibility that he could have been killed. Of one thing she was certain: if he hadn't been there, she'd be dead.

Was Egan's injury on the mend, or was he simply putting up a façade and acting tough, like the majority of her male patients? She sat still and listened. No one stirred outside. Only the sounds of rustling branches reached her ears. She gazed at the brazier, its fire long since gone out. It would take but a moment for a divination spell.

Did she dare?

Her heart rate kicked up its pace. She glanced at the entrance of the tent. The flap was closed, no one would see her. But what if someone barged in? She could claim she was cold and was rekindling the fire. She swallowed against the constriction in her throat and prayed no one would enter.

She stood up from the pallet, her booted feet making no sounds on the soft, mossy ground as she crept over to her portmanteau. She silently opened it and removed the pouch of Fire of Azrael, then slid over to the brazier. Nervousness caused a slight tremor in her fingers as she glanced back at the flap.

Breena had never performed a spell for a patient before. But she couldn't help herself now. Was she just desperate, or was she starting to trust in her skills?

Breena quickly lifted some of the coal from the brazier to create a small space. She pulled the strings on the pouch open. The sweet, exotic, woodsy scent of the Fire of Azrael drifted up to reach her nose. She sprinkled the yellowish-brown grains on the small space of the brazier, then pulled the string to close the pouch. Using the nearby flint and steel, she struck again and again until sufficient sparks fell onto the Fire of Azrael. As it burned, the exotic scent spread throughout the entire tent.

She gazed into the small fire, blinking against the slight sting of the smoke. "Will Egan heal from the wolfpack injury?" Her voice barely a whisper.

Breena wrung her hands and waited for the small fire to die down. After it did, she gazed at the clear, glowing ash. Her brows furrowed as she angled her head left and right, trying to decipher the symbol. It resembled an S. She exhaled in a rush of frustration. Was it the rune symbol Eihwaz or Sowulo? One foretold of stability and the other of success. She straightened as something warm settled on her insides. They were both positives. Her lips stretched into a smile. She still wasn't sure she believed in signs, but she'd accept this as a positive one. Knots eased in her belly.

Just as she returned the coals to the brazier and the pouch to her portmanteau, slow shuffling sounded outside. The men were awakening.

What a stroke of luck.

Breena brushed and braided her hair, got dressed, and lifted the flap of the tent with the intent of seeking privacy by the freshwater burn to perform her morning ablutions. Her eyes widened at the sight of the two intimidating Dunbars standing guard on either side of the tent. With the threat of the Campbells, it was a sight she had to get used to.

She eyed some of the men as she strolled. Some nodded amicably at her, and some even smiled. At least their wariness of her had dissipated. She'd even witnessed a glower or two filled with blame right after the wolfpack attack.

She lifted her chin and smiled back, thankful the glowers were gone.

On her way back from her ablutions, she encountered Ian and Craig, also headed in the direction of the camp, their four Dunbar shadows not far behind. Ian moved more proficiently with his walking staff now.

Craig threw her a conversational glance. "I looked in on Egan earlier, he's healing well. Bone broth will not satisfy him for much longer, however."

"Should I start him on something more substantial today?" she said.

Craig nodded. "Yes, I think it's time."

She considered both Craig and Ian. She was thankful they were together so she could speak to them both. But then she paused. Had she really settled on going to Eileanach to be Egan's mistress under the guise of being his healer? Had she given up her dream of marriage, a husband, and bairns of her own? If she went with Egan, her already slim chances of procuring a husband would be reduced to naught. As it stood, her independence was not a desirable trait, and neither was the fact that she was twenty and five. She was considered by some to already be on the shelf. But if she went to Eileanach with Egan, that would brand her forever as a fast and loose woman.

Her chest tightened and something twisted in her gut. What about the MacIntyres? What if she got with child? Would they accept a disgraced woman as their healer? Would her family disown her? Something cold speared her chest, for despite all the reasons not to go to Eileanach Castle, she still wanted to be with Egan.

Breena was about to open her mouth when Craig posed a question of his own.

"Now that the lad is on the mend and your head is clearer, I have to know. What were you two doing out in the forest that night?" His voice was a whisper, as he gave the guards behind them a cursory glance.

Breena froze despite the drums that had started to boom in her chest. Heat rushed into her cheeks. "We . . . I was casting a spell, and Egan somehow took note I'd left camp and tracked me down." She kept her voice low so just Craig and Ian could hear.

Her uncle's face turned white, no doubt with an altogether new concern. "Did he witness your casting?"

She'd been pondering that same question since Egan had come upon her in the forest. "I couldn't say for sure."

"Do you think he suspects about the witchcraft?" She didn't miss the way her father's shoulders had stiffened.

"I can't rightly say." She shrugged, regretting that she couldn't give them a more definitive answer.

"But did Egan say anything to you? Did he confront you?" Her uncle's whisper was insistent.

"He didn't confront me, nor did he say anything. I told him about the MacNeils in passing and he insisted something like that would never happen at Eileanach Castle, even more so since the Witchcraft Act was repealed," she said.

When Breena's eyes landed on her father and she took in his raised eyebrows, she recounted the story of her childhood friend, Rowan Mac-Neil.

Ian shook his head, his expression downcast. "So many face such inexcusable and unwarranted targeting."

"Since Egan didn't confront you, it's more likely than not, he didn't see anything. Nevertheless, you must be more careful in the future. I know you are grateful to the lad for what he's done—we all are—but you must not forget propriety, nor what happens to witches."

Breena sighed out aloud. "Yes, Uncle."

Breena's earlier boldness about asking to go to Eileanach was dwindling fast, so she opened her mouth before it left her all together. "I should go to Eileanach Castle, to help with Egan's bandaging," she said, with purposeful nonchalance.

Even as she spoke, she was certain an illustrious place such as Eileanach had its own healers and even physicians.

"Of course. We're all going," Craig said.

She fumbled with the linen and soap in her hands. "We are?"

"Egan proposed just this morning that we all stay with the Dunbars until they are certain the Campbells won't retaliate," Ian said.

"Oh. Of course." Breena's step faltered.

She caught herself falling behind and quickened her pace to keep up with her father and Craig. She was an utter imbecile! Here she was, thinking Egan had asked her to come to Eileanach to be with him because he cared for her. Why else would he call her *mo ghaol* and *leannan* if he didn't care for her, if the thought of being separated from her didn't fill him with an unimaginable twisting in the gut, as it had filled her? Because he'd gotten caught up in their lovemaking, that's why. Words like *Leannan* and *mo ghaol* had been uttered in the heat of passion. He'd no doubt already forgotten.

CHAPTER
28

*E*gan was in hell. He caught a glimpse of the crimson color on Breena's cheeks as she applied the grassy-scented salve to his naked flank. Did the intimacy of the act strike her as it had struck him? His hands and fingers itched to touch her, to hold her, to draw her nearer to him. But he couldn't do a damn thing because Craig was eyeing them like a hawk. Craig now came around whenever Breena tended to him, as if Egan were the fox and Craig was on guard at the henhouse. It appeared that the gossip from Egan's men had reached Craig's ears and he was now intent on disallowing any appearance of impropriety.

In fact, hell would be a stroll in the forest compared to what he'd had to endure over the past sennight. Breena's soft little hands touched and scorched his skin as she changed his bandages. Her blossom-scented hair tantalized and tormented his senses as she bent down to rub salve on his flank. The feather-like feel of her delicate fingers as they grazed his thighs while she applied a poultice, all the while causing pressure to build at the base of his spine. Egan could do nothing but fidget, squirm, and agonize, imagining her soft hands tightly wrapped around something entirely different.

Perhaps conversation would distract him. "Why'd you become a healer?" he said as she rebandaged him. Craig narrowed his eyes at them both from across the wagon.

Breena threw Egan a cursory glance as she continued to wrap the linen around him. "I come from a long line of healers, my grandmother, my mother, and my uncle."

"You didn't answer my question." He said wryly.

She gave him an imperious tilt of her chin. This time she paused and seem to carefully consider the question. "It gives my life purpose. There's so much satisfaction and contentment when I am able to relieve someone's pain or help mend a broken arm or deliver a bairn."

He took in her poignant expression. "I can see it means a great deal to you," he said.

Egan had come to see firsthand what a gifted healer she was. She wasn't simply good at mixing potent sleeping concoctions, she had a wealth of knowledge concerning antiseptic plants, plants that dulled pain and aided healing, stopped bleeding, and kept infections at bay. She also had the ability to soothe with a caring smile and wasn't afraid to exert her authoritative side.

It all told him he was in good hands.

"I had good teachers." She threw Craig a smile.

"Craig?" he asked, avoiding the other man's eyes. Egan wondered what would happen if Craig found out what they'd done that night, right before the attack of the wolfpack.

"Yes. And my grandmother, Sorcha. She died two years ago." A pained look crossed her soft features.

"I'm sorry," he said.

"Grandmother Sorcha was my anchor. She was sensible and serious and knew everything about healing. She tried to pass it on to me. Some things I took to and some things I didn't. She had the most tranquil presence and no matter what, always managed to put me at ease. It felt good just being around her."

"You were close?" It was a rhetorical question, for it was clear to see from the emotions etched in her features that she cared for her grandmother a great deal.

"When I was thirteen, Balor died, my deerhound. I cried for days. She looked at me one time and said, Breena, my child, death is a part of life and life a part of death. You cannot have one without the other. You loved him when he was alive, and you won't stop now that he's gone, but life continues. And then she had this look in her eyes, it's a look that only she had the ability to give. It told me everything was going to be all right. I miss that constant in my life. I miss her."

Egan ached to touch her. He reached for her, but Craig chose that very second to clear his throat rather loudly. Egan even caught the shuffle of the other man's feet in the dirt, as if he were preparing to hurl himself at Egan and tackle him away from Breena. Egan withdrew his hand. He wanted to growl at Craig, but he didn't. Apparently, Craig shared the common consensus that any connection, appropriate or otherwise between his niece, a lowborn, and Egan, a highborn, was forbidden. He respected Craig for doing his duty as Breena's guardian and for wanting to protect her, but that didn't mean he had to like it.

Which was more than he could say for himself. The conversation he planned on having with his sire wasn't going to be easy: at worst it would be an excruciating and agonizing battle of wills and at best, a painful reminder of his burdensome duty. Duty to his clan and to his sire had always been a source of pride and strength for Egan. But ever since Coll he was starting to understand what Atlas must have felt like, holding up the sky for so long.

Egan left the wagon and started to not only move around but also join practice sessions with his men within the next three days, despite the objections of Breena. The pain was minimal, and an ugly brownish-red scab now covered most of the hole in his flank. Her tinctures, salves, and poultices seemed to have done their magic.

"You must not overexert yourself or your wounds will reopen, risking another infection," she called out, her voice resonating through their camp as his men prepared to leave the next day.

He turned to her, winked, and whispered, "Then you'll get another chance to have your hands all over my body again."

Her eyes narrowed at him even as a deep blush appeared on her cheeks. She scoffed. "Fine, kill yourself. See if I care." She swung around and walked away.

Egan chuckled and took in the glorious sight of her swaying curves, much like a wee bairn with a sweet tooth staring at shelves of candy.

⸻

They came to a compromise. If he agreed to take regular breaks, kept their travel time light, allowed her to tend to his wound, and promised to drink the tinctures, then they could set out for Eileanach Castle.

The next day, before the break of dawn and two weeks after they'd made camp, Egan guided their party due east toward his home. They left the green of Glen Brittle Forest while the dark azure of predawn sky turned a lighter blue mixed in with pinks and yellows. They passed the banks of the Glen Brittle waterfalls, its skeins of rushing silvery water pounding the rocks into the beginnings of a ravine. They kept to the flat moorlands, traveled parallel to the water where possible, passed the fairy pools with the red-and-black igneous and basalt rocks of the Cuillin Hills in the background. And as the sun rose to hit the hills, their colors changed from black to gray and from red to brown.

Egan wore a dark woolen waistcoat over his clothes, plus an off-white cravat. The days had gotten shorter and chillier. It was now the second week of November, with just nine hours of daylight.

The compromise he'd worked out with Breena was going well, because he'd forgotten all about it, until she popped her head out of her uncle's moving wagon to remind him.

"You promised to take regular breaks and keep the riding light."

"We've only been traveling a few hours," he said. His voice more like a moan, a weak attempt to avoid that devil's brew she called a healing tincture.

Her eyes narrowed and cut into him. Bollocks! He was starting to think of her authoritative side as the dreaded glare of the dirks. Egan swallowed and raised his leather-gloved hand in the air, signaling his men to stop.

A few minutes later he sat on the hard stump of a dead oak tree. He inhaled the mustiness from the ground below as he tried not to smirk. Craig stood next to Breena like a sentinel and eyed him the way an eagle eyed a mouse's hole waiting for the burrower to emerge. Breena took a peek at his shoulder bandages, then, seeming satisfied, she pushed aside Egan's coat, unbuttoned a few buttons on his waistcoat, then tugged up his léine to inspect his flank. He inhaled her blossomy scent as his fingers itched to tangle themselves in her radiant dark silky locks while she bent down in front of him.

He wanted to tell her he was fine, and she didn't have to fuss, but then he wouldn't have her soft hands on him, sending shudders of heat down his spine. It was an acute torture of deprivation, having her hands on him and not being able to touch her in return, but if this was all he could get at the moment, he would take it.

The need to smirk was erased, because after she'd finished her inspection and he was tucking his léine back in the waist of his kilt, she unscrewed the top off a flask and held it out to him.

He shrugged. "Why waste it? I feel fine." His protest was weak, and he knew it.

Her eyes narrowed at him. "Drink."

Bloody hell. "You're a very autocratic healer." He grumbled.

"Bottoms up." She gave no quarter.

One hand rested on her spectacular hips, and the other one continued to hold the flask out to him. Despite the impatient tapping of her right foot on the ground, he saw the twinkle in her eyes. And he knew no amount of bellyaching was going to get him out of this one.

Egan huffed out a breath and took the flask from her. He was a highly trained, fearless Highland warrior—a few sips of this horrid-tasting tincture shouldn't frighten him. He pinched his nose with one hand, tilted his head back, and brought the open flask to his lips with the other. He took fast, huge gulps in hopes that the quicker he got it over with, the less the foul taste would linger on his tongue. But when he was finished with the last gulp and brought his head forward, his eyes widened. Something was different. It wasn't as bitter, foul, or congealed as the last few times, nor did he recall the burn as it went down his gullet.

He threw her an inquiring gaze. "What did you change?"

Those inviting lips of hers curled up.

"You'll find out shortly."

What kind of an answer was that? She took the empty flask, screwed its cap back on, and sauntered back to the wagon. This time, when he stared after her swaying derrière, he exhaled in a long, slow, heated breath and felt like a rutting bull with just-contained lust pumping through its veins. Then it hit Egan, a lightness in his head. Something started to hum in his blood, and he grinned. She'd put whiskey in the devil's brew to coat its taste. Clever wench.

At Breena's insistence, they set up camp early that night under the stars. The lulling rumble of the surf of Inner Sound meeting Loch Alsh's calmer waters made sleep restful during the night.

The next day, they chartered several fishing doggers to take them across the Loch to the mainland. Four sails on each of the fishing boats made the crossing smooth and fast, facilitated by a steady easterly wind. Once they disembarked, they headed east at an ambling gait toward Eileanach Castle.

An hour after night blanketed the land in darkness, Eileanach Castle came up on the horizon. And as they left the soft earthen ground and clopped onto the narrow stone bridge across Loch Long, warmth radiated in Egan's chest. But then something else corded the muscles on his shoulders: his duty. He clenched his jaws as disquieted frustration slammed into his chest in anticipation of the conversation he'd soon be having with his sire.

CHAPTER
29

*B*reena's mouth slackened as she gazed at the grand structure that was Egan's home. Her head tipped back to take in the full scale and lush details of the stone castle, illuminated by the countless flickering torches against a backdrop of the bluish-black skyline.

Ian, who sat next to her, craned his neck stare out of the wagon. "Look at that. I've never beheld its equal."

The first words that came to her mind were *impressive* and *magnificent*, but they were an inadequate description for the towering, earth-toned stone walls that formed three lofty rectangular towers and the elegant main keep, with its decorative glass-paned windows. She knew glass-paned windows to be a highly taxed item only the wealthy could afford. She'd learned this from her conversation with Lady MacIntyre last year when Laird MacIntyre had tried to have the windows replaced at Duntulm.

Breena's eyes widened as she counted at least fifteen cannons sticking out from atop the battlements and double the number of patrolling sentries. Several colorful flags flapped in the night air from the tops of the towers; the two tallest were the blue-and-white Saint Andrew's Cross, and the red, white, and blue Union Jack. Were the Dunbars trying to appease both the nationalists and the royalists?

If a structure could radiate power, strength, and wealth bordering on restrained opulence, this would be it. She'd thought a sea of unsuitability roared between Egan and herself; now she was convinced it was more like the entire expanse of a universe.

Her eyebrows arched. "The Campbells won't dare come after us here."

Ian narrowed his lips. "That's one of two good reasons for us to be here."

She sent her father an inquiring look. "What's the other reason for being here?"

"You and Egan are not fooling anyone, my dear."

She ignored the constriction in her throat. "Whatever do you mean?"

Ian's features arranged themselves in what can only be described as a sympathetic expression. "We have to be here because we lack any way of protecting ourselves from the Campbells. It's unfortunate the Mac-Raes and Maxwells were part of the Highland Clearances, and from what Craig told me, there's nothing but crofter's cottages on our lands now. But this will also give you and Egan the opportunity to bring a conclusion to this inappropriate friendship you have."

Something tightened in her belly. Friendship? Was that what was between the two of them?

Breena huffed. "I don't think there's much to conclude."

Ian's brows gathered, and he looked like he was about to say something but then decided against it.

Egan rode up alongside their wagon. He sat tall and effortlessly in control of Heimdall.

"Now that I see your home, I can imagine the pride that swells inside you every time you return," she said.

"It does. Although the fanfare is owed to Kenneth Dunbar, who constructed it. He ruled these parts in the thirteenth century and held the land from the Earl of Ross."

"Didn't the first Jacobite Rebellion flatten most of the castles in these parts?" Ian asked.

Egan pointed to the structure on the left while his right hand gripped the reins.

"Just the west wing was destroyed when the Spanish occupied it in 1719 in support of the Jacobites. That's when the redcoats bombarded the structure. However, afterward, it was rebuilt to its original specifications."

Breena's gaze followed Egan's gloved finger and spotted the barest hint of a darker shade on the stones of the west wing when compared to the rest of the structure. A difference that would have been indiscernible in the night had it not been for the countless torches.

Breena's stomach hardened and her muscles clenched, making her glance down at her nondescript black cloak and her ordinary green travel dress. Her hands shot up to trail the length of her simple braid, now slightly disheveled from travel. She was underdressed, unprepared, and out of her element.

<hr />

Breena stood in the courtyard of Eileanach amid the warm glow of the torches. A deafening gaggle of conversations, shouts, and laughter filled

the air. She looked on as families sprinted into the courtyard from the main door, greeting the Dunbar retainers with hugs, claps on the back, and kisses on the cheeks.

A twinge of something cavernous caused images of Aunt Madeline, Eva, and her friends at Duntulm to flash across her mind's eye.

Many of the families pouring into the courtyard waved a hearty greeting at Egan and sent welcoming smiles toward Breena. She nodded and smiled back, not missing their subsequent critical stares and curious glances in her direction. Stable hands and squires took several of the horses from the retainers and led them away to the stables. The slow clip-clop of the hooves joined the boisterous clamor.

"Welcome to Eileanach Castle."

The lilting voice made Breena shift around to eye Egan, the upturned corners of his mouth caused a smile to tug on hers.

"How's your injury?"

"A little stiff, but nothing to worry about."

"My recommendation is a long, warm bath. After which I'll reapply the salve and rebandage."

"I'm all yours."

His deep voice and devilish smile made something hot settle in her belly. Would he always have such an alarming effect on her temperature?

Sharp barks startled her. Breena broke eye contact and pivoted around on her heel. Two deerhounds bolted toward Egan from the direction of the stables. Their ears flopped and their bodies rocked back and forth like Grandmother Sorcha's old rocking chair. Breena smiled at the sight of their comic pink tongues lolling out of their mouths, even as her chest tightened when thoughts of Balor flashed across her mind. She missed his scruffy face.

The dogs' piercing barks and heavy huffs were audible as the first one approached Egan. The dog's tail wagged as he lowered his front and opened his mouth, allowing a long pink tongue to hang out. Egan laughed and reached out to ruffle the dog's neck and withers.

"How are you, Loki? How are you, boy?" His voice was smooth with a warm singsong cadence.

A sigh joined Breena's smile as she took in Egan's greeting of the dog. Who'd have thought that deerhounds would bring out a vulnerable streak in the formidable Egan Dunbar?

"I take it this one is mischievous?" she said, considering the name.

"Don't leave your knickknacks lying around this fellow. You'll never find them again. He's partial to shoes. Isn't that right, boy?" Egan ruffled the dog's mane.

The second dog was slower in arriving.

He whined more than barked as he kept his head bowed low. He wasn't as vigorous and upbeat as Loki. The color of his coat put him at a similar age as his companion, so age wasn't the reason for his sluggishness. He didn't have any visible signs of injury, but Breena did take note of his pronounced pot belly.

She knelt by the second dog after he approached her and held her hand out to him. He sniffed with caution, then deciding he liked her, licked her hand. Something warm and welcoming fluttered in Breena's stomach. She petted his hairy head and ran her hands along the length of his back. His coat was soft but his frame bony.

Something heavy settled on her chest as her fingers trailed the indentations of his ribs. She'd observed something similar with Balor years ago.

"And what's your name, boy?" She attempted a singsong cadence, one she hadn't used in twelve years. His tail wagged from side to side.

"That's Odin," Egan said.

Breena refrained from laughing at the pattern of the names of Egan's animals. "These are your dogs?"

Egan nodded as he reached over to ruffle Odin's head. "Odin is fierce and loyal. He was the alpha of the two until of late. Now, I'm not sure what ails him."

Loki approached her. She stretched out her palm. His wet nose tickled her skin as he sniffed. She then ran her palm down his back as his tail wagged from side to side. His body felt lanky but compact. His energy pulsated beneath her hands, unlike Odin's.

"You've made two new friends," Egan said.

The sound of footsteps on the stone floor approached them.

"Welcome home, Master Dunbar." The voice was warm and resonant.

The newcomer was a short, round woman, her salt-and-pepper hair neatly pulled back from her smiling face. Her complexion was pale, as if she weren't fond of the outdoors. Her brown eyes twinkled beneath thick eyebrows. Her linen cap with its wide silk bow and her plain gray gown and pinafore were neat but not those of a lady.

Egan stood up, smiled, and planted a kiss on each of the woman's cheeks.

"Agnes! How are you faring this fine evening?"

"I'm well, sir." Her smile lost some of its shine as she scanned Egan up and down. She even took a step back and eyed him like a disapproving mother. "Have you not been eating properly?"

"A few days at home with your cooking ought to fix that."

Agnes blushed at his compliment. It was clear that whoever this woman was, Egan didn't want to worry her with mention of the wolfpack attack. Egan faced Breena just as Craig and Ian returned from having taken their wagon and horses to the stables and getting George set up with the stable hands.

"Breena, this is Agnes. She works miracles in the kitchen, among other things." He then turned to Agnes. "Agnes, this is Breena MacRae. She is the MacIntyres' healer."

Breena curtseyed as a sign of respect. "It's a pleasure to meet you, Agnes."

"You have pretty manners, my dear, but there's no need for formality with me." Her expression was warm and curious.

Egan introduced Craig and Ian, then asked, "Where are my parents?"

"The Laird and Lady are at Castle Inbhir Garadh with the Mac-Donells. We expect them back in a day or so."

"Well, it's been a long day . . . and we've no doubt missed the eventide meal." Egan cocked an eyebrow at Agnes with what looked like hope to the contrary.

"Not to worry, we have plenty of food in the kitchen."

"In that case, can you please attend to the comfort of our guests? I need to speak with the marshal on guard duty."

As they followed Agnes toward the entrance, Breena's eyes widened when she caught sight of the canopied balcony high above the main door. Her mind jumped to Shakespeare's tragedy *Romeo and Juliet*. She hoped she wasn't living in a similar love story; life was too precious.

She held her chest in awe at the elegant, lofty doorcase as they crossed the threshold of the massive mahogany main door. It was arched, with a decorative fanlight framed in black cast iron. It was a door that promised more grandiosity inside, worthy of such a palatial castle.

The air in the castle was crisp and clean with floral undertones and a hint of fresh-baked bread.

"As my kitchens are about to be mobbed by fifty noisy, ravenous retainers, I'll show you up to your chambers and have baths and food sent up. I am sure you'll appreciate the privacy and quiet after your journey. Would that be agreeable?" Agnes gestured for them to follow her past the great hall. Several lanterns hung along the walls and cast a shimmering glow to guide their way. Breena's mouth slackened, and her gaze followed the lines of the polished stone walls up to the lofty vaulted ceilings. And she couldn't help but stare in awe at the great hall, which looked like it could house two hundred guests and still have room for a spacious ballroom.

Several long rectangular trestle tables stretched evenly across the hall, covered in gleaming white tablecloths, atop which stood down-turned silver trenchers, utensils, and glass goblets. She could easily picture Egan's imposing presence on the dais, which stood, majestic, above all else with its long decoratively carved mahogany table and red cushioned chairs appraising everything below.

An image of a grand ball with twirling ladies in elegant gowns and lairds in their colorful tartans, a world she had little experience with, flashed across Breena's mind. It dawned on Breena that Agnes awaited an answer. "Your suggestions are very agreeable. In fact, it sounds like heaven, after where we've been," she said, thoughts of Carragh souring her stomach.

Craig pivoted away from gazing at the intricate tapestries hanging high above the hall to chuckle at Breena's response.

Breena blinked, and she sucked in a breath as she peered up at the large, gilded paintings along the walls, the images of imperial men and women of the distant and not-so-distant past all superbly adorned in grand Dunbar regalia.

Agnes eyed Breena, following her line of vision.

"All these portraits are of past Dunbar lairds with their ladies." She pointed to one of the grandest images, in the center. "That is Kenneth Dunbar with his wife Isobel. He was the third Earl of Seaforth and an old clan chief of the Dunbars. He was great friends with King Charles II. They called him *Coinneach Mor*."

The Great Kenneth.

As Agnes spoke of the Dunbars' history, she smiled and stood a little taller, with her chin raised, the pride easy to spot.

They followed Agnes up a dizzying staircase with a shallow rise and slim stone treads that seemed to hover in space with no means of support. The metal banister beneath Breena's fingers was hard and cool. Ian handled the stairs with his walking staff as if he'd been doing it for years, tapping as he climbed the steps. When they reached the fourth floor, Ian and Craig were shown to their adjoining bedchambers.

"The garderobe is at the end of the hall to the left. Food and your trunks will be up before long," Agnes said, before leaving them and leading Breena across the corridor.

Agnes pushed open polished mahogany double doors set in a deep paneled doorcase and gestured for Breena to follow. Breena took two steps in, then stilled at the interior's lofty luxuriousness. Agnes scuttered across the room toward the fireplace.

One of the largest four-poster beds Breena had ever seen was at the center of the chamber, with two steps on its right side, needed just to climb in. The fine damask curtain woven with a floral red and orange pattern hung from the canopy and looked like it belonged in a royal palace. After spending the past two weeks on a straw pallet in a tent, Breena wanted to weep at the sight of the bed's plush counterpane.

When the light from the fire Agnes lit started to throw the entire bedchamber in a shimmering golden glow, Agnes turned toward Breena.

"Mistress Phoebe Dunbar occupies this chamber when she's in the Highlands. I hope it's to your liking."

Breena sent the other woman an inquiring glance. "Isn't Mistress Dunbar currently in residence?"

"No, she spends most of her time in the Lowlands, hobnobbing with courtly folks."

Agnes proceeded to light two candelabra with a splinter from the fireplace. The fireplace had a stone Palladian chimneypiece in the shape of the Dunbar crest, a horse's head, reined and bridled. Below it, the

Dunbars' motto *In Promptu* carved into the stone. In Readiness. Dunbar pride not only shone bright on the faces of its people, but it also shone from the walls of their castle. She'd first experienced that shared sense of pride when she'd gone to work for the MacIntyres. The MacIntyres weren't as illustrious as the Dunbars, but their sense of shared identity and honor was no less.

The inviting scent of the beeswax candles joined the pleasant scent of oak from the fireplace, with its now popping and crackling fire.

"Master Dunbar has never brought home a lass before." Agnes's cheery voice boomed around the chamber.

Breena's eyes widened and her breath lodged in her throat. When realization hit her that she was gaping at Agnes, she swallowed. "Egan hasn't brought me home . . . I am not his . . . that is to say, we're not . . ." Breena exhaled audibly, at an utter loss for words. She ended up frowning. Why was she here?

Was she here to be kept safe from the Campbells, or was she here because she was Egan Dunbar's mistress?

Agnes's features dropped. "Forgive me, Mistress MacRae, my comment was too forward."

"No, not at all. I was just taken by surprise."

"I've known Master Dunbar since he was a wee bairn, and he's never come home with a lass before. It gives me hope for his future." Her smile was that of a hopeful mother.

Breena didn't want to quash the woman's ebullience, so she said the one thing she was sure of. "We ran into some difficulty with the Campbells. Egan brought us here for protection."

Agnes's eyes went round. "Just a month ago the Campbells killed Edna's and Emily's husbands while they were out on patrol. God only knows what the Campbells were doing this far from their keep. He was right in bringing you here."

"Yes, we're much obliged for Egan's help. What will happen to the families of the two men the Campbells killed?"

"Master Dunbar went to Coll to demand the Campbells make amends. But no one expects them to. The Campbells are animals."

"Indeed, they are."

"Many here want to go to war with the Campbells over the killings. But some, like the Dunbar himself, think there's been too many deaths already from the great wars. He's trying for a peaceful solution."

"Let's hope one can be found."

Breena let her gaze rove over the polished tallboy next to a dainty lady's dressing table complete with mirror and an accompanying pastel-cushioned stool. But as she advanced on said mirror, she cringed at her reflection. Her hands shot up to smooth down her disheveled braid.

She exhaled in a defeated rush of breath. But when her gaze traveled across the room, past the open shutters overlooking Loch Long, and fell on the immaculate writing desk with its matching chair, topped off with paper and a quill, goose feather no doubt, she forgot about her hair.

"Is it possible to send a missive?"

Agnes threw her a purposeful glance. "Alban or Master Dunbar can arrange it for you, mistress."

How long will Egan be taken up with the marshal on duty? He was no doubt apprising the man of a possible Campbell threat. Although the Campbells would not only have to be reckless but foolish as well to attack such a fortress as Eileanach Castle.

"Do you know where I might find Egan, after I've had some time to settle in and eat?"

Agnes scratched her head. "If he's not in the courtyard speaking with the men, he might be in the kitchen or the solar. I doubt he'd go up to his bedchamber anytime soon, his is one flight up. Should I tell him you need a missive sent out right away?"

"No. It's not urgent."

"I'll have your trunks brought up, along with a bath and some food. I can also send up a lady's maid, Mistress MacRae."

Breena waved away the suggestion. "No. My gowns are not that complicated. I don't require a lady's maid."

Agnes threw an assessing glance at Breena's hair and looked like she wanted to insist on something but then decided against it. She instead headed for the door. "If you change your mind, I can have one of the chamber maids tend to you. Just let me know. I'd better go down to the kitchens before the chaos starts."

Breena ate her fill of salted ham and fresh bread with cheese after a maid arrived with a food tray. She took a warm bath and donned a simple smoke-gray overdress with self-indulgent ruffled three-quarter-length sleeves over a matching silver-embroidered underdress. She then set to vigorously brushing her hair to a shimmering shine and rebraiding it. Two hours later, Breena left her chamber and went in search of Egan. She carried bandages, a jar of salve, and the last of the tincture.

She started down the stairs with the intention of asking someone where the solar was, but then paused, turned, and looked back up the stairs. From the loud ongoing conversations flowing up from the general direction of the kitchen below, Breena suspected Egan was where the crowd was, but she thought it prudent to check one flight up before heading four flights down, remembering what Agnes had said.

She dashed up to the fifth floor and surveyed the corridor. She had no idea which bedchamber belonged to Egan, but since a crack at one doorway emitted a warm flickering light, she took a chance and headed toward it. She knocked.

She may have knocked harder than she realized, because the door slid further open. Her eyes widened, and she stilled as something warm seeped into every cell of her body, heating her from the inside out. She shouldn't have come to his bedchamber. It was highly improper and most assuredly forbidden.

Egan reclined in a large wooden tub filled with water, his back toward her, his auburn hair wet and slicked back. His muscular arms glistened with droplets of water, they reclined atop the edges of the tub. He hadn't turned around. Perhaps he'd not heard the knock.

She considered going back to her room to wait but stopped in her tracks when he spoke.

"Come in. Are you here to bandage me up again?" His voice sounded relaxed, with the barest hint of amusement.

She slowly stepped in and swallowed against the rush of moisture in her mouth. The air was sultry, and it smelled of a woodsy pine soap and maleness. She was having difficulty breathing, but it couldn't just be her, for a light mist rose up from the surface of the water like hot breath on a cold day. Her gaze was drawn to the surface of the water, taking in how the soapsuds concealed what was underneath. When she caught herself staring she blinked and looked away.

She followed his line of vision and ended up staring at her own reflection in a wood-framed mirror atop a mahogany shaving stand. He'd been looking right at her the entire time.

"Should I come back later?" Her eyebrows rose, her voice winded.

"Don't you already know what I look like naked?"

Breena inhaled a long, deep, measured breath in an attempt to lower her rising pulse.

By the Gods yes, she'd caught him in all his scintillating magnificence before. His chiseled body was indelibly etched in her mind from that night at Glen Brittle Forest. And the things he'd done to her had kept her awake with an aching, hungry need many a night since. She shook her head to dislodge her sultry thoughts, recalling the reason for her visit.

"I came with more salve and bandages, but I also have a few questions."

"Questions? Sounds ominous," he said with a wry grin.

She took in his chamber, which was almost twice as large as the one she'd come from, its tones and colors less pastel and warmer. More masculine. It was imposing yet cozy, bold but not ostentatious. And while there was a book out of place here or a piece of clothing thrown over there, they didn't take away from the room's beauty. On the contrary, the strewn-about items added to its rugged charm. Much like the man himself.

A fire crackled and snapped in the far corner fireplace, which didn't help her current state of feverishness. She drifted over to the large chest of drawers, leaned against it, and folded her arms, going for a pose that suggested nonchalance even though she was anything but. Her eyes scanned his writing desk filled with various papers, leather-bound books, and a globe. It was flanked by two armchairs carved with cabriole legs. Her eyes lingered on the books. What was he reading?

She took a peek at one. Alexander MacDonald, *The Sugar Brook*. The perfect book for a Jacobite sympathizer. She'd expected something practical, like *Transactions of the Honorable Society of Improvers, In the Knowledge of Agriculture in Scotland*. Laird MacIntyre was forever flipping those pages whenever she found him in the MacIntyres' library.

Egan eyed her with a lazy, assessing expression. "What would Craig or Ian say if they knew you were here?"

Mirth tugged at her lips even as she imagined the severe tongue-lashing she would receive. "They would run you through, despite what you did for Ian."

Her eyes unwittingly found his extraordinarily large bed. She imagined sinking into those fine plush garnet sheets and lavish counterpane which was no doubt infused with his clean male scent. She snapped her eyes away from the bed when she realized the direction of her thoughts.

"Then you must bandage me up so I can escort you back to your bedchamber."

Water sloshed about the tub. Her mouth went dry as she swung around.

Holy Saints, he'd risen.

No amount of swallowing got past the resistance at the back of her throat as she gazed, transfixed by the rivulets of water running down the length of his magnificent body, like golden honey warmed by the flickering candle. He stood unapologetic and unabashed in his rippling nakedness. Her breath came fast and shallow as heat suffused the entire length of her spine.

Her eyes widened as her gaze dipped over his sinewy muscles, from his broad shoulders and wide chest down the ridges of his abdomen. His midsection was built like a centurion's breastplate except for the dash of short reddish-brown hair. Breena's chest constricted, and she had to remind herself to breathe. Heat burned her cheeks and hummed through the rest of her body.

She uncrossed her arms and grabbed the chest of drawers to steady her teetering legs, forgetting she held a small jar and roll of bandages. The smooth round glass jar slipped out of her fingers and clanked on the stone floor, then rolled, stopping when it bumped into the wooden leg of a chair. She scurried to retrieve her items and deposited them on his desk.

Taking a deep breath and straightening her shoulders, she turned back to face him. It wasn't as if she hadn't had glimpses of naked men before during her practice as a healer. But she couldn't recall any of them affecting her like this. Heaven knew why, but her eyes landed right below his waist this time. She bit down on her lip, trying to quiet an unwitting whimper.

It took her a second to realize he'd cleared his throat, twice. Her eyes flew up to meet his dark, hooded ones. Waves of energy vibrated and hummed in the air between them. She shook her head to dislodge the improper thoughts, then it registered that he was pointing to the chair next to her.

"The linen?" His voice was gruff.

She blinked and turned to the chair, her mind moving at the speed of an utterly soused sailor. She reached over and tugged at the linen, leaving the nearby clothes, then fought her sluggish knees to take one step after the other until she reached the tub and held out the linen to him.

Breena's eyes flickered from the bite marks on his shoulders to those on his left flank, where a number of ugly scars were visible, some still covered with brownish scabs. The scars tinged his hardness with something dangerous, even savage. Her eyes ran down the tight bulge of his thighs and the firm slabs of his calves as she recalled their strength while he'd straddled Heimdall earlier that day.

She felt his eyes boring into her as he dried himself. Heaven help her, but her body pulsated, ached, and burned to touch him, for him to touch her. She itched to run her fingers over every wet, hard contour and crevice of his body, but instead she bit down harder on her bottom lip.

"Questions?" he said, with an amused dark stare.

"Pardon me?" Her brain refused to function at full capacity, at any capacity, for that matter.

"You have questions for me." He stepped out of the tub and slung the linen over his shoulders.

She was nothing but a hot plethora of dark urges and wicked needs. They thrummed and reverberated through her, rendering her speechless and senseless. And he hadn't even touched her.

She took a long, deep cleansing breath. "Why am I here, Egan?"

She pivoted around with the intention of returning to the prop of the chest of drawers, but his hand took hold of her arm, stilling her. His touch sent shock waves through her body, inciting something akin to a pyre in her. She made a move to turn, but his other hand took hold of her free arm, keeping her back toward him.

The damp length of his warm body connected with the entire length of her back. It sent a conflagration of mind-numbing tingles down her spine, weakening her knees and making her lean back into him. She closed her eyes as her breath came in quick, noisy bursts. Her hips instinctually moved back, pressing against him, seeking contact and friction. Her body screamed and roared with desire, needing more of him around her, in front of her, on top of her, inside of her.

His warm breath tickled the back of her neck just before he nudged aside her braid and brushed his lips against her nape. Her world collapsed into an abyss of wickedness and pleasure.

"Why do you think?" His voice rasped as he nibbled at her nape, then he made his way to her ear, tugging with his teeth in gentle pulls.

"To protect me from the Campbells?" Her voice sounded hoarse and breathless to her own ears.

"Yes. Why else?" His voice was deep and muffled against her skin as he continued nibbling at her now oversensitive skin.

Her breath sounded like she'd been racing. Her dress was now two sizes too small, she couldn't think, she couldn't even move as he pressed against her.

"Because you needed a healer?" Dear God, he was making her mindless with need, a veritable wanton.

"Yes. And?" His tongue joined the gentle assault of his teeth and lips as his hands encased her breasts. Breena's head fell back with a scratchy moan.

"Because you want me in your bed?" she whispered.

"Without a doubt." His mouth suddenly lifted from her neck and he stilled. And somewhere through the fog of her muddled mind and sluggish thoughts, she heard footfalls.

Egan released her and cursed under his breath as he reached for his clothes.

CHAPTER
30

*E*gan slipped out of his bedchamber hours before the gray clouds lit up with the climbing sun. He walked down the stairs, pushed the door to his solar open, stepped inside, and closed the door behind him. Nothing sounded but the rustling wind, the occasional owl's hoot, and the muffled clanking of a patrolling sentry's weapons.

There were lengthy livestock reports to review, hay and grain inventories to evaluate with the seneschal, correspondence from their Edinburgh solicitors on trading ventures to respond to, meetings with tenants to be scheduled, bank drafts to be signed, and clan matters that needed attention. But none of that had brought him down here. No. It was thoughts of the bewitching lass sleeping in a guest bedchamber above who had him spellbound. His desire for her fueled him with an intense need to shatter the conventionality of his position as future chief to the Dunbars.

Since Coll, his burdens threatened to bury him alive beneath a mountain of dark earth and heavy rocks. He wanted to forget what had happened to Alex; fifteen years of guilt was driving him mad.

He wanted to pretend the rebels hadn't lost. It blackened his mood. Why couldn't the British understand that everyone was entitled to their own culture, their own choices? It shouldn't matter, as long as they'd harmed no one.

Then there was his damnable duty.

Duty to the clan comes first, son.

Duty to his clan shackled his hands and cut him off at the knees. He wanted to avenge not only Callum and Brodie, but the tortured men in Alasdair's dungeon.

Most of all, Egan wanted to forget his infernal duty to marry a laird's daughter, one with peerage title to elevate the Dunbars' prestige and add to their coffers. None of them had ever boiled his blood, matched the core of his spirit while unburdening his conscience, like Breena did.

Egan now sat behind his desk and glanced at the unfamiliar penmanship of the three sealed missives on top of a pile of paper. He picked them up and brought them to his nose. The woodsy smell of the paper was laced with the faintest tinge of heather undertones. He looked down at the cursive and smiled, beautiful sweeping strokes, dainty yet sure, but then he paused at the left slanting letters and remembered Breena had secrets. Were the secrets about her mother, or was there something else? Egan exhaled aloud and replaced the sealed missives. He'd have Alban assign messengers for each as soon as the lad showed himself. Since sleep was illusory, he dug into the first pile of work on his desk.

When morning finally came, there was a knock on the solar door. He looked up from the report he held in his hands.

"Come."

Agnes stepped into the solar carrying a breakfast tray. Egan's groggy mood from his lack of sleep lifted, and a warmness expanded his chest. The meaty smell of black pudding and bacon, the buttery scent of scones, and the sharp, earthy aroma of coffee wafted into the solar.

Her smile was affable. "You missed breaking your fast in the hall."

He reclined in his chair and eyed her as she approached his desk, cleared a small space, then set down the tray. Egan's brows were knitted. "No reprimands?"

She gave him a look he was only too familiar with, like when he was seven and he'd stolen meat pies from the kitchen, or when he was thirteen and he'd said it was the stew that had made him sick when they'd both known it was the four bottles of ale he'd guzzled down. Ale that he wasn't allowed to drink. She'd never said a word to his mother.

"The fact that you're asking me that question means you ken what you should and should not have been doing. What if your sire or lady mother had walked in on the two of you?"

He averted his gaze. "She was there to take care of my bandages."

"The lass may have had good intentions, but I know you too well to know yours weren't."

Egan scoffed and refrained from rolling his eyes. He reached for a slice of cheese lying next to the scones. She swatted at his hand.

He contorted his features in feigned offense and snatched his hands away with the purloined cheese. A grin tugged on his face as he popped it into his mouth.

"If you care for her reputation . . . I don't need to tell you the servants' gossip, and naught is kept secret for long in a castle." Her voice was tinged with solemnity.

"It's not as dire as all that, is it?" Egan frowned as he took a second piece of cheese.

"If you plan on marrying her, yes."

Egan paused his chewing for the briefest of moments, ceasing to register the buttery taste of the cheese.

Agnes gave a heavy sigh and lowered her head. "Your sire was married and already had you when he was your age."

Egan recalled the way Breena had avoided his question when he'd asked her to come to Eileanach and the way she'd been fidgeting in the wagon as they'd approached his home. She'd seemed lost. There hadn't been time to discuss anything with her and her hovering watchdog Craig. He still wanted to know about her mother, about what else she was hiding. He didn't know if she trusted him. Did he trust her?

There had been time to talk last night, but he was ashamed to say his baser urges had pulverized his need for conversation when she'd appeared at his bedchamber door.

Egan cleared his throat. There was no reason he should squirm under Agnes's gaze now. "As you've been reminding me," he groused. He reached for the mug of steaming coffee.

"I like her. She seems to have a good head on her shoulders."

Ease settled over him at Agnes's words. While he wasn't looking for her approval, he was delighted he had it, nonetheless. Agnes's opinion mattered a great deal to him. He gave a noncommittal grunt as he brought the mug to his lips.

"If you two decide to marry, you'll have a hell of a time convincing your sire."

The hairs on the nape of his neck stiffened. When the acrid taste of the black coffee hit Egan's throat, he almost choked. He managed to push the scalding liquid down. His insides squeezed; the coffee and cheese threatened to retrace their steps up his gullet.

What a bloody understatement.

"Thank you for the breakfast, Agnes."

Agnes nodded in response and headed for the door. Her hands paused on the doorknob.

"In case you're wondering, the lass has been in the stables with your deerhounds since the break of dawn. She treated Odin with some strange smelling mixture she prepared after she visited the apothecary. She claims to know why he has not been eating."

A jolt of hope settled in his gut. Breena cared for dogs, it had been there in her face and eyes when she'd met Odin and Loki. His dogs weren't easy to win over, yet she'd done it in a matter of minutes. Optimism for Odin's recovery warmed Egan; if the dog could survive the vile taste of her concoctions first.

After Egan attended to some correspondence and spoke to the Dunbars' overseer regarding stocking up on grains and hay for their herds, he sat back in his chair. Duncan, their head pastoralist, gave his report. Duncan was in his forties and had never taken a wife. He had a thinning, pale brown mane above a round nose with a full, thick beard covering half his face. His beetle brows covered his eyelids and hung over his narrow eyes, making him seem in a perpetual foul mood.

Duncan's father had been head pastoralist for many years, and when he died, Egan's sire thought to give Duncan the chance to prove himself in the position out of respect for his father. Egan always thought Duncan's vice wasn't that he wasn't an excellent pastoralist, but that he was a zealot when defending the Dunbar name.

Duncan had gotten into too many fights with their neighbor's sons, the Rosses, claiming they had, at one point or the other, besmirched the Dunbar name.

Egan regarded Duncan across his desk as the man spoke.

"No fear of lice for the next few months since we completed the winter dipping. All the markings on our flocks have been retouched, so those damn bellyaching Rosses cannot accuse us of thieving their sheep again. And three ewes gave birth this week." The scowl on Duncan's face got particularly hostile whenever he mentioned the Rosses .

Egan steepled his hands on the desk. "Were all the male lambs castrated last season?"

"All the shepherds did their castrations except Greer. He complained he was too busy with the shearing last season and didn't have the time. I already told him if he can't get the job done right, we'll give it to someone else. I think he'll be more careful in the future."

Egan quirked a brow at Duncan. "Where are we keeping all these newborn lambs?"

"In the stables, sir."

Egan's insides vibrated, and his pulse spiked. His drab day brightened at the mention of the stables. Was she still there with Odin? Egan pushed himself up from his desk.

"Let's go take a look."

Duncan's eyes rounded in surprise. "You wish to inspect the lambs, sir? Now?"

"I do."

"Oh, of course, sir."

Egan led the way into the courtyard. He momentarily paused, raising his hands to shade his eyes from the afternoon sun, which stretched its shadows below the spectacular mountain peaks of the greenish-brown Five Sisters of Kintail. Egan continued his stroll into the stables. It seemed he'd wasted most of the day in his solar.

The scents of horse sweat, hay, and manure loitered in the air, and the sounds of neighs, bleating, and conversation swirled around inside the stables. Familiar barks rang out. Egan braced himself as Loki shot out from behind the stable door and pounced on him with his front legs. The dog's head was high, tail relaxed, ears up, and his mouth open letting a long pink tongue hang down. Musky dog breath, licks, and eager huffs assailed Egan as he chuckled, ruffling the dog's mane.

"How are you, boy? And how's your pal Odin doing?"

Loki barked as if in answer and jumped down.

Egan strode after Loki, around the corner of the stalls to find Breena, Craig, Ian, Alban, and George looking down at Odin. Alban glanced from Odin to Breena, his gaze lingering a bit too long, his face flushed and his eyes glossy, then his gaze snapped back to Odin. Even though Egan knew the lad was harmless, something raw grated at his nerves.

Alban's brows furrowed. "Is it supposed to look like that?"

"Yes." Breena's features were pensive.

"Why is it moving?" Ian's lips were pressed into a fine line as he scratched his chin with one hand and leaned on his walking staff with the other.

"He's purging the worms," Breena said.

Craig was crouched over Breena, who knelt on the ground with her head bowed over Odin. Odin reclined on the ground, his neck raised, his head tilted down, while his eyes looked up at Breena, his ears upright and forward.

"It's working then, isn't it?" Ian asked, shooting an inquiring gaze from Breena to Craig.

"It would appear so."

"Yes, but it will still take time." Craig's tone was reassuring.

Breena gazed down at Odin and gently stroked his head, her expression softening. She wore the dress from last night. Egan took in her shimmering onyx curls and the enticing way the delicate tresses framed her fair face, a stark contrast to her apricot lips. The sight of her made Egan's skin tighten.

Something irrational surged through him like cannon fire: to hell with his responsibility to marry a lass with a title. He wanted to take Breena far away, away from her dark secrets, from Alban's admiring gazes, from the threat of the Campbells, from her hovering uncle, to somewhere they could be alone and he could have his devilish way with her.

Odin turned his head and half barked at Egan, and his tail wagged wide, but the dog remained in his position. Something tightened in Egan's chest. He remembered when Odin had boundless energy. He looked down at Odin, then he recoiled, seeing the sludgy pool of matter next to him.

"What in Hades . . . ?"

It was grayish-orange, watery, and it wiggled around. A faint hint of something odoriferous drifted up. Which end had that come out of?

He dragged his eyes away from the sludge and glanced at Breena. "What is that?" He gestured to the muck.

"I've been mixing Odin's food with apple cider vinegar, carrots and chamomile, to rid him of the worms. He's been passing them."

Egan stooped down in front of Odin and ruffled his head. The dog gave a pathetic bark. Egan's brows gathered.

"Worms?"

She nodded, her smile encouraging.

"Is he taking your concoctions well?"

"Yes. He was hesitant about the strange taste of his food in the beginning, but I think he's getting used to it now."

"How long before he's his usual self?"

"A couple of weeks, depending on how long he's been infested."

Warm hope for Odin's recovery seeped into Egan's belly. He cocked a brow at Breena and Craig, for they both appeared familiar with the treatment for worms.

"How'd he come by these worms in the first place?"

Craig shrugged his shoulders. "Hard to tell. Depends on where the dogs play. Could come from fleas, rodents, infected soil, or a number of other places."

"Could they get worms from running around with the sheep?" Duncan said.

Craig shook his head.

It had slipped Egan's mind that Duncan stood behind him. He stepped aside and introduced Duncan to Craig, Ian, and Breena.

Duncan scowled. "You're both MacRaes?"

Breena nodded with a congenial smile.

"Yes, we are," Ian said.

There was something about the way Duncan stared at Breena and Ian that gave Egan pause, but before he could consider it, the bells on the east tower started to toll. Egan turned toward the stable doors. Retainers sprinted past on their way to the gate. The bells tolled five times, then stopped. Egan's neck muscles corded as he swallowed a tightness at the back of his throat.

"Five tolls. Laird and Lady Dunbar are returning," Alban said.

"It would appear so." Egan nodded.

He stole a glance at Breena. Her expression was impassive. But then he noticed the tremor in her hands as she stood up and smoothed the front of her dress. Something heavy weighed on Egan's chest as he turned and went to welcome home his parents, Alban and Duncan at his heels.

◆—◆—◆—◆—◆

Egan sat at the dais with his father and his foster brother Daegan Mac-Donell. His parents had arrived with Daegan and his wife Eva that afternoon from Castle Inbhir Garadh. The great hall buzzed with chattering and chairs grated against the floors as they were pulled out from under

tables. The Dunbar clan drifted into the great hall, sat down, and awaited the eventide meal. Servers and cup bearers hustled with purposeful
footsteps to attend service on the long trestle tables covered in gleaming
white tablecloths and silverware.

Agnes had just left their table after she'd fretted that even though
they'd given her only four hours' notice, she'd managed to put together
a small feast in honor of their guests and the return of Laird and Lady
Dunbar, which she hoped would be to their liking.

"How did you find the Campbells?" Daegan said, eying Egan.

Seeing Daegan always filled him with warm nostalgia, perhaps for all
the mischief they'd gotten into and out of during his fostering days. With
his easy smile and dark good looks, Daegan had been a favorite of the
lasses, until he'd fallen head-over-heels in love with Eva.

"Mean and ornery as ever," he said scowling at mention of the
Campbells.

Daegan's dark eyes twinkled. "My sire and I thank you for the warning you sent from Coll."

"Have the Campbells been on your land as yet?"

"We increased our patrols after your men Leith and Camdyn came
to warn us. It may have scared them off. But if they ever decide to hunt
Jacobites in our territory, we'll make sure we give them a well-deserved
welcome." Daegan winked.

Egan's father craned his neck toward Egan. "Will the Campbells
make restitution to Callum's and Brodie's families?"

A muscle twitched on Egan's right jaw as he turned to face his father, a man he'd known and respected all his life. A man who was fair yet
firm, gallant but didn't balk at the occasional covert maneuver, a man
who never raised his voice to his wife, no matter how boiling mad she
made him, yet had no qualms about biting the head off Egan's tutor when
she'd lost track of him in the gardens, years past. A man whose iron will,

impressive skills, and determination had served him in the old clan wars and made him victorious, heroic, even legendary. A man who had cried like a bairn at the death of his second son, Alex.

A man he'd never disagreed with, until now. Until the Campbells had killed two of his men, leaving two grief-stricken widows with father-less bairns, had tortured and murdered Jacobites for the redcoats, and had imprisoned Ian MacRae without just cause. But still his father stuck to this new dream of peace.

"They will not. Under the claim our men started the skirmish." Egan's voice was harder than he'd intended.

Daegan glanced from Egan to his father. "Uh-oh. I know that look, Padraid; the Campbells have put Egan in a foul mood."

Egan's sire harrumphed and rubbed his belly. "I'm not discussing this further on an empty stomach."

A hushed silence swept across the great hall. Heads turned in the direction of the lofty double doors that served as the entrance, where faint footfalls approached.

Three elegant ladies glided in, dressed in vibrant finery that would be at home in any Scottish court.

Of the three ladies who approached the dais, Egan focused on the one at the back. His eyes widened as he took in Breena. Though she held her head high, her step faltered for a split second. Eva MacDonell took her hand and ushered her along.

She was dressed in a patterned French-style gown, a style his sister harped about ad nauseam the last time Phoebe had visited from the Lowlands. It was a dark shade of cherry red, sprinkled with patterns of tiny, shimmering leaves. Despite the gown's perfectly alluring silhouette, his first thought was her enticing figure beneath.

Her lustrous raven-colored hair was in a loose chignon, with errant tiny curls framing her face and one single, fat lush curl extended toward her delectable décolletage. Egan had a preposterous urge to untie the golden-flowered ribbon and pluck the pins from her hair, just to see it tumbling down, soft and wild. Something primal inside him grunted. *Mine.* He was unable to utter a word as he stood up and gazed down at Breena. The three ladies offered deference, then stepped onto the dais.

After everyone greeted one another and was seated—Egan and Breena to the Dunbar's left, Egan's lady mother, Abigail Dunbar, to the Dunbar's right, and Daegan and Eva to his lady mother's right—Padraid leaned over and eyed Breena.

"How do you find our home, my dear?"

Breena smiled cordially at his father. "It's majestic and grand, my laird. Your clan is prosperous and must be remarkably busy managing these vast lands."

The Dunbar smiled, raised his chin, and puffed out his chest. "We are involved in a number of profitable ventures."

"It's quite evident, pastoralism is one of them," Breena said.

"Yes. We are one of the largest sellers of wool and shearling in the Highlands."

His father then ran through some of their other business ventures, from their trade with local tradesmen to their overseas shipping ventures with international partners, for both ordinary and luxury goods.

At the end of a long-winded speech about teas, silks, tobacco and the like, Breena seemed to consider his words, then quirked a brow. "Don't the British levy high taxes on such trade?"

"They do, my dear, but as our overall yield is a net profit, it's quite sufficient to appease the British taxes. And we do try to appease them, for they have their uses." Padraid Dunbar cast a hard glance in Egan's direction, then continued. "They have valuable trading routes with the East India Trading Company, which we are looking to expand our ventures into."

Egan curled his fingers as he listened to his father. He had a fairly good notion of his father's underlying point with mention of the British.

"My dear, please don't bore our guests with talk of business ventures." Abigail Dunbar cut in. Egan knew that tolerant countenance too well, and her uncanny ability to keep the peace.

The servers entered the hall, and the scents of piquant roasted mutton, fresh lemon-glazed salmon with turnip greens, and fresh-baked bread filled the air. Ale soon filled every goblet. Egan asked a server to bring the *uisge-beatha* right after the meal, and his sire concurred. At least they agreed on that. A minstrel was ushered in with his clàrsach by one of the servers and given a chair. The man sat down and started to pluck the strings to the melodious sounds of "Sir Patrick Spens."

After Egan swallowed his first mouthful of food, he leaned over to Eva.

"Where is wee Torquhil?"

It was Daegan who answered. "The journey here from Inbhir Garadh knackered the little fella out. He's sleeping under his nanny's watchful eye."

"He's a remarkably beautiful bairn," Breena said, her lips turned up in what looked like a wistful smile.

"He takes after his mother, then," Egan said, just before taking another bite of food.

Eva laughed out loud before she raised her goblet, cheered Egan, then sipped. Daegan shook his head and rolled his eyes, his mouth too full of food for a witty comeback.

"Aren't your father and uncle here?" Eva said, looking at Breena, as she picked up her knife and fork again.

"Yes, they're seated at a lower table."

"They are most welcome to sit at the dais, my dear," Abigail said, her brows arching with concern.

"It would be against propriety, Lady Dunbar. We are not highborn. I myself am only here because of the insistence of Eva, whom I am incapable of refusing because she is my dear friend, and she means well." Breena's tone was soft yet firm.

His mother leaned across from his father and eyed Breena. "I insist you call me Abby, my dear. We have never stood on ceremony at Eileanach Castle. You are all our guests, even more so after you and your uncle treated Egan's injuries from the wolves. I dare not to think what would have happened had you not been there to tend to him."

Breena's eyebrows shot up as she turned to face Egan. A crimson stain appeared on her cheeks. There was no denying the accusation in her expression. She thought he'd told them everything.

Egan gave an infinitesimal shake of his head.

She seemed to relax, then faced his mother again. "It would be indecorous for my family to sit at the dais, my lady . . . Abby."

His mother huffed. "Fiddlesticks, my dear, I am the illegitimate daughter of a baronet. The concept of decorum is quite preposterous to me." His mother waved her hand with a gesture of imperious dismissal before picking up her goblet.

"I think it's rather refreshing the lass adheres to decorum. A trait some of us could use more of." Egan wasn't surprised when his father threw him a narrow gaze, which he promptly ignored before popping a spoonful of turnip greens into his mouth, eager for the whiskey at the end of the meal to settle his stomach.

Egan became aware that the harpist had begun to strum "The Witchery O' Cora" on the clàrsach. Why in Hades had the man started to play that song? It was the story of Cora, a beautiful young lass who couldn't be trusted. It chronicled the dark devilry in her blood, the conniving trickery in her stare, and the evil witchery in her actions. Something made Egan shift to take in Breena. His body tensed as he took in her ashen expression, the tremor in her bottom lip, and the way her chin had dipped.

"Pardon me," Egan mumbled.

He pushed up from his chair and stepped down from the dais. He marched over to the harpist. The occupants in the great hall seemed oblivious to the tune and its possible implications for his guests, with the exception of Duncan, who was turned in his direction. Egan narrowed his eyes at the man. Bloody zealot.

Egan leaned toward the harpist's ear. "Play something else."

The music stopped. The harpist, a mouse of a man with short gray hair, widened his eyes at Egan and nodded. When he resumed his playing a few seconds later, it was "Tam Lin."

Egan returned to his seat. His sire threw him an inquiring glance, but Egan offered no explanations. It was a second before he realized Breena was no longer seated at the dais. He frowned as something tightened in his chest. Egan spun around to take in the entire expanse of the great hall. She was nowhere to be seen.

CHAPTER
31

*B*reena dashed down the long, narrow corridor, her slippers tapping against the stone floors. Her heart was dancing an erratic beat against the walls of her chest as cool air brushed past her. She ran into no one—they were all in the great hall.

She now understood Sorcha's words from a dream she'd had the previous night.

Beware, someone knows.

She'd started to think her status as honored guest at Eileanach wasn't so preposterous. It wasn't outrageous or absurd that the future chief of the Dunbars had brought her, a baseborn healer, along with her father and uncle as his guests, to his lavish and luxurious castle. But someone had taken note of how outrageous it was. Someone who'd asked the harpist to play that horrid song, someone who knew she was baseborn and a witch. Someone who knew the wretched secret of her family.

Breena bolted further into the darkness. Her breath came shallow and fast. She slipped into the shadows of a dimly lit alcove and bent over as she held her stomach. She tried to catch her breath within the confines of her corset stays. She waited until the knots in her gut loosened, until the pain that stabbed her insides subsided.

After several long breaths, she straightened and leaned back against the cool stone wall. The heat of shame bubbled up from her stomach and inflamed her cheeks. Fiery humiliation and hurt warred inside every cell of her body. Uncontrollable tremors blazed through her, from head to toe. She squeezed her eyes shut. Pain shot from the backs of her eyes into her head. But she kept them closed, fighting the weakness of tears.

Four hours ago, she'd been overcome with the warmest of joys at seeing Eva, who'd received her missive. It'd been several months since she'd last seen her dear friend.

Her introduction to Egan's parents, Abigail and Padraid Dunbar, had been innocuous. They'd welcomed her like a friend of the family, although Padraid seemed reserved, careful of what he said as much as his wife was outspoken. Abigail Dunbar was a refined lady in every respect of the word, being the daughter of a baronet, albeit an illegitimate one. And while Padraid Dunbar was not as refined as his wife, he was the epitome of what Breena imagined Egan would be in thirty years.

Then it'd been four hours of nonstop engaged chattering with Eva about all they'd missed in the past several months. It was a delight to meet Eva's beautiful new son Torquhil, a meeting that was tinged with a sweet wistful yearning. Was she herself carrying? Her courses were now three days late.

Eva had cocked an eyebrow at one point while eying Breena.

"I'd expect you to be at Duntulm. How'd you end up at Eileanach Castle?"

Breena had stumbled for an answer. "Egan was hurt after wolves attacked two weeks ago. I treated his wounds, and somehow ended up here."

"Oh no! That sounds rather horrific."

"He's all healed now." She won't be applying any more salve, considering where it had led the previous night.

Then Eva had made the comment Breena dreaded.

"I thought your father had died from an accident when you were a bairn, which is why I was stunned . . . and pleased to be introduced to him today."

Breena had considered carefully before speaking. She ended up telling Eva the whole sad, painful tale of her parents she'd recently found out, leaving out the part about the witchcraft. She wasn't ready just yet to reveal that part.

Her friend's eyes had welled up with tears of concern and outrage as Breena had spoken.

"My poor dear, how dreadful for you. The Campbells are the most deplorable barbarians!"

Eva had held Breena in a comforting embrace as they'd both brushed away tears. Then she'd asked the next logical question.

"But why didn't your uncle and aunt reveal all this to you before now?"

"They claimed it was for my own protection."

"But that's infuriating and makes absolutely no sense!"

Breena might have laughed at her friend's apropos response if this whole episode of her life wasn't so dark and disastrous. But somehow their conversation had validated her anger ever since her aunt came out with the truth. That had settled something deep inside her for the first time in weeks.

Eva had later insisted Breena use her lady's maid to help with her dress and hair. A battle she'd already lost this very morning when Agnes had brought in a chambermaid to help her dress. And Eva had stood firm in Breena having her choice of any of her fine, elegant gowns for the evening.

Breena now glanced down at the dazzling taffeta gown she wore. She'd never had anything so fine and beautiful. But she was a fraud. Time for make-believe was over. Whoever had requested "The Witchery O' Cora" in the great hall had doused her in ice-cold reality.

Clipped footfalls jarred Breena from her mulling. She smoothed her skirts and straightened even as pure fear jarred her senses. Was it the person who had requested that horrid song come to confront her? But if she slipped out of the alcove now, she would be caught. The footsteps, like a death knell, grew louder. They'd come to shout obscenities and shake wooden staves and pitchforks at her just like they'd done to Rowan. Or worse, they would drag her, yelling and screaming, to strap her to a tall stake before they lit a blazing pyre at her bound bare feet, like the Campbells had done to her mother.

But what if this was all in her head?

The problem was she couldn't get her feet to move, even as cold ice coated her skin. The footsteps grew louder still, and then they were upon her. Tremors assailed her body. A tall figure cast in shadows walked pass her. She gasped, then held her breath. The sound must have been audible, for the figure stopped and circled back. Breena closed her eyes and said a silent prayer.

The footfalls stopped in front of her. She opened her eyes to meet her fate. But when she caught the familiar silhouette, air rushed out her lips in a breath of relief.

"I asked the harpist to play something else. I'll deal with the person who chose that song later," Egan said, his voice soft.

His shoulder-length auburn hair was pulled back in a queue. He wore a plain waistcoat over a white léine, in stark contrast to the close-fitting, immaculate midnight-blue velvet jacket with embroidered cuffs.

Had he witnessed everything that night in Glen Brittle Forest, when she'd cast the spell?

"You know, then?" she asked.

"About your friend Rowan? You told me."

"Rowan? No. About me." The words slipped out before she considered what she was saying.

Her entire world was caving in. Perhaps it was time to give up one of her secrets.

She couldn't make out his features, for they were concealed by the long shadows stretching across the corridor. His larger callused hand enveloped her smaller one, and he nudged her back toward the great hall. His touch was warm and solid, and the contact sent little tingles straight through the center of her palm. But then he stopped and shifted toward her. He brought her fingers up to his lips and pulled her closer, then frowned.

"You're cold. Did the song upset you that much?"

Despite the chill now starting to ebb from her skin, she shook her head.

She didn't know how to explain the bout of irrational madness that had just gripped her like a tornado. She'd been flung about like a helpless scarecrow, and nothing but pieces of crumpled, broken straw were left in its wake. A lifetime of hiding her family's secret had taken its toll.

Egan considered her for a few breaths, then turned in the opposite direction of the great hall, prodding her along. She sprinted to keep up with his long strides.

They made two quick left turns and then stopped in front of a set of towering mahogany doors. She recognized the entrance to his solar, where Agnes had shown her to leave her missives the night before.

With one swift motion, he pushed the doors open. Their hinges creaked, and the wood scraped against the stone floors. He ushered her inside, then pushed back the doors and bolted them. The solar was filled with the scent of books and papers mixed with the sweetness of beeswax.

He turned to face her, his gaze uncompromisingly direct. "What should I know about you?"

"Pardon?" She was stalling, and they both knew it.

"You said it wasn't Rowan, but something about you."

"Oh. Yes, so I did." It seemed he hadn't witnessed her spell casting after all, or did he just want her to say it? Breena was at a loss for words, she needed time to think. She bit down on her lip and surveyed their surroundings. It had been dark yesterday when she'd slipped in here with the missives. A fire popped and crackled in the fireplace. It was warmer in this room than the great hall, or was it just the braw imposing Highlander who stood behind her that had thawed her chilled blood?

She stepped past his desk and chair toward a drum table with four matching chairs atop an earth-toned Savonnerie rug. The table held a spherical model of the earth on an oak stand and several leather-bound books. The light from the lanterns was just enough that she could make out the names David Hume and William Dunbar as she ran her fingers along a textured cover. Should she switch their topic of conversation to poetry and philosophy? *Coward.*

She took a long, cleansing breath, then turned to face him. She had to answer the question. She could no longer hide, could no longer avoid it.

It was her time of reckoning.

His dark hazel eyes bore into hers, waiting. The wall she'd built between them was no longer there, it'd been reduced to dust. "Talk to me." The twang of pleading in his voice wasn't something she'd ever expected from him.

Since her parents disappeared nineteen years ago, she'd dreamed of a family of her own, a husband and bairns. And if she were being honest, coming to Eileanach Castle, it was a dream she'd given up to be a future laird's mistress. She'd given up her dream to be with him, something she'd never thought possible. Egan had become entangled within the threads of her life to such an extent, since Coll, she couldn't fathom a life without him, even if it meant she had to share him with his future wife. She'd shared secrets with him that she'd never shared with another living soul, and perhaps in the process she'd given a part of herself to him. She'd unwittingly melded their souls together. But she couldn't give up being a witch. It was in her blood, in her bones, intertwined with every fiber of her being. Inseparable.

Breena took a deep breath and forcibly pushed the words out her lips before she changed her mind. "I'm a witch."

She was surprised at the relative steadiness of her voice even though the revelation distorted the very essence of her existence. She'd never revealed her secret to another living soul before. It almost felt anticlimactic. She'd expected the walls to fall in around them, the roof to crumble down on their heads and bury them, the ground to erupt and swallow them whole. But none of that happened. Her voice simply lingered in the air, mingling with the crackling of the fire, even as her heart was at risk of jumping out of her chest.

She braced herself for the backlash, for his striking face to become distorted in disgust and repulsion.

"Yes, I know. I suspected as much since that night in the glade when you'd slipped away from camp." His tone was matter of fact.

Her eyes widened. His casual response dumfounded her. "You know?"

He nodded and took measured steps toward her, stopping a foot away. She stood her ground and raised her eyes to meet his. His expression held nothing but concern as his eyes explored hers.

His manner was so calm and accepting, it confused her. For she'd expected the worst, for him to turn from her. But there was none of that. His countenance suggested this was the manner of conversation he took part in on a regular basis. Whereas with her, it felt like her entire world and future were being decided here, in this very moment. And it shook the very infrastructure on which her world stood.

She swallowed back the rush of emotion. "Doesn't that fact shock you, fill you with loathing?"

"Why should it?" His voice was low, his tone curious.

She'd spent her entire life hidden in the shadows. She practiced her craft at night. She pretended to be someone she was not, pretended the twisting fear in her gut didn't kill her every time she cast a spell, thinking they'd come for her. And the most painful had been the way even her closest friends equated witchcraft with evil, unaware that she was a witch. And here Egan Dunbar asked her why it should matter that she was a witch.

A disbelieving laugh escaped her lips.

He sent her a poignant look, perhaps sensing she needed the full account of his opinion. "I suppose, witchery is a way of life like any other. Like being a Druid or a Manx. I understand witchery, in particular, is a practice that is feared by many and because of that some spew hatred against it. But it's because they are afraid. Or perhaps ignorant. I imagine there are good witches and bad witches, like there are good Druids and bad Druids . . . like with any other group of people."

What a modern idea. One she admired a great deal. One that shed light on her very dark life thus far. Peacefulness settled on her insides. It eased the knots and twists from her head to her toes. It even eased something in her soul. It was a peace she'd never experienced before. As if she'd taken flight somehow, even though her feet were still on the ground.

She offered a thin smile. "If only the rest of the world was of that opinion."

A solemnity washed over Egan's expression. "It's unfortunate that some people discriminate or look for unfounded reasons to discredit others. They pull others down, because in doing so they believe they rise, become more worthy. More worthy to live and breathe on this earth, in all of their self-righteous arrogance, bigotry and false piety. You shouldn't give these people the satisfaction of taking your peace of mind away. Of taking away your equal right to live and breathe on this earth. Because if you do, bigotry wins."

Breena swallowed against the tightening of emotions that were rising up. The gravitas of what he'd just said hit her like a stampeding herd of cattle. It left her weak and tremulous. Shaking with the force of a stark realization. She had a right to her witchery, to her heritage, to her way of life, as long as she harmed none. But the realization wasn't that she didn't know this, it was that she'd forgotten. She slowly shook her head, hugging herself. Words rumbled in her chest, came up through her throat and then ejected themselves from her lips like shards of glass. Sharp, slicing, and painful.

"I'd . . . I'd actually allowed myself to be ashamed of who I am."

The words were a reflection of the deepest and blackest burrows of her soul. They left her raw and vulnerable.

He looked stunned for a breath. But then his brow wrinkled, and he closed the distance between them. His warm palms gently brushed her upper arms in a soothing and comforting motion.

"I don't want you to be ashamed of who you are. My God, that's like me being ashamed that I am a Scot, when amongst the British. I would never . . . it's unfathomable. I feel nothing but a singular sense of pride. It's my right. No, my privilege to be born a Scotsman. And it fills me with nothing but honor and fortitude to practice and preserve the Gaelic culture. Nothing on this earth will ever make me feel differently. And I pity the man who tries to convince me otherwise."

His words were laced with the force and vehemence of someone who disliked the British. Perhaps even hated them. She jutted her chin at him. "The British never burned us alive at the stake for being Scots."

He harrumphed at her. "That's because we would never stand for it."

Despite herself, she smiled.

His hands had stopped brushing her upper arms, but instead he maintained his gentle hold with his thumbs stroking. The motion sensitized her flesh. The warmth from his hands now seemed to seep into her skin. To warm her from the inside out.

"I don't want you to be frightened. I will shelter you. You are safe here. You are safe with me," he said.

His words caused a tiny pull in her chest. She realized it was her heart, and it was amalgamating itself to him. It was forming an unbreakable bond, critical to her life and to her very existence. But even though she was grateful for his vow of protection, she wondered how long it would last.

Perhaps sensing she had an unspoken question, he continued. "And I shan't let any harm come to Ian or Craig either."

When Breena's chin lowered a fraction, ashamed of her own cowardice for not speaking up, the cruck of his finger lifted it.

"You were born a witch lass because you were fated to be one. Just like you were fated to be standing in front of me here, in this very moment. And I was fated to be standing in front of you."

His finger moved from her chin to the curve of her jaw where his knuckle gently brushed. Caressed, almost in reverence. His finger lightly traced her brows, one after the other. Then moved on to the arc of her cheeks. His touch was soft. Slow. Then the pad of his finger brushed her bottom lip, back and forth with the pressure of a butterfly's wings. It did something to her, for her breath hitched, and then quickened. Her body, having a mind of its own, leaned into him, seeking his warmth. Like a rosebud in the spring seeking the sun.

His gaze now rested on her lips, and hers dropped to his, recalling their sensual softness. Recalling their expert ability to tease and torment her until she lost her head, until all she could focus on was the molten fire of need for him. He lowered his head and his lips replaced his finger as his arms smoothly encircled her waist.

His lips skimmed hers, then his tongue traced the seam of her mouth just before their lips gently fused together. He kissed her with such tenderness, her insides melted. As their lips sampled each other's, the solar felt like it had started to whirl around. Like the very air around them had become fiery. She slid her palms up to spread her fingers on the refined smoothness of his lapels.

Why did she feel light-headed? It was the same reason her skin grew hot at his nearness and the same reason she arched her back toward him. He lifted his head. His pupils had darkened. Her own breath came in soft pants.

"You'd have to be a witch, lass, for you've bewitched me, mind, soul, and body." His voice touched every secret part of her and flowed like warm honey through the not-so-secret parts.

And any reservations about their unsuitability she might have had, after hearing that song in the great hall, was burned to ashes.

She inhaled the smell of him. It was the clean scent of soap and freshly laundered clothes mixed with his particular intoxicating male scent. It weakened her knees.

A raw urge stirred inside her. Her body hummed and sizzled. Something sultry speared through her core. She tipped her chin up and she held her breath as his head came down again.

His lips were soft. They sweetly and slowly seduced her. The kiss drew a low heated sigh from deep in her throat. Then the kiss became fierce and desperate as their embrace tightened. Or was it her own desperation? Desperation to make believe that what she wanted here and needed now was all that mattered. His hands went down the length of her back, and she pressed into him. Her fingers dug into his shoulders, then somehow found their way up to tangle in his thick hair.

Ever since the night in Glen Brittle Forest, Breena had been incapable of ridding herself of the images of what they'd done under the silvery moon. Perhaps she hadn't wanted to. It had ignited a blue flame deep inside her, that simmered and scalded her very thoughts.

The kiss stoked that flame to an unbearable aching need. He tugged on her bodice. Her hands went around his neck to pull him closer when cool air brushed against her bare breasts and his fingers started to knead the delicate skin. He broke the kiss, his gaze following the ministrations of his hands. Dark desire was chiseled into his expression, mixed with awe and adoration. Breena closed her eyes, let her head fall back, and gave in to his delicious caresses.

His expert touch ravaged her senses, seared her blood and melted her bones.

She felt the silkiness of her hair fall loose and weightless on her shoulders and realized that he'd pulled the pins out. Her eyes flickered open, and her hands tightened their hold on him as she straightened her head. He took her mouth with his again. She wanted him closer. She needed him closer, needed him all over her. Her behavior might have shocked her if the need to feed this maddening urge didn't squeeze the very breath from her.

A dark craving unlike any she'd ever experienced before speared her body, a hunger so cavernous it made her weak. Her skin was overheated, her limbs too unsteady, her breath too ragged, her core too bare.

"You are wearing too many clothes," she said, her voice a muffled murmur.

Egan wiggled out of his jacket, unbuttoned his vest and dragged it off, and let the garments float down to the rug. He lifted his head away from hers to pull his léine up and off his body. It joined the rest of his discarded clothes.

"Now *you* are wearing too many clothes."

He carefully turned her around and undid the stays on her dress, as her world raced at a dangerous, dizzying pace.

"Raise your arms," he ordered.

She did as he bid, and soon her dress joined his clothes. He smoothly whirled her back around to face him.

Breena's eyes widened as she took in Egan's bare chest. She reached for him. He was solid and warm; inviting and mesmerizing. His skin was smooth and slick. She tangled and knotted her fingers amid the modicum of ruddy hairs. Something visceral and fiery jolted her senses. Breena's breath hitched, and time stood still as her heart pounded like a manic drummer.

So many things about him drew her in, his sense of honor, the way he championed her father, how he'd maneuvered the Campbells, his sense of duty, his formidable strength, and his impressive physique. But most of all what drew her in was the way he made her feel. Cherished. Desirable. Exquisite. She reached in and pressed a kiss on his chest. Her curiosity got the better of her as she licked and nibbled. Salty and sweet. A low groan came from him. The right side of her lips turned up in a wicked smirk.

He enjoyed her touch, and the knowledge filled her with the confidence to try something, something she'd never thought to do but had heard stories from the maids at Duntulm. Her fingers moved down over his warm sculpted abdominal muscles and continued further. She scraped with her fingernails in gentle playfulness, even as she stroked and kneaded his chiseled perfection. She knelt before him, unbuckled the leather belt holding up his kilt and let it fall to the ground.

"*Leannan* . . . ? His voice was hoarse.

"It's your turn." The wicked intonation in her voice lingered in the air as she proceeded.

"Jesus Christ," he hissed as his head fell back, and his fingers gently tangled themselves in her hair.

The growls he made, interspersed with his groans were pleasing to her ears. They were the sounds of someone who was being utterly pleasured, whose senses were being ravished, yet they were greedy for more. And Breena found that she not only liked how he responded to her intimate ministrations with such intense passion, but it also gave her a degree of control. And so she continued at a leisurely pace, reveling in her power.

But then Egan withdrew his fingers from her hair and eased himself from her. When his eyes found hers, the raw heat in his dark gaze speared her like a bolt of lightning right down the middle. "As decadent as that feels, if you go any further, you will unman me. I need you."

Before she'd taken another breath, Egan had her flat on her back, atop the pile of soft clothes that lay discarded on the floor. He lifted the soft hem of her shift and teased her with his warm lips and tongue until liquid heat pooled at her core. Until she was dizzy with it. And just when he had her at the point where she was prepared to beg, he nestled himself between her legs. They worked in unison as his body glided in and out of hers. His grunts joined her moans. And when her climax came, she cried out as deliciously molten waves of pleasure consumed her.

⬩—⬩—⬩—⬩—⬩—⬩

Breena floated back to reality. They'd made love a second time, and her head and back now leaned against the wall as she reclined bare bottomed on a polished sideboard. Egan's sweat-slickened naked body was at rest between her legs, his forehead resting on her crown. She moved to get up, but Egan's limbs were tangled with hers, and he pulled her back as he encircled her in his arms. He was warm and cozy. The pull to stay in his arms was strong.

Her own body was sweetly achy and heated, like after dancing too close to a campfire.

"I don't want you to be unsettled here at Eileanach Castle," he said.

The reality of her situation came back to her. "That's difficult, since I've lived most of my life in fear of what I am."

His arms tightened around her, and he kissed her forehead. "Duncan means no harm, he just happens to be a zealot when it comes to outsiders. I'll have a talk with him."

She couldn't afford to get pulled into this dream again, into this beautiful fantasy of make-believe.

He was a future chief and she a baseborn healer and a witch. This wasn't a world where they could be together, despite his modern ideas, offer of shelter, and his sweet words. This was a world that burned witches alive. She needed to make him understand. She had to tell him the truth.

"My life would be filled with less dread, apprehension, and anxiousness if everyone thought the way you do. But they don't "

She slipped down from the sideboard and walked over to the pile of clothes on the rug. As she bent down to pick up her shift, her stomach churned. She pulled the garment over her head and then pulled up her stockings. It took great effort not to look at his tall, hard body as he came toward her and picked up his léine.

"And how is that?"

"That witchcraft is acceptable. That witches aren't heathens, an abomination, easy targets."

"These are not simply my thoughts, it's a matter of law." The muscles of his jaws twitched as he considered her. "You haven't told me the whole of it, have you?"

She shook her head. "Not entirely."

"Then talk to me." The pleading in his voice had returned.

She picked up her gown, stepped into it, and pulled it up. She gave him her back. He proceeded to fasten the stays. When he was finished, she took a few steps away from him and sat in the chair farthest from where he stood. She couldn't be within reach of the tantalizing heat of his body, look into his dark eyes and expect to continue a rational conversation.

She eyed him from under her lashes as he tugged on his kilt.

Quick and painless, the best way to remove bandages from a wound. She took a deep breath. "My mother was a witch."

Something icy ran down Breena's spine. She waited for that painful hollowness that always twisted her insides at thoughts of her mother. But only coldness settled on her body. She wondered if the absence of the hollowness, that ever-present void since she'd been six, had anything to do with the return of her father or the Highlander who now eyed her.

Calm consideration was etched in his features. "How did she die?"

Something painful clawed at her stomach, and her gaze dropped. "She was burned at the stake by the Campbells." Her voice sounded weak to her own ears.

She became aware Egan had stilled. She looked up at him. Even as his brows drew together, his eyes were steady on hers, almost comforting. Somewhere deep in her bones, the coldness and numbness started to thaw.

"Dear God. I'm so sorry."

But then something in his expression changed with a twitch of the muscles on his right jawline. He looked away, but she caught a glimpse of his raised chin and flared nostrils. He started to pace, but then bared his teeth as he stopped at the table, bunching his fingers into huge fists. He brought them down with a loud bang on the table. The globe in its oak stand rattled against the tabletop, the books clattered, and the table's feet protested with a muffled rumbling against the rug.

"Those bloody bastards!"

Egan's knuckles remained resting on the tabletop, still in fists, and his head hung down for a few seconds before he drew in a deep breath. He raised his head. His expression had turned dark and lethal.

If she didn't know him, that look would make her tremble in her shoes.

CHAPTER
32

*E*gan eyed his father. The man sat behind his prodigious desk like an old lion in a high-back carved mahogany chair. The golden morning sun streamed through the stained-glass oculus like celestial rays behind him. Egan beat down the urge to wring his hands as if he were a lad again. Was it because he'd stood in this very spot twenty years ago, with his chin dipped, as his sire gave him an earful for leaving a bad-tempered pine marten in his tutor's hutched desk?

Or was it because his father leveled the same narrow-eyed, sanctimonious gaze eleven years ago, when he'd skipped out on the MacDonell's curfew to go horse racing with Daegan? His father was more venerated and seemed larger back then.

Or was it that he himself had been smaller?

Egan took a deep cleansing breath and opted to pace in an attempt to dissipate some of the rawness racing through him. Nothing he'd just reported affected his father's placid, self-righteous façade. Egan had laid out the Campbells' torture of the Jacobite prisoners, Beth's murder and Ian's imprisonment, the cruelty of the Campbell to his own clan, and the sorrow of Edna and Emily, Callum's and Brodie's widows.

His father pushed aside a stack of papers on his desk and tilted his head to consider Egan.

"You're not telling me anything I don't already know."

Egan had visited Edna's cottage earlier that morning, half an hour's ride south of Eileanach Castle. He'd had a hell of a time convincing the widow to come live in the servants' quarters in Eileanach with her three bairns.

"Callum built this cottage with his bare hands. He built it for us. I can't leave here, I can't abandon him . . . desert his memory," she'd said.

He'd tried to persuade her right after Callum's death, but she'd been so distraught, she'd been unable to hold a conversation without bursting into loud sobs. After two hours of talks this morning, however, during which time Egan had started to doubt his negotiating skills, Edna had agreed to leave the cottage. Egan told her he'd send retainers to help with her move. He didn't think it was safe for her and her bairns to be there alone anymore.

Egan had also spoken with Emily after returning. Emily and her two bairns had already moved into the castle three weeks earlier to be near her brother Rory, who was one of the Dunbar retainers. Emily still had a vacant look about her, and her hands shook whenever she mentioned Brodie.

"I miss his laugh the most. The towering ox had a big, barreling laugh that shook the rafters, made the children giggle . . . made life full, busy, bright. Now, it's so quiet," Emily had said.

Considering that she now lived at Eileanach Castle, one of the liveliest and most boisterous places Egan had ever known, her claim of its quietness was saying something about her frame of mind. Egan was worried about the woman. She'd lost considerable weight in the past few weeks. He was pleased, however, to see her bairns were healthy and in good spirits. Egan planned to speak with Rory to see what else he could do for Emily.

Egan paused his pacing to eye his father. "You knew about Breena and her parents?"

His father steepled his hands on his big desk and eyed him. His calm manner irritated Egan.

Why wasn't he outraged?

"I was unaware of the lass and her parents. But, now that I think about it, there was talk some nineteen years ago that the Campbell burned a MacRae witch at the stake for killing his wife, more for the killing and less for the witchcraft. The MacRaes are known witches. Duncan's father delivered wool to them in the old days, before the Highland Clearances. He'd always come back from the MacRaes' keep with stories of witchery."

A sudden prickling ran down Egan's spine. He took a step back and peered at his father. So that explained how Duncan had guessed Breena was a witch. Egan recalled talk of witchery in the old days by Duncan's father, but he'd never paid attention to the stories. Egan himself had guessed the MacRaes were witches, but he had a hard time believing Breena's mother would kill anyone, even though he'd never met the woman.

Had she?

"Are you sure?"

His father gave an imperious nod.

"The Campbell was after Beth MacRae. He might have even taken advantage of her. When Ian MacRae tried to protect and defend his wife, he was imprisoned."

His father's mouth turned down, and he shrugged. The gesture was dismissive, it simmered Egan's blood.

His sire threw him an inquiring glance. "Was Ian MacRae imprisoned when you found him? Did the Campbells release him to you?"

Egan cleared his throat, fighting the urge to squirm or shuffle his feet like he was a lad again.

"I broke him out, unbeknownst to the Campbells."

That narrow-eyed, sanctimonious gaze returned. "It's unwise to provoke the Campbells. They have the ears of the British. Nothing must hinder our chances with the East India Trading Company."

"I only offered my protection from the Campbells."

His father grimaced. "First and foremost, your duty must always be to our clan. Offering protection may be a fine thing, but not at the expense of clan business."

Egan clenched his jaw as a stiffness cramped his neck. He no longer cared to calm the rawness inside him. Did his father intend to forsake justice for additional trading revenue? He shook his head, as if to dislodge the mountain of realization that had just crashed down on him, the weight of it unbearable. He wanted to smash something. He'd been a fool, gullible.

Taking his father at his word.

"If we allow the Campbells these acts of barbarism, we are no better. It's simply not enough anymore to stand by and let them have their way," said Egan.

His father huffed out a breath, but then his gaze pierced Egan like a hawk's. "This is about the lass, isn't it?"

The challenge in his father's curled lips and raised chin was clear. The gauntlet had been thrown down.

Was the challenge against his ability to make sound decisions as future chief, or was it about Breena?

Discussing his affections for Breena would weaken him in his father's eyes. His father valued a man's fight, his actions, his demonstrations of bravery, not weakness. And just how should he categorize his affections for Breena? Truth be told, they terrified him, but he'd come to one conclusion last night: he didn't want her to leave. Discussing affections was unwise but what about final decisions?

Defensiveness made Egan draw himself up to his full height and lift his chin. "I intend to marry her."

His father shot up from his seat, several sheets of papers fluttering to the floor. The chair's legs scraped against the uneven stone, grating on Egan's nerves. If the deep scowl and reddening of his father's face were any indication, Egan had not only broken through the man's calm veneer but he'd also managed to get a rise out of him.

"Have you gotten her with child?" The pitch of his father's voice vibrated in the air around them.

"No." She would have told him if she was with child.

"Then why marry her? I forbid it. You know what your duties are for your future wife. Your wife must be of the correct pedigree. This MacRae lass is most definitely not. Do you need to be reminded of your duty?" His father's harsh tone drilled into his eardrums.

He had always done his duty, honored his father, done what was best for the clan, and done it with pride, but for what? Had his father always had underlying motives for his past acts of valor? Had his part in the old clan wars been for justice? Or had it been for the appearance of justice? Mayhap it had been for an altogether different reason: glory. Jesus Christ.

The temperature of Egan's blood notched up from simmer to boil. He leveled his own glare at his father. "I've always done my duty."

"Until now. Alex would never have gone against me for a lass."

"Alex was ten."

"If he hadn't gone to see you that night, he'd still be here."

Something jagged and cold pierced his gut, tore, and ripped his insides. Nausea kicked in. Egan swallowed hard to push the rising bile back down. His sire had just given voice, for the first time in fifteen years, to the blame Egan had carried inside since the accident. It was his fault his brother was dead.

Alex had taken that horse that night and was on his way to see Egan, because he'd failed to keep a promise.

Something inside Egan shifted, something that had never shifted before. It placed him and his father on opposite sides. Heat swept over him, and he struggled to get a grip on his temper and on the gut-twisting guilt. Egan flexed his fingers at his sides. He fought to override that lad from twenty years ago still inside him, who still strived to honor his father, who still tried to do his duty, and who still looked for approval from the man who now glared at him.

"You overlook the barbarism of the Campbells, and instead choose to remind me of my duty? What about your duty, your famed fight for justice during the clan wars? Is justice now forgotten for some trifling trading routes?" Egan's voice shook with the force of the blood that surged through him.

Padraid Dunbar's face hardened as he bared his teeth, every bit the fierce old lion getting ready to pounce.

"How dare you challenge my dictate for . . . for a bloody woman. And one that is beneath your station. You forget your place." The crescendo of his sire's voice boomed in the solar.

Heat flushed through Egan's body like a rampaging herd of cattle. His vaunted control was shattered to a million pieces, like shards of a glass window after being struck by a hammer. Nothing but rawness and heat raged through him.

"No. You forgot yours. But I intend to remind you. I'll return to Coll posthaste, and I have no intention of keeping the bloody peace."

Egan swung around and barged forward. His fists smashed against the closed double doors of his father's solar. The door swung open, rebounding off the stone wall with a loud echoing crash.

That diligent lad inside Egan had been exorcised.

"Come back here. I'm not finished."

Egan ignored his father's bellows and charged forward in search of Dougray and Keith. He wanted his men armed, saddled, and ready. He was the head of the Dunbar retainers, and they would follow his orders, despite his father's opinions. He'd damn well make it so.

They were setting out for Coll within the hour.

❀ ⸺ ❀ ⸺ ❀ ⸺ ❀ ⸺ ❀

Egan and his men were concluding preparations to depart Eileanach Castle, when Abby Dunbar's graceful figure was seen rushing into the stables. She approached Egan and placed her hand on his arm. Her pained stare and wrinkled brows made Egan brace himself, even as something constricted in his chest.

"Why did you two argue? I've never seen him like this. You must go back and apologize."

"It has gone too far, Mother."

"He's your father, and you are his son. Whatever it is, it can be mended."

Egan looked into his mother's watery hazel eyes, so much like his own. For the past fifteen years, he'd been too afraid to ask a question, for fear of the answer. But the time had come for him to know, in spite of the fear.

"Do you also blame me for Alex's death?"

The skin bunched around her eyes. It was rare for her to cry and even rarer for her to look her fifty years. His mother always comported herself as a lady, cultured and composed in speech, manner, and dress, no matter the situation. She took his face between her palms and shook her head.

"I don't blame you. Neither does your father. I don't know what he said to you, but it was in anger."

"One of you is a liar." His voice was barely above a whisper as he tried to look away.

Her hands gently nudged his face back toward her. "Where are you going?"

"We're returning to Coll. The Campbells must answer for the deaths of Callum and Brodie. And for Breena's parents."

"I already lost one son. Losing the second one will kill me."

He eyed her beautiful, aged face, seeing the streaks of silvery gray amid her flaming red hair, and something weighed on his chest. He was thankful she'd never once questioned Breena's presence at Eileanach but had instead been charming and welcoming. Perhaps she already knew. He didn't want to cause her worry, but he had to make a stand against the Campbells and against his father.

"Please don't worry, Mother. I've no intention of dying."

Amid his mother's protests, Egan kissed her on the cheek, turned, and mounted Heimdall. He left explicit instructions for Alban to stand guard over Breena, then departed Eileanach with the rest of his men.

◆──◆──◆──◆──◆

Egan and fifty Dunbar retainers rode their horses at a full gallop south-west, back to Coll. With no wagons to slow their pace, they rode with the wind. Hooves pounded the ground, and crisp air whisked by as graying and bare trees, snow-peaked bens, and deep glens were reduced to a blur. The briskness of the air around them did nothing to temper the heat that pummeled through Egan's veins. His father's harsh words still rang in his ears.

If he hadn't gone to see you, he'd still be here.

Egan wanted to howl and roar as he raised a hand to massage the vein throbbing in his temple.

He had replayed that night fifteen years ago in his head so many times, it was like yesterday. His chest had been puffed up with so much ego and self-importance at being the next chief back then, it's a wonder he hadn't toppled forward from the sheer weight of it.

It had been Alex's tenth birthday and Egan had promised to take him riding. Alex had wanted to show off his equestrian skills. But Egan had been sparring with Daegan and other trainees at Castle Inbhir Garadh. He'd forgotten that he'd responded to Alex's missive.

Alex had taken a horse from the stables at Eileanach and ridden off by himself toward Inbhir Garadh.

The horse had been too green and too wild for his little brother, and it threw him. A guest from the Ratagan Inn found him. The physicians said the break in his neck had caused instantaneous death, there wouldn't have been time for pain. Or disappointment. The unnatural lines of his still little body were ingrained in Egan's mind. And despite the countless times Egan had tried, he couldn't forget the gray tint or coldness of his brother's skin that day.

Laughter sounded, jarring Egan back to the present. They'd slowed to give the horses a rest. One of the Dunbar riders ahead must have said something amusing to Dougray. Dougray was in riotous spirits because he'd been itching for a fight with the Campbells since they'd gone to Coll twenty-three days ago.

"The first two guards are mine. No. The first three are mine, I'll need the third to clean the blood off my sword from the first two." Dougray guffawed.

Rory, who rode alongside Dougray, sniggered. "I'll use the backs of the next two for target practice with my *sgian dubhs*. On second thought, they're used to stabbing men in the back, they'll be expecting that."

Gregor, who rode behind him, grunted. "Quick deaths are too good for these bastards, let's throw them in their own dungeon to rot and toss away the key."

After a while, the horses' hooves drowned out his men's revelry as his mother's words replayed in his head like a practicing pianist jabbing repetitive notes on a pianoforte. *I don't blame you. Neither does your father.* But every time they repeated, her words were smothered by a flash of his father's angry glare.

◆——◆——◆——◆——◆

It was dusk when they arrived at Kilchoan, on the Ardnamurchan Peninsula across the bay from the Isle of Coll. Egan slipped down from Heimdall to survey the wide expanse of Sanna Bay. His retainers reined in their horses behind him, several conversations about attack plans ongoing. The neighs and snorts of their horses joined the multitude of resting weapons that clinked as his men dismounted.

Egan walked toward shore. An ethereal mist hung in the air just above the water of the bay. That, coupled with the fading light, made it difficult to catch what was beyond the docked fishing doggers in front of them.

He turned to face Keith.

"We'll have to see about chartering boats from the locals."

Keith considered Egan for a few seconds too long, his lips pressed together in a disapproving grimace. "I've never known you to not have a plan before. Or is the plan to charge the Campbells first and ask questions afterward?"

Egan snorted. He didn't need Keith's level-headedness right now; he wanted Dougray's itchy fight hands. His bloody head throbbed. He wanted one of Breena's healing tinctures. Bollocks. He hadn't spoken to her before he left. Hadn't even told her he was returning to Coll. Just as well, she'd tell him he was being too cocksure of himself.

Sharp shuffling sounded behind him.

"What the hell is that?" Rory shouted.

The sharp slicing sound of at least twenty swords being drawn echoed around him. Then quietness followed, the energy-infused kind, like between lightning and the cracking of thunder.

Egan looked around until he caught sight of them. Heat spread through his body as excitement surged in his veins. "Steady, men." His voice rang out amidst the quiet.

The curled snakelike figureheads of three wooden bows pierced the cloudy white mist on the bay, one after the other. They floated like quiet specters on the calm waters. Then the rest of the birlinns emerged from the mist as their mainmasts came into view. The mist hid their flags. Egan made out the threadbare blue-and-green tartan of the Campbells as they dropped anchor and jumped into knee-high water. His fingers curled around the hilt of his claymore, but he didn't draw, for the man in front of them came into view amid splashes and shouts as they waded onto shore.

"Shouldn't we attack?" said Dougray. The air around them sizzled and vibrated with readiness and anticipation.

Egan moved his hand away from his sword. "Stand down."

If it had been Alasdair Campbell, he would have given the order to attack. But Egan had started to make out the dark hair and stubby chin of William Campbell as he approached, ahead of fifteen or so other Campbells, some of whom he recognized from their recent trek to Coll.

William waved, seeming to take note of Egan. "We come in friendship."

Egan strode toward the shore to greet William. Dougray and Keith bracketed him on either side.

Egan reached out and congenially shook hands with William. The side of William's mouth quirked up in an amiable half grin.

Concern and curiosity needled Egan. "What in Hades are you doing here?"

"I was on my way to find you and Breena."

Something squeezed Egan's gut at his mention of Breena. "Why would you be looking for us?"

A full grin turned up William's features. "Alasdair Campbell is dead. The bastard was done in by consumption yesterday."

Dougray laughed out loud, turning toward the Dunbar retainers. "The Campbell is dead!"

A loud cheer rang out, along with hoots and repeated thuds of swords against targes, although it was tinged with disappointment, for his retainers were charged with energy in preparation for battle.

Yet some of the tension in Egan's gut relaxed. "Good. Consumption saved me the trouble."

Keith and Dougray both sniggered. Egan narrowed his eyes at his two men and their giddy upturned faces. He didn't need a bloody audience if he was going to ask William what Alasdair's death had to do with Breena. Egan clasped his right arm around William's shoulders and drew him a few feet away from their men.

William put up no resistance. He hooked a thumb into his belt as he shifted to fully face Egan.

"On Alasdair's sickbed, he told me he'd brought me to Coll to kill me . . . me being his half-brother and top contender for his position as chief of the Campbells. The Campbells have long been dissatisfied with the way he ran things. The bastard was giddy when he admitted the poison that made Rosalin sick was meant for me."

Egan's eyes widened. "Is your wife still ill?"

"She is well now, thanks to Breena. She got all the poison out."

Egan's jaws slackened, recalling when Breena stayed at William's cottage to nurse Rosalin back to health. "That was poisoning?"

"Aye. Didn't Breena tell you?"

Egan shook his head. "She said Rosalin had eaten something that didn't agree with her."

One thing was certain, Breena MacRae knew how to keep a secret. But then, he imagined she had to as a healer when it involved intimate information about her patients.

"Yes, poisonous berries the Campbell left."

"Is that why you came looking for Breena and me?"

"No."

Impatience burned Egan's gut as he waited for William to elaborate.

After an interminable pause, William continued. "Alasdair also revealed that he sired a daughter twenty-five years ago with a MacRae witch. The witch hid his daughter from him for six years before he found out. Once he found out, he ended up killing the witch and throwing her husband into the dungeon. But he kept the husband alive for nineteen years, hoping the man would reveal the location of his daughter, no doubt to exploit her powers. But the witch's husband escaped around the time you and Breena left Coll."

Egan blinked at William, a coldness settling in him.

Pieces of a puzzle started to fall into place. Alasdair had indeed taken advantage of Beth MacRae. Bloody swine. And Breena was the result? The coldness in his belly made him want to wring a dead man's neck. Did William suspect the daughter was Breena? That William himself was her uncle?

Egan cloaked the icy shock that shook him to the core as his gaze wandered to the surface of the bay. Alasdair Campbell is . . . was Breena's father. *Bloody hell.* Alasdair Campbell had no shortage of enemies, even among his own clan. Would revealing that Breena was Alasdair's daughter put her in danger?

Until he could be certain, he would say nothing.

Was this another secret Breena was keeping from him? No. She wouldn't have snuck into the Campbells' keep to free Ian MacRae the way she'd done if she'd known. Would she have?

Egan faced William. "And of course, you remembered the man in the trunk and now suspect him of being the witch's husband."

"Isn't he?"

He had to admit to that much for this to play out. Egan nodded his yes.

William pursed his lips. "I never told Alasdair you had the prisoner. And the guards from the flanking tower couldn't identify their attacker. But the Campbell was no fool. He didn't think it was a coincidence the witch's husband escaped confinement while you and Breena were on Coll."

Egan exhaled a breath of frustration. "So, he suspected."

"He wanted to ride with his men to strike back at you by recapturing the prisoner. If he couldn't find the prisoner, he planned to take Breena instead. But his health deteriorated. However, the men still loyal to him left Coll to carry out his last request." William gestured to the Campbells that came with him. "These men who travel with me are loyal to me. They have accepted me as their new chief."

Something dark and icy pilfered Egan's breath. For a second, he froze with the cold shivers of dread running down his spine. He had to head home. Now. Blood hammered through his veins. She was safe at Eileanach Castle, wasn't she?

"When did the Campbell's men leave? How many?"

"On his deathbed yesterday, he told his men to carry out his plan. Fifteen of them left this morning. They planned to hit Kilmuir and Eileanach Castle. I don't know where they will strike first."

"This morning?" Egan gripped the hilt of his dirk so hard his knuckles cracked. He quickly calculated in his head the length of time it would take fifteen retainers to reach Eileanach from Coll.

"Where is Breena?" William asked.

"At Eileanach Castle."

"I assume the lass is guarded well?"

Bloody Hell. Shite. Shite!

Fear cut Egan's gut like a knife, twisting and knotting. Alban alone just wouldn't do. What had he been thinking assigning just Alban? He hadn't been thinking when he'd left Eileanach Castle. That was the problem.

"I need to return to Eileanach forthwith." Egan swung around, but William stayed him with a hand on his shoulder.

"My men and I are at your disposal. If you have need of us."

Egan eyed William. "On your way back to Coll, can you stop by Kilmuir to ensure they're not there, causing trouble for the MacRaes or Maxwells?"

William nodded. "Consider it done."

Egan turned and made a dash for Heimdall.

In the wee hours of the morning, as the new moon threw the sky in onyx like blackness, Egan and his retainers charged into the courtyard of Eileanach in a storm of dust and pounding hooves. They'd ridden straight through, only stopping for short breaks to rest and water the horses.

Egan ignored the tiredness in his limbs and the knots in his shoulders as he bolted up to Breena's bedchamber on the fourth floor. He swung open her door. His heart stopped cold. Something choked the air and life from his lungs. She wasn't in her bed. Glacial iciness speared

Egan's gut. The bed looked like it hadn't been touched. Egan frantically scanned the entire chamber. He half expected her to pop her head from behind a desk or a drapery. Dougray and Keith rushed in after him.

"She's not here." Egan's voice sounded like a low croak to his own ears.

A bitter coldness unlike anything Egan had ever experienced before threatened to drown him in blackness where he stood. He resisted the overpowering urge to crumple to his knees like a sack of grain and howl like a crazed, injured beast.

He spotted a candle, and with tremulous fingers he lit it. He had to make sure. His gaze darted around the chamber. But he already knew, even as the candle's flickering light filled the empty chamber. The jabbing iciness in his gut was his answer.

Egan's father marched into the chamber, finishing a knot at the waist of his dressing gown. His lady mother and Eva stumbled in seconds later, both in their night clothes, worry splashed across their features.

"We haven't been able to find Breena or Ian since eventide meal. We found Craig and Alban. They've both been severely injured. Blade and musket wounds. Physicians have tended them, and they will live," Padraid said.

"Daegan and a handful of Dunbars are out looking for Breena. I pray they find her," Eva said. Her voice cracked with the same dark emotion Egan had just embraced. Gut-wrenching fear.

Egan pinned his father with a glacial stare. "The Campbells?"

Equal parts agony and regret were etched in the man's weathered features. The urge to ask if he still wanted peace dissipated.

His lady mother chose that moment to clear her throat rather forcefully. Both Egan and his sire faced her. She was glaring at his sire. Something passed between his parents before his sire shifted toward him once more, resolve inching his chin up.

"Forgive me . . . you were right about the Campbells. Alban confirmed as much before he passed out." His sire had never asked his forgiveness before. Ever. What had his mother said to his father?

"Why would the Campbells want to hurt Breena?" Abby said.

Egan shook his head even as his lips curled into a snarl. "How does one explain the reach of Mephistopheles, even from hell?" He walked to the window, grabbed the sill with both hands, and dug his fingers into the wood as he let his neck and head hang down. He'd only known her for a short time, twenty-four days to be exact, not counting their first meeting at Castle Duntulm. But already she'd become as essential to him as the very air he breathed, the sun that shed light into his days, and the heart which now pummeled his chest.

Something dark and lethal unfurled inside of him. He was going to squeeze the life out of each one of the Campbells who'd taken her, with slow, methodical precision. He clenched his fingers tighter and tighter around the wooden sill. Egan growled like a wounded animal, uncaring of his audience. The wood in his hands gave way. He hurled it against the hearth. It crashed and splintered.

When the image of one of them putting their grimy hands on Breena flashed through his mind, it all but decimated his insides.

The Campbells who'd taken her were already dead men. Egan swung around and headed for the door.

"Egan?" Abby asked.

"Where are you going?" Padraid said.

"To find her!" Egan said.

Dougray and Keith sprinted to keep up with him as he charged down the stairs.

"What's the plan?" Keith asked.

"I need someone who can sniff out the Campbells' trail. And I know just the animal for the job."

CHAPTER
33

reena forced her eyelids open through the haze of uncon-
sciousness. The gray darkness that met her as she blinked and squinted
discombobulated her. Terror and dread in equal measure seeped into
every molecule of her body at her last memory. She'd been tossed over a
horse and a coarse sack of some sort pulled over her head.

With each gallop of the horse beneath her, she felt a jarring pain
as her feet and head dangled. Horse sweat, dust, and odious body odor
assailed her senses. It choked the breath from her. Through the coarse
material she made out vague shadows and movements, unsure if it was
day or night. She tried to cry out for it to stop, but her voice came out as
a muffled groan. Something foul had been stuffed in her mouth and tied
in place; it tasted like chalk.

The rest of her memory came flooding back as tears dampened her cheeks. Alban had been shot and Craig stabbed in a chaotic nightmare of threadbare blue-and-green tartan. The colors of the Campbells. What had become of her father? They'd all been running and playing with the dogs outside Eileanach Castle's curtain wall when the silent attack had come.

She struggled against her restraints and tried again to yell, but when something slammed into her head, causing black spots to register on her vision, her body fell limp. The blunt pain of it was unlike anything she'd ever experienced before. As the salty iron taste of blood registered in her mouth, the dampness on half of her dress puzzled her. Chilled gooseflesh assailed her entire body, then she recalled that she was wearing no cloak.

"Stop your bloody squirming, wench," someone barked.

That voice! Finlay, Squinty Eyes. Where were they taking her? Was this retaliation for freeing her father?

Someone bellowed for them to stop. She wasn't sure how many of them there were. She'd gotten a glimpse of five Campbells before the sack had been pulled over her, but the hooves pounding the ground were of more than just five horses.

The horse she'd been flung across was reined in. Then its odiferous rider dismounted and left her belly down on what she'd come to guess was the horn of a saddle. She was dragged down to stand on her weakened legs. She wobbled and fell against her kidnapper's rank body. She was shoved unceremoniously back against the belly of a horse. Just so, for she preferred the uncertainty of a thousand-pound beast, which could break her with one stomp of its hooves, to a murderous Campbell.

Her captor hauled her body up over his shoulder like a sack of grain. She twisted when the fear of unsteadiness speared through her gut.

"Be still!"

"I am trying." She said, which sounded like "hm m mm m" with the mouth restraint.

When someone delivered a sharp blow to her derrière, Breena went limp.

Someone else nearby guffawed. "If the bitch is too much for you, Finlay, I can take her off your hands."

"Bugger off, Glenn."

She landed sideways in a painful, loud crash on the cold ground, her shoulder and hip taking the brunt of the fall. It knocked the air right out of her. Footsteps receded, and the grassy dankness of terra firma filled her nostrils. Her head ached from the earlier blow, as if a blacksmith's hammer pounded it, and her neck, back, and shoulders were sore from the ride.

Even though she was bruised, Breena knew worse things could be done to a woman.

She was able to make out pieces and bits of conversation that seemed to come from twenty to thirty paces away.

"Do you think the Dunbars will follow us?"

Breena's first thought was Egan. He would move mountains to get to her. That somehow gave her a sliver of confidence.

"They'll have a difficult time tracking us across the loch."

That explained the dampness in her dress, splatters from when they rode through said loch. Which one, and how far from Eileanach Castle, she had no idea.

Just then footsteps approached, and by the grunt and thud, someone was dropped next to her. Her father?

"Athair . . . Athair?" Breena said, which sounded like "hmm . . . hmm," to her own ears.

The only response was a blow to Breena's stomach. The blunt pain of it made her heave, gasp, and cough all at once, and her eyes and nose watered.

"If I have to tell you one more time to shut up, you're not going to like it," Finlay said.

Had he kicked her?

Breena stilled and waited for the footsteps to recede. When she was certain Finlay was gone, she inched her body toward the noise of someone breathing. The process was snail-like because of her restraints. Was it Ian? After a few minutes she stopped and listened. Breathing sounded low and wheezy. He was unconscious?

Fear that her father was injured overpowered her, which dulled in comparison to her fear of being hurt. She couldn't lose him after she'd just found him.

She needed to get their attention, to somehow convince them to let her tend to her father. Breena thrashed about and shouted as loud as she could, which didn't resonate exceedingly high, thanks to the mouth restraint. She shouted until vibrations from the muffled sounds resonated and throbbed painfully in her skull, until her eyes watered and her throat hurt.

After a long while, she was about to give up because of the ringing in her head, when heavy footfalls sounded.

Someone grabbed a bunch of material from the bodice of her dress and hauled her up to her feet in one single swoop. The sack was yanked off her head. Breena blinked and squinted as the sharp light of day shot into her eyes. What time was it? Blurred images came into focus. Finley's meaty hand held her up by the front of her dress, the fabric bunched in his grip. They were in a small glade surrounded by tall, thick trees. Fifteen or so unsavory-looking Campbells sat around a campfire about thirty paces away. A few of them eyed her with curled lips and sneers.

"I told you you'd be sorry. Now we're going to have a little fun."

He dragged her by her dress toward a huge tree. As he did, she glanced down. Ian lay on the ground, bound with a wheat sack over his head. Something fierce speared her gut when she caught sight of his bloodied left leg. Breena twisted and jerked at the same time she was viciously hauled up and slammed against the tree trunk. The lascivious gleam in Finlay's eyes made Breena's stomach roil. He grinned, and his bloodshot yellow gaze slithered down the full length of her before coming back to rest on her chest. Breena swallowed the onset of queasiness. She shook her head against the sensation of a hundred insects crawling on her bare skin.

"I am a healer. Please let me tend to the injured man over there." Attempting words over the mouth restraint remained useless.

Breena recoiled when Finlay pulled out a knife from his boot. Did he mean to cut her? No. If that were the case, they wouldn't have gone through the trouble of tying her up and bringing her along. She raised her chin as fear and anger notched up the frequency of the blood surging through her veins.

Finlay brought the blade of the knife up to her face. "I'm going to pay you back for all the trouble you caused me."

His corpulent face twisted into a hideous chuckle as he bared his crooked teeth. He pressed the sharp tip of the blade against her face and trailed the cold steel across her left cheek. She jerked back when he nicked her skin. He slipped the knife behind the ties of her mouth restraint and sliced through it.

She lowered her head, coughed, and sputtered as the foul thing fell away, even as Finlay's meaty left hand pushed her up against the tree.

"I am a healer. I have to tend to that man over there. He's injured," Breena said, as she glanced toward Ian's still body and tried to regain some level of moisture in her chalky mouth.

"Are you now? Well, why don't you scratch my itch first." His mouth twisted into a laugh. The malicious sound of it made her swallow her rising dread.

He stooped down and yanked up her skirts as he pressed his revolting body against hers in a suggestive manner. Breena's jaws tightened as she jerked her legs within the confines of their bonds, as if to shake off a crawling roach. But then full-body tremors hit her all at once when realization sunk in.

She shook her head. "Stop it. Get your hands off me."

Daylight glinted off a gleaming surface a few paces away, momentarily blinding her. Breena blinked and looked over Finlay's shoulder.

All the fear and tension seeped out of her. Relief and joy ballooned in her chest at the familiar broad-shouldered silhouette that emerged from the trees. Egan's right hand held a glinting silver-handled dirk. When she saw him flex the fingers of his other hand, she ducked behind Finlay's pudgy body. A loud thud sounded, and Finlay yowled. He dropped her and grabbed the back of his neck. Breena landed hard against the unforgiving ground. Her eyes widened at Finlay as he stumbled back. Blood seeped through his fingers still gripping his neck. He gurgled in an attempt to speak.

Within seconds Egan was behind Finlay. He took hold of Finlay's head from behind with one hand on his chin and twisted upward. There was a sickening crack of bones as Finlay's eyes went up into the back of his head. The unfazed look of a trained warrior etched on Egan's face as he eyed Finlay's crumpling body was something Breena was grateful for. The look evaporated as his eyes fell on her.

"Are you hurt? Jesus Christ, I thought I'd lost you." His voice was laced with a tremor, as he took his dirk to her bounds.

"I'm fine, but Ian . . . I have to tend to Ian."

Egan worked on slicing through the ropes until they fell off her ankles and wrists. The second the bonds were gone, she threw her arms around his neck, filling her lungs with his familiar male scent. An onslaught of emotions surged through Breena's entire body, the force of it almost ripping her apart. Tears of gratitude came as the warmth of love squeezed her lungs so tightly, she thought she would lose consciousness.

The sweet balm of relief was the only thing that kept her from falling to pieces as the steadiness of his arms around her assuaged the unsteadiness in her knees.

"Thank the saints you came when you did," she said through her sobs. When she finally released Egan, awareness of the mayhem thirty paces away hit her. Swords clashed against swords, loud swearing and shouts filled the air, battleaxes tackled blades, and flintlock rifles fired as the Dunbars took on the Campbells.

Egan released her and drew his claymore.

"Take cover, *mo ghaol.*"

As Egan lunged into battle, Breena scrambled to Ian's side. And as she tended to her father, the Dunbars obliterated the Campbells.

CHAPTER
34

reena opened her eyes and blinked up at the damask canopy surrounding her large plush bed. She shifted, burrowing further into the luxurious mattress. The warmth and softness of the counterpane covering her night rail-clad body lured her into staying in bed.

But then flashbacks of last week's kidnapping by the Campbells instantly assailed her mind.

The battle between the Dunbars and the Campbells a week earlier had been a brief one. The Campbells had been outnumbered by more than two to one and it had been evident, from their weak defense, that they were neither as well trained nor as well equipped as the Dunbars. Given the fact that none of the Campbells survived, Breena suspected the Dunbars were taking revenge for their two previously murdered comrades.

She swallowed, remembering to be grateful for the safety Eileanach Castle, Egan, and the Dunbars now provided.

Judging from the faint sliver of light piercing the darkness of the bedchamber through the window, she estimated it would be dawn soon. She slipped out from under the counterpane, dragged the damask curtain aside and stepped onto the rug. Its coolness seeped into her bare feet. She grabbed a dressing gown from the back of a nearby chair and donned it. As she walked toward the shutters, she recalled Sorcha's voice in the dream she'd just awoken from.

I'm proud of the path your life has finally settled on, my dear.

Breena unbolted the wooden shutters and threw them open, gazing beyond the glass at the lightening, blackish-blue sky and the distant dark, rippling surface of Loch Long. She hugged herself as coolness from the outside settled on her torso and shimmied down the rest of her body. Puzzlement filled her as to why the dream made her feel peace and calm. Why was Sorcha proud of her? Granted, she was living in a luxurious castle, but she was doing so as the leman to the future laird.

And she didn't know how long this would continue . . .

She strode over to the fireplace, added a log and kindling to the ashes, reached for the flint and steel, and struck a few times before a small steady flame broke out on the kindling. The pleasant scent of the crackling fire joined the faint smoky scent of the fireplace. Breena strolled to where her portmanteau stood leaning against the wall by the desk and withdrew the necessary herbs, along with the pouch containing the seven stones. She sat at the desk. Equal parts anticipation and dread needled her belly. Breena pulled open the strings of the pouch, sprinkled the herbs, blew her witch's breath on the stones, and pulled the strings closed.

For the first time in a long time, she lacked the fear or anxiety of discovery of performing witchery. She knew she was safe among the Dunbars and with Egan currently asleep just one flight above.

Her dread and anticipation instead stemmed from what the stones would reveal.

She swallowed. "I am happy you're proud of me, Grandmother, but why?" she whispered.

Breena shook the stones within the soft pouch, hearing their faint clinking. She became aware of her heartbeat booming in her ears as she closed her eyes, pulled the strings open, and drew out the first stone her fingers connected with. She opened her eyes and blinked down at the green aventurine. Love. But Sorcha had never told her if it meant that she loved someone or that someone loved her. Breena sighed softly. Of one thing she was certain: she was irrevocably ruined for marriage to any other man besides Egan Dunbar. And since marriage to Egan was impossible for someone from her particular social standing, then one undeniable fact remained. She was ruined. And desperately in love with Egan.

✦─✦─✦─✦─✦

The golden rays of the mid-morning sun streamed through a high corner window at Eileanach as Breena sat next to Ian in the bedchamber in which he'd been convalescing.

She'd been grateful that the Dunbars had sustained only minor cuts and bruises from the battle. Even though Alban, Ian, and Craig suffered serious wounds, their recovery was well underway. As a fire crackled in the bedchamber's fireplace, Breena eyed the brownish scab that had formed over the pistol wound on Ian's left thigh.

"It's healing along nicely. You'll have use of the leg once it's fully healed, but you will need crutches now. I fear a single walking staff will no longer be sufficient."

She sent him an encouraging smile as she spread the herb-scented salve on his skin.

Ian scratched his chin. "Maybe I can get a nicely carved pair. If I must use crutches, I'd at least like them to have some style. And my gratitude to you, my dear, for taking such good care of an old man."

As she rebandaged his leg, warmth spread across her chest, for despite everything, she was well aware that it could have been worse.

"You're not old. You're seasoned. And you're not just any man. You're my father."

He lowered his chin, and the expression that passed over his face puzzled her. But he was no doubt worn out from the past nineteen years and overtaxed from the recent kidnapping. He'd been through so much, and yet he still found a reason to smile. Craig was right, her father had an unshakable core.

"Have you and Egan settled things?" he asked.

Breena swallowed the sudden tightening in the back of her throat. "Settled things? What are you referring to?"

Did he mean the fact that she was a lowborn witch and Egan a highborn future chief? Or mayhap he referred to the fact that entire worlds separated their respective social standing. Worlds that could never be bridged if one were to face the cold reality of things.

He shrugged as his gaze fell to the bandage around his thigh.

"I thought you might have discussed the future."

Try as she may, the only future Breena saw with Egan was to continue as his leman. She would then have to step aside once he took a highborn wife. He would go on to build a beautiful family of his own, while she was left bereft and broken.

"There's nothing to talk about," she said in a quiet voice.

Breena jerked her head up as the door to the bedchamber opened. Craig and Egan stepped inside. Her belly did a strange little oscillation at the sight of Egan's formidable stature. The room seemed to vibrate with the restless sort of power that always surrounded him. Egan took

Craig's weight as they went to the red-cushioned chair across from the bed, where he assisted Craig to sit.

Breena eyed Craig. "Uncle, you shouldn't be out of bed."

Craig's reluctant gaze made her pause.

Egan went back to the chamber door and pushed it closed. He leaned against the door and crossed his arms over his chest.

The shared solemnity of their three gazes caused her pulse to pick up its pace. "Is Alban all right? Did something happen?"

"Alban is fine. He's resting," Egan said.

Breena exhaled a breath of relief but still eyed the three of them with suspicion.

"One of you ought to tell her, or I will." Egan speared Craig and Ian with a determined gaze.

Breena's shifted to face her father. "Tell me what?"

Ian cleared his throat and lifted his eyes to meet Breena's.

"My dear, your mother—"

"Ian, we swore to Beth we'd keep her secret. We cannot renege," Craig cut in.

"The bastard is dead. I think that releases us from our promise," Ian said.

When Craig remained silent and then lowered his eyes to the floor in what looked like acquiescence, Ian turned to Breena.

"Beth never wanted you to learn the truth because she loved you so much and was trying to shield you from the foulness of the Campbell. She knew if Alasdair got his hands on you, he would corrupt you, use your witchcraft for his personal gain, and lead you down a forbidden path of black magic. Mayhap, even marry you off to one of his barbaric friends."

A cold shiver ran up Breena's spine as she stared into Ian's lined face.

"No one had to keep me from that savage. I'd do that for myself. What is it you're not telling me?"

Ian took a deep breath, paused, then opened his mouth, but closed it again without a word.

"If you don't tell her, I will," Egan said. His voice was edged with hardness.

Ian faced Breena once more. "Alasdair Campbell raped my wife . . . your mother. You are the result."

Even though his voice was a whisper it hit Breena with the force of a pistol shot.

Her eyes widened, and strange chills climbed up her body. She stared at Ian for the longest while. She'd come to know him well these past few days, recognized that dark look of pain plastered all over his features, the one he got whenever he spoke of Beth. She recognized the look enough that she didn't now ask him if he was jesting, a jest that was in poor taste indeed.

Breena suspected that if the events of a week ago hadn't happened, her reaction would have been different. The truth was, their kidnapping had left her numb and cold, yet in a constant state of heightened awareness, as if she were holding her breath waiting for the rest of her life to resume.

If she weren't numb, she'd have screamed at him and told him to take the words back.

"It's not true," she said, staring at the floor, not understanding why the joints between the stones suddenly looked blurred.

"Forgive us, my dear, for keeping it from you. We only thought to honor Beth's last wish and to protect you," Ian said.

Alasdair Campbell was her father? She'd stood there in his solar a month ago burning with ire as she'd looked upon his despicable face. And all this time he'd been her father? Holy saints. Her father had not only killed her mother, but he'd also dismissed her, his own daughter, like a common trollop from his solar.

His reptilian face flashed across her mind. No, she shouldn't refer to him as her father. He wasn't. He was a miserable monster who'd raped her mother. Her mother had made the right decision in trying to protect her from him. She shuddered to think of the life she would have had on Coll with the Campbells, if it weren't for the promise her mother had asked of Ian and Craig.

"Did he know who I was?" she whispered, shaking her head, trying to dislodge the coldness. But the answer hit her, even before Ian spoke.

"No, my mission was to keep him in the dark. It's a mission that kept me alive for nineteen years," Ian said.

Breena's chest tightened. Had Ian sacrificed nineteen years of his freedom to keep her safe? She swallowed the painful guilt. This was the worst kind of torment, but she had to know once and for all.

"Why did you and my mother go to Coll? Why not stay far away from the Campbells?"

Ian seemed to contemplate his words before he spoke. "Beth and I lived in Portree, where you were born. We were happy, the three of us, a perfect little family for the first six years. She'd told me who your real father was just before you were born, told me what Alasdair had done. I was away when it had happened. I had thought you were mine, up until then. Every fiber in me had wanted to kill the bastard. But she'd made me promise . . . promise not to. She said he'd sired you despite what he'd done."

Pain lined Ian's face as he stared at some invisible point beyond Breena's shoulders. Despite the shock of it all, threatening to crumple her where she sat, she wanted him to continue.

She reached out and took his hand in hers and gave it a gentle squeeze. "What happened after I was born?"

"Six years after you were born, Alasdair returned with his wife to negotiate the sale of some horses with the Gordons of Portree. The Campbells would visit Portree on occasion to conduct business with the

Gordons. That was when his pregnant wife took ill. Beth was the only healer in Portree, so she was summoned. Alasdair later ordered Beth to go to Coll. He threatened to kill you if she didn't. He had no idea he himself had sired you. I was no match for the bullying tactics of the Campbell and his retainers, but I would never have left Beth's side. Right before we left for Coll, unbeknownst to anyone, we sent you with a trusted neighbor to Craig and Madeline in Kilmuir with instructions."

Breena took a long cleansing breath, trying to absorb it all. For the first time in nineteen years, she felt as if the fog that had been her life was starting to clear. Almost.

"But how did he come to find out he had sired me?"

"After we arrived on Coll, a maid overheard Beth and I saying Alasdair could never find out he had a daughter. The maid went straight to Alasdair. Soon after his wife died with their unborn bairn, he wanted you. Beth and I refused to tell him your whereabouts. That's when he concocted the fictitious murder of his wife and child and blamed Beth. It was a vile tactic not only to get Beth to give you up but to give in to his depravities. But Beth never would have yielded. He found that out and he hated her for it. She was executed a week later, and I was thrown in the dungeon."

Breena fought against the tears burning the backs of her eyes. "Dear God, what you must have gone through. Both of you. I can't even begin to fathom."

Ian's mouth stretched into a dry smile. "I am grateful I had the strength to never yield. In the end, I think Beth and I won. He never found out who or where you were."

Breena rose and collected Ian in a tight embrace. Unable to hold them back any longer, tears of gratitude tinged with pain, regret, and love rolled down her cheeks. She wiped them away. "Even though I am grateful, it still breaks my heart that you sacrificed your life to protect mine."

"I would do it again without a moment's hesitation, just to prevent Alasdair from getting his way."

Breena released Ian and avoided Egan's gaze. She couldn't process the sentiments that must be etched in his features just yet. With the chaos of emotions that rioted through her, it would rip away what little composure she had left.

Her eyes found Craig's. "So, this is what you've been keeping from me all these years?"

The remorse etched in his features squeezed her chest. "You can't imagine how ashamed I was at not being able to shield my sister from Alasdair. It chipped away at my soul. The least I could do was to carry out her last wish and protect you from the Campbells and the truth."

"I could never fault you for keeping my mother's promise or for trying to protect me. Where would I be without you and Aunt Madeline?"

She shuffled over to her uncle and threw her arms around him. It was good to hold him. He anchored her even in the worst of times, even when she wanted to scream at him. The exhalation from his chest sounded like relief.

She strode back to Ian's bed. He needed to rest. She had put him through enough reliving a dark past for now.

He eyed her as she pulled the covers over his bandaged leg.

"I am sorry too, my dear. You asked Egan to rescue me, thinking I had sired you."

"You have nothing to be sorry for, the Campbell stole your life. I would still have rescued you, knowing what I know now. You gave up nineteen years of your life for me, for my mother. You will always be my Athair."

Ian's eyes softened, then searched her face. "There is so much of her in you. She would have loved the fact you share none of Alasdair's traits."

Thank the saints for that. "My greatest regret is I never got the chance to know her."

"To know her is to know yourself. I see her in you," Ian said.

She leaned down and kissed Ian's forehead, then bid him rest. She promised to procure two impressive crutches for him so he could be back on his feet soon for the journey to Kilmuir now that the Campbells were no longer a threat.

After they left Ian, Breena and Egan saw Craig back to his own convalescence chamber. As they were about to leave, Craig eyed Breena.

"I sent a missive to Madeline two days ago, letting her know we were fine. I told her we would be coming home in a couple of weeks. So she wouldn't worry."

Caught off guard by Craig's comment, Breena stared at him for a few breaths before nodding mutely.

Because his comment more than anything meant they would all be leaving.

CHAPTER
35

Breena and Egan strolled side by side down a pebbled path through the gardens. They were surrounded by box hedges with rows of drying reds and browns of autumn foliage. He gently slipped his hands into hers, intertwining their fingers.

The contact sent a warm jolt through her body despite her forlorn thoughts of leaving Eileanach Castle.

She shot him a glance. "You never did tell me how you found us so soon after the Campbells kidnapped us."

The corners of his mouth turned up in a wry grin. "Loki set us on the Campbells' trail."

She spun around expectantly. "I'll have to thank him with an especially nice treat. Where are the two rascals?"

"They're not allowed in the gardens. It's a long story, one involving some dug-up rosebushes and my mother almost wringing both their necks some time ago. Plus, you have my gratitude. I am thrilled with Odin's progress. The stable hands tell me George has been feeding him a special diet, per your instructions."

Her eyes were drawn down to where Egan's larger hand was laced with her smaller one. Her thumb traced the sinewy skin of his forefinger's knuckles, enjoying the rough feel of it.

"How long have you known?"

He shot her an inquiring glanced. "About the Campbell being your father?"

"Uh-huh."

"I found out a week ago from William, when he delivered the news that Alasdair was dead. I wanted to tell you, but I thought it best to come from your uncle or Ian."

"I was relieved when you told me of the Campbell's death. That relief hasn't diminished, now that I know he was my father. Is that terrible?"

Egan stopped under a willow tree, half its yellowing leaves scattered on the soft ground beneath their feet. Rigid lines replaced the relaxed demeanor of his posture. "He raped your mother; that doesn't mean he is your father."

She stopped beside him to consider his words. He was right, of course. Ian was her father, even if he hadn't sired her. Breena took in the warm depths of Egan's eyes; it dawned on her that in this light they were more gray than hazel.

His right thumb brushed the cut on her cheek Finlay had gifted her. "Does it hurt?"

She shook her head. "No, I'm treating it with a concoction of bilberry, lavender, and rose hips. It should fade. Although I wouldn't mind having matching scars with you."

They'd somehow ended up a hairsbreadth away from each other. She brushed her lips against his Adams apple, where the whitest skin of his scar ended. She thanked the saints, all the ones she could name, that the injury from the redcoat who'd manhandled Phoebe hadn't gone deeper. She thanked them that Egan now stood in front of her, addling her mind with his nearness and heating her blood with his gaze.

And as she sensed the protection his body would always offer hers, she was most of all grateful he'd purloined her heart, even if he could never be hers.

"My scar is infinitely more impressive," he teased.

She dipped her chin. The thought of him sharing those teasing glances with a future wife sent a dirk straight to her heart. Egan reached out to nudge her chin up until her eyes met his. The emotion there glistened, stalled her breath, and radiated heat through the length of her.

"Marry me," he whispered.

She blinked up at him, doubtful she'd heard correctly. "What?"

"When I thought I'd lost you, my world was reduced to a very dark and cold place. It all but ripped the life from me. I love you, *leannan*. If I can't have you by my side each and every day for the rest of my life, I don't think I'd want to go on."

Weakness shot through Breena's entire body, settling in her knees. She feared she would collapse despite the fact that her blood hummed with something soft and dulcet. But she couldn't afford to get caught up in this exquisite dream again.

"But . . . but you're the future chief of the Dunbars, I'm a lowborn heal . . . er." Her voice trailed off as realization slammed into her chest. The fact that Alasdair Campbell's blood ran through her veins made her want to retch, but it also meant she wasn't entirely lowborn. She was even related to William, and by virtue of marriage, Rosalin as well, and despite herself, she drew a few easy breaths.

"My father gave me his blessings. I can speak with Craig if that causes you worry. I have a feeling Ian won't object."

Breena wanted to laugh and cry all at once. In fact, she was sure the light-headedness his words brought on could make her take flight at any moment.

"You . . . you spoke with your sire about me?"

Egan nodded. "Right after he came back from Inbhir Garadh."

Incredulity made her shake her head. "Didn't it bother you I am low-born? That is, when you first asked your sire, you didn't yet know the Campbell had sired me."

Egan exhaled in a rush of breath. "You're like my father in that respect, preoccupied with lineage and propriety. Truth be told, he was angry at first. And when he found out that the Campbell had sired you by raping your mother, he was outraged. Then Ian explained that your mother had naught to do with Lady Campbell's death. That knowledge settled him a bit."

"Ian spoke to your father?"

"Yes. My sire wanted to know what happened on Coll. After he took some time to consider, he agreed. He said that while the Campbell's actions were repugnant, criminal, and morally reprehensible, it did make you the daughter of a laird. We also resolved a misunderstanding regarding Alex at the insistence of my mother. She can be an exacting, effective, and merciless negotiator when she wants to be. I even suspect she had much to do with my father's change of heart regarding you being my wife."

Breena was intrigued. "Merciless? Oh my. But Abby struck me as being so lighthearted."

Egan leaned against the trunk of the willow tree and seemed to consider the clouds for a few breaths before speaking. "She is very lighthearted when she wants to be and merciless when she has to. When I was a boy, the redcoats were on the brink of garrisoning Eileanach while my father was away fighting in the great wars. My mother went to the Earl of Sutherland himself and demanded he tell the redcoats to back down. The rumor is that she bargained by threatening to turn his tenants against him. Many of them were farmers who sold grain to Clan Dunbar to feed our flocks."

Breena's jaws slackened in amazement. "Your mother sounds like the perfect match for your father."

He grinned. "She is that indeed. Like you are the perfect match for me."

A wide smile tugged at her lips. So much love, tenderness, and adoration overflowed inside her for this man, she thought she would drown in it.

Egan pushed away from the tree and took both her hands, brought them up to his lips, and started to press light kisses to each of her knuckles.

"Will you marry me, *mo ghaol*?"

"I love you, Egan Dunbar. I love you so much it hurt to look at you when I imagined I couldn't have you for myself. You rescued Ian, you protected me from the wolves and the Campbells. I wouldn't be here if it weren't for you. You are the most honorable man I've ever known."

"For you, I would gladly venture to hell and fight Mephistopheles himself."

She pressed into him, and the delicious length of him sent warm tingles down her spine. She rose up on her tiptoes, wrapped her arms around his neck and touched her lips to his. The kiss was sweet and soft, tasting of salt from her tears of joy and his particular delicious male flavor. It seared her senses and eroded any remaining reservations she had.

When Breena lifted her lips from his, she became aware of his chest rising and falling with rapid breaths. As the sultry haze ebbed from her brain it occurred to her when Egan mentioned her mother, that hollowness that had always plagued her since she was six no longer pierced her innards. She was sure now, it had been filled by the Highlander standing in front of her.

She threw Egan an inquiring gaze. "Since your sire is preoccupied with propriety and lineage, I am surprised, albeit pleased, he gave you consent to marry the illegitimate daughter of a laird."

"Well, he could hardly object on the grounds that you are illegitimate, born out of wedlock, since he fell in love with and married the illegitimate daughter of a baronet."

"Does your sire know then, that I am a witch?"

Egan tucked an errant lock of her hair behind her left ear and nodded.

"How'd he put it? 'It's naught but load of ancient pagan beliefs of times gone, inconsequential to the present.' As we are addressing witchcraft, I did have a talk with Duncan. He admitted to requesting 'The Witchery O' Cora' that night in the great hall. He claimed he was drunk, and he apologized. An apology, he assured me this morning, he will deliver to you in person. I told him if he ever does anything like that again, he'll be relieved of his manhood."

Breena was not looking forward to the conversation she would have with Duncan, but it was necessary. Just like a number of similar conversations she'd likely be having with others in the future.

The green aventurine stone she'd plucked from the pouch during the wee hours that morning came back to her. It had meant not only that she loved, but that she was loved. If she stopped trying to make the stones tell her what she wanted to hear and simply listened to what they were saying, mayhap there was hope for her divination spell casting and witchery after all.

But what about all the times the signs and her dreams had confused her? Her mind skipped to Sorcha and the dream she'd had the night in

Glen Brittle Forest when she'd left camp to carry out the protection spell for Egan.

"What is it, *mo ghaol*?"

Breena relayed to Egan her dream of Sorcha. That he was in danger, explaining that's why she'd rushed off to perform a protection spell in the dark of night. Breena concluded the story by adding, "I just can't decide if I have the gift of second sight or not."

Egan considered her story for several breaths before a smirk appeared on his lips. "When I was training with the MacDonell, he asked a few of us to ride over to Ardgarry Farm to round up a flock of sheep and bring them back to Castle Inbhir Garadh. Many of us protested that we were there to train as warriors, not as sheep herders. He then told us of the farmer's three beautiful daughters and how it was such a shame we wouldn't get to meet the lasses. Of course, we all promptly took off for Ardgarry Farm."

Breena narrowed her eyes at him. "How are these beautiful lasses relevant to my grandmother?"

"Well, when we arrived at Ardgarry Farm, we found out that the farmer in fact had three sons and no daughters. The MacDonell told us what he had to get us to go the farm. But since we were already there, we rounded up the sheep and brought the flock back as he'd asked."

"Are you saying Sorcha just wanted me to leave camp, but that you were never really in any mortal danger, even from the wolves?"

"Well, if she is as cunning as the MacDonell, then yes."

"But the only other thing that happened that night was that we . . ." Breena broke off as her cheeks warmed.

"Was that we made love. You gave yourself to me fully that night and I gave myself to you, mind, body, and soul."

Breena's jaws slackened not only at his words of love but at the implications of what he was saying.

Disbelief surged through her. "Are you saying that Sorcha meant to throw us together with that dream?"

He half shrugged. "I'll leave that determination up to you."

Perhaps she did have the gift of second sight after all, and Sorcha was not only trying to tell her that, but she was also playing matchmaker.

She exhaled in a rush of realization. The rest of her life had resumed. Even though her courses had arrived two days ago, and she wasn't with child, the prospect of having Egan's children filled her to the brim with a warmth and weightlessness unlike anything she'd ever experienced.

Her mouth stretched into a wide smile, for her dream of a husband and bairns of her own was at last within her grasp.

"I'd like to have lots of bairns, at least five to begin with," she said.

"I can't wait to get started, as soon as you agree to marry me, of course."

"It would be my honor and privilege to be your wife, Highlander. And it would fill me with immeasurable happiness to stand by your side each and every day from this moment onward, until I am no more."

"Aww, an answer, at long last." His eyes darkened as he bent down and took her lips in another mind-numbing kiss that weakened her knees to the point where they could no longer hold up her body.

But with Egan there holding her tightly, she knew she would never fall.

Acknowledgments

hank you to my mom, for staying up with me countless nights on a different continent by candlelight when I was little to teach me parts of speech and the like. You are my strength.

And to my husband, for his unwavering support and patience these past fifteen years and for reading all my drafts, discussing each at length with me, and for accompanying me to Scotland. You are my inspiration.

My gratitude to Val Matthews, for her kind words, encouragement, and direction. Thanks also to Jamie Evans and Elisabeth Nelson for their invaluable feedback. And to Starr Waddell and her beta readers at Quiet House: your readers' perspective helped fine tune this story.

My sincerest thanks to my publisher, CamCat Books: Sue Arroyo and her team granted me an outlet for my passion. And thank you to my editor, Bridget McFadden, for your enthusiasm in helping to make this book shine.

And in memory of my dad who taught me to never settle:

May flights of angels sing thee to thy rest...
—*William Shakespeare*

About the Author

Roma Cordon was introduced to romance novels in her teenage years and instantly became a voracious reader of the genre. In the 1990s, she came to live in New York where she earned her undergraduate and graduate degrees. After taking a writing course at New York University with Anne Rice, she dived into the world of writing while testing the waters at public speaking at her local Toastmasters club. By day, Roma works in the finance industry; in the evenings and weekends, she is a passionate romance writer. She also writes on her blog romacordon. com. Inspiration for Roma's debut novel, *Bewitching a Highlander* came from trips to Scotland with her husband. Roma is an active member of the RWA-NYC Chapter and lives in New York with her husband where they care for two adorable furry friends adopted from local shelters.

Author Q&A

What would you consider to be your main character's strength and weakness?

Breena is courageous, especially when she is terrified. She risks her safety and in some cases her very life among a murderous and treacherous clan for a chance at finding and freeing her imprisoned father. And despite the fact that witches are burned alive at the stake in her world, she stays true to her witchery heritage, when it would be much easier to abandon it altogether. Especially given the fact that her abilities are anything but stellar. She confronts her own insecurities and fears head on. The thought of abandoning her mission and returning home never enters her mind. On the other hand, perhaps she is too courageous and bold. She is quick to temper and is forced to bear the consequences of her actions when she slaps an ornery sentry in retaliation for an insult. But then again, if it wasn't for her boldness, she wouldn't pursue a forbidden relationship with a future laird and her story would end before it had even begun.

What inspired *Bewitching a Highlander*?
This book was inspired by a trip to Scotland with my husband. There's something unexplainable, intangible, and inspiring in the air in Scotland, especially on the Isle of Skye, that makes one think of fairies, witches, and forest nymphs. It might be all that fresh air, lush greenery, open vastness of thistle and heather, rolling bens and deep glens, or possibly the impressive Scottish history and culture.

Here, the story of Breena was born, a lass with witchery in her blood, who is terrified of being burnt alive at the stake. But I had to insert some reality into the story, and the reality was that in Scotland in 1563 a Witchcraft Act was passed, making witchcraft a capital offense. Before this law was repealed in 1736, 4,000 to 6,000 people were tried for witchcraft and more than 1,500 executed by strangulation or burning in Scotland. In Europe at large, where similar laws existed, approximately 50,000 people were executed for witchcraft. It was out of these statistics that Breena's paranoia was born.

What was the greatest challenge in writing *Bewitching a Highlander*?
Tying up loose ends was a challenge in this book because the story took on a life of its own along the way. There ended up being a backload of information toward the conclusion of the story when I realized certain revelations had to be made. For instance, Breena's witchcraft and second-sight abilities and its connection to her grandmother was revealed at the end. Another included an answer to the burning question; why did Breena's parents initially go to the Isle of Coll? There was Alasdair's

true identity to be revealed and Egan's father's opposition to Breena's low-born status to wrap up. There were also the results of Odin's (the adorable deerhound) treatment to discover. And last but not least, the forbidden relationship between Egan, a future highborn laird, and Breena, a lowborn healer, needed a happy ending.

What would you consider the key theme(s) of *Bewitching a Highlander*?
The forbidden love between Breena and Egan is a key theme in this book. Egan risks the wrath and good opinion of his father, whom he'd idolized, to save Breena. His esteem for Breena forces him to break the bounds of societal propriety that would forbid him from getting involved with a lowborn healer. Breena gives up her dream of a husband and children of her own, a respectable endeavor, by becoming Egan's leman/mistress, thereby branding herself a morally "loose" woman. And she goes further still, by ignoring the advice of her uncle and father to pursue a relationship with Egan.

Witchcraft is another big theme. Witchcraft has an unfair and inaccurate stigma attached to it. Some equate it with devilry, Satan worshiping, blood sacrifices, black magic, hexes, and the like. But this is a remnant of the Middle Ages and bad propaganda hatched-up by religious zealots. Others equate witchcraft with Glenda, the good witch from Wizard of Oz; a beautiful and ethereal fairylike female, who masterfully grants wishes of the worthy few. But what about a witch who is a typical woman? One with reverence for nature, spirituality, and life?

In Breena's world, witches are burned alive at the stake, and though it would be much easier to give it all up, she stays true to her heritage, despite the shortcomings of her abilities and the fear of discovery. This is in part due to the special relationship she has with her grandmother who taught her the practice, as well as witchery being so ingrained in her persona, separating the two would be impossible.

The notion/definition of "family" is an underlying theme in this book. The reader follows Breena on a journey where she risks her life for the chance to rescue her imprisoned father. On her journey, she discovers that family is not always defined as blood relations. In the end, Breena embraces the fact that family includes those we hold dearest in our hearts—those we are prepared to sacrifice everything for, even life itself.

I sought out to empower women readers with a strong heroine. Women readers are very astute and can easily spot a strong woman as opposed to an ill-tempered shrew. I found this line a little tricky to tread. While a strong woman can come across as a shrew, a strong hero comes across as formidable, commanding and heroic. How does one thread this dual-edged sword? I strived to show Breena's strength's but to also showcase her vulnerabilities. One might even say I emphasized the latter. I strove to show her as a courageous and capable woman, who also makes mistakes, like the rest of us. I want my women readers to know they can overcome obstacles in their lives just like Breena. But in the end, I'll leave it up to the reader to determine how Breena comes across on the pages. Courageous and bold, or an ill-tempered shrew?

How did you do research for *Bewitching a Highlander*?
Research is a fun part in the process of writing. For this book, I traveled to Scotland and visited places like the Isle of Skye, Dunvegan Castle, Eilean Donan Castle, the Isle of Harris/Lewis, etc. I spoke to tour guides and shop owners. I consulted with spell craft reference writings by Scott Cunningham, Ann-Marie Gallagher, Marion Weinstein, etc. For period costumes, I found Millia Davenport's *The Book Of Costume* helpful and for architecture Lady Henrietta Spencer-Churchill's *Classic Georgian Style* was a wonderful source of information. Plus it goes without saying, but where would we writers be without Wikipedia, Google, and Pinterest?

What do you want a reader to take away from this story? A thought? An idea? A hope?

Based on my research, witches are spiritual people with a reverence for nature and life. Witchcraft is by no means limited to black magic, hexes, blood sacrifices, etc. In every population of people there are law-abiding citizens as well as lawbreakers. But the actions of a few criminals shouldn't define the population at large nor should it be a representation of the entire population. Likewise, those that dabble in black magic, blood sacrifices, and hexes shouldn't define the entire world of witchery and spell craft.

What was the most fun about writing *Bewitching a Highlander*?

The connection between Egan and Breena was fun to write because of how it emotionally impacts the story. Breena and Egan are both strong characters who lead eventful, exciting, and dangerous lives. Their coming together was romantic and even explosive at times. The redefining of their relationship from physical attraction to something deeper and more meaningful was satisfying. The change in their relationship was gratifying to put down on paper because of the hurdles jumped and the distances traveled for them to reach their ultimate destination; a happily ever after.

For Further Discussion

1. In what ways do you feel Breena's characters developed? Egan's?

2. Breena's witchcraft is different than the typical witchcraft you see in books/tv/movies, as she uses nature to ignite her powers. What were your thoughts on Breena's form of witchcraft?

3. Do you think Egan made the right choice to disobey his father and almost start a clan war?

4. If you were in Egan's position, would you choose love or duty?

5. What made you interested in reading this book?

6. What was your favorite scene?

7. What are your thoughts on the family dynamics in this book?

8. How did Breena's family react differently than Egan's family about their budding romance? Who do you think was right?

9. If *Bewitching a Highlander* became a movie, who would you cast as Breena and Egan?

10. Were you rooting for Breena and Egan to end up together? Or did you feel they would be better apart?

If you enjoyed

Bewitching a Highlander by Roma Cordon,

you will enjoy

Daughter of the Salt King by A. S. Thornton.

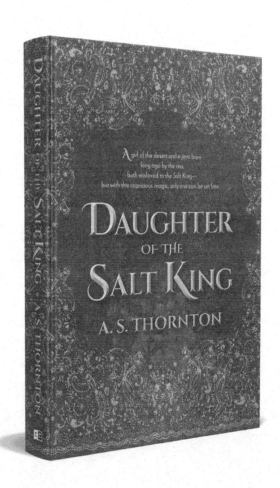

PROLOGUE

*T*here was an immense tree that gave strong wood and sweet fruit. *The goddess Masira thought, This tree makes life too easy. Man grows weak. She tore it from the ground and shook out its roots, spilling grains of sand and drops of water. From the sand, Eiqab was born. From the water, Wahir.*

She was fascinated by her Sons and grew so possessive over them, she desired that none else should have Sons of their own.

From this point forward, Masira said, there shall be no more trees that give life. And so, the desert was born.

The Sons were exhausted by the world's bleakness and angered by the weak people who caused it. Mother is right, Eiqab said, People must be made hard from a hard life. So Eiqab crafted a great light above his head, so hot the ground desiccated beneath his feet. Now, Eiqab said, the people will suffer as they deserve.

Seeing his brother's searing light and dried earth, Wahir was repulsed. He said, Mother, Brother, man cannot live in the world you have made, and cruelty will not lead to strength. He stepped through the sand, and in his footsteps, people found cool water and a respite from the sun under the small trees that grew there. Seeing how man swaddled his body in cloth to protect himself from Eiqab's light, Wahir fashioned a dark sky and pale light that split the world so that they would have cool nights to break from the day.

Masira watched her Sons and saw that they were both right. She was satisfied, for her Sons were of her spirit, and she proclaimed all living things, but man most of all, shall likewise be of both light and dark.

—Excerpt from the *Litab Almuq*

CHAPTER
1

These cards were worn to fatigue like everything we had, and I cradled them with my fingers, the better to keep them secret from my sisters. Three cards lay on the ground between us, awaiting mine—the last. The images had long ago begun to fade, so I surveyed them carefully before making my next move: a spider in a glistening web, a buzzard above its carrion, a vessel of fire.

I looked back to the cards in my hand, and a greedy smile spread across my face. Next to the others, I placed a golden eagle soaring beside a blue moon. My sisters groaned.

I had won, again.

"Praise Eiqab for this embarrassment of riches!" I held out my hand, and they dropped their chipped glass beads and cowries into my palm.

The cards were collected and shuffled while I added the tokens to my pile, now the largest. My smile widened as I picked up my new hand.

There was a rush of air and shock of sunlight as the tent's entrance was pulled open. Our attendant, arriving just as I won, of course. I huffed and turned to her, waiting to see whom she would call so we could return to our game.

"Emel, come." She did not look at me. She tossed my name at the twenty-six of us who sat inside—daughters of the Salt King, my full and half-sisters—and disappeared behind the fabric that sealed the entrance.

Sons, I was not prepared to hear my name. My heart quickened, and like the sand of an hourglass, dread filled me. I had hoped the suitor would choose one of my sisters so I would not have to endure another failed courting—to face lengthy preparation before an evening of pretense, only to conclude in a morning soaked with failure. Then again, a suitor was the only answer to my wish for escape. Sighing, I set down the limp cards.

"Open that tent back up, eh?" Pinar called to the guards outside. "We could provide drink for the gods if you collected our sweat!" She wiped at her hair, a wet lattice on her forehead.

"Store it in silver bottles and perhaps Father could sell that for dha, too," Tavi muttered under her breath.

The request would go unanswered. We were not allowed to draw open the tent, lest palace visitors glimpse us in our home. We were the Salt King's most protected jewels. The mythical ahiran, whom powerful men from across the desert came to bed and, if satisfied, carry home astride their camels. Each daughter married was another jackal leashed. Father's reign strengthened every time he transformed a would-be contender into a son.

I pushed my winnings to the center of our circle with shaking hands, the pile spilling.

"Better to end when the sun is high. Let's all remember that I was the winner, eh?" I stood slowly.

"Good luck tonight," Raheemah said as she divided my prize among the remaining players. My sisters watched me go. Some mumbled under their breath, wishing they had been chosen in my stead.

"If you aren't choking on his dagger, you aren't doing it right," Pinar said. The girls giggled from their sand-strewn mats. My lips twitched.

"If he talks too much, just shove those udders in his face," Kadri added, "Or your kuz."

Riotous laughter now. Even I succumbed. "Quiet!" I hissed. "You'll get us all in trouble." My sisters fanned themselves with the corners of thin blankets as they bantered about the best bedding techniques, ignoring me. I lifted a dark wool abaya from the basket and patted sweat from my brow with its embroidered edge. The intricate designs marked us as belonging to the King, but the tattered and fraying hems revealed, to the keen observer, our worth.

I shook my head at my sisters' ribaldry, but I was grateful for their distractions.

"Maybe this time you can get him to request you for a second night?"

My smile disappeared at Sabra's bitter words. She always found a place to sink her stinger. I did not acknowledge her and pulled the cloth quickly over my head so that my amber-dyed fustan was completely covered. I tied a threadbare black veil over my hair. The setting sun sizzled outside of the tents. Though our walk would be short, the sun punished those who did not protect themselves from its glare.

My attendant waited for me outside. The veil covering her face did not conceal her disapproval as she listened to the advice my sisters were still hollering through the fabric walls.

An adolescent boy, as swathed as the attendant beside him, was more discomfited by the obscenities. He shifted his weight from side to side, absently brushing his fingers against the hilt of his rusted scimitar. He was one of my many half-brothers. He was also my guard. Our eyes met. His shoulders tensed, and I quickly looked away. Make no mistake, he was not there to protect me from others.

I nodded to the pair. "Hadiyah. Bahir. Shall we?"

Hadiyah strode away with a huff, her robes billowing like clouds behind her. Indecent shrieks and groans emerged from behind me now. I looked back to my tent. Beside the entrance, two guards' eyes watered and shoulders shook with mirth.

<hr />

We walked briskly through the narrow path between rows of palace tents. Bahir trailed close behind me, his chest puffed and chin raised high.

The servants' homes were held open with thick camel's hair rope, in hopes that the wind would find ingress to carry away the heat. Goats were spun over fires, milk poured into big vats for cheese, and pots set out to harden in the sun. Servants called to one another, shoving reels of fabric into each other's arms or dousing the flames of the smelting fires with sand. The flurry and sounds of the palace collided around us. All for the Salt King.

My stomach turned on itself as we walked, my nerves a pestle to my insides as I prepared for my role in the King's court. I envied the servants in that moment—how simple their lives must be, to roast or weave or hew, then be done for the day. Sure, there was no great glory, but too, there was no great risk. And security, a clear future, was favorable to my unknown.

The servants looked up from their work as I passed, carefully positioned between my attendant and guard. This procession, the embroidered clothes on my back, revealed what I was, and they knew what awaited me. Did they watch me, thinking of my past failures? I'm sure they laughed behind my back—a waste of time for the King. I was to be a "forever ahira," until I was twenty-three and thrown into the streets as used and useless as the playing cards.

A little girl ran from her home into the path, shrieking with laughter, chased by two boys not much older. A red birthmark trailed from her eyebrow to the edge of her lip. I remembered when she was born, how I had thanked Eiqab I was not cursed with the same mark upon my skin. But now, I saw that it was she who was lucky. The trio whipped past Hadiyah, who grunted in disapproval, before they flew past me and further down the lane. A laughing woman emerged from the tent behind them, and upon seeing us, fell to her knees.

"Forgive me, forgive them," she mumbled over and over, brow pressed to her clasped hands.

Bahir barked at her, his boy's voice suddenly harsh like a man's. A bird cried out as it soared above us in the purpling sky. Oh to be that bird.

Finally, we arrived at a large tent the color of sunrise—the zafif —where I was to be prepared. I followed Hadiyah in, leaving Bahir to stand guard outside. It was time.

Scents of crushed roses and warm honey met my nose. Attendants in flowing, colorful fustan stood from cushions and thick mattresses at my arrival. They rushed to greet us as Hadiyah whisked off her coverings, revealing braided graying hair and a camel-colored dress, which I eyed enviously. Because she was a servant, her clothes were simpler than mine—no bright patterns nor embellishments that signified she belonged only in the palace. She could go anywhere in those.

Hadiyah's eyes softened when she smiled—the stern charade had been cast off with her abaya and veil.

"Beauty." She smoothed the hair from my face. "It's been too long." Her hand moved down my back. She tapped my bottom and winked.

"You should listen to your sisters; they give good advice." She walked off and began fussing with the various jars and vessels they would need to ready me that evening, calling over her shoulder. "This will be your husband, I just know it. Eiqab has given many signs today."

"Did you see the clouds on the horizon this morning? They were so dark, perhaps promising rain," Adilah said.

"And the vultures that circled the bazaar," another attendant added. "There were three. One who searched for his mate." The women trailed off, discussing the good omens bestowed on us that day. Of course, I had seen none—ahiran were forbidden from leaving the palace.

Their hope smoothed my unease, but still, the pressure of the evening was too great to smile, the knot in my chest too tight to speak. I had met the suitor that afternoon at the courting where he surveyed my sisters and me like a meal to be savored. He was stiff and proud, and when he finally spoke to me, even his curious accent was not intriguing enough for me to take interest. Evidently, I had played my role well. He'd chosen me tonight.

Hadiyah saw my face and banged her open hand against the copper basin, a loud ringing startling us all.

"Well, come on then! The prince needs more than a hand to keep him company."

I slipped off my sandals and flexed my toes into the soft, woven rug before I went to the jasmine-scented water.

The water's surface rose to my neck as I lowered myself into the bath. The pain in my chest eased as I relaxed against the basin wall, my shoulders falling back. I listened to the attendants' gossip, their words a calming cadence as I closed my eyes.

Then, "A runner arrived today."

My eyes flew open.

"The caravan arrives tomorrow," the attendant continued excitedly.

"From where?" I asked.

"Emel," Hadiyah warned as she scrubbed my skin.

The woman pursed her lips. "North, I think."

North! Hoping she was right, I mused about what and who the caravan might be bringing. Hadiyah dunked a bowl full of water over my head. I sat forward, sucking in a startled breath.

"Look at you. A woman of the court." She emphasized the last words. "I remember when you were just a girl." She took my hand to clean under my nails. "You were so excited when you were requested the first time."

"Must you remind me?" My free hand covered my eyes.

"You talked and talked about what kind of wife you would be for him and how you would please him. Where has that girl gone? Now you want to talk of salt trade and politics." She tutted disapprovingly and pulled my hand from my face to clean that one, too.

"I was naive. Not such a fool now."

"You weren't a fool," Hadiyah said. "You were smart, focusing only on that which affected you." She narrowed her eyes at me. I bit my tongue as she continued. "And you were hopeful, too. As you should be still."

It was true. I was not yet finished as an ahira, with over a year left before my father would cast me out. There was still a chance a man would choose me for a wife, still a chance I would finally leave the palace. But finding hope was difficult when it was buried beneath the rejections of dozens of suitors who had come before. Perhaps I'd have better luck if I doused flame with salt.

What was it they saw to make them turn from me every time? I looked at my knuckles. Too boney? My palms. Too many lines? Or did they see that I did not want them? That I only wanted what they could offer me, that I only wanted to be free from the palace?

When my bath finished, my skin dry, Hadiyah brought me a large goblet of wine. I consumed it dutifully, barely tasting it.

An attendant waved a fan of palm fronds toward me as I lay back onto the feather-stuffed mattress. I shivered beneath the breeze.

"Thank you," I sighed. I wanted to stay there forever, never feeling heat again.

The wine hit me swiftly, and the world began to shimmer and spin. I closed my eyes and smiled lazily as my worries began to recede. A sharp burn splashed against my thigh and my eyes flew open. Hot honey wax. With a terrible rip, it was removed. I clenched my teeth and my eyes watered. It was repeated again and again and again.

"You need a stronger drink," Hadiyah grunted when the women finished. She mixed two liquids in a curving vessel and decanted it into a small goblet. Arak. It smelled of anise and looked like camel's milk. My father's favorite spirit could unsteady even the strongest carouser. I sipped it slowly, disliking its bitter taste but needing it to soothe me. I knew with it, I would perform better. The world twisted and tilted.

"Stay still," Hadiyah put her hands on my shoulders to stop my swaying. Hadn't the world been moving under my feet? My hair was braided as she held me, kohl was lined around my eyes.

"He will want to devour you whole," Adilah said as rose-scented oil was smoothed into my skin.

"And I will let him," I purred, touching a droplet of the oil and pressing it to the bow of my upper lip.

I stumbled when I stood, Hadiyah's quick hands holding me up. "Careful."

An unblemished, diamond-studded garment of shining green silk was taken from a copper box. Besides the jewels that decorated our necks and wrists, it was the nicest thing an ahira would wear. All loans from our father for courtings only. Strings pulled at my back, tightening the clothes onto my breasts and hips until I could take deep breaths no longer.

Soft slippers cocooned my feet. Hadiyah placed my headpiece, from which hung delicate chains that veiled my mouth and jawline and tickled my skin.

"Everything sparkles, and I sparkle, too," I slurred as I gazed at my reflection on the basin-water's surface. The attendants sighed in admiration.

Hadiyah said, "How can he say no to a beauty like you?" Then whispered into my ear, "Don't spoil anything by talking of that which doesn't concern you, and you will be sealed into marriage."

There it was again. Marriage. Like a hook, it pulled back all of my dread, my fear of failure.

"The Buraq?" I searched around the room for that which I knew would help.

Adilah rushed to a table to collect a tarnished silver tray. Hadiyah worked efficiently with the metal instruments there—igniting, scooping, adjusting. I watched, entranced by the deftness of her hands. She held out a curved pipe, and I slipped it between the strands of my veil, seating it between my lips. Tasting the tang of metal, I leaned over the lamp until the dried petals burned.

Hungrily, I inhaled.

Charred honey filled my mouth, filled my lungs. The burning desert rose was named after Buraq, the winged steed of legends, for its effects on the mind. The one who inhaled the rose would feel light enough to fly. I gulped in the smoke, eyes closed, clutching the pipe like it was my only tether to the world.

"Take me to him," I said when I was finished.

"Good girl," Hadiyah said, her hand rubbing my back. "Can't take your pride into those halls. Best to leave it here with us."

Alcohol swirled in my blood; smoke spun in my chest. I floated inches above the ground. This suitor was my only chance out. I could not let my fears and worries of failure tarnish my performance. Tipping up my chin, I left the zafif and strode into the palace.

I was an emerald goddess and ahira of the Salt King.

And I would find my freedom.

◆———◆———◆———◆———◆

My steps were silent in the hallway. Only the chink, chink of the chains hanging from my clothes could be heard as I staggered through the narrow corridors, trailing the guard. Mesmerized by the torch flames that danced in the air, the patterned carpets that covered the sand, and the pristine fabric walls that towered above me, I took slow, unsteady steps. I was within the opulent heart of the palace, the King's tents. It was the most heavily guarded, entered only by wealthy visitors and royalty.

Holding my arms out to the side, I spun in the hallway, pretending to be a bird flying through the sky. I was a kite with green feathers soaring above the tall, white peaks of Father's tents. Circles of servants' quarters and workrooms surrounded Father's private chambers.

I imagined how it would appear on a map. How *did* maps get made if people could not fly? I stopped to consider this seriously. Birds were somehow involved. I strutted around like a walking bird, a map-making bird. I giggled.

The guard whipped his head around. "Sons be damned," he muttered. "Stop that!" He stopped and reached his hand toward me. I backed away from his grasp.

The drunken fantasies fell away. "Forgive me," I mumbled. I took measured steps forward, now using my arms only for balance.

We entered a soaring room that glowed golden from its glinting metal lanterns. Servants waved palm fronds toward the center. The softly moving air sent the fires into violent fits that demanded my attention.

"Not bad!" boomed the King. I jumped at the sound and tore my gaze from the flames. My father sat upon an immense gilded throne, peering at the goblet in his hand as he licked his lips. "They said they'd be bringing more?"

"Twenty bottles, and if you found this to your liking, you get first pick before they're sent to the bazaar," Nassar, my father's vizier, said from his seat at a small table nearby.

My father took another long drink. He was not a large man, but in that chair, he was tremendous. Heaps of white crystalline granules and stacked gray slabs surrounded him.

Salt. His wealth displayed so all who visited could see the worth of their ruler. It was why the caravans came, and what the rest of the desert needed so desperately.

The Salt King was the only one who had it.

Neither he nor Nassar acknowledged me, though I now stood before them. They continued their conversation about the runner that Nassar met earlier in the day and what the caravan promised to supply. Father nodded absently, tapping his goblet until Nassar filled it again. Finally, as if an afterthought, he turned to me. I stared at his feet, willing the world to stop its revolutions, and knelt before the Salt King.

"My King," I said, sweetening my voice. I pressed my forehead to the rug, my palms flat on the ground. Tightly closing my eyes, I stretched my arms in front of me, slowly reaching until I felt it: the edge of a salt pile. Moving slowly so I wouldn't be seen, I pushed my fingertips into the heap until the coarse salt swallowed them.

"Very good. Up," Father said, bored.

I curled my fingers and scooped the fine crystals into my palm. Standing, I raised my eyes to him slowly. His white, silk-lined boots had rubies that sparkled at the end of curling toes. The folds of his red and ivory robes cascaded around his large belly. A long beard draped from his face of deep, waxy creases. His black eyes—the eyes we shared—were yellowed from life at a decanter. He stared at me with furrowed brow.

Cold panic swept through me, washing away the liquor, and I dropped my gaze to the ground, chewing my cheek behind the veil. Had he seen my theft?

"Aashiq will be pleased with her." The vizier's voice dripped with honey. I nodded toward Nassar, but Sons, I wanted to spit on his silk slippers.

The King set the goblet on the table and dabbed sweat from his face with his handkerchief. "They are never pleased," he said. His thick bejeweled fingers twirled the fabric, his long nails snagging the threads as he leaned back in his chair. The accusation in his gaze was quickly replaced with apathy.

So he did not see me steal his salt, he simply wanted to remind me of my inadequacy. Of course. I stopped grinding my cheek between my teeth.

"Aashiq's time has begun," the King said, gesturing to the tall hourglass whose narrow stream of sand was just beginning to fill the base. "But your own time is short, Emel. If he is not satisfied when I speak to him tomorrow, I will urge him to request one of your sisters and not waste further time with you. No doubt with another, he will find his wife."

One night? My heart sank. If the suitor desired it, I could have three nights to show how I would be a suitable wife. If my father convinced him to choose someone else after the first night, there would be no hope for me.

Nassar butted in, flailing his hands. "When you have had such successes with your other daughters, we must ask if perhaps it is not the sire, but the dam."

Anger burned through the rest of my high. I collected bloodied spit in my mouth, rolling it between my cheeks, imagining a life where I could really do it. Where I could reach his feet from where I stood, damn all the consequences.

"It is no flaw of mine, of that I am sure." The King waved his hand toward his vizier, keeping his gaze on me. "Emel, let me remind you that these men are threats to our home. Weak ones, sure. I could destroy their settlements if I wanted. But what good would that do me? Your mother will be so ashamed if two of her daughters fail. Sabra? Well." He shrugged, dismissing her so casually, even I felt stung. "You're almost what, two and twenty? I cannot bear the thought of throwing such a beautiful bird out to the foxes." He pouted and looked down at his sash, from which several blades and trinkets hung. Carefully, he detached a glass vessel wrapped in golden bands.

I said, "I will try harder. I will not disappoint you or Mother." I pressed my hands together and took a step toward my father.

He paid me no more attention, distracted by the vessel he held in his palm. Inside, tarnished gold smoke churned lazily with nowhere to escape. His eyes followed the billows and swirls of the smoke possessively. I followed his gaze. I could not deny its allure as I, too, was entranced by its beautiful movement. Even Nassar peered at it curiously. My father was never without the thing, and I did not let myself linger on the thought that my father found wine and a trinket more worthy of his attention than his own daughter.

Tearing his gaze from the vessel, he said, "Aashiq is from a strong family. He would be an asset to me, and it is your duty to secure him. Eiqab has blessed you by allowing you to share his bed tonight. Do not squander this gift." He waved his hand to dismiss me and rose, unsteadily. Nassar jumped up to support him.

"Isra!" My father shouted, and with Nassar at his side, left the tent, a train of slaves at his heels. His absence sent a ripple of relief through me, and my shoulders fell forward as I waited.

A woman entered the room, and I turned eagerly toward her. Her flowing dress, fastidiously decorated with bright stripes and zig-zagging lines, barely concealed the curves she had acquired as a mother and a wife. She held her head high, the coins and colored beads on her beautiful veil—the veil of a king's wife—glinting as she approached. I mirrored her strong posture. The kohl lining her eyes swept up to her temples. The corners of her mouth pulled up into a tight smile, as if secrets were waiting to tumble from her lips.

"Mama!" I ran to her.

She stepped forward, arms stretched wide, and we collided. Frankincense clung to her hair and clothes.

"You're lovely." Her fingers pressed the jewels on my head, my hips, passed over the skin of my arms, my shoulders. Her touch lingered on the metallic veil that covered my mouth. "And, how are you?" She asked with eyebrows raised. A test.

"I am much better now—"

"You do not sound sincere," she interrupted. "Try harder."

"Mama . . ."

"I am trying to help. Don't get mad at your mother."

"This is pointless," I spat. "It isn't my fault they don't choose—"

"I don't want to fight. I just want . . ." She hesitated and closed the distance between us. "For you to be wed—to get out of here." She said it quickly and quietly into my ear. To any guard it would have seemed as though she had simply pressed her cheek to mine. She stepped back, "Are you ready to meet him?"

"Of course." I squeezed the salt in my left fist more tightly.

She put her arms around my shoulders and pulled me close, her scent surrounding me.

"Be your very best tonight, Emel." I did not understand the plea I heard in her words. Why did she seem a touch more desperate to see me gone than before? Had she heard that Father was allowing me only one night with Aashiq?

I pulled away, not wanting to hear more when I seemed destined to fail. Unable to meet her eyes, I dropped my gaze to the golden medallion she always wore around her neck.

She grasped my shoulders one last time, taking in every detail, then she said, "Show him why he must take you home."

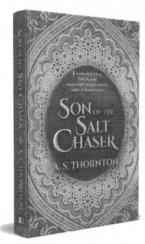
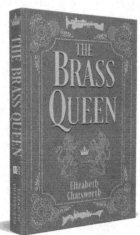

CamCat
Books

VISIT US ONLINE FOR MORE BOOKS TO LIVE IN:
CAMCATBOOKS.COM

SIGN UP FOR CAMCAT'S FICTION NEWSLETTER FOR
COVER REVEALS, EBOOK DEALS, AND MORE EXCLUSIVE CONTENT.

CamCatBooks   @CamCatBooks   @CamCat_Books   @CamCatBooks